Lost Paradise

The Promise Me Series, Book 8

By

Tara Fox Hall

Published by
Melange Books, LLC
White Bear Lake, MN 55110
www.melange-books.com

Cover Art by Caroline Andrus

Lost Paradise
Tara Fox Hall

While the vampire Devlin rejoices at news of his impending progeny with Sar, werecougar Theo braces for more challenges to his Ranked title, content that after Sarelle has the dhamphir child Devlin will be out of their lives forever. Yet when The Lust reappears, Sar's world again turns upside down as old hatreds make themselves known, resulting in a steamy affair with the weresnake Lash, a new friendship with the werecoyote Serena, and the severing of Sar from the last remains of her old human life in favor of a new Paradise with Devlin.

To TOR, for all her tireless work helping me edit the Promise Me series.
Thank you for being my friend.

Chapter One

When I woke up the next morning, my werecougar lover Theo was still sleeping beside me.

The problem was likely all that scotch my stepfather had plied him with in celebration of us becoming parents. Deciding to wake him after breakfast was ready, I left him sleeping and went out to my hungry and vocal pets.

After I got the sausage cooking more than a half hour later, I began to be concerned. Usually Theo was in the kitchen by now with plate in hand, waiting for the first piece to be done. But he hadn't emerged from the bedroom. Hoping he wasn't sick, I went in to wake him.

"Theo," I said firmly, shaking him.

He didn't respond.

Even if the scotch were to blame, his body would've metabolized it by now.

"Theo!" I said loudly, then felt for his heartbeat. It was beating, but slowly, much too slowly. His skin was hot to the touch, burning with fever. He wasn't sleeping; he was unconscious.

He'd been poisoned! Theo had almost the same symptoms my vampire paramour Danial had when he had been poisoned years ago. Danial had mentioned the assassins after him and Theo only days before, when we had celebrated our recent Oathing—a vampire version of marriage—with a late honeymoon at Letchworth State Park. One of those assholes had gotten to Theo somehow. But this time, I couldn't save the day. My blood that had once helped a stricken and dying Danial was useless to Theo.

Panicked, I ran for the phone. *I needed sorcery to undo this. I needed Titus!* Thank God for Danial having a brother who wielded considerable power...and that Devlin was also my lover, under the terms of the same Oath that bound me to his brother. Devlin's demon sorcerer was sure to know an antidote. At this moment, it didn't matter if Titus ate people so long as he saved Theo's life.

1

I clutched the phone, started to dial Hayden, then stopped. *Was it better to just teleport to Titus at Devlin's estate, or call him first? What if this was some type of were poison? Could it affect other weres besides cougars...Oh God, Elle had been around Theo all night. God, please let her not be sick, or dead!*

I called Danial's cell immediately. It went to his voice mail.

"Shit! Danial! It's Sar. Something's wrong with Theo. Shit! I'm going to try Terian."

I dialed Terian, Danial's half demon/half faerie bodyguard. He answered after seven rings, his voice heavy with sleep. "Hello?"

"Terian!" I screamed. "Get to Elle now! I think she's been poisoned!"

"What the hell?" he yelled. "What?"

"Keep her away from other weres if she's sick!" I gasped, hyperventilating.

"Theo's comatose, he's not responding. I'm taking him to Titus now!"

"I'll meet you there!" Terian replied, and hung up.

I held onto Theo and teleported, ending up in the kitchen at Hayden. We scared the hell out of some blond woman.

She ran out of the room screaming, "Hayden is under attack! Help! Help!"

"Help!" I echoed at the top of my lungs. "Titus! Devlin! Help! Help!"

There was the sound of feet running down the stairs, then Devlin was before me, his dark shadow of a guard Lash right behind him. He lunged in front of Devlin and faced me, his gun drawn.

"Get back!" I yelled at him. "This might be were poison! I need Titus!"

Lash—a were himself, of the cottonmouth persuasion—stopped in his tracks at the word 'poison'. To my relief, he nodded and backed out of the room, his non-human snake eyes on Theo. Devlin came past him to my side and crouched down. "What happened to him?" Devlin asked, the expression on his handsome face half worried, half irritated.

"Theo's unconscious," I gasped, then toppled over myself onto the floor.

"Sar!" Devlin yelled, all traces of his arrogance gone. He punched buttons on his cell, then screamed into it, "Titus, get your ass here now! Sar's sick! It may be poison!"

Seconds later, the demon Titus was beside me, a red light emanating from his hand bathing my skin. "Poison for sure," Titus said with a lot of hostility. "Were poison. It's affecting Sar because of the child she's carrying."

"Heal her!" Devlin demanded. "Do whatever you have to. Don't let her die!"

"I can't do anything," Titus said, cutting Devlin short. "The cure might hurt the baby. Sar will be fine if she rests. She'll just feel as if she has a cold. I need to work on Theo, though, Dev. He'll die if he isn't treated soon."

Devlin glanced down at Theo, then his gaze beheld me a second before his golden eyes looked away.

"Save him, please," I beseeched him. "Take my blood, if you need it—"

"Save him, Titus," Devlin said with a sigh. "She might die if he dies."

"Rest, Sar," Titus said, his deep voice soothing. "I'll draw out some of the poison that's in Theo. It's most likely just cougar-targeted, so everyone else should be fine even if some of Danial's men were around Theo at your house."

Elle...I moved to get up, then lay back, sickened. Devlin crouched near me, murmuring soothing words as Titus worked on Theo, incanting some spells that seemed to have no effect. Then, miraculously, Theo stirred slightly. He sat up at once, opening his grey blue eyes which fast became incredulous.

"What the hell? How did I get here?"

I went weak with relief. Devlin and Titus moved back, rising to their feet.

Theo noticed me prone beside him. At once, he pulled me up into his arms, cradling me. "What happened to us?" he asked. "Are you okay?"

"You were poisoned," Titus said in his low grating tone. "You were near death when Sar brought you here. I gave you an antidote which will draw it out of you. You should be fine in a few days."

"I'll pay you," Theo said stiffly, not smiling. "Thanks."

"I'll send the bill to Danial," Titus said disdainfully, his red eyes unfriendly.

Terian appeared, holding Elle in his arms. "Hurry, Titus!"

I let out a scream, Theo started, and Devlin rolled his eyes in disgust. "Just great!" he said accusingly, glaring at Theo. "How many others did you infect?"

"How is she?" I asked hysterically, my eyes all for Elle. She looked pale as death.

"Elle!" Theo cried, staggering as he tried to get to his feet.

"Keep back from her," Titus warned. "You'll re-infect yourself, cougar."

"She's conscious, just barely," Terian said worriedly. "Danial is beside himself. What happened?"

"Poison," Devlin said, getting to his feet. "Meant for Theo, probably."

"Give her to me," Titus said, motioning to Terian. "I've got to make more of the antidote. Come with me to my lab, son, and I'll show you what to do. Odds are, you'll be making it again soon."

My skin crawled at his surety. Theo had more than one hit out on him. *What if Titus was right. What if this happened again?*

"You'll be fine, Theo," Devlin stated, glaring at his rival, whose eyes were all for Titus as he took Elle downstairs. "Go home and get some clothes on before we all go blind. I'm going back to bed."

"Here." I handed Theo my blue velvet bathrobe. He took it, covering

3

himself.

Devlin helped me to my feet. "Did you get anything in the mail, Sarelle?" he said, his worried eyes searching mine. "This poison came in contact with you somehow. You and Elle wouldn't have gotten sick just from being near Theo unless he had some on his skin."

An enemy had tried to poison Theo with something similar only last Christmas, sending a package for Theo through the mail to my house. The deadly missive had been intercepted, barely. "Nothing, there was nothing—"

"It was the cat," Theo interrupted, running his hand through his hair. "I'll bet anything it was on the cat I found in our woodshed."

"Danial's new cat?" Devlin said angrily. "Someone put poison on it? Bad enough they abandoned it in mid-winter—"

"How could they do that?" I asked. "Wouldn't the cat just have licked it off and died?"

"Remember, it was sick," Theo said bitterly. "It's probably known you like cats, that you have some as pets. Someone left it there for you to find, figuring you would bring it inside to take care of and I would be exposed. After I found it, we kept it in the garage because it was sick. To ensure your cats didn't get sick, I washed my hands and changed my clothes after I took care of it every time. That must have delayed the poison affecting me. I haven't felt sick or weak until I woke up on the floor here."

"Makes sense," Devlin supposed. "But risky. What if it got killed before giving the poison to you or managed to groom itself enough to get the poison off?"

"There's been nothing else out of the ordinary," Theo said, rubbing his eyes. "This explains why the cat had a cough when all its tests were negative. The vet said he wasn't sure exactly what had caused it, that maybe the cat had inhaled some chemical?"

"This stinks of that bastard Robert," Devlin interrupted. "You know he's after you—"

"I know," Theo said irritably. He took my hand. "Let's go home."

"Please have Terian call us the moment Elle awakens," I asked Devlin.

He nodded. "Get some rest. I'll call you later." He turned and walked back upstairs.

Lash went to follow him, then stopped suddenly, watching Theo and I. Theo growled at him. Lash just smiled a little, then looked pointedly at me for a long moment, a smirk on his face.

I reddened. Since the early days of my current pregnancy—and the previous one with Danial's half vampire child, I had been afflicted with The Lust, a desire that hit me in odd moments. It compelled me to rash actions of a sexual nature, usually eliciting violence along with the coupling. Lash had been the target only weeks ago, an event the weresnake clearly hoped to rub in everyone's face as much as possible.

Theo growled louder, his warning obvious. Lash shot him an easy grin, baring his fangs, gave me a final look, then went after Devlin.

I teleported us home to find the house stinking of burned meat.

I ran into the kitchen, and moved the burned sausage off the stove. It was little more than a black mess in the bottom of the pan. I put it in the sink with detergent and water to soak, then looked for the bacon. I found only the chewed remains of the empty wrapper on the floor. While we'd been gone, the cats had knocked it off the counter, and the dogs Ghost and Darkness had eaten it.

"I hope you guys are proud of yourselves," I said sarcastically to them. "There will be no more treats for either of you today."

Looking at the stove, it all seemed too much suddenly. Resigned, I got out some more bacon and sausage, and then eggs and bread for toast. "What and how many?" I asked Theo tiredly.

Theo finished letting the dogs outside, then turned to me. "You don't have to cook, Sar. We just had a traumatic event."

"Good," I said gladly, grabbing some cereal bowls. "Cheerios or Raisin Bran?"

* * * *

"I haven't ever seen you eat so much," Theo said as he watched me finish my cereal. "That's your second bowl."

I laughed. "Pregnancy tends to do that."

He reached out to take my hand in his. "You did good," Theo said softly. "You saved me, Sar."

"Titus saved you," I corrected gently. "I just got you to him."

"He wouldn't have saved me if you hadn't asked him to," Theo said roughly. "Not for any price. He dislikes me as much as Lash does."

Theo's bitter words sunk in as I finished my cold but filling breakfast.

Robert, the third Ranked—a hierarchy of those who made their living from jobs of everything from bodyguards to assassins, would likely be trying again, once he found out his attempt on Theo's life had failed. Rumor was—à la Danial—that Robert was eager to take Theo's number two spot in the Ranking. Usually that occurred after a challenge of some kind, and a fight to the death. But it seemed like Robert meant to take his prize by any means necessary...no matter how many other lives were collateral damage.

If I didn't know Titus, or he wasn't my friend, Theo would have died. I'd initially balked at Titus, worried at his reputation as a poisoner, his association with Leri—an evil witch who'd threatened me—and his somewhat scary admission that he thought of me as kin now because I'd been exposed to some demon blood from his son, Terian. But after this morning, I no longer cared what Titus was, or what he was into. He'd saved Theo. From now on, I was going to be nice to him and turn a blind eye to what he had to do to live. He couldn't help what he was. And I needed him now more than ever.

* * * *

Despite Titus's grave words, there were no more problems with poison or attempts at harming Theo in the next four weeks. What did quickly become a problem was Theo's over-protectiveness of me in my condition. I didn't lose my temper until he told me I wasn't to walk the dogs anymore.

"I'm pregnant, not an invalid!" I yelled in frustration. "I want to try to keep in shape. Already I can't fit into my jeans—"

"I'll buy you a treadmill," Theo said smoothly. "You are not walking outside, not until the ice is gone."

"Fine," I said reluctantly.

True to his word, Theo came home with a treadmill the next night, and set it up for me. I got used to using it in time, and it was easier than walking outside on ice, though I missed my walks with the dogs.

In all other ways, my current pregnancy was the same as my previous one. The Lust presented itself regularly, though it was Devlin who now raised it and sated it without fail. He got great pleasure out of the latter. Though I still found that disquieting, I was grateful for his help, as it allowed me to control my otherwise out of control desires. Better yet, The Lust did not present itself with either Theo or Danial again.

Some of that may have been the chaste way with which Danial acted toward me now, or the restraint that Theo showed in the few times we were intimate. I didn't call attention to either behavior, content to cross my fingers and hope that my luck held. Lash still shadowed me whenever I visited Hayden, unless I was with Devlin. I wanted whatever miracle had allowed me to elude a repeat encounter with him to continue for the remainder of my pregnancy.

Not that I hadn't grown used to Lash in all the hours we'd spent in each other's company. I was accustomed to his silence and stillness by now. His reptilian snake eyes still made me uneasy, but he was never rude or coarse, as he had been to Danial that one morning in Letchworth. He never mentioned to me that we had been intimate at all, or acted as if I was anything other than a friend's girlfriend he was watching over. As time had passed, I had relaxed sufficiently to feel easy in his presence, enough so I began to talk to him when he was in the mood to talk, which wasn't often.

6

One afternoon, I noticed he'd finally neared the end of his book about the Tibetan Dead. "What's it about?" I asked, filing another birth certificate in the correct drawer.

"It's about life after death," Lash hissed, not looking up from the page. "About what the Tibetans believe."

Why don't you vague that up for me some more, Lash? "What do they believe?" I asked, holding back my retort.

"Why do you want to know?" Lash inquired, looking up finally.

I turned to him, leaning on the filing cabinet. "I believe in God, but sometimes I wonder about good and evil. I know Devlin can be bad, but I love him, despite what I know he's done. I like Titus, even though he told me what he has to do in order to live."

Lash flicked his tongue out at me, tasting the air. *Perhaps he was tasting for truthfulness?*

"I think I'm a pretty good person," I continued. "But I wonder what will happen when I die. Will Dev be where I end up? Will Danial? Will I meet Theo in another life, now that we're bound?"

Lash nodded. "The Tibetans believe that you are reborn when you die," he hissed. "But not immediately. Your spirit wanders around for a while to various couples creating life, and you have to choose your parents, and hope you learn something by living life as that child. You only stop being reborn when you reach the level of perfect harmony with the universe, and then you aren't reborn anymore."

"Do you believe that?" I asked.

"No," he hissed. "I like to believe I'm going to end up in a bar run by loose weresnake women for eternity, so I can drink heavily and enjoy myself forever."

I burst out laughing. After a moment, he laughed, too. "I'm kidding," he hissed. "I'd be happy to end up somewhere warm and sunny, someplace where it wasn't ever cold. That would be enough. That would be a kind of Heaven."

There was yearning in his words, enough to make me feel self-conscious. He'd accused me months ago about not seeing him as a person, and he'd been right. Sure, he was a badass, but he had the same fears I did, and probably some of the same hopes, too.

I turned back to my work. "I think I would want to go on living, go on being reborn. I like living. There's always something new to see and do. But I'd be happy to be in the sun, too. I hate being cold, not to mention the ice and snow of winter."

"You are going to live a long time," Lash stated, regarding me intently. "You're part vampire now, or so Dev says. You probably won't age."

"That's what Danial told me," I said quickly. I still hadn't come to terms with that. Every time I thought about it, I worried. And that wasn't even counting whatever impact my exposure to demon blood would have on my longevity, much less my soul.

"Why are you working so hard?" Lash hissed angrily. "Devlin didn't bring you here to work, Sarelle."

What was this about? Why was he angry? "I like to work," I said stiffly, not turning around. "I like to do things. Theo lets me do nothing now. And I can only lie in bed for so long."

There was no reply. I looked over my shoulder to find Lash gone.

Had he left in anger? That was odd. He'd never acted angry since that time he'd thrown the glass in the kitchen, when he'd been pissed off at a previous lovers' unfaithfulness to him. Putting down my work, I went after him.

I walked to basement stairs and bumped into Leri coming down the steps.

Chapter Two

She dropped her eyes immediately. "Hello, Sarelle."

"What are you doing here?" I accused. "You were forbidden from entering the grounds of Hayden, or so Dev told me."

"What I did was wrong, I know that—"

Like Hell. "Don't," I said, holding up one of my hands. "I'll never forgive you, even if Titus has."

She sighed. "I can't forgive myself."

"Why didn't you just kill Terian when he was born?" I said bluntly. "You would have spared him a lot of pain."

"He was Titus's son," Leri replied. "I couldn't kill him. I panicked. I wasn't ready to be a mother, especially to a half-demon child. I thought it would be easier, just giving him a life away from me—"

"Leri," I interrupted. "If you really want Terian to forgive you, tell him the truth about Keriam."

Leri stared at me, shocked.

God, I hoped I was doing the right thing by telling her this. "You've got to know Terian wants to find his family. He tried that vampire Danial knew out west, but they can't find anything about Keriam's real family. You have to know the answer."

Terian had been to Dallas, Texas, the first place he had remembered living when he was a child. Though he had scoured the local files, even expanding his search to include surrounding towns, there was no record of a college kid who had disappeared fitting Keriam's description. Having no way to discover the true identity of the mortal man that Leri had bespelled into caring for her supernatural child more than seventy years previous, Terian had returned to New York State, dejected and hopeless. Sundown's presence in his life was helping ease his depression, but not much.

"He won't talk to me."

9

Terian had refused to see his faerie mother Leri after an ill-fated attempted reconciliation by his demon father, Titus. He had cut himself off from the one person who could give him the answers he was looking for. *But then if my mom had tried to kill me, I'd probably have done the same.* "Then write him a letter," I retorted glaring at Leri. "Telling Terian Keriam's real name would go a long way toward healing some of the damage you did. I'll take it to him."

"Why?" she said suspiciously. "You don't like me, so why help me?"

"I'm not doing it for you, I'm doing it for him," I said disgustedly. I longed to really light into her verbally, but was afraid of her magical power. "That's all you need to know." I walked past her and up to the kitchen, before my anger got the better of me.

Lash was waiting for me outside the cellar door, leaning nonchalantly against the wall.

"Did you already eat?" I asked, moving past him. There was no point in asking if he wanted any of what I'd make for myself; he always refused.

"Yes, earlier," he replied, following me into the kitchen. "I was listening to you talk to Leri."

Another fellow listener at doors. Something to remember. "Then it's okay if I eat?"

His head inclined, puzzled. "Why wouldn't it be?" he hissed.

"You left all of a sudden, without saying anything," I said, irritated. "I thought there might be a problem."

"Someone was in Titus's workshop," Lash said. "I knew it wasn't him by the movements. I expected to find someone who needed reminding the basement is off limits. It was only Leri, getting some things for Titus."

His tone hadn't been apologetic, but it also wasn't sarcastic. I nodded in reply, then went about making lunch.

I was pleased at my progress at Hayden. I'd painted half the guest rooms and gotten through ten of the boxes to be filed. I still had at least thirty boxes to go, but progress had slowed a lot today. I had entered older records from the 1940's and before. Inside those stacks of cardboard boxes weren't just receipts and documents, but also older photos and memorabilia.

In retrospect, I should have expected that. Danial, keeper of secrets, had never showed me the contents of his gray memory boxes. I'd never asked, worried about how I might feel to see his other lives, the loves he must have had over the years. Yet Devlin had never balked at telling me about the past, or anything else I asked him. It made sense his memories weren't locked away, but jumbled together with everything else where anyone could see them.

While I had been eager to see some of the history of Devlin's long life, I'd been ill prepared for how it had made me feel. There were photos of Danial and

Devlin together, sometimes with one woman, sometimes with two. The women were not of one type, and so far, none of them had looked like me. I was both happy and worried about that.

There were also photos of Devlin alone with several women, and other men, sometimes couples, and one of him alone with a younger man. It didn't look like anyone I knew, although something seemed familiar about the face. In all the photos, Devlin looked almost the same, though most of the clothes he wore in the photos were old fashioned and dated.

That upset me more, irrationally. I didn't know who any of these people were, and most of them were likely dead. But they must have meant something to Devlin to have their pictures stored down here. *How many had he loved? How many did he still remember? One day, would I have a file that was the same? Looking at Cia's face a century from now, would I remember her name, or how much fun we'd had last week with the weight of a hundred years dimming the memory? Or was I doomed to stare at the faded picture, struggling in vain to recall not only her name, but ever being there with her at all?*

"Are you going to warm up that soup?" Lash hissed. "If so, let me help." He turned on the stove burner, and set it on low. Startled out of my musing, I prepared my sandwich, then put the soup in a bowl. I walked into the other room to eat. Lash followed me, sitting across from me, his arms crossed over his chest.

I had been unsettled by his watching me eat at first, but he never did anything more than that and he never initiated conversation. That made it easy enough to ignore his flat eyes fixed on me.

When I'd finished, I took the plates back to the kitchen. "I have to leave now for my doctor appointment. I'm going to teleport. I'll be back in about an hour."

Lash nodded. "I'll be here when you get back. You'll be at least an hour, right?"

"Yes," I said, giving him a smile.

To my surprise, he gave me one back. "I'll be here," he said, then turned and left.

* * * *

All went fine until Dr. Camlyn left with a sample of my blood to test. He was back in a few moments, his face worried.

"What is it?" I said, alarmed.

"Nothing. I just need to check something," he said vaguely. "Lay down." He rubbed goopy gel all over my abdomen, and then slid the scanner around. I looked at the screen with him, but I couldn't make heads or tails out of what I was seeing. There were shadows, blobs, and some faint movement.

"Yes, there it is," Stephen muttered.

"There what is?" I said stridently.

Stephen looked up at me. "Congratulations, you're having twins."

"What?" I stammered.

"You need to brace yourself."

"For what?" I said quickly. "Spit it out already."

"Only one of the babies is werecougar. The other's dhamphir."

My eyes went wide as chills went down my spine. "No," I breathed. "That can't be possible—"

"Your blood has the same markers now that it did before with Danial's child," Stephen said, putting his hand on my shoulder. "This is going to be another one for the record books."

"This can't really happen!" I said shrilly. "This is like an episode of daytime TV—"

"There is nothing contrived or impossible about this," Stephen said patiently. "You said Titus gave you a fertility spell. Your body released two eggs as a result. Then you were with Theo less than forty-eight hours after you were with Devlin. Each of them fertilized one of your eggs, Sar. The twins are fraternal, not identical."

Thank God Theo had gone with Danial overnight on a trip to Akron yesterday, and hadn't come with me to this appointment. "Can you tell if they are male or female?" I managed.

"No, not with any certainly," Stephen said with a smile. "But just my confirming that one is his should make Devlin very happy."

This had to be wrong. He had to be. "Could it be a mistake? You didn't test my blood right after Devlin brought me back from the brink of death—"

"Sar, the last time vampire DNA was in your blood was when you were pregnant with Theoron. The DNA is very close to Devlin's." He paused. "Odds are that with them being fraternal, one is a boy, though I can't say which one."

I gave him a weak smile.

"See that?" he said, and pointed to the screen. "Here is one baby," he said, pointing to a small blob. "Here it the other, almost hidden behind the first." He pointed to a smaller blob.

"If you say so," I said slowly. "You're the doctor."

"Sar, I'm going to prescribe more vitamins for you to take. You're going to have to be very careful. Carrying either of these kind of children would be taxing. Carrying them both at once is going to be a tremendous strain on your body. You need to rest and eat as much as possible."

Like that would be a problem. At this one moment in time, nothing mattered except getting back to Devlin and telling him our plan hadn't failed, it had worked. "Can you give me some samples for now? I really want to get back to Dev and tell him."

Stephen nodded. "I'll call in the prescription and give you some samples for tonight and tomorrow." He turned to go.

"Stephen, please make a copy of the ultrasound for me and write something out to take to Devlin," I said, managing a smile. "He's not going to believe this either."

* * * *

As I waited in the lobby for my vitamins and papers, I thought about the best way to tell Devlin. We had all night, but I wanted it to be perfect. Devlin had waited two hundred years to be a father and now it was finally happening.

A few minutes later, I arrived in the kitchen at Hayden. Serena rushed over to me immediately, as if she'd been lying in wait. "Sarelle, quick, get out of here!" she urged frantically, trying to propel me towards the garage.

"What is it?" I said, grabbing her hands and prying them off. "Calm down and tell me what's happened."

"That Ruler, Perseus, he's here! He's looking for you!"

"Where's Dev?" I gasped. "What happened?"

"A few minutes ago he showed up at the front door and burst in," Serena said, her head darting to check the door behind me. "Harriet got pregnant, but she miscarried. She's alive, barely. He was shouting at Devlin, telling him he was going to kill him for his treachery and take you. Lash killed at least three of the weremonkeys he had with him before Devlin headed to the ballroom to draw him off." She clasped my hands in hers. "There's a weresnake Perseus brought that bit one of the bears. He's already feverish. Devlin told me to wait for you, to make sure you escaped—"

No. Now that Dev's plan had worked, I was getting that bastard Perseus to back the hell off. "Stay here," I said, heading to the door. "I'm going to go see Perseus—"

"No!" Serena yelled desperately. "They'll take you! You're my only friend!"

"Shh," I demanded. "Once Perseus hears what I've got to say, he'll back off."

"What?" Serena asked, her eyes wide and frightened.

"I'm having twins," I said proudly. "One of them is Devlin's. Now come on!"

Her expression shifted rapidly from shock to resolute, then she hugged me hard. "Lead on," she said, giving me a determined look.

We walked quickly towards the ballroom, the yelling becoming audible before we were anywhere near the door.

"I know you did something, Dalcon! Harriet miscarried, and she shouldn't have. Your instructions were lies!"

"Shut up, Greek!" Devlin's voice replied mockingly. "I told you what to do. You should've tried one at a time, and not pushed it. Sar miscarried once herself. That may be the result the first time a woman tries. Harriet survived, and no other woman who miscarried has done that in recent history, except Sar."

"More lies," Perseus growled. "Sar is having that werecougar's child, not yours. We expressively forbade it, Dalcon! Why did you stand for it? She is Oathed to you!"

"Sar may miscarry," Devlin replied easily. "She should not have gotten pregnant as fast as she did. I'm waiting for her to bear one child successfully before making her pregnant with my own, that it will have the better chance—"

"You're a fool!" Perseus hissed. "A fool in love with a human! You were such a fine vampire once, Devlin. It's a shame you've gone soft."

"I'm neither a fool, nor soft in any way," Devlin laughed. "Sar knows that well—"

"Spare me your sexual escapades," Perseus spat. "Your excesses are legend."

I put my hand on the ballroom door, then paused. *Legend?*

"And yours are nil! At least I know I can father a child!" Devlin answered arrogantly. "You have never even managed to make a child, have you? It was Samuel's child Harriet lost, wasn't it? Not yours, Perseus. You were probably sterile back when you were human—"

With a look to Serena to stay outside, I took a breath and pushed open the double doors.

Perseus looked over immediately, as did Devlin, the latter looking instantly scared to death, sure I'd walked into a trap. Lash was there, serrated knife in hand, facing a muscular man with a similar knife. Both of them cut their eyes to me, and then back to each other. Perseus faced me and grinned like the Cheshire Cat. "Ah, Sar," he said, advancing. "I'd hoped you would arrive—"

Devlin was between us in a second, blocking Perseus as he reached for me. "Back off, Greek!" he growled, shielding me with his body. "You aren't taking her. She is Oathed to me."

"I'm taking her Oath tonight!" Perseus hissed menacingly. "I have a doctor ready to abort that were—"

"You're taking Sar over my dead corpse," Devlin growled back furiously.

"Kill him," Perseus ordered. His weresnake went for Devlin, even as Lash moved and blocked him, their knives meeting in a clash of steel. Both backed off, and began circling, slicing at one another.

"You want to fight, Greek?" Devlin hissed, eyes red. "I'm right here. Sar, get out of here; run!"

"You won't stop me this time," Perseus said, baring his fangs. Devlin braced himself, baring his own wide, and snarling.

"Stop this!" I yelled. "Stop this male bullshit!"

Everyone looked over at me.

"I'm having his child," I said, handing Perseus the papers. "I've just been to Camlyn, and he confirmed it."

"This is a trick," Perseus hissed. "Another trick, like Harriet—"

"Not one of my making," Devlin said, trying to put distance between me and Perseus as he backed away, pushing me behind him.

"Heteropaternal superfecundation?" Perseus said slowly, reading the papers.

"Two fathers, two eggs," I explained, flushing. "You should be aware of the possibility, as it might happen to Harriet. She is subject to the same conditions I've been in."

Perseus crumpled the papers and threw them down on the floor, glaring at me. "I will check this out with Camlyn, Sarelle," he hissed. "It had better be as you say."

"Go ahead," I said defiantly, staring him down. "I'm not lying."

"At least the dhamphir will have something to feed on while he's growing," Perseus hissed nastily.

Dizziness overcame me, then sudden worry. *What if he was right?*

Devlin grabbed hold of my arm, steadying me as he watched Perseus. "By law, you can't take her from me," Devlin said with relish, flashing Perseus a fang-filled smile. "There is no way in Hell Samuel would stand for it, not and set a precedent that might cost him his own heir. You can't fight the both of us, Greek. Now get the Hell out of my house and don't come back."

"Let's go," Perseus said, with one last look of hate toward Devlin. He strode out, his weresnake henchman following him, sheathing his knife as he gave Lash a last parting hiss.

Lash ignored him, sheathed his own knife, then went to the papers and picked them up. He smoothed them, then handed them to Devlin. Devlin skimmed the papers, then slowly looked down at me. "Is he sure?" he said joyously. "There's no mistake?"

"Yes," I said happily. "You're going to be a father."

Devlin hugged me tightly, then lifted me in the air as he whirled me

15

around a few times, laughing, smiling radiantly.

"Congratulations," Lash said, giving him a wide smile.

Devlin hugged him fiercely. "We have to celebrate," Devlin said, turning from Lash to me. "Let's go out!"

"Davy's?" Lash suggested.

Devlin looked at him, then said carefully, "Do you mind?"

"Cin has left the state," Lash said with a shrug. "I don't mind."

I looked at the floor uncomfortably. Cin had been a weresnake waitress at Davy's, and Lash's lover. Their breakup had been precipitated by his one liaison with me, which had led to his discovery of Cin's unfaithfulness to him through sordid means that had affected me. He and I had never talked of it, after his apology…

Don't think about that.

"Davy's it is." Devlin turned back to me. "Does Danial know?"

I forced a smile. "You're the first to know," I said warmly, hugging him again. "I came straight here from Dr. Camlyn's. No one else knows except Serena and Lash."

"Good!" Devlin shouted with glee. "I want to be the one to tell him." He pulled me close, then lovingly sang, "Here is all I need!"

"A book of verses underneath the bough,

A jug of wine, a loaf of bread, and Thou,

Beside me singing in the Wilderness,

Oh, such a Wilderness would be Paradise enow!"

I gave him a giddy smile, happy that he was so happy. "Your own creation, Dev?"

He shook his head. "From the Rubaiyat." He offered his arm. "Come, Sar. This night will be filled with many songs, all of them in your honor."

* * * *

We had a great night at Davy's. I had a glass of wine to celebrate, two grilled cheese sandwiches, and some chocolate peanut butter pie.

The guys got trashed. From the first, Devlin and Lash toasted the baby, downing one drink right after the other. Within an hour they were singing drinking songs loudly, both their voices out of tune. The wearbears Nick and Jazz had taken up positions by the doors, but weren't in much better shape, despite they'd had plain beer instead of the concoction Lash and Dev were drinking.

Devlin couldn't drink much alcohol, or at least, that was what he'd always told me. Still, Lash and Dev were drunk on something mixed with blood. I suspected some type of drug possibly, though Devlin refused to tell me what it

16

was they were imbibing, his only answer a gleeful smile.

After the first round, Devlin called Danial and excitedly informed him he was going to be a daddy. Terian showed up at Davy's with Danial ten minutes later.

"Bro!" Devlin cried, jumping up and hugging Danial hard. "Another round!" he called to Gary.

Gary brought over some more mugs, giving me a happy smile. I gave him a halfhearted one back.

"You are wasted, Dev," Danial said rolling his eyes and smiling. "What have you been drinking?"

"Blood, laced with a little something," Devlin said raucously. "Want some?"

"Just one," Danial said, gingerly taking up a mug. "I'm only doing this because I'm so happy for you."

By the time Danial had finished his mug, he was singing along with Lash and Dev, his notes pretty much on key. I'd never heard him sing before. I tried to listen, but it was hard to make out the lyrics, even though there weren't many other people in the bar. Giving up, I went over to the bar where Terian was chatting up a brunette.

I tapped him on the shoulder. "Got a minute?"

"Sure." He said good-bye to the woman, then turned to me. "Congrats."

"Thanks. You must have been here before."

"Once, with Titus, after I met Leri with him the first time," Terian sighed. "I needed a drink, and I think he did, too. He brought us here."

"That's what I wanted to talk to you about." I produced the letter given to me by Lash a couple days ago. "Here."

Terian took it. "What's this?"

"I know this isn't the time. But I don't know when I'll see you next. Going to Danial's and Devlin's every weekend is fun, but I'm starting to feel like I never see anyone but the three of them anymore." I gave him a half smile. "I hope Sundown is adjusting okay?"

I'd met Sundown a week ago. Theo had been right; she could've been my sister, something I found upsetting, but didn't know how to address, not that it was my place to do that anyway. It was Terian's business who he dated. But I'd seen in her eyes when she'd met me that the resemblance between us hadn't been lost on her, either.

"What's this, Sar?"

"A letter from Leri."

He made as if to crumple it. I stopped him. "Wait, read it."

"I don't want to hear anything she has to say," he said vehemently, and made to crumple it again.

"It's about Keriam's real identity," I said quickly. "She is the only one who knows, Tears. Read it. You can always burn it later."

Terian nodded, stuffed it in his pocket, and then walked away abruptly.

I'd done my good deed for the day and it had left me in a foul mood, feeling unappreciated. It was about midnight by now; past time to leave. I walked over to Danial, Lash and Dev, who were singing When a Man Loves a Woman.

"I'm ready to go home."

Devlin staggered to his feet. "My Lady," he said gallantly.

"I'm not letting you guys drive," I said, holding out my palm. "Keys, please."

Dev handed them to me as Terian teleported Danial home. A little while later, I arrived back at Hayden with Lash, Devlin, and the bears, all of whom were now coherent. Leaving the keys with the bears, I followed as Lash and Devlin walked upstairs together, supporting each other.

"Think Danial will tell Theo?" Lash hissed snidely, as he went inside his room. "Won't he be surprised."

Guilt hit me. It wasn't right that Theo didn't know about the twins. In all the celebration, I'd forgotten to tell him. A phone call was out of the question.

"Love!" Devlin called loudly from his doorway. "Come to bed!"

Screw it, I'd teleport home quick and tell Theo. Elle was at our house tonight, but I shouldn't wake her if I was quiet.

I went up to Devlin. "I'll be right back."

"No!" he sang with longing and volume. "Come to bed, my love. Come and be with me! Thou are flesh of my flesh!"

"Go take a cold shower and brush your teeth," I said sternly. "And maybe I'll think about it when I get back."

With deliberate effort, Devlin headed to the bathroom. Reassuring myself that as a vampire he couldn't drown, I teleported to my bedroom at home.

"Theo," I said softly.

"Sar?" he said, his words heavy with sleep. "What are you doing here? Is something wrong?"

"I saw Stephen today. I'm having twins."

Theo's face lit up. "That's wonderful! I wanted—"

"Only one is yours," I said quickly.

He rolled onto his back, staring at the ceiling. "Is Stephen sure?"

"Yes," I said, apologetic. "I didn't think it was right that you didn't know."

"It's okay," he said in a tone that meant it really wasn't. "This is good. You're not only having my child, you're having his, too. We'll be rid of him that much sooner."

He was deluding himself, but I was too tired to argue. "I'll see you tomorrow. I've got to get back."

"Elle and I'll be there at the horror movie," Theo said, rubbing his eyes. "Elle has macabre taste. Must be from Tawny. I never had a taste for horror movies."

Was mentioning her a dig at me, because he was angry over my news? "I watched too many of them with her when she was young, trapped in her cougar form," I replied. "I didn't think it would warp her, but I guess it did."

"I don't think that was it," Theo said, raking his hand through his hair and giving me a smile. "But maybe it was. Go. I'll see you tomorrow, Sweetheart."

Maybe I was being too sensitive. "Sleep well," I said. "I love you."

"I love you too, Sar," Theo said.

I teleported quickly back to Hayden. Devlin was still in the bathroom. I got undressed and slipped into bed. He came out a moment later, looking ill.

"Are you okay?" I said, concerned.

"I will be," Devlin said, sighing. "I'm out of practice. It's been a while since I did drugs that heavily."

Many, many possible replies crossed my mind, but I held my tongue on everything except, "Go to sleep."

He laid down in my arms, one possessive hand on my belly, stroking it softly.

* * * *

The next day, I didn't see Lash in the kitchen when I went down for breakfast. Concluding that he was also not feeling well, I ate quickly and teleported to Danial's.

It was mid-March now. Business was back in full swing, and Solutions Inc., Danial's detective company, was booked solid.

I worked hard for the first four hours, even though it was Saturday, then took a break about lunch. Danial was still sleeping. Hesitant to disturb him in case he also was feeling ill, I brought my hastily made sandwich over to the werecompound, eating most of it on the way. Then I sought out Elle and Theoron to break the news to them that there were going to be two babies born in late summer, instead of one.

Theoron was amazed one of the babies would be like him. "A dhamphir?" he said incredulously. "I thought I was the only one."

"You were. Don't worry, you're still special."

Theoron looked mournful. I hugged him.

"It's Devlin's child, isn't it?" Elle said astutely, her blue eyes looking at me with Theo's exact calculating stare.

She still looked nine, but she was maturing faster and faster. "Yes," I answered honestly. "You know he and I are Oathed, Elle. There is nothing wrong with him being the father of my baby."

Elle shrugged nonchalantly. "Dad is happy about it. I saw him last night when he came in with Terian."

Apparently to her, Danial's opinion was all that mattered. *That was a blessing.* "Let's take a walk, kids, while we wait for your father to get up."

During the walk, Elle and Theoron both eagerly pointed out tracks to me, and also named some birds we saw and heard. Though the weather had been cold and there was still snow coating the ground, the first signs of spring were evident in the budding trees.

When we returned, Cia and Aran were waiting for us. Aran Jr. was there, too, in his fox form.

Cia greeted me, her eyes dancing with pride. "He's changed for the first time. We're letting him spend time as a fox for a while to learn how to use his other form."

"He's adorable," I said, petting Aaron Jr.'s soft reddish fur. He made little yips and barks, then jumped up on my legs. I picked him up carefully. He licked my nose, then began struggling to get down.

Danial came out of his bedroom, dressed. "Please go get on fresh clothes," he told the kids. "Hurry now."

Theoron and Elle ran to get ready, as I said my goodbyes to Cia and family. When I returned to the great room, Danial was there alone, reading a book.

I looked him over skeptically. "How are you feeling?"

"Okay," he said, his tone off enough from normal that I understood his response to be a positive exaggeration. "I take it Devlin was hurting last night?"

"Yes," I announced, smiling. "He said he was out of practice."

"That drug the blood was laced with is very potent," he said, wincing slightly. "You can lose your reason easily with just a glass." He paused, gathering his courage. "Is it true I was singing?"

It was in his voice how much he wanted that to not be a true memory. "Your voice was good," I praised, giving him a kiss. "You should sing more often."

Danial blushed. I watched him with relish. "You should blush more, too," I added, kissing him again. "You are unbearably attractive when you blush."

He tugged me down on the couch next to him with unnatural swiftness and tickled me. "Is that so? Well you are unbearably attractive when you wriggle about and shriek—"

"Stop!" I shrieked, laughing. "Stop! I need to breathe!"

Danial stopped tickling me, giving me a quick hug before releasing me and standing up. "We should go, Sar," he said, offering me his hand. "Where's Theo? He should be here by now."

"Here!" Theo called loudly, striding in. "I was getting these for Sar." He handed me a large bouquet of white roses.

He had never gotten me flowers before, ever. I was so touched, I started to cry. Danial handed me a tissue. I took it gratefully, then went into the kitchen to put the roses in some water.

Theo came in behind me. "I didn't mean to make you cry," he said, resting his hand on my upper arm.

"They aren't sad tears. They're happy tears. Thank you, they're beautiful." I leaned in close to some of the beautiful blooms, hoping to catch some fragrance, but there was none. Masking my disappointment, I followed Theo back to the great room where Danial and the kids waited.

* * * *

We made it to the theater in plenty of time to get our tickets. I stood in line for candy and popcorn, while Danial and Theo went with Theoron and Elle to get seats. I had just finished giving my order to the attendant when I felt a hand cup my buttock and squeeze.

Danial would never do something like this, especially out in public. "That had better be you, Theo," I said darkly, turning to look. My eyes met an expansive chest. I raised my head to take in laughing golden eyes and a winning smile, laced with more than a little triumph. "What are you doing here, Dev?" I said in surprise.

"Seeing a movie," Devlin said, smirking, as he put his hands on the counter on either side of me. He leaned in, then rubbed me gently with his lower body. There was a shifting beneath his jeans, then a gentle flexing motion against my groin.

"Stop that," I said sternly, trying not to laugh. Devlin smirked wider, then rubbed again. Crimson with embarrassment, I looked over at the cashier to see Lash paying for the food I had ordered, along with some extra bottles of water.

"Where are you sitting?" Devlin said, moving his body away from mine casually, as if nothing had happened. "We want to sit near you."

If I said no, he'd do it anyway. "Follow me." I grabbed my food, Lash grabbed his water, and we three headed into the theater.

The movie trailers hadn't started yet. Theo and Danial both turned to me with a smile, then both of them looked annoyed. "What are you two doing here?" Theo accused, irritated.

"Seeing a movie," Devlin restated. "Blood by the gallons and songs to boot. What could be better?"

"The ratio of guards to kids is two to four with just you two," Lash hissed to Danial, ignoring Theo. "With us its four to four. Better odds."

Lash was right, in that I was human and vulnerable...making my half-human children within me equally vulnerable. "He's got a point," I added half-heartedly.

Danial rolled his eyes. "Sit down, then."

Theo growled as Lash and Devlin sat behind Theoron and I, but didn't protest further.

I was able to relax during the film, knowing they were both watching my back literally. While I enjoyed the movie, the blood and gore was a little over the top. Devlin, the kids and Lash laughed through much of it, while Danial and Theo did not. When it was over, we all walked out together.

"If they ever make a movie of my life, I want Depp to play me," Devlin said. "He's a great actor."

"He would play me instead, Dev," Lash said, grinning with his one fang bared. "He looks more like me, anyway. You're too tall and blond."

Johnny Depp didn't look a thing like Lash, but I kept my mouth shut, not wanting to antagonize him.

Devlin gave him a good-natured shove. Soon they were tussling in the parking lot. After a moment, they broke it off, then turned to face us.

"Where's your SUV?" Devlin said to Danial. "We'll escort you."

Uh-oh. "We have to go," I said, giving Dev a smile. "We'll be fine, it's just down—"

"To your parents, yes," Devlin said, grinning. "Lead on. We're coming, too."

I gaped at him. "What?"

"No way," Theo growled.

"Yes," Devlin said, grinning widely and baring his teeth. "Sar's having my child. It's only appropriate that I meet her parents. It's positively overdue."

God, I should have seen this coming, as soon as I saw him tonight.

"Dev—"

"He's right," Danial interrupted. "Your mom and dad should meet him."

"You told him about this outing," I rebuked, putting my hands on my hips. "Last night."

"I may have let something slip," Danial admitted slowly.

"He invited me," Devlin purred.

Danial looked at the ground.

"Good going, Danial," Theo said sarcastically. "You're going to make her parents think Sar's landed herself smack in the worst crowd possible. They've accepted a lot already with you and me. Now you're going to announce that she's having your brother's baby, oh and by the way, he's a vampire, too."

"I'm just going to say I'm Danial's brother, for now," Devlin placated. "When they know me a little better, I'll tell them I'm the father of one of her children and that we're sort of married."

"You will not!" Theo growled loudly. "Sar's my wife, not yours—"

"She's got on two pair of wedding rings, Theo," Devlin said, folding his hands across his chest. "And you are not the only man wearing the matching partner."

Devlin now wore a band on his right ring finger. It was the same kind of band with the metals swirled together that Danial and I still wore.

Theo's eyes went wide. "You bas—"

I clapped my hand over his mouth. Theoron and Elle didn't need to be taught yet another swear word. "Stop," I said, then put down my hand. "He's right, Theo. I'm bound to he and Danial almost in the same way I'm bound to you."

I turned to Devlin. "But I'm not "sort of married" to you, Devlin. You could never be married to any one woman, as you've told me before. We are Oathed, and you are not going to say anything about it to my parents until I say it's okay. Do you understand?"

Devlin looked at me defiantly, his eyes glowing, and didn't answer.

"That's not going to make it any easier," Danial said, sighing. "Your mom will notice our bands, Sar. She's sure to say something."

"There is no easy way. We'll try it Dev's way. For now." I turned to take in both Danial and Devlin. "But no innuendoes, nothing, from either of you," I said, giving them the look of death. "My mom will pick up on anything, no matter how small. Don't say anything."

"All right," Lash and Devlin assured.

They followed us to my parents' house. My mother came out to meet us, the perplexed look on her face indicating she was curious as to who Lash and Devlin were. After Theo, Theoron, and Elle had hugged my mother, Theo took the two children inside. By that time, Danial was beside me.

"Tina, Chris, may I present my brother, Devlin, and his bodyguard, Lash?" Danial said courteously.

Devlin kissed my mother's hand. "It's good to meet you."

Lash just nodded.

My stepfather shook their hands, eyeing Lash like he was bad news.

"Is he a vampire, too?" my mother asked. "He must be, if he's your brother."

Devlin whipped around and looked at Danial. "They know about you?"

"Yes," Danial said. "Lash is a were too, as Theo is. But he is a snake, not a cougar."

Lash looked over at Danial and said mockingly. "Thanks, Danny. Appreciate it."

My mother nodded like this was all normal. "Come in," she said, leading the way inside.

"You didn't tell me her parents knew what you were!" Devlin hissed low to Danial.

"You wanted to come crash our visit," Danial hissed back. "Part of crashing is not to know what to expect."

"Thanks so much," Devlin said sarcastically.

The kids and Theo were already having pie. I took an offered glass of wine from my mom.

"Want some scotch?" my stepfather said to Danial, Devlin, and Lash.

"I'm driving tonight," Danial said, declining.

"I'll have a small one," Devlin said, smiling politely. "I'm used to drinking wine, but I like single malts, on occasion. Do you have any Laphroig?"

"Ten year or fifteen year?" my stepfather said imperiously. "Cask strength, quarter cask, or regular?"

"Sweet," Lash hissed with a wide smile. "I'll try the fifteen year and the cask strength. I've only ever had the ten."

My stepfather widened his eyes at Lash's snake fangs. Forcing a smile, he led them both over to the bar.

I took a long swallow of my wine. *Please, God, let this evening go well.*

* * * *

"I think it went well," Danial ventured to me hours later, as we sat on my couch, Ghost and Darkness sleeping at our feet. "I'm sorry if you were ill at ease."

"Dev was right to come. My mother will tolerate him once she knows everything, even if she's irritated with me for having his child. She'll love my babies, of course."

"I'm glad there wasn't a scene. I was sure your mom would find out about 'everything,' as you put it so well."

"She confronted me in the kitchen," I admitted. "She was curious about why they came tonight, but never before now."

"What did you tell her?"

"That we couldn't bring Lash before because he can't hide what he is. That he was Dev's best friend, and we were waiting until they accepted Danial and

Theo to have your family visit."

Danial nodded. "Well done, even if Lash isn't what I consider family. What did Devlin want? He followed us to your house to kiss you goodnight."

"To assure me that he would behave himself, that he liked my parents, and that he was looking forward to them becoming part of his family. Nothing bad."

"Good. Rest," Danial said, holding me close. "You need to keep up your strength, Sar."

"I'm just glad we got a vacation before you got so busy."

"Me, too," he said, satisfied. He hugged me close. "Me, too."

* * * *

Two more weeks passed quickly.

On the last day in March, I put the finishing touches on the final guest room at Hayden. Putting down the brush, I surveyed the room.

Pride washed through me. I'd taken my time doing the guest bedrooms, and all had come out gorgeously. Each room had patterns on the ceilings, done with rollers. While none of them were as elaborate as Danial's night sky ceiling with all of its constellations, each one was eye-catching. The purple room had blue, blue-violet, and light gray on the ceiling in swirls. The orange room, a.k.a, the flames room, had a similar one with red, yellow, and light orange on the ceiling. I'd done others as well: green with a gold and shades of brown and tan ceiling, and dark gray, with a blue sky and clouds on the ceiling, similar to the one painted on Elle's ceiling years ago. At Devlin's request, I'd done the last four rooms in shades of gray, with glazed ceilings all in white and gold and silver.

That had left one final room, this one. For my finale, I had gone all out, doing the walls in metallic silver, with glitter all over the ceiling. When the overheard light was lit, the entire room shone. Today, I'd finished up the last of the pearl trim.

Congratulating myself on a job well done, I washed my brush in the adjoining bathroom. This afternoon, after lunch, I'd get started on Hayden's gardens. There wasn't too much time left before spring. And being pregnant, the more time went by, the less and less I'd be able to do. Thankfully that restriction wouldn't apply to baking and sewing.

Serena and I had become good friends in the few weeks I'd known her. She was a decent baker now, so it was on to a new skill. To my dismay, no one had eaten the baked goods she left out for general consumption. I guessed that the other women who lived at Hayden had told their mates not to, and consoled myself with her assurances that some of her patrons who had been privately gifted with her creations had given her a lot of praise for her efforts.

Our first sewing project was going to be making catnip cat toys for Phantom, not that he needed more spoiling. Having never visited a grocery store, Devlin had not known there were such things as cat treats. Now Phantom had a row of treats in a special plastic case.

I smiled. Phantom was an odd cat. He curled at the bottom of Devlin's bed each day, but spent his nights someplace else. Though he'd always been sweet and loving with me, he was destructive, destroying the cat treat bags, chewing them apart to get at the treats, prompting the special plastic case. His temperament was similar to Dev's. Maybe that was why Dev loved him so much.

I packed up the painting paraphernalia, and put it to the side. I'd carry it down to one of the storage rooms tomorrow. Taking my cell phone out of my pocket, I dialed Lash.

As usual, he answered right away. "Lunch?" he hissed querulously.

"Lunch," I affirmed. "You ready?"

"I'll meet you there. Don't hurry; I'll be a second or two finishing up."

"Okay. Five minutes?"

"More like two," he hissed.

"Sure. Bye."

I hung up, then caught sight of myself in the mirror. I had paint in my hair, a few silver streaks near one ear and also at the crown of my head. I put my fingertips to the paint, which was dry.

"Nice. I'll have to scrub it out later." Wincing, I shook out my hair from its clip and rubbed my scalp. It hurt from having my hair up so long. "I need a hair appointment, too," I added under my breath, then headed for the door.

Just as I grasped the knob, The Lust reared up within me.

Chapter Three

Lash.

I wanted Lash.

Devlin was sleeping upstairs, but I didn't want him. He wouldn't drink me down like water. He hadn't taken any of my blood for weeks now. But Lash likely didn't know that he shouldn't. If I told him to, he would.

I threw open the door, and bolted into Kev in the hallway, knocking him off balance. "Sorry," he said, then did a double take at my wanton expression.

"Where is Lash?" I drawled, giving him a smoldering look.

His eyes widened. "I'll take you to him," he said, grabbing my hand.

He walked fast down the hallway toward the ballroom, pulling me along after him. Pushing through the doors with a shove of his hand, he started across the wide hardwood floor.

I registered my surroundings, scanning eagerly for Lash. The cracks in the walls had been fixed. Scaffolding had been erected to reach the ceiling cracks, but it was empty. There was no one here, least of all the person I was looking for. Fury rose up in me in an all-encompassing wave.

"Where is he?" I snarled.

"Lash is upstairs," Kev said quickly, dropping my hand. He turned and ran for the door.

I ascended the stairs, and began looking around. There were a lot of supplies up here, but no Lash.

God damn it, I need him! He must have left for the kitchen. I would have to go after him. When I found him...

"Sarelle," a voice called teasingly.

I turned around. Kev and Vince were there at the top of the stairs, blocking them.

"Where is Lash?" I hissed angrily. "He's not up here, like you said!"

Vince and Kev didn't reply. They spread out, and began to advance toward me slowly. Both of them were big men, burly and muscular, and the way they moved was meant to be menacing. If I had been in my right mind, I would've been afraid, would have known immediately what they were planning.

Instead, I was pissed off. "Get out of my way!" I shouted, grabbing a claw hammer from the stack of tools beside me. "Now!"

"We just want to give you what you need, Baby," Vince growled eagerly. "We won't hurt you, if you let us have you—"

I dashed between them. They lunged for me as one. I hit Vince solidly in the teeth with my hammer. The entire front five caught the impact, breaking several as he let out a scream more surprise than pain.

Kev grabbed me around the waist. I kicked him hard in the balls. He groaned and went down hard, holding himself.

I sauntered down the stairs in search of Lash, full of myself. I held tightly to the hammer, liking the weight of it in my hard. *Hitting Vince had felt good. I liked the shriek he'd made when I hit him. Maybe I would get a chance to swing my hammer again on the way to the kitchen. If Lash didn't behave, he could have some of this, too...*

I'd forgotten there were two sets of stairs, that the men I'd hurt were werebear, not human. As I reached the last five stairs, Vince was suddenly there before me, his partly healed teeth bared.

"I want Lash, not you!" I snarled at him, and swung.

He evaded me easily. "Grab her!" Vince hissed.

Kev, who had come down silently behind me, grabbed hold of me.

I kicked him, but he was ready, turning his body to protect himself even as he tore the hammer out of my grasp.

"You Fuck!" I hissed. "Release me!"

"No more," Kev ordered, tossing the hammer away. "Now behave—"

"What a joke!" I laughed. "As if either of you could satisfy me—"

Vince slapped me hard. The blow rocked my head backward, the force of it enough to break The Lust's hold over me.

Instantly recognizing the danger I was in, my fear crashed down over me like ice water. I went still in Kev's arms. "Let me go. I'm okay now. I'm sorry about hitting you."

"Not a chance," Vince said, growling. "We've waited a long time for this, Sar. Hold her."

Vince began fumbling with my pants, growling softly in anticipation. I screamed. Kev put his hand over my mouth, stifling me, as Vince tried to slide my jeans over my hips. Lucky for me, I'd squeezed my vain ass into my skintight stretch jeans. They clung to me like a second skin as he tried to pull them off.

"We were all told to stay away from you," Kev growled furiously in my ear. "Dev decided he loved you, so we were just supposed to forget how you shot six of us dead, how your boyfriends killed another eight of us over at Danial's house that same night. But that doesn't fly with me."

I struggled, frantic.

"Devlin may have forgiven you, but we haven't. I'd rather snap your neck here and now, but raping you is the only payback I'm going to be allowed to have. Get ready for a wild ride, Sar."

Vince gave up trying to shove down my pants, and instead turned them inside out, peeling them off me like a skin, even as I thrashed.

"Everyone knows you get horny," Kev continued, his hate palpable. "We've all been briefed. If you asked, we were supposed do whatever you asked, so long as it didn't threaten your life or the fetus." Kev leaned in closer. "That gives us all kinds of leeway. Dalcon's a big believer in rough trade anyway—"

I bit Kev's right hand hard. He jerked back from me, gritting his teeth, blood oozing from his hand.

"Stop it! Don't do this!" I got out.

He slapped his hand over my mouth again. "Shut up! No one will believe you didn't ask for it! You've fucked Lash! If you'd let that snake have you, you'd let anyone have you!"

I closed my teeth on his hand again, biting deep. But this time he didn't let go.

Kev hissed, "You bite me again, and we'll fuck you until we can't get it up anymore. You bed a were regularly. You know how long we can make this last. Now hold still."

I stopped trying to bite him as tears slid down my face. Kev eased down on the stairs with me, so I was lying on his legs and his body. I struggled harder, trying to get up.

"The best part of this won't be doing you," Kev hissed in my ear. "It will be seeing you for months afterward, years, us both knowing what really happened and that no one believed you didn't want it. I'll cherish your screams, Sar. They won't bring my best friend back, but it's something."

I flailed hysterically, frantically, moving desperately, trying to get free of him as Vince unzipped his fly, and dropped his pants.

"Hurry up," Kev said, his breath hot on my neck. "After you have her the first time, she'll settle down. Then you can hold her for me. We'll trade off after that."

Vince stepped out of his pants, his penis already erect, a drop of semen glistening on the tip. I began to whimper with fear. *What Devlin had done to me hadn't been this. Dev had been gentle, even considerate. These men just wanted*

29

to hurt me. I kicked harder at Vince, thrashing.

"Hold her still," Vince said roughly, as he began to ease his body down on mine.

There was a hiss of air. Vince fell forward onto me, shrieking in pain, a huge hole in his right shoulder, the edges bloody hamburger.

Kev sprang to his feet, and pulled out a knife, holding it against my throat. "Stay back!"

Lash stood there near the ballroom door, his eyes flat and cold, a silenced gun smoking in his hand. "Kevin," he hissed. "You know better than this, to think you can fight me. Drop her."

"Stay back!" Kev said, digging the knife into my neck. I let out a cry. "I can knife her before you can shoot me."

Lash stopped and holstered his gun. Then he uncoiled his whip, pulled his knife in the other hand, and began advancing.

"Want to share her, Lash?" Kevin called out.

Lash moved closer. With the speed of a striking snake, he curled the end of the whip around Vince's right arm, and jerked him off of me. With a flick of his wrist, he loosened the whip from him, and began closing the twenty-five feet that separated us.

Kevin began to back up the stairs, still holding me. "Stop!"

I felt the point of a knife again against my throat. Lash stopped where he was, but didn't put down his whip or his knife.

"I know how good you are!" Kevin called. "But you can't get this out of my hand before I cut her artery. Titus is off with Leri. She'll bleed to death in moments. Now be reasonable."

Lash didn't reply.

"We'll share her with you, Lash. I know you haven't been with anyone since her. That was months ago! I just had some last night, and I'm already horny just from feeling Sar struggling against me. You must be in agony, going that long without any—"

Was that true? Shit, I hoped not.

Lash was motionless as a statue.

"Come on," Kevin growled. "I can smell how much you want her. You can even have her first, if you agree to hold her for us after."

Lash resheathed his knife, and coiled his whip up, snapping it back on his belt. "Hold her for me," he hissed lustily.

"Yes!" Kevin shouted with relief.

I struggled in his arms, but he held me easily, the knife still at my throat.

"I want to go first," Vince growled from the floor. "I'm hurt—"

Lash looked down at him. Vince shut right up, and didn't move, staring up

30

at Lash with fear.

Lash strode over and stood before me, his flat eyes staring into mine. "Put her hair in front of her body, so I can see it," he hissed. "And take the knife away from her throat."

"You said to hold her," Kev said suspiciously.

"Hold her arms. She's afraid enough that she won't move. I don't want to feel anything but her body against mine, Jerk."

Kev put away his knife. Shoving my hair to fall over my chest, he took firm hold of both of my arms. "You should have known better than to put your faith in a celibate were," he murmured in my ear. "There's no vampire here to save you this time, Sar."

"Be quiet already," Lash hissed at Kev, as he grabbed hold of my shoulders and bent his head to my neck.

I held still, praying the man I'd come to know wouldn't betray Devlin, even if he still hated me. His fangs pierced me, and he began to drink. The moment he did, The Lust washed over me again.

Yes, God, Kev could hold me, anything to feel this again, to feel Lash drinking me down like water...

"Yes," I murmured, letting my head fall back as I clasped Lash closer. "Please—"

Kev's grip abruptly loosened. Lash groaned and pulled me against him hard, his arms going around me, grinding his hips into me. I let out a moan, then reached down for his zipper.

Lash exploded into action. Without warning, he yanked his fangs out of me, shoved me aside, and sank them into Kevin's neck. Kevin shrieked, trying to push him away. I was painfully wrenched back towards them, my hair caught in Kev's belt. Lash gave me another push, tearing me free. Kev shrieked loudly over and over in absolute terror as I rolled to lay on the ballroom floor, dazed.

Pushing myself up with my arms, I saw Lash let go of Kevin. The werebear slumped to the floor, his eyes rolling up as he convulsed. His mouth was agape, drooling as he jerked spastically. Vince was screaming over and over, his eyes wide with fear, as he tried to crawl away from Kev and Lash. Lash went for him next. With a hard snap, he broke his neck and Vince's scream cut off. He fell to the floor to lie in a pile of bloody arms and legs.

"He healed," I murmured. "There's new skin showing through the hole in his shirt."

Lash left them where they lay and walked over. He put his hand gently on my shoulder. "Are you all right?" he hissed softly.

"Yes," I said brokenly, and began to cry.

Lash took my hand, and pulled me to my feet. "Come." He took me into the nearest bedroom down the hall and shut the door.

I looked about me at the red walls, dazed. "This is the flame room."

"Sit for a moment."

I sat. *It was good to sit.*

Lash went to the bathroom sink and washed out his mouth, taking something from his pocket, and mixing it with water. He did this several times, spitting whatever it was into the sink. After, he came back over to me. "Do you want me to call Dev or not? He can come here—"

It seemed hard to think. Why couldn't I understand his words? "What were you doing?"

"The poison I shot Kev up with won't kill him, but he won't be able to move for the better part of a day. It would have killed a human." He looked at me intently. "I needed to get any traces of poison that were left out of my mouth, just in case you were still in the mood."

My terror eclipsed my outrage. "You said that your bite was only poisonous in snake form!" I said shrilly. "You lied to me!"

"My fangs don't change," Lash said blatantly. "If they went back to human teeth, that would be true."

I shrank back from him. "So any time you drank from me, you could have killed me—"

Lash's hand shot out to grip my face hard. "I won't hurt you," he hissed, his flat eyes staring into mine. "I promised Dev I'd keep you safe. I can bite without injecting poison, as you well know."

I curled up into a ball, making myself small. "Why'd you lie to me?"

"That night I said that I wanted your blood. You wouldn't have let me if—"

"You scared me."

"I had to," Lash hissed. "I had to make Kev believe that I was going along with their plan to get close to him. He was right, he could have cut your throat before I could stop him. Titus is too far away to save you. You would have bled to death."

"No, I wasn't scared then," I whispered. "I was scared of you before, but not now. I trusted you to save me."

He let go of my face. "I saw that you did in your eyes, before The Lust came."

I wanted to tell him that it meant something that he had had me there in his power and he hadn't taken advantage. *Right now he was probably regretting he hadn't...*Embarrassed at my unkind thought, my face flushed.

"Why were you in there anyway?" Lash hissed. "You said you were coming to meet me for lunch. How am I supposed to keep you safe if you don't do what you say you will?"

"I went looking for you," I replied, coloring further. "Kev lied to me, told me you were there." I sank down to the floor, sitting cross-legged.

Lash eased himself down beside me.   "But you don't want me now, right?"

While Lash had made sexual remarks before, they'd been teasing or hostile. His words now were polite, laced with an undercurrent of passionate need. What Kev had said about his celibacy had most likely been true.

Disgust rose in me at the thought of Kev, at what he'd tried. But more disgust was for me, that in the midst of attempted rape I'd still managed to get off on the idea of fucking Lash. *What the hell was wrong with me?*

"I'm going crazy," I said brokenly.

"Maybe," Lash offered, after a moment. "But it's not like you got there by yourself. For a human, I think you're handling things really well."

I wiped at my tears. "I hit Vince with a hammer. I enjoyed it. I was hoping to hit others—"

"If I were you, I'd have hit him, too," Lash said drolly.

I looked over at him. "I'd have hit you if I found you, if you hadn't done what I wanted."

"No hitting me," Lash said, giving me baleful eyes. "Not that you'd have needed to. I'd have done what you asked, whatever it was."

I looked back at him, biting my lip. He stared back at me, unmoving.

I looked away. *What was it about him that called to The Lust?* It had always wanted violence, back from the first. But Lash had never hurt me. I'd witnessed him hurt Theo, but that was it. None of this made any sense…

What did I know for a fact? Only that The Lust had risen today when Lash had drunk my blood. But The Lust rose and was sated with Devlin without Devlin doing any blood drinking. Maybe it was Lash's fangs entering me that had incited The Lust to rise?

I cast another quick glance over at him. Lash looked back, clearly still hoping.

If he kissed me, would The Lust rise? There was only one way to find out. But did I really want to go there again on purpose? Sure I'd fucked up his life, driven his girlfriend to another state, and he'd been celibate now for months. But that didn't make sex with Lash a good idea.

On the other hand, what if he didn't need to touch me for The Lust to rise? The first time I'd just looked at him. I'd been minding my own business this very afternoon when I'd been driven to seek him out. *What if we left here, and The Lust came back in the kitchen during lunch, or worse, a couple days from now when I was home with Theo?* For whatever reason, it clearly wanted Lash this time. If I denied it again, I might be even more violent the next time it overtook me. *What if I picked up a gun then instead of a hammer?*

I had to control this. It was better to get it over with now where we had a little privacy.

I reached for him, my eyes a little scared. "Come to me."

Lash looked at me in surprise, and then moved closer, coming into my arms. He pulled me tight against him, molding his body to mine, the press of his erection straining to be free against my groin. I reached down between us then, hesitantly, and very slowly ran my hand across the hardness. He let out a loud hiss, his pelvis contracting against me.

The Lust rolled over me like a steamroller, squashing my resistance flat, making me feel like I had not been with anyone in years. Without a word, I unzipped his jeans and reached inside. He was hot and swollen, already a little slippery in his readiness. I curled my hand around his shaft, and he thrust into it, hissing with eagerness. I brought his penis out of his jeans, stroking him quickly. Lash hurriedly unbuckled his belt and unbuttoned his jeans, baring himself fully to me.

I looked at him with hot eyes, savoring the sight of his engorged flesh. I hadn't been wrong about his width, and his length was good, too, though nowhere near Devlin's. I stroked his hard shaft gently, rubbing the tip. He responded immediately, moving frantically in my hand, letting out groans with each thrust.

I wanted him somewhere else besides my hand. Moving my hips closer to his, I put the head of him against my underwear, wanting him to feel how wet I was for him, how ready my body was to accept his. Then I moved them aside just enough to rub the head of his cock on my clit. Lash shifted with a jerk, then went still. I pushed my pelvis toward his, sliding the head of his penis inside just a little. Lash made an agonized cry. I braced myself for him to grab me, eagerly anticipating the shove of his flesh into mine. But he remained where he was, breathing rapidly.

What was he waiting for? Suddenly it hit me: he was waiting for me to tell him what I wanted.

"Please, Lash," I whispered. "Take me."

As soon as I said the words, Lash was in motion. He yanked off my underwear and pushed down his pants further, almost ripping them off in his desire. A half second later, he rolled me on top of him, settling my hips on his as he slid in with a loud hiss of pleasure.

"Ahh!" I cried, throwing my head back, grabbing fistfuls of his T-shirt in my hands.

Lash began moving at once in long purposeful strokes, even as he reached his hands up to unfasten my bra. My breasts swung free, my bared nipples stiffening instantly. He slid his hands up to cup my breasts, rubbing his hands over my nipples as he thrust. I tried to push up his shirt, wanting to feel his chest, but he quickly stopped me with his hands. Grasping my hips, he pushed me down on him forcefully, driving into me over and over. I grabbed hold of his T-shirt again with both hands, moaning loudly.

God, he felt so good! "Kiss me," I groaned. "I want to feel your tongue—"

Lash pulled my upper body down on his immediately, sliding his arm around my shoulders as he kissed me deeply. His tongue caressed mine, licking eagerly, exploring as his mouth devoured mine. He made no noise, except a soft hiss now and then of pleasure.

Muffled cries escaped my lips as waves of pleasure washed over me. *God, I was so close! I needed him to bring me!* "Bite me!" I gasped yearningly. "Please!"

Lash broke the kiss and moved his head down to my neck, sinking his fangs in. I came screaming. His hand snaked out quickly and covered my mouth, muffling my cries. I shook hard in his grip.

Before my climax faded, he rolled over onto me, covering my body with his. He moved frantically, shoving himself inside as far as he could. He jerked suddenly, spilling himself with a soft cry. As before, he withdrew from me almost immediately and lay on his back making soft hisses, jerking as his orgasm ebbed. He didn't touch me at all, or say anything.

Slowly, in the space of several minutes, rationality returned. Before I had entirely come back to myself, Lash pulled on his pants, got up, and left the room.

Feeling sordid, I used the opportunity to clean myself up the best I could, and put the little clothing I was wearing back the way it should be. I was just finishing washing my face when Lash appeared with my jeans, socks, and sneakers.

Ah. "Thanks," I said as he handed them to me.

He nodded. "Are you ready for lunch now?" he asked politely.

"Yes," I said, pulling on my jeans and the rest. As I followed him to the kitchen, neither of us said anything.

I was grateful he was making this easier for me by not talking. Or maybe he didn't want to talk. This wasn't a romance: what he'd done was just another part of his job, even if he did enjoy it.

No one was there when we got there, even though it was noon. Either someone had overheard us and everyone had cleared out, or some crisis had happened. Either way the silence was great. I needed time to think.

My plan to control myself had worked, giving me a theory: The Lust had chosen Lash because it had wanted someone to drink my blood. The question was why.

There was also the weirdness that Danial had spoken of back on vacation: *why was I able to climax when The Lust hit me during this pregnancy, when orgasm had been impossible during my previous pregnancy?* Devlin usually bit me during The Lust, but his drinking my blood wasn't required; at least, it had been sated without me asking him to. Also, as it had been with Danial, sometimes The Lust came and went without my climax, as its goal seemed to be Devlin's orgasm. Lastly, Dev's bites usually caused substantial pain after The Lust left. In contrast, Lash had bitten me twice. Neither wound had been painful; in fact, I didn't even feel the bites now. Yet his biting had brought me immediately both times.

Why was The Lust interested in him at all? Lash is no vampire.

"Sar," Lash hissed, closing the kitchen door behind us and locking it. "I need to go back to the ballroom. Stay here while I'm gone. Don't let anyone in, unless it's Dev. I'll call him and tell him to come down and get you."

I nodded. "Thanks."

"Always a pleasure," he hissed with a small smile, then turned to go.

"Wait," I said suddenly. "I don't know what Devlin may have said to you about taking blood from me, but—"

"Shit!" Lash swore, stopping and turning to me. "I'm not supposed to take any, am I? Dev was bitching about it."

I touched my neck. "I'm fine. Your bites aren't even bleeding."

Lash flicked his eyes to my neck. "You heal faster now, because of the blood Dev gives you." His tone was annoyed. "All the same, I shouldn't have."

"Camlyn said my blood levels were fine. No one is taking my blood now but you. It's okay. You seem to like it."

"It's not the taste, though you taste good," Lash said hesitantly, then stopped.

There was something he didn't want to tell me. What? "And?"

He looked at me a moment, as if weighing his response, then closed the door, locked it, and came back to stand in front of me. "You remember the night I first tasted you?"

When you were being an asshole. "Yes."

"Remember how I fell asleep?"

I nodded. "Yes."

"It wasn't because I was just warm, and comfortable, though I was both of those." He paused. "I have what you might call a mild headache, from the potion I take. It's present all the time now; day after day, month after month.

I've gotten used to it over the years, so much so that I didn't notice a difference when I first drank your blood. But as I was watching Titus heal you, it suddenly hit me that it was gone. The relief from finally being free of the pain was so good, I relaxed completely, falling asleep."

The constant pain he was in was probably the reason why he was so irritable most of the time. Now he was pain-free and he'd just been laid for the first time in months. No wonder he was verbose. "How long did it last?"

"Almost a week." His tone was wistful.

What he'd taken had been insignificant and I owed him big for saving me. "Then take some each week when I come here to see Dev. The small amount you take won't hurt."

"Why are you offering it to me?" Lash said suspiciously. "I'm not that good of a lay compared to Dev, at least from what I've done with you so far—"

"I don't want you to be in pain," I said, flushing at his bluntness. "And your bites are—"

"I'll take it if we have sex," Lash said, getting up. "Otherwise, no."

"Why not?"

Lash shoved the chair, sending it sliding to crash into the table. "Because you're running some angle by offering me your blood." His words were cold, and hard, all trace of gentleness gone. "What do you want from me?"

I knew I should keep my mouth shut, but I didn't. "The Lust seems to like you best," I said quickly. "It was thoughts of you that brought it, those first times it rose with my other lovers. You almost brought it when Kev was holding me, even though I was terrified. I thought if you took it every week, maybe between that and Dev—"

Lash backed away from me a step. "It can't like me better than Dev. I'm not a vampire. I don't believe you—"

"I don't know why, either!" I replied desperately. "It doesn't make sense. But the only angle I'm working is to control myself." I swallowed. "I don't want what happened this afternoon to happen again."

"You're telling the truth," Lash hissed. "At least what you believe to be the truth." He came closer to me. "As for Devlin's other guards, don't worry. I plan on making a harsh example this evening. They don't always remember verbal warnings. They always remember bloodshed, particularly when it's their blood staining the floor."

His casually evil tone sent a shiver down my spine. "So you won't consider my offer?"

"I'll take some if we have sex again," he agreed. "I won't take more than I did today, a few swallows or so. If my pain gets worse, I'll ask you for some when you visit. Good?"

I nodded. "As long as you take some if I ask you to."

"Well, of course," Lash replied irreverently. "I'm not anxious to be hammered."

I let out a snort of laughter. "Sure—" Abruptly I remembered the hammer smashing Vince's teeth, then Kev grabbing me. I sat down quickly, sickened and upset.

"Are you okay?" Lash said, laying his hand on my arm.

When he touched me, The Lust rose its head high. *Yes...He could have me here on the kitchen table, just like he had Cin on the pool table at Davy's...*

Madness engulfed me. The sex hadn't helped! The Lust still wanted him. Shaking my head, I reached out, and gently pushed his hand off me. "No."

Lash moved back from me, leaning against the counter.

Yes, this was just like in the kitchen at Theo's old place. Lash had been great that night. He'd be even better here...

I trembled, trying to push my urges away. I fought my desire to touch him, to have him, to open my mouth and tell him to take me now. Slowly the feeling passed, leaving me shaky and weak.

The Lust had never risen so quickly again after being sated. Never. Devlin had tried one night, being in one of his moods. He had been unable to raise it once he had sated it. Lash had raised it again within minutes, with almost no effort. What was going on?

"I smell your desire," Lash hissed softly. "If you need me again, just say so."

"I do," I whispered. "And I'm scared to death."

Lash came over to me, grasped my arm, and pulled me to my feet. His arms went around me. "Why are you scared?" He began backing me slowly toward the table.

I wiped at my eyes, even as desire flooded me. "We just did this—"

Lash pushed my pants down carefully, then lifted me to sit on the table's edge. "That's okay. A man likes to be in demand." He leaned in and kissed my neck, his fangs pricking me.

I leaned back from him, then raised a hand to his face. Carefully I touched the tip of one hooked fang that was always revealed by his scar. "You're not a man."

Lash smiled wider, both curved fangs glistening as his forked tongue snaked out to stroke my cheek. "You're right, I'm not. But I'm what you need—"

The Lust engulfed me. Frenzied, I went for his belt buckle. Lash kissed me feverishly, as I dropped his pants. He grasped my rear with both hands, then pulled me forward quickly, impaling me. I let out a moan, and he kissed me again, devouring me as he began to thrust.

Lash stroked my tongue with his, then ended the kiss. Baring his fangs, he sank them into my neck. Heart racing I clasped him to me, kissing his neck, his face, anything within reach.

"Deeper," I hissed needfully. "Harder."

Lash lifted my ass, then moved backwards while supporting me, easing us down into a chair. He drove in another few inches, then began to move fast, straining. My orgasm built quickly. In seconds it burst. As I began to scream, Lash withdrew his fangs and covered my mouth with his. Where I ended he began, his muscles clenching beneath me as he came.

As The Lust faded, I pushed back slightly from him, panting, not sure what to say.

He grasped me and gave me a chaste kiss, then released me. Carefully I stood up.

As he came free of me, Lash let out a soft hiss of satisfaction. Then he was all business as we both put our clothes back on.

When I was dressed, I turned to him. "I'll stay here and wait for Devlin."

"You won't have to," Lash hissed, going towards the door. "He's heard us."

Devlin's room was above the kitchen. I flushed as Lash unlocked the door to admit Devlin, his golden eyes tinged red.

"What happened?" he asked snidely. "You get her this far and give up?"

Lash faced Dev accusingly, his normal humor oddly missing. "What happened is your favorite asshole grabbed Sar. He and Vince planned to rape her and blame The Lust. In the process of handling that, The Lust rose—"

Devlin snarled, his eyes glowing red like hot embers. He gripped the doorjamb, sinking his nails deep into the hardwood with a creak. "Did you kill them?"

"They're in the ballroom," Lash hissed. "I'll take them to the dungeon."

"They said it was payback for me killing some of them that night you came for me," I whispered.

"Take them to the dungeon!" Devlin thundered. "Now!"

Lash nodded. "Kev's out cold for today, but Vince will recover as soon as his neck is reset. You want them healed up for you, or you want me to take care of it?"

"Just take them there now," Devlin answered curtly.

Lash nodded, then left.

Devlin grabbed hold of me, crushing me against him. "I'm sorry this happened," he murmured. "Teleport now to Danial. Tell him you'll spend tonight with him. I'll come to you later on tonight, be with you there at his house—"

There wasn't going to be a later for us, but I felt too much guilt rejecting him right here after he'd just heard me have sex with Lash. "It was close, Dev. I'm all messed up."

Devlin was still apologizing. "—I'll punish them for this, Sar. You won't see either of them again, ever, so don't worry. Nothing like this will ever happen again, not to you, not here at my home—"

"Before I leave, I have to tell Serena what happened," I interrupted, remorseful. "She cared about Vince a lot. She needs to know."

"I can have someone else tell her, Love," Devlin said, drawing back from me. "You don't need to."

"No," I persisted, resigned. "A woman should tell her. I'll do it, before I leave." I'd be damned if would let one of those women who hated her tell her. It was going to be hard enough to hear it from a friend, especially as there was no way to downplay the circumstances.

"Come upstairs," Dev said, taking my hand. "She's in her room, sleeping."

I followed him, glad of his hand steadying me. "Kev said I'd killed his best friend. That was the real root of it, at least for him. Vince…I don't know why he went along with Kev."

Devlin released me. "It's true, you did kill his friend. But death is one of the risks of working for me. You were only defending yourself."

I hadn't been looking for a pep talk on the rightness of my actions. *Maybe this was him trying to make me feel better?* "I'll see you later."

Dev kissed me, then gave me a hard look. "Tell Theo, if he wants to come, I'll leave one of them for him. He has a right for vengeance. You are his to protect as much as mine."

I nodded, trying not to give into the surreal feeling his words had created. "I'll tell him."

Devlin went downstairs. I knocked on Serena's door.

She opened it, her face streaked with tears. "Lash already told me, Sar."

Damn it, Lash. "I'm sorry—"

She got up and hugged me. "It's not your fault," she said. "Lash told me what happened."

I hugged her back, and didn't say anything.

"I should've known," she said softly. "Kev had fantasies; he asked me to—"

"Stop!" I said harshly. "Please Serena, I don't want to know."

"Vince never said or did anything. I don't want to believe it."

I hugged her harder. "I'm sorry. I know you cared about him—"

"I do, but that doesn't mean I blame you for this," she whispered, letting go of me and stepping back. "I'll see you when you come next time." She closed her door gently in my face.

We both needed some time. "I'll see you then," I said aloud, and turned away.

I teleported to Danial's, ending up in the snow on the lawn. In my haste, I'd forgotten my coat and my keys.

Fuck, who cared? My first priority was getting to a shower before anyone smelled snake scent on me. I went to the front door and knocked lightly, praying Mary was on duty.

Instead, Danial opened it a moment later dressed in his robe, clearly annoyed. He took one look at me and knew immediately something was wrong. "What happened?" he said, reaching out to enfold me in his arms. "I can smell that snake on you from here—"

As soon as he touched me, my strength evaporated. I dissolved into tears. "Some of Devlin's bears tried to—"

"Shh, Sar. I can guess the rest." Danial walked me to the nearest phone, picked up the receiver, and began dialing.

"You don't need to talk to him," I said, irritated. "He said he'd be by later." I moved out of his embrace, then walked to his bathroom. "I need a shower."

Danial put down the phone and came after me. "The Lust raised with Lash?"

I nodded, stripping off my clothes. "Don't tell Theo. I don't need him to have another hissy fit."

Danial nodded once. "He won't hear it from me. Relax in my room when you're done. No one will disturb you." He turned and left.

Had it been my anger or the scent of sex with Lash that had caused him to leave? It didn't matter. I was a big girl. I would go shower, cry, and pull myself together.

I took a long hot shower, wrapping my arms around myself as I sobbed out the delayed shock and fear. The familiar scent of my favorite blackberry shampoo soothed me, telling me I was safe, and that it didn't matter what might have happened, only what had happened. *I had gotten away from Kev and Vince. Lash had saved me. That was all that mattered.* I told myself that over and over until I believed it.

When I emerged, Danial was gone. I went looking for him and stumbled across Theoron and Elle in her room, playing a board game, Dark Tower.

The old game was from my youth, back when computers were new and did only small things. The object was to journey completely around the board picking up keys and loot, and then when you'd made it back to your starting

41

point, to challenge the tower. The most fun was going to tombs and ruins looking for treasure, because the computer chose for you at random what you would find.

Once in a while, the tomb or ruin was empty. Sometimes there was gold, or a dragon-killing sword, or a flying horse. Often there were bad guys waiting for you in the dark, protecting those treasures. There was no way to know how many bad guys you'd have to fight. Most times there were only a few waiting when the door of the ruin creaked open. These could be easily beaten. Sometimes there were too many to fight, though. Then, like in life, you were doomed.

Chapter Four

Elle was the first to notice me standing at the door. "Mom!" she cried happily. "Today's not your day to visit. I thought you were coming tomorrow!"

"I'm early," I said, forcing a smile. "Is that okay?"

They both left their game and ran up to me. "Yes!"

It felt so good to feel their little arms around me. I hugged them back, then quickly let them go, not wanting them to suspect how upset I was. "How's your game?"

"I'm beating him," Elle said proudly.

"You are not," Theoron said snidely to her. "I'm using good strategy." He looked up at me. "Want to play? We're halfway through, but we could start again—"

That meant he *had to be losing.* "No, you guys play," I said, giving him a smile and ruffling his hair. "I'll watch for a while." Dark Tower was a long game. Sometimes it went on for three hours or more. Devlin wouldn't have patience to wait if he arrived in mid-play.

Two hours passed, Elle emerging the victor, though Theoron had only been a few moves behind. Through it all no one came looking for me or disturbed us.

As they put the game away, I debated taking the kids out to an early dinner as a treat. But for that we needed a guard of some kind. Also, Danial wouldn't like it if I left. Devlin would expect me to be here, too. I knew better than to think he'd understand. *He wanted me right where he told me I should be...*

I pushed my bitter thoughts aside. Devlin hadn't been anything but understanding, really. I was just grumpy—not that I wasn't entitled to that—and I wanted nothing more than to spend tonight quietly with my family. I wanted comfort, love, and comfort food, too. I'd missed lunch.

"Want me to make you some dinner?" I asked.

"Yes," they chorused. "We're hungry."

Elle still ate raw meat as Theo did, just Theoron drank blood like Danial. Tonight however, it was going to be normal food. "Come on. I'll make some sandwiches. After, we'll make cookies."

* * * *

We had just put the last batch of gingerbread cookies into the oven when Devlin walked into the kitchen.

"Uncle Dev!" Theoron yelled. He ran to Dev, who had crouched down, his arms open to receive him. Devlin grabbed hold of Theoron, and swung him up into his arms. "We're making cookies," Theoron informed him.

"So you are," Devlin said with a smile. "Did you make me any?"

"You don't eat cookies," Theoron laughed.

"True," Devlin said, laughing himself. "But I'd like some anyway, if you made them." He put Theoron down, and came over towards me. "And how's my lovely—"

Elle blocked him.

Annoyed, Devlin crouched down in front of her. "Little Lioness," he purred softly. "What do you think you're doing?"

"I don't want you by Mom," Elle growled. "Not until Dad comes back."

"Its okay, Elle—" I started.

Devlin held up his hand. I fell silent.

"Why not?" Devlin said, his golden eyes fixed on Elle. "Your Mom likes me to touch her, Elle. It's my right to, as well. You know what the choker she wears means."

"I know what it means," Elle hissed, bearing her fangs. "But I don't trust you. I smell—"

"Quiet, child," Devlin said authoritatively. "I don't have to explain myself to you. You will obey me—"

"Stop it," I ordered. "Dev, where are Theo and Danial?"

"They came to help me," Devlin said, making it clear to me by his tone what they had been helping him with. "Danial said he had a right as well. Kev and Vince are dead."

"Thank you." My words were polite and clipped. Though I was happy those asses were gone, I'd assumed that and wanted not to ever hear their names again. Would Titus be disposing of the bodies? It was much better for me if I didn't know.

"You're safe, Love," he said softly, caressing me with his voice. "Lash had a talk with the others as well."

Most likely none of the bears, male or female, would be coming within ten feet of me for the foreseeable future. That was good, but it also ensured I'd never become friendly with Devlin's guards the way I had with Danial's. My sole friend there would be Serena. Maybe that was for the best, too. "Good."

"You were baking," Devlin prompted. "For whom? Theo?"

I'd just been keeping the kids and myself busy, but his comment reminded me I'd been going to make a cake for Theo's birthday in May. I hadn't decided if he'd want a surprise party. He'd spent so many birthdays alone. He might still look twenty-seven, but his face was growing older. There were faint lines on his brow now that had not been there when I'd met him years ago. Soon, despite his were genes, we would look almost the same age. After a few more years passed, he would began to look even older than me...

"Sar?"

I was scared about that. When Theo was very old, things would change between us. At the least, he would resent Danial and Devlin for keeping their youth. *Would he come to resent me, as well?*

"Sar?" Devlin said sternly. "What's the matter? You look ill."

What was wrong with me? "I'm okay." I forced a smile. "Do you really want some cookies?"

"I'll take some for Lash," Devlin said meaningfully. "If you don't mind."

I began putting some into a bag. "Of course."

Lash might be my lover, but he was not my friend. Still, I gave business associates cookies, so giving him some wouldn't be too odd. We were coworkers of a sort, with me still feeling like a guest at Hayden instead of its mistress. After all the work I had done there, it didn't feel like home to me. Now, after what had happened today, I doubted it ever would.

Maybe that was best. Dev was going to get bored with me in a few years or so, just like Theo had said. There would come a time when my attention and love wouldn't be enough, even with him getting more on the side. When he told me it was over, I wouldn't be going to Hayden anymore. I would be missing him enough; I didn't need to miss friends, too.

"Love," Devlin said, enfolding me in his arms. "Please don't look so sad. Tell me what's wrong. Tell me what I can do to help."

I tucked the bag in his pocket. "I'm all over the place," I whispered, worried. "My mood shifts in seconds from happiness to depression. I felt like this earlier today."

He kissed me gently on the cheek, then turned me to face him. "You've been through a shock. This is normal, Sar. Just remember you are loved and safe. I'm here for you."

I gazed at him. It was hard not to be spellbound. He was so handsome with his golden hair, his molten gold eyes, his features that were sculpted, but unquestionably male.

"I love you," he said passionately, touching my nose with his. "Yes, you."

It was his charisma that really drew me to him, the way he posed so casually with that gleam in his eyes inches from my lips. His bearing said he was here for me, that he was already thinking of the many ways he wanted to caress me. *God, it was enough just to watch him like this and think...*

"Mom, the cookies are burning!" Elle said loudly.

I jumped, startled. "Take them out."

"Theo and Danial should be along shortly," Devlin purred. "They are showering." He smiled slightly. "It was necessary."

Eww. I busied myself with the cookies, removing them from the baking sheet Elle held..

Devlin crouched down and beckoned to Theoron, who ran into his arms with glee again. "You, Little Prince, are going out with Theo, Lash, and your sister to a movie tonight." He handed Theoron fifty dollars. "That's for treats," Devlin said generously. "Make sure you get enough popcorn for everybody, including Theo."

"Yes!" Theoron yelled. "When does the movie start?"

"In about an hour and a half," Devlin said happily, eyeing me and grinning. "Theo and Danial should be back within the hour."

"Why aren't you going?" Elle asked, her eyes narrowed.

"I and your father have business with your mom tonight," Devlin answered.

Elle glared at him. My cell phone rang suddenly.

It was Terian. "Sar, can you come over to the lab? I need to talk to you."

"Now?" I said, trying not to be abrupt. "I'm kind of in the middle of —"

"Now!" Terian said forcefully.

Sigh. "I'm coming now," I said. Hanging up, I faced Devlin, Elle and Theoron. "I need to go talk to Terian. I'll be right back. Call his lab if you need me."

"Okay," Elle said, pleased that I was leaving and Devlin wasn't going.

He was not pleased. "I'll walk you over."

"No, I'll be right back. Please, stay here and watch the kids."

Devlin gave me a smoky glance, then nodded.

I arrived immediately in Terian's lab. He was waiting for me, his suitcases near him.

"What's going on?" I asked.

His cherry wood colored eyes were determined. "I read the letter from Leri."

It took you this long? I'd have read it that same night with a bottle of wine handy. "Where are you headed?"

46

"Leri didn't know much about Keriam," Terian said sadly. "Except that his real name was Matt Mairek. That's why she called him Keriam; it was an anagram of his last name. She liked that it was similar in sound to her name, too."

"Do you want to talk?" I said, sitting down and hoping he didn't.

Terian sat down in a nearby chair. I shifted, uncomfortable. This little alcove he kept for reading in his lab was comfortable enough for one, but close quarters for two.

"Leri knew she was going to deliver soon. She teleported to Las Cruces, New Mexico, and went to a community campus in one of the surrounding towns, searching for someone to entrust with my care. She wanted to find a smart young man. She was worried about leaving me with a woman, that a female wouldn't be strong enough to handle the kind of baby I'd be. She finally found a medical student. He had just gotten off the night shift at the local hospital, and was walking home to his fiancée." He swallowed hard. "She told him she was scared, that she was going to deliver soon. He could see both of those things were true.

"He took her back to the hospital. She went into labor before he could do more than secret her into an unused room. She put a compulsion spell on him when he tried to leave to get help—"

I grasped and squeezed Terian's hand.

"She used her magic to help speed up the birth. She was able to heal herself, though she lost a lot of blood. He cleaned me up. While he was occupied, she performed another spell, a very complex one she'd worked on for months, taking a bit of his hair and blood. She told him his name was Keriam, that he was her son, and I was his brother. She told him to take care of me, then gave him a few hundred thousand dollars. Teleporting him to Texas, she got him settled in a hotel there. Then she left.

"The potion she gave him made him forget who he had been, though it didn't change the kind of man he was, or his hopes and dreams. Leri made him forget everything he'd been before they had met. He lost his fiancé, his entire life, everything he'd wanted! It was all my fault!"

Terian was crying now openly. I hugged him, though his tears were almost boiling in their heat.

"It wasn't your fault," I soothed. "It was hers." I handed him some tissues.

"We've come full circle," he said, using them. "I remember that first day we met, that day I handed you those tissues. I felt so bad that day that I'd made you cry."

"I needed you to tell me what you did back then," I replied. "But sometimes crying is good. I always feel better afterward. You must feel better too, to finally let it out."

"I'm leaving tonight," Terian said, standing. "Sundown is coming with me. This time I'll find my brother's family, and put his spirit to rest." He hugged me hard. "Thank you. I owe you one for this. You need some spell or a potion for something, just let me know."

"Thanks," I said automatically. "You don't have to—"

"I want to," Terian said firmly. "You're my best friend, Sar. I've never had a friend like you. I love Sundown, but it's not the same."

"You've been there for me too, my gallant sorcerer always ready to save me," I teased.

"I always will be," Terian said gently, kissing my forehead. "I just wish you wouldn't get into all the trouble you do. I'm good, but there'll come a day when even I can't save you."

A shudder went through me. *That day had come: it had been today*...Quickly I masked my feelings. I didn't want him to know any of it. "Hopefully not. When will you come back?"

"I'll be back in a week or so," Terian said. "If I'm longer, I'll call. Danial knows. He said he'd work out something with Brian and Theo."

"That's okay," I said steadfastly. "Do what you need to do. I can arrange to have Lash guard me if I have to. Dev won't mind—"

Terian gave me a look. "You won't mind?"

"He's not a jerk," I said defensively. "Lash takes his job seriously."

Terian shrugged. "Maybe he's not the fuck that Theo has told me he is."

I thought of several descriptive replies, but held my tongue, mostly out of surprise that Terian had sworn so casually. Maybe he was spending too much time with Theo.

Sundown came in. "Hi Sar. Tears, we've got to go," she said, shooting me a polite smile. "We're going to be late if we don't leave right now. That fucking plane will leave without us."

Maybe it wasn't Theo that was influencing Terian's language. "You'd better go. Be safe."

I teleported back to Danial's kitchen. Elle was packing the cookies into bags. Being used to Terian popping in at odd times and places, she didn't even flinch when I appeared.

"Dad's back," she said neutrally, her eyes upset.

"What's wrong?" I asked, concerned.

She shook her head, and didn't answer. I went to go to her and muscular arms enfolded me from behind.

"Sar, are you feeling any better?" Theo asked tenderly

I turned to him instantly and hugged him, his wet hair cold against my arms. "Yes." I took a deep breath, smelling prairie grass, pine woods, and wide blue skies. "I'm glad you're—"

"We need to go," a hissing voice said.

I turned to see Lash there, regarding us, dressed in a grey shirt, his weapons at his sides. Elle threw down the cookies, and stalked out, growling at Lash as she went by him.

Someone had let slip to her that Lash had been my lover. I went after her.

"No one told her," Theo said, grabbing hold of me. "Lash still smells like you—"

Lash shot Theo a smile, then slipped out the door.

"—Elle smelled your scent on him. She accused him of hurting you. He didn't know that she didn't know about the two of you, so he told her the truth. She was very angry. Danial heard the shouting from inside his bedroom and came out to see what was the matter."

God, this was a nightmare. "What does she know?"

"He told her that what Lash had said was the truth. She's been in the kitchen ever since, trying to come to terms with it."

I sat on the kitchen stool and put my face in my hands. "Jesus Christ."

"I'll talk to her later tonight," Theo said, putting his hand on my shoulder. "She's old enough to understand what happened, and that it isn't your fault."

It wasn't, but that didn't matter, did it? At least Theo was being nice this time. "Okay."

"I'm going to go now," Theo added. "I'll probably be gone until at least three a.m. Danial's arranged for Ivan to go and watch our pets tonight. I'll come back here after the movie with the kids and crash in the basement. Tomorrow, we'll go home."

I wanted to tell him to take me home tonight, that I just longed to go home with him, watch a TV movie, and have him hold me. I was tired of all the intrigue, The Lust, and Devlin's constant demands. But I couldn't. There was no way out of what had to happen here, and I had my own duties to perform. He couldn't save me from this.

I gave myself a sudden mental slap. *What the hell was wrong with me?* I didn't need a savior; I was strong enough to deal with my situation on my own. "Be safe," I cautioned, hugging him. "I'll make you breakfast in the morning."

"You're on," he said. He shot me a last grin, then left.

There was a soft meow at my feet. The black cat Theo had saved from our woodshed was there looking up at me. "Are you hungry?" I said, reaching down and picking him up. "You want some food?"

"I gave her several cans of cat food this morning," Danial said, flashing me a smile from the doorway. "Plus a few bites of ham. She's well fed."

I petted the purring cat. "What did you name him?"

"It's a her," Danial said, coming over. "Her name is Briar."

"Briar," I said, stroking her. She purred, kneading my shoulder.

"They've left," Devlin announced gleefully, coming through the door and over to us. "It's about time, too. I thought they were never going to go."

Danial shot him a nasty look. Devlin ignored him, putting his hand on mine. He ran it up my arm to clasp my neck loosely. "Sar," he whispered. "Why don't you slip into something more comfortable?"

Startled, Briar leapt out of my arms and ran out of the room, ears flattened.

"Knock it off," Danial said, giving Dev a shove. "We have hours. You don't have to rush things."

Devlin snarled, baring his fangs. "Why don't Sar and I go to Hayden, then, and leave you here? It's my night anyway."

"Did it ever occur to you that Sar might not want to have sex?" Danial said, clearly exasperated. "She had a full day already with what she went through."

Devlin was quiet, looking from Danial to me and back. It was obvious he had not thought about it, just of himself. "Do you not want to be with me?" Devlin said tentatively.

Despite myself, him, and everything that had happened today, I found it humorous that he could be so full of himself one moment, and so vulnerable the next. It was one of the things I loved most about him. "Are you ever not in the mood?" I said with a roll of my eyes.

"No," Devlin said, grinning. He pulled me close and began kissing up my neck.

"He is *always* in the mood," Danial said, irritated. "You'd think after centuries, after thousands of—"

"Shut up," Devlin ordered, breaking away from me. "Or I won't let you join us, Danial."

I opened my mouth, but nothing came out. Devlin had said he and Danial had business with me. As I suddenly understood what that meant, my eyes got as big as saucers.

Devlin caught my look in my eyes and nodded. "Danial told me about your fantasy," Devlin purred, kissing my cheek. "Both of us at once. Your fantasy is going to come true tonight, Sar."

Suddenly, I was in the mood completely, the desire all my own. I pulled Devlin close and kissed him hard, slipping my tongue into his mouth. He responded instantly, kissing me deeply, his hands roaming my body.

Danial pried us apart. "Hey," he said firmly. "I'm not doing this in my kitchen, and I'm part of this tonight. Let's go into my bedroom where we can

50

all get more comfortable."

Devlin looked at me, his eyes melting gold now, hot with love and lust. "That sounds good," he purred. "I've brought something for Sar to wear."

Looks like I wasn't the only one who had fantasized about this.

"I have something I want her to wear," Danial said mildly. "And it's my bedroom, Dev."

That was a surprise, yet on reflection, it shouldn't have been. I hadn't been the only one getting hot and bothered over the idea of a threesome when Danial had first broached the delicious idea. "No fighting, gentlemen."

"Fine, you can have your fantasy first," Devlin said easily. "Mine can be later, when we can take longer."

First? Later? Longer? What was I getting into? I followed Danial and Devlin into Danial's bedroom. Danial locked it behind us. "Go and change Sar. What I'd like you to wear is on the back of the door."

I went into the bathroom. There on the back of the door was a bra and panty set, made entirely out of bits of red lace. There was almost nothing to it, it was so scanty. Closing the door, I put it on with trepidation. To my surprise, it fit fine. Those daily treadmill workouts were working to control my pregnancy weight gain. There was only the small swell of my tummy to give proof I was pregnant at all.

I wrapped myself in my robe, then looked in the mirror. *Could I do this?* It was one thing to take several lovers. It was another thing entirely to have lovers plural at the same time.

Screw it. I wanted to try it. I took a deep breath, then opened the bathroom door.

The light had been turned off. Now several candles burned around the room. Danial and Devlin were both on the bed, reclining there naked in the flickering light, their eyes on me. The sight of them together waiting for me was enough to make me pause.

We watched each other for several minutes in the candlelight. I wanted to remember this always, to capture the moment and commit it to memory. It didn't matter what the night brought, or if other nights like this one followed. I would never feel this way again; eager and shy equally, hesitant as a virgin.

Danial got up from the bed and came to me. "You're trembling. What's wrong?"

"I'm a little afraid," I whispered, awkward. "Just nerves, I think."

Devlin came to stand at my back. He clasped my arms with his hands, then slid them up my shoulders to my neck, massaging gently. "Why are you afraid?" Devlin whispered, kissing my neck lightly. "Is it because of the last time you and I were together in this room?"

The night he'd tried to drain me dry. "Stop it, Dev," I said angrily, tensing. "I've been trying like hell to forget that other night, and you casually bring it up..."

"She's not scared of us, or you," Danial said calmly, as if I'd not spoken. "She's afraid of having her fantasy come true." He kissed me on the lips. "Don't be."

"Yes, don't be scared," Devlin added. He began kissing me on the side of my neck.

Feeling their familiar touch, my fear passed like it had never been. I knew these men. I loved them both. Nothing was going to happen tonight that I didn't want to happen.

Danial deepened his kiss, sliding his tongue into my mouth as his hands slid up under my robe. He undid the sash and pushed my robe off my shoulders, revealing the red lace outfit. "You look beautiful," he whispered, his dark eyes hungry. "Just as I imagined." He kissed me again.

Devlin kissed the nape of my neck, his naked body pressed against mine, his erection hard against the small of my back. With a groan, he held my hips and rubbed, flexing persistently. Letting go of my hips, he moved his hands upwards to cup my breasts, squeezing gently. I groaned loudly, breaking away from Danial's kiss. God, this was already overwhelming and we hadn't gotten past the foreplay...

"Let's move to the bed," Devlin said huskily. As one they lifted me together, setting me down in the middle of the bed on my knees. They immediately took up positions; Devlin behind, Danial in front. Devlin unhooked my lace top, and Danial slid it off my shoulders. I was momentarily uneasy, remembering that long ago night with them. Then Devlin gripped my head with his hands, turning it to kiss me from behind as Danial kissed and caressed my breasts. Overwhelmed by pleasurable sensation, I relaxed into them, luxuriating in the feel of their lips.

Devlin intensified his kiss, his tongue darting into my mouth to taste me. He reached down with his hand and opened me, rubbing the head of himself on my wet folds.

"Please." It was too much to have to wait any longer. "Please—"

"She's ready for you, brother," Devlin growled throatily. He kissed me again, sighing gently, then drew back as Danial lay down. His breathing hard, his hands urgent, Danial guided my hips to straddle his. Danial thrust upwards, burying himself in me with a loud cry. I arched my back, pushing back against Devlin, who slid his hands up to hold my breasts, as he began to kiss me hungrily, his erection throbbing against my back.

Danial thrust slowly and deeply into me, crying out each time, watching me kiss Devlin above him. His hips held mine, moving me in rhythm, helping me to stroke him over and over. I began to moan softly from all the pleasure I was feeling, my breaths ragged. Devlin was breathing hard now, too, his hand tangled in my hair, his mouth devouring mine, his swollen shaft moving against me in rhythm with Danial and I.

Danial lost his rhythm suddenly, shaking a little as he tried to resist climax. I didn't want him to. At once I bore down with my hips hard. In two strokes, I pushed him over. He soared, arching his back as he clutched my hips hard, screaming out my name. "Sar!"

Devlin drew me off him at once, pulling me to one side. Danial let out a gasp as he came free. Devlin quickly lay down beside Danial, then settled my body on his, penetrating me with a loud cry. I was relaxed and open now; Devlin's length entering me easily. Closing my eyes in bliss, I let my head fall back, a sigh of pleasure escaping my parted lips. Devlin gazed up at me, his fangs bared slightly, every move deliberate as he gave himself to me again and again.

I was so close now from what they had done to me it was almost torture. "Now," I moaned, clutching at Devlin's chest. "Yes."

Arms came from behind, pulling my upper body back from Devlin. Danial had taken up Devlin's former position; caressing and kissing me as Devlin made love to me. I began to tremble with tiny jerks, the pleasure so good, so total...*God, this was just as mind-blowing as I'd dreamed...*

Devlin laughed softly, still thrusting regularly. "I can feel how close you are," he groaned. "You need only a little push to send you over the edge. Do it, Danial—"

Danial broke the kiss, and ran his fangs down the edge of my neck, gently pressing. At once I moved faster, crying out eagerly as Devlin thrust into me hard and swift. Then I shouted, almost sobbing in sweet release as the orgasm washed though me.

Danial sank in his fangs just a little. I jerked hard, the sensation of him drinking intensifying the orgasm. Devlin suddenly erupted beneath me, shouting my name as he spent himself, pulling my hips hard against his. "Sar!"

The synergism of Danial and Devlin together had left me weak. Danial gently pulled me off Devlin, who let out a moan, then pulled me into his embrace, spooning me from behind as I faced Devlin's heaving chest.

Devlin rolled onto his side to face me, breathing hard. "Were we everything you hoped for, Sar?" he said confidently, reaching out to stroke my face.

"Yes," I said, when I could talk. "Being with you both like that, it was better than I imagined it would be. I'd never...I've never done this before."

Devlin gave me a satisfied smile, then cut his eyes over my shoulder to Danial. "I think she's lying about us surpassing her fantasies," Devlin said, moving closer to sandwich me tightly between his body and Danial's. "What do you think, Danial?"

Danial kissed my shoulder once, and then spoke, his words soft in my ear. "I think Sar enjoyed us, but I know you, Dev. What we did is not elaborate enough for you. And you are right; we could do much more."

"More? God, I'll die," I joked. "I'm tired."

"Rest, Sar," Devlin replied, snuggling close. "We'll make love again later, when you're ready. We have hours yet."

I luxuriated in the feel of both of them against me, surrounding me. In a few minutes, I was asleep.

* * * *

Brian woke us, banging hard on the door. "Danial, call for you."

"Fuck off..." Devlin said, yawning, then stretched against me.

"Who is it?" Danial said, not moving. "Take a message, unless it's critical."

I cut my eyes to him in surprise. He obviously didn't want to leave. *Must be jealousy.*

"Your accountant," Brian replied. "He said it's urgent."

Danial swore, then got up, put on his robe, and went to the door. "I'll be right there."

"Trouble?" Devlin said, giving Danial a serious look even as he maneuvered my body under his.

"Tax issues," Danial said, making a face. "I'm a father now. He advised claiming Theoron as a dependent. And there's the usual question of how much to over pay to balance out the off-the-book jobs."

"Got it," Devlin said, even as he began to kiss me. "Take your time; we won't wait for you to get back—"

"You had better wait," Danial said warningly as he shut the door behind him.

As soon as he'd gone, Devlin moved back off me. "Sar, are you willing to try something?"

"What?" I said teasingly, running my hand down his hip. "One on one?"

"No. Are you willing to let us both inside you at the same time?"

I bit my lip as Devlin watched me, saying nothing. I hadn't expected this. I should have.

"I've never done what you're asking," I said finally. "I've never even thought about it."

"I understand that just by the look on your face," Devlin said, grinning slightly. "My question is are you willing to try it?"

"Have you done that before, you and Danial? You've had to have done what we already did before; you were too coordinated not to have had practice."

"No, we haven't actually," Devlin said, chuckling. "Danial is a little prudish when it comes to this sort of thing. Myself, yes; I have done this with other vampires and mortals." He paused. "You needn't worry. Your body can accommodate—"

I had a surprise for Devlin. "I know it can, Dev. Danial did to me once what you are really asking me permission for. I asked him to under the power of The Lust, back when I was pregnant the first time. You should know he didn't enjoy doing it. After I came back to myself, I was...well, let's just say I regretted it."

Devlin stroked my arm gently. "I'm sorry your first experience of that kind of sex was not pleasurable, Love. It's possible that Danial had never done it before. You also weren't prepared to have him enter you that way. I know what to do. It doesn't have to be painful, or messy. This won't hurt you, if it's done right."

I already didn't like the sound of that. "Why are you asking for this?" I said defensively. "Don't you like what we did?"

"I liked it very much," Devlin said earnestly, holding me tightly against him. "But we must take turns with you that way. I didn't want to wait to have you. Sharing anything is hard for me. Sharing you is hardest of all."

"I'll try it," I said with hesitation. "But if I feel uncomfortable, I want you to stop."

"We are here together to pleasure each other, Love," Devlin said, kissing me. "No one wants you to do something that hurts you, or that you don't want done to you. If you tell me to stop, I will. I promise."

I had reservations, but I nodded. "What do I have to do?"

Devlin grinned and took my hand. "Come with me to the bathroom."

Chapter Five

Devlin showed me what needed to be done. Although I was a little apprehensive, I agreed. After he left me in the bathroom to give me privacy, I did what he'd told me to do. I was in there a while, getting it all sorted out. By the time I exited the bathroom, Danial had returned, and he and Devlin were waiting on the bed for me, once more naked.

I paused, posing. "How does this look?"

I was wearing what Devlin had brought for me; a sort of thin but strong gold metal lingerie. It had bracelet cuffs and a shaped, belt-like band that fit under my breasts, raising them slightly. The outfit resembled jewelry, with delicate, sparkling chains that attached between gleaming cuffs and belt. Yet another chain that ran up from the belt between my breasts to my choker. Devlin had attached that last somehow, the links sliding together like my choker did. There was also a tiny skirt-like bottom, make of gold lame embroidered with gold thread held on by more sparkling chain. This wasn't underwear, as it left me completely accessible.

"You're beautiful," Dev purred, his tone dripping desire.

I felt utterly beautiful, seeing in his eyes how much he thought that I was, dressed this way for him. This had to be some kind of vampire lingerie made specifically for an Oathed human to wear. *What did something like this cost? And where did you get it?*

Danial got up and came over to me. "Yes, you are beautiful." He touched my shoulder. "Devlin told me what he intends, Sar. You don't have to do this if you don't want to."

I hugged him, the chains clinking slightly. "I want to try it. Just stop if I say to."

Danial kissed me gently. "Stop me at any time, if anything I do hurts."

"Of course."

Danial led me back to the bed, then sat down with me cradled me in his

56

arms. "Well, it's your fantasy," he said. "Tell me what to do."

Devlin bared his fangs and grinned. "I want to love Sar as thoroughly as possible."

Danial laughed lightly and uneasily. "Dev, I don't have your level of self-restraint—"

"You don't need it," Devlin replied, smirking. "I've taken that into consideration." He leaned in close, kissed me, and then turned to Danial. "Do whatever else you like, but stay out of her for now. Begin."

Danial kissed me. Pulling back my hair gently, he bared my throat and began kissing down it, grazing me gently with his fangs. I shuddered in pleasure, leaning into him as Devlin began to sing. It was "Unchained Melody," the tune Danial had played for me that night back last fall. Danial and I deepened the kiss, remembering the night we had made love to this very song. I felt dizzy with wanting. It was already too much to feel Danial touching and kissing my body, while Devlin's voice set my nerve endings shivering. All the love, lust and need Dev felt was laced in every note he sang, intensifying our emotions, making each sensation that much more powerful.

By the end of the song, I was uttering soft cries and Danial was trembling hard, thrusting his hips against me, so excited he couldn't restrain himself. Neither of us could wait; we were at our breaking point, Danial's fangs pricking me gently in his arousal. As Devlin finished singing, I grabbed hold of Danial's engorged flesh, and moved myself into position to slide onto him.

Danial threw his head back, gasping, "Please—"

Dev's hands closed on my shoulders, pulling me gently away from Danial. "It will not be over so easily, Sar," Devlin said throatily. He cut off my reply with a passionate kiss, holding me tightly as I wormed against him, desperate.

Danial kissed the side of my throat from behind me, then pricked it again with his fangs.

I writhed, trying to get hold of Devlin's inflamed erection. He moved deftly, keeping himself just out of reach.

I couldn't stand much more of this, or I'd go mad. "Let me touch you," I whispered. "I've got to feel you, Dev—!"

"Say please, Love," Devlin whispered, kissing my throat, and biting gently. His fangs pressed hard, but didn't break the skin.

"Please!" I cried.

"Touch me," he said, moving within reach.

I reached down and stroked him, gripping him tightly in my hand. His eyes closed as a tremor went through his body. "Feel that, Dev?" I said hungrily. "I can feel how much you want to sink yourself into me." I stroked him faster, and his body helped me, lubricating him.

He kissed me ardently, moving himself in my hand hard and fast, grunting softly.

I pulled back my hand suddenly, letting him go, then grabbed a fistful of his hair. "Tell me what you want to do to me!" I said, yanking it back hard so he cried out. "Tell me, Dev!"

Dev's tone when he spoke was terrifying, his desire for me was so strong. "Danial and I are going to have you together, and then we both are going to bite you, as you come!" he roared, his golden eyes burning hot. He grabbed me and pushed me to the bed, rolling quickly under me as he impaled me on him, thrusting into me hard enough to hurt.

Letting out a shout of pleasure, Dev held himself there with effort, straining to hold still, shaking hard. "Quickly, Danial!"

Danial moved into position behind me, then came the soft sound of liquid noises as he applied lubricant. Carefully, he eased inside me as I held as still as I could, Devlin twitching under my body as he watched us. Finally, he was also inside me fully.

"Ready," Danial said softly.

"Now," Devlin said, the words tortured in sweet agony.

Slowly and deliberately, they began to move as one.

I went weak almost instantly from the new incredible sensation, my jaw going slack.

Devlin eased me down on him without breaking rhythm, holding me close. "You feel so good, Sar!" he groaned, rough with need. "So good around me."

"Oh, Sar, you do," Danial cried out, each word guttural with raw ecstasy. "You're so tight for me, my love, so wonderfully tight. It's like nothing I've ever felt."

Both of them trailed off into moans as they fought not to break their rhythm, their hands suddenly clutching me tight. Danial held me by the hips, thrusting into me on his knees. Devlin held me at my waist and shoulders, still thrusting into me in time with Danial.

I let out cry after cry, my ability to form rational words gone.

"Tell us we feel good to you, Love," Devlin whispered seductively. "Tell us how much you want us there within you, together."

I found my voice. "Yes," I groaned. "God, yes! Just like this, to feel you both. Please, don't stop, please—"

"We don't intend to," Devlin purred. "Take as long as you want, Love."

Wave after wave of pleasure hit me as they made love to me in slow strokes. As much as I wanted the bliss to last, the wave we were riding was already cresting, turning, ready to break over us.

Danial began to shake. He was close. I was close, too. *Just a little more…*

"Hold on," Devlin ordered. "Just a few more seconds!"

Danial groaned, slowing slightly, still stroking me.

Devlin speeded up suddenly. A second later Danial did also, than leaned into me. The weight of him pushed Devlin that much deeper into me, grinding my hips against his. My climax was immediate, all-consuming, flooding over me, making me scream raggedly over and over as I spasmed around them both, digging my fingers into Devlin's chest.

At my first scream, Danial bit into the right side of my neck and Devlin the left side, as they had done years ago. Both began drinking from me, sighing in pleasure. In the next instant, Danial and Devlin both bore down, thrusting into me deeply. I felt them both come, jerking hard, their cries of ecstasy muffled.

As they finished, Danial slipped his fangs out with a last grunt, then held his lips to my neck for a second before he collapsed on me, still jerking. Quickly, Devlin slipped out and eased me to the right side of him and moved Danial off to the other side. We were all gasping in air, trying to control our still shuddering bodies.

As my panting eased, Devlin sat up, and pulled me close, healing the bite marks. "They aren't deep, Love, but it pays to be careful." He looked them over. "All set."

Lying back down, Devlin held me gently, Danial again spooning me from behind. "Now that was what I had in mind," Devlin said contentedly. "How about you, Sar?"

I didn't reply. I was too busy still trying to get my mind around what we had done.

"You were right," Danial said contentedly. "Being with her like that with you was wonderful. It was more than wonderful; it was ecstasy."

"I told you decades ago to try it with me," Devlin said richly, laughing. "But no, you—"

"Maybe I should've listened," Danial admitted, kissing me. "But maybe not. This felt as good as it did because it was her, Dev; because I love her."

"I know," Devlin said tenderly as he looked over at Danial and I. "I feel the same. I have done this before many times in my life. It never felt as good before as it did tonight."

"I love you, Sar," Danial whispered softly.

"We love you, Oathed One," Devlin said, giving me a gentle kiss.

"And I love you, both of you," I said softly, reaching out to grab both of their hands and put them to my heart.

The three of us snuggled together and slept, sated. Just before I drifted off, I wondered if Danial and Devlin had ever been truly happy sharing anything like this before in their long lives. I was betting not, that for them this was the first time.

* * * *

I awoke about midnight on Devlin's chest, shivering. Falling asleep with the covers off hadn't mattered when I'd been hot with exertion. Now I was chilled from sleeping sandwiched between two vampires.

I shifted backwards slightly, rubbing up against Danial at my back.

"What is it?" Danial asked softly in the darkness.

"I'm cold," I answered. "Can you pull the comforter over us?"

"Dev, move your leg and grab your side," Danial said, sitting up and pulling his side of the comforter upwards.

"Okay," Dev mumbled. He shifted, then sat up just enough to grab the comforter and yank it over he and I.

"Thanks," I whispered, trying to wrap the blanket around my cold toes. Two vampires was two too many for my human heating system to handle alone. *We needed a non-vampire in here for added heat...*

Blushing slightly, I wondered if Theo and Lash were back from the movies. Probably not; they'd only left a few hours ago. Even if Theo had come back, he wasn't welcome here.

Depression flooded me, then a sudden burning anger. I'd just had the most amazing night of my life so far, a fantasy come to life, and here I was missing another man. What the hell was wrong with my brain?

Maybe it was that I had found out too late what I really wanted: a peaceful life, not a fantasy complete with villains and love that threatened to swallow my soul. I'd done my best to adapt to what my life had become, yet more and more, I was tired of its complexity. I'd always been a simple woman with simple needs and desires. Nothing was simple anymore. There were too many people to please, and most of the time I felt like none of them was me. The constant traveling to and from other houses each week was exhausting. I wanted back the quiet life I'd once had with Theo of going to work, spending the evenings with him watching movies, eating pasta, and making love...

"Sar, why are you not sleeping?" Danial asked, worried. "You smell anxious. Are you hurt?"

I scrambled quickly in my mind to come up with something, anything, because I couldn't say I'd been thinking about Theo. Bad enough Danial would be hurt, but Devlin would be apoplectic with rage. For all that Theo had let go his jealousy of Devlin, at least most of it, Devlin's had only seemed to get stronger with time.

"I'm wondering why Dev came to me on a bike in the middle of winter," I said lamely. "There had to be warmer ways, even in daylight."

60

"You are thinking of that now?" Dev said, surprised. He struck a match and lit one of the bedside candles.

"Sar often thinks this way," Danial said casually, giving my neck a gentle kiss. "I am not surprised."

"I am," Dev said, snuggling close, his golden eyes searching mine. "I told you, I had to get to you in time, Love."

That wasn't an answer. "But why not come to me in something safer? Sunlight hurts you badly. What if you had gotten in an accident on the way to me? Why not bring at least one guard to follow you and keep watch? Just a small tear in your leather might have made you a crisp."

Devlin hugged me tight. "I had to get to you, Sar. There's danger in everything worth doing. I needed you to think I was Aran, so I could get inside your house and save you. Even if you wouldn't let me be with you, I needed to give you some of my blood. But I did bring a guard, of course."

I furrowed my brow. "Then where was he?"

"Nick was watching from the quarry road the entire time I was with you. When we left, he followed at a discreet distance. He froze his ass off, he said. After I gave him a large bonus he got over it."

That was why Devlin had gone with me to the door when Brian showed up. Nick hadn't called to warn him. "You were worried Brian was someone Samuel sent to collect me?"

Devlin nodded. "And before you ask, Nick has been told to keep the snowcapades to himself."

Nick had gotten an eyeful when Devlin had chased me out into the snow naked. I blushed faintly, then stammered, "If you ever do get burned, what do I do? Should I give you blood like I have in the past?" My tone was guilty, remembering the burn I'd given Dev.

"Hush," Devlin said easily. "I told you to forget that. It was nothing."

"Yes," Danial said from behind me. "Blood would heal Dev or I, if we were burned, as long as we could get out of the sunlight. But if it ever happens and it's bad, don't try to save either of us, Sar. We might savage you, as I did the first time I took your blood. For anything more than a slight burn, call for help instead."

"He's right," Devlin said, old hurt in his tone. "I killed a little girl once. I didn't mean to. I'd been burned when the house I was staying in collapsed in a earthquake. It was agony. I waited in shade for hours, writhing in pain. When she stopped to rest on her way to the local well, I grabbed her, and drank from her. I only meant to take a little, but there was so much relief to feel the pain ease that I took too much. She died healing me. I had never killed a child, or even hurt one before that. That still haunts me."

I shivered, Devlin's memory calling back Lash's words of how good his relief from his pain was. Then I told myself to get a grip. If Lash had wanted to drain me, he would have already. The only important thing to remember was to take some of my vitamins first thing in the morning. Between letting Lash drink my blood and now Danial and Dev, I had to be running a half pint low.

"Sar, get some sleep," Danial said softly. "Morning will be here before you know it."

I snuggled against him as Devlin settled himself against my back, drifting quickly back into pleasant nothingness.

* * * *

Elle woke us at ten a.m. with a gentle knock on the bedroom door. "Mom?"

I slept right through it, but Danial heard and shook me gently. "Sar, Elle wants you."

"What is it?" I called sleepily.

"Can you come cook us breakfast? Theo said that you would this morning."

I shot a glance at Danial, and his eyes met mine. This wasn't about breakfast. Elle knew Devlin was in here with us, and she wasn't happy about it.

"Mom?" Elle called again more loudly.

Devlin stirred beside me, and opened his golden eyes. "Tell her no," he said, kissing me lingeringly. "I don't want you to get out of bed yet, Sar. I want to hold you in my arms, and remember last night, how good you felt. God, you were amazing—"

"You promised, Mom!" Elle growled fiercely, each word close to a shout.

Devlin's patience snapped in a split second. "Listen, you were b—"

Danial slapped his hand over Devlin's mouth. "No."

I shot Dev a look of aversion. "Elle, I'll be right out, as soon as I shower," I said tiredly, rubbing my eyes. "Go defrost the bacon and sausage. Make sure you get out enough for Theoron your father, me and you."

"Of course," she said sweetly.

Danial took his hand off of Devlin's mouth.

"What?" Devlin said grumpily. "I have a right to be here."

"Dev, Elle had a problem with Theo at first," I interrupted, moving to sit on the bed out of his reach. "Now she's got to deal with you having a piece of me after she found out about Lash and I yesterday. Give her some time. This is a lot for her to deal with."

"She isn't a child—" Devlin started.

"She's my child," Danial said with red-tinged eyes. "I'd better not ever hear you call her what I think you were going to, Dev. She's just protecting her mother the only way she knows how."

"Danny, I don't care!" Devlin sang derisively. Danial's eyes began to glow red.

"I'll talk to her," I interceded. "Dev's right. She needs to accept this. Theo said he would talk to her last night, but he must not have. I'll talk to her this morning, alone. I want the both of you to stay in here for a half hour after I leave, okay?"

They both nodded.

"And Dev," I said sternly. "You need to get used to this. You'll have a child soon yourself. That child's needs should come before your needs. I won't be able to help you until the baby's older—"

"I'll hire a nanny or two," Devlin said smoothly, folding his hands under his head and lying back on the bed. "It worked well for Danial. Theoron is a well behaved, well-adjusted child."

That wasn't what I meant, but I was too burnt out to explain. "I'll be in the shower," I said, shutting the bathroom door firmly behind me.

I carefully removed the metal lingerie, rubbing at the slight red marks it left on my skin, and then placed it back inside its box, irritated. Last night had been so wonderful, a magical fantasy come to life. This morning it was back to reality and all the trouble that came with it.

As I dressed, I kept wondering what last night would mean for me. If Dev and Danial had their way, our threesome would happen again. I'd enjoyed it, no question. But instead of excitement, the prospect of a repeat sometime soon left me feeling uneasy and worried. *What was wrong with me? What had changed? What we'd done had been my fantasy, hadn't it?*

After showering quickly, I dressed, then saw to my wet hair, conditioning it and coiling it up out of the way. When I reentered the bedroom, both Devlin and Danial were reading some old books of poetry. To my surprise, it was Danial who held a copy of Dante's Inferno, and Devlin that was perusing Paradise Lost. "A little light reading this morning?" I quipped. "What happened to love and passion?"

Devlin lowered his book, giving me a smoky gaze. "Our state cannot be severed. We are one, Sweet Sar."

I smiled. "Not at all the sentiment I expected from those pages, Dev."

Danial took the book from Devlin, then flipped a few pages. "Here is one of the more quoted verses, Love." He cleared his throat. "A mind not to be changed by place or time. The mind is its own place, and in itself can make a heaven of hell, or a hell of heaven."

A dark thought, and one that mirrored my own disquiet this morning. Did

63

Danial suspect my omission of last night? I kept the smile on my face with effort. "More what I was expecting."

Devlin shot Danial an annoyed look, then took the book back, flipping pages. "All is not lost," he intoned grandly. "The unconquerable will and study of revenge, immortal hate, and the courage never to submit or yield." He turned his eyes to me, his forceful tone changing to sensuous. "What is dark within me, thou illuminates. Grace is in all your steps, Heaven in your eyes, in every gesture dignity and love."

Danial rolled his eyes. "He who overcomes by force overcomes but half his foe, Dev."

It was going to be a poetry quoting war shortly in here. I headed for the door. "Remember, stay here. I'll be back shortly."

"Give me a kiss, before you go!" Devlin said, tossing aside the book and reaching for me.

Danial pushed him back down roughly. "Shut up and give your libido a rest, for once."

I laughed at the dark look Dev shot Danial as I closed the door after me. Turning, I jumped, startled to see Lash lying on the couch under several blankets, his clothes in a pile on the floor near his whip, knife, and boots.

He was devoted to Dev, no question. I ventured closer, knowing he had to be awake after Elle's tirade earlier. Since I was making breakfast. I might as well see if he wanted any.

I went over and crouched next to him, but didn't touch him. "Lash," I said softly.

He opened his eyes. "You woke me," he hissed, stretching under the blankets, and yawning just a little. "Not very nice."

"You're full of it, Liar," I said, giving him a half smile. "Do you want any breakfast?"

"Only if you have blood," he said, reflecting a half smile back at me.

I should have seen that coming. "I'll check and see. We should have raw chicken, or beef?" I offered.

"The latter will do," he said. "Especially if you put a little in the blender for me, liquidate it, then heat it up a little."

Was he serious? Yuck. I looked at him, and decided he was serious. "I'll see what I can do," I said cautiously.

Lash saw my hesitation. "I can do it," he said, and began to get up.

He had to be naked. What if it a flash of skin brought The Lust again? "Stay here, please!" I said emphatically, gesturing for him to sit.

He sank back down on the couch, amused.

"I need to talk to my daughter. Please just stay here and keep everyone away. If you see Theo come up, tell him to wait, too."

Lash nodded once. "Sure. But aren't you going to ask Theo about breakfast?" he hissed, his smile baring one fang. "We wouldn't want him to feel left out."

I laughed, trying to ease my sudden tension. "I already know he wants some, and what he wants." Quickly I turned away from him, and went into the kitchen.

Elle was there at the counter, dressed and looking stonily at nothing. Theoron was in his pajamas, trying to get the bacon out of the package, but it was frozen into a hard block and wouldn't come out.

"Theo, go get dressed," I said. "We have guests for breakfast, and it's not polite."

"It's just Uncle Dev and Lash," Theo said softly, still prying at the bacon.

"Do what I said," I repeated harshly. Theoron gave me wide eyes, and went.

I closed the kitchen door. *Time for the Big Talk.* "Elle, I think we need to talk—"

"They'll still hear all of this, your four lovers!" Elle shouted, her face was filled with tears. "Don't bother closing the door!"

I grabbed her hand. She tore it free of mine, but not before I had teleported her to Terian's lab. "Why bring me here!" she yelled at me. "Are you going to tell me he was your lover, too?"

"No," I said quietly. "But you are right that we need privacy, and we weren't going to get any in the kitchen. I have some things to say to you—"

"What, to tell me something I don't know? Why don't you tell me you're not a slut—!"

I grabbed hold of her and then shook her a few times, as hard as I could, screaming "Shut up!" She looked at me in shock, and shut her mouth. I took a deep breath, trying to calm myself. "Elle, I am your mother, and you don't have to love me—"

"You aren't my mother, not really," she said nastily, her eyes yellow.

That hurt. A lot. "I'm the only mother you're ever going to know," I retorted angrily. "Now sit your ass down and shut your mouth for a moment."

Elle sat down, tears leaking from her eyes.

I sat across from her, and took one of her hands. "I'm sorry I yelled at you. But your brother is going to come back soon, and we have to be there when he does. I—"

"How can you let him touch you?" Elle wailed, crying hard. "I smelled you on him! He's not even handsome, and Theo and he don't like each other at all, they were trading insults all night—"

65

Great. "Lash and Theo have some kind of feud—"

"—and you told me you didn't trust Devlin! Theo said you had to have the baby for him, that you didn't have a choice, but you clearly wanted to be with him yesterday—"

"Elle, please!" I said raggedly.

"—and I found out that Devlin's had other women besides you! I smelled one on him last night! You're pregnant with his child! He doesn't love you, Mom! He doesn't even respect you! How can you love him, let him treat you like that?" She was crying hard.

I hugged her to me, blinking back tears in my eyes. Everything she'd said was true, but that didn't change anything for me.

"Elle, I kept most of the hard facts from you," I said finally. "I thought you were too young to know."

"Know what?" she said, sniffling.

"When I'm pregnant with a vampire's child, I channel some of the lust that they feel when they take blood. But because I'm not a vampire, my lust is for sex, not blood."

"That's why were you with Lash?" she asked, making a grimace.

Okay, try not to sound defensive. "The Lust likes him for some reason. But I don't want you to let this get to you. It's a normal part of having a dhamphir. When I was pregnant with your brother this happened until the pregnancy reached four months. I'm almost four months now, so this won't last much longer."

"So you don't love him?"

"No, I don't," I replied. "When The Lust is done, I won't be with Lash anymore. He knows this, Elle. He's only doing this because Devlin asked him to, as a favor."

"But you love Devlin," she said coldly. "You're Oathed to him."

"Elle, I made a deal with him, one I explained to you already, But you're right, I do love him, and I did make him a promise." I swallowed hard. "I know about the other women, and gave him permission for it. I know it's odd, with what I always told you about how you should always walk if a man cheats—"

"He saved you so you owe him sex?" she interjected angrily. "You owe him a baby for your life?"

How had she learned so much so fast? Listening to the weres? Overhearing Danial? "I don't owe him anything," I replied. "But I need him and he wants me. It might not be that way forever—"

"Why couldn't you just be with Dad?" she said, pulling back from me, a hard look in her eyes. "You love him more than Devlin, I know it."

"Because Devlin didn't give me that choice!" I shouted. "The other Rulers

66

were going to kill your fathers, both of them! You would never have seen me again. I made the only choice I could, Elle. Stop berating me for it!"

"Can't you get out of your Oath?" Elle began, her eyes filling again with tears.

"No! Elle, if I told Devlin that I refused to be with him anymore, he would not just say that was okay! I know that from firsthand experience, because I refused him once before!" I let all my memories of Devlin's threats flood into my eyes. "Do you understand what I'm saying, or do you need me to spell it out for you?"

She hugged me hard enough to hurt me a little, then began crying hard again. I comforted her, wiping away some tears of my own in the process. "I'm sorry," she said finally. "I didn't know. Dad never told me that."

"Your dad didn't want you to know. Neither did I."

Elle nodded. "I understand that," she said. "But I hate him," she growled. "I don't want him near me, Mom."

I knew who she meant. "You don't have to like Dev. But you have to let him touch me, if he wants to. I can handle him. And no more scenes like this morning," I added gently. "Devlin may spend the night again like he did last night."

"Dad doesn't like sharing you—"

"That depends on who is involved, Elle," I said meaningfully. "But that is his business and mine, not yours, and we will handle it."

Her face went white. "Dad is jealous—"

"No, he isn't," I lied, telling myself it was partly true. "Danial is happy that I'm Oathed to both him and Devlin, Elle. He's happy I'm having Devlin's child. You need to know and accept that your father wanted Devlin here last night. Devlin will probably come here again. All you need to do when he does is be polite when you see him and excuse yourself. Now can you handle that or not?"

Elle nodded slowly. "I guess so."

I stood up. "We should go back. Your brother has got to be in the kitchen by now. I don't want him to turn on the stove and burn himself. It will hurt, even if he heals."

She blew her nose a final time. "I'm ready."

I teleported her into her room. She turned to me in surprise.

"You look like you've been crying," I said. "Cool down your face some, and then come out."

"Thanks," she said softly, hugging me. "I'm sorry…what I said. You are my mother. I wouldn't want another, not ever."

I hugged her hard, knowing I was going to have to get a cold cloth of my own for my face now, because my cheeks were flushed, my salty hot tears running down them in a river.

* * * *

When I teleported back to the kitchen a few minutes late, Theoron was there working on the sausage. He had gotten all the bacon defrosted somehow, and it waited in a moist pile on a plate. The sausage was defrosted, too, at least most of it. I watched him put one piece at a time in the microwave and hit the button, and bit my lip, holding in my amusement and affection.

"Good job," I said lovingly, going to the fridge and taking out a steak. Tossing it into the large blender, I hit liquefy. Carefully, I poured some of the meat juice into a large mug, and then put it in the microwave. Theoron watched me hungrily.

"Watch that for me," I said to him. "Taste it when it comes out, and tell me if it's hot enough." He nodded eagerly.

I got the meat and eggs cooking, then started in on the waffles. When the microwave beeped, Theoron got out the mug, and tasted the contents.

"Warm enough?" I asked.

"No," Theoron said, making a face. "Though it's really good!"

"Nuke it again," I said, and then added as an afterthought, "and please put the rest in another mug as well, and heat that up, too."

Theoron hastened to comply. When the microwave beeped again, the mug was steaming, the coppery tang of blood scenting the air. I was relieved it didn't smell good to me. I worried sometimes that one day it was going to.

"Is it warm enough?"

Theoron tasted both mugs and nodded.

"Take the bigger one in to Lash then," I said. "The other one is for you."

Taking them both carefully, Theoron walked out of the kitchen. I heard him say, "From Mom," to Lash, and then Lash's hiss of thanks.

When Theoron didn't come back, I surmised he was sitting with Lash, though I didn't hear them talking. *Well, that would make Danial pop a gasket...*

The cellar door opened. I heard Theo greet Theoron, though he said nothing to Lash. He came into the kitchen, giving me a sunny smile.

"Good Morning," I said.

Theo gave my cheek a kiss. "I knew I smelled bacon," he said, inhaling deeply.

"I made the whole package," I said. "How many eggs?"

"Five," Theo said hungrily. "I ate too much popcorn last night. I need to have a good breakfast."

"I'm making waffles," I said, even though it was obvious. "Elle should be in shortly."

"I tried talking to her last night," Theo murmured. "She got angry, and so did I. It didn't end well. I said some things I probably shouldn't have. She went to bed angry."

"She got up angry," I said, turning over some sausage. "But I talked to her this morning. I think things will be a little better now."

"What did you tell her?" Theo said, coming over to stand behind me, and rubbing my shoulders.

"I'll tell you later," I said quietly, motioning that we should zip it, because everyone was sure to be hearing what we were saying.

Theo nodded. "So are you ready to go home after breakfast?"

I put down my fork, and put my arms around him, kissing him thoroughly as an answer.

He broke it off, his blue-grey eyes surprised. "Does that mean yes?"

I loved his eyes better than anyone else's, even Devlin's. "It means yes," I said, nodding.

"You seem different this morning," he said happily. "Like your old self."

"Maybe," I whispered. "Or maybe I just finally remembered who I really am."

Titus had been right. It had just taken longer than a night for the bond to solidify between us. Maybe because I'd already been pregnant by then with Devlin's child, maybe because I'd been so close to dying. But I'd had enough of lovers plural, and waking up in different beds. I wanted only one man, the one standing before me. I reached out then gently, and held Theo's cheek in my hand.

"And who are you?" Theo murmured.

"I'm yours," I said emotionally. "I always will be."

"Mom?" Elle said hesitantly, walking into the kitchen.

I dropped my hand from Theo's face, as we both turned quickly to the kitchen door to Elle. I noticed Lash was behind her, dressed, watching us intently from the dining room, sipping from his mug.

"Do you want some help?" Elle said, offering a tentative smile.

"Yes," I said, giving her a grateful smile. "You can start bringing in the food."

"What is Theoron eating?" Elle said, smelling the air. "It smells good."

"He's having some liquefied steak," I said. "Would you like some—?"

Theo growled, surmising rightly that I'd made Lash breakfast.

"Will you go and get Danial and Devlin?" I asked him. "They should both be awake reading."

"Will do," Theo said curtly, his eyes still watching Lash.

"Theo," I said pointedly.

Theo shot me an irritated look, and went to wake the vampires, studiously not looking at Lash as he went past him.

Sigh. Well, at least they weren't fighting.

Theoron ran back in the kitchen, followed by Lash. "Can I have some more?" Theoron said hopefully.

I looked at Lash. "Do you want more, too? I can split it again like I did the first time."

"I always want more," Lash hissed meaningfully.

I flushed as Elle cast Lash an angry look, a soft growl filling the air.

I went to the fridge, and unwrapped another steak. "Why are you only polite when we're alone?" I said cheerily, my eyes shooting daggers at Lash as I prepared the meat juice.

"I'm sorry," he hissed, nodding once. "I should not have said that to you here in front of the children. I'll be in the dining room." He turned and left.

Apparently, he had manners after all. Elle looked as surprised as I was, but didn't comment.

"Here," I said, handing the mugs to Theoron. "You know what to do."

* * * *

As I was cleaning up after breakfast with Elle's help, Theo put his arms around me from behind. "Great job, Sar."

"Thanks," I said tiredly, handing Elle a clean dish to wipe.

"We can leave anytime you want to," Theo whispered. "I'm off for today, and you have that appointment tomorrow with Dr. Camlyn."

"Sounds good," I agreed. "We can—"

"Doesn't sound good to me," a melodious voice said coldly.

Theo, Elle and I looked up, startled. Devlin stood there in the doorway, his hands gripping the doorframe above his head. He was smiling, his eyes tinged with red. Abruptly, he let go of the door and glided toward me, beginning to sing. The full effect of his voice enfolded us as we stood motionless, enraptured.

"Oh can't you see, you belong to me? How my poor heart aches, with every step you take..." As Dev reached the word "take", he put his arms around me, pulling me close.

"It's too early in the morning to be ripping off Police songs," I said sarcastically.

"I'm not singing them idly," Devlin replied. He bared his fangs in a smile. "I mean them, Love."

"Let her go," Theo growled. "Sar's tired and I'm taking her home."

70

"You leave," Devlin growled back. "I'll say when she—"

"Stop it!" I shouted suddenly, hysteria lacing my words. "Dev, I'm going home with Theo after breakfast. Now leave us in peace!"

Devlin opened his mouth, and I put my hand over it. "I'm pregnant, I'm tired, and I'm sore," I said firmly. "I need to rest. All I would be doing if I stayed would be sleeping."

Devlin reached up and gently removed my hand. "But we could sleep together. I told you before how much that means to me."

"Not today," I said firmly. "I'll see you Wednesday."

"Very well," Devlin said gruffly. "Wednesday." He turned and strode out of the kitchen.

"Mom," Elle wheedled. "You said during breakfast about the sleepover—"

Parenting, the job that never ended. "June," I said firmly. "And this time, pick only a couple of good friends, Elle."

"Violet and Susan," she said quickly. "They're my best friends."

Violet, I remembered; I'd liked her. "Is Susan in your dance class?"

"She's in the advanced class. She's cool."

"Then that sounds fine," I said, trying to be cheerful. "Pick a Friday or Saturday, but give me notice, so I can work it out with Devlin and Danial."

"Thanks, Mom," Elle said happily, then left the kitchen.

"What about you?" I asked Theoron. "Did you get enough to eat?"

"Yes," Theoron said earnestly, smiling up at me. "I heard Lash said he wanted more. I told him he could have most of mine, too, but he said for me to drink it."

"That was thoughtful of you," I said to Theoron, resisting my urge to scream. "Why don't you go and watch some TV?"

"Okay," he said, hugging me. "Thanks for breakfast, both of them."

I pulled the unraveling edges of myself back together, and smiled down at him. "You're welcome."

Theoron ran out of the kitchen.

"Why does Devlin always have to be so over the top?" Theo said irritably, putting plates away.

Danial walked in and went to the oven, setting it to self-clean. "I don't know," he replied wearily. "Jealousy doesn't explain the mood swings he's always had, either." He turned to me. "Is there anything else I can help with?"

"No," I said, giving the kitchen a quick summation glance. "There weren't that many dishes with you and Dev not eating."

Danial nodded, then cracked a smile. "We're low maintenance in some ways." He gave me a hug. "If you get to the point you want to work from home, just let me know. I can have my tech guy set you up, so you can do the e-mail."

I hugged him back. "It's not you I need a break from," I whispered meaningfully.

"I'm know," he said softly. "Take care."

* * * *

Theo put his hand in mine as we walked, the dogs bounding around us, sniffing. "Janice and Ivan certainly seemed happy."

I nodded. Janice had become lovely overnight, the glow of fresh love suffusing her face, making her eyes sparkle. Ivan was also looking much better. He was no longer the ghost he had become after his brother's and Suri's deaths. "It's good to see them in love." I squeezed Theo's hand. "It's also good to see some signs of spring. It's good to see some ground, not just unending whiteness." I glanced at him. "How about a movie later? There's that new remake out—"

He made a face. "I don't like the ending. There's no justice."

Darkly, I thought to myself that was realistic. Sometimes the wronged didn't find justice, even after a long hard road, being brave, and fighting like hell.

"We need a feel good movie instead," he continued. "Something like—"

I suddenly stopped walking and faced him. "Thank you."

He took in the tears in my eyes, and quickly hugged me. "For what?"

"For staying. For not reconsidering, and deciding that dealing with Devlin is too much."

"Stop, Sar," Theo said firmly. "I promised you, remember? Devlin is too much for me to take most of the time. Seeing Lash is worse. But I'm not ever leaving you, especially not like this. I'll still be here beside you, years from now—"

"Hold me," I said jaggedly, as my control quickly slipped and I began to cry. "I'm a mess, I feel like I'm falling apart."

Theo held me in his strong arms and stroked my hair. "Things will be okay," he said softly. "Believe me."

I wanted to believe him, yet I felt deep in my heart he was wrong.

Chapter Six

The next morning when we arrived at Dr. Camlyn's, Lash and Devlin were there waiting for us.

"Hi," I said, smiling with effort. "Come to see your child?"

"Of course," Devlin purred lovingly. "I haven't been to any of these appointments with you since we found out. I should have been here for them all. I apologize for that. You were right yesterday in your criticism. I'm going to be a father soon, and I need to be more serious about that role. It matters to me that I show you that, Oathed One."

How could he be so annoying one moment, and so tender the next? Dealing with him had been so much easier when I hated him.

"Come with us then," Theo said curtly.

"Lead the way," Devlin retorted, unmoving, his warm expression crystallizing.

Irritated, I strode past them into exam room one. "Let's get this over with."

A few minutes later, we were all watching the monitor, trying to make sense of the images. "I see two tiny blobs, I think," Devlin said finally. "Which one of them is mine?"

"We can't be sure," Stephen said patiently. "We won't know for certain even later on without doing a blood test, unless Theo's child is in cougar form—"

"Can we make sure Sar doesn't have to deliver naturally if that happens?" Theo interrupted.

"Yes," Devlin added, his eyes cutting to Theo. "If my child is born as Danial's was, Sar's going to be hurt like she was last time. Let's plan to do a C section."

"It's not that simple—" Stephen started.

"It is that simple," Devlin said firmly. "Sar doesn't want any more children after these. If possible, she would like sterilization surgery right after the births;

if not, as soon after as it can be done. I'm giving my permission for that right now, and I speak for Danial as well—"

Theo looked so stricken I wanted to crawl under the table. *Good going, Dev.*

"Camlyn," Devlin continued, looking pointedly at Stephen. "This is also a chance for you to rectify your mistake."

Stephen looked at him warily. "What mistake?"

"Your papers on Sar's recovery put her in danger," Devlin said. "Those papers exposed the fact that she was healing. If you hadn't published them, Perseus and the others would have left her alone, thinking her barren."

Stephen shifted uncomfortably. "I didn't know—"

Devlin glided over to stand in front of Stephen. "But you do now," he hissed. "You are going to report that this pregnancy scarred her so badly that you removed her womb. That she can't have any more children, as there's nothing to heal. You are also going to make sure surgically, so she and Theo can't have any accidents that would show that statement to be a lie."

Stephen glanced at me. "Sar, is this what you want?"

"I want not to be pursued anymore," I said wearily. "This is the only way."

"He's right," Theo growled. "I wish there were another way, but he's right. And it's what she wants. Do it."

"I might be able to do it a week or so after she gives birth," Stephen said slowly. "Or directly after the birth, if everything else is normal..."

Like that would happen. This birth was probably going to be as abnormal as it got.

"Good," Devlin said curtly. "So everything is fine, then? Sar's healthy?"

Stephen looked back at me. "Have you been spotting at all?"

"Yes," I said, feeling very self conscious and wishing everyone else would leave the room. *Why the hell was Lash in here anyway?*

"I would like to do a pelvic exam, just to check," Stephen said. "You'll need to get undressed."

"I'll wait outside," Lash hissed quickly, and left, shutting the door behind him softly.

I was so grateful, I almost cried out with relief as I slipped off my jeans and underwear.

The next few minutes felt like an eternity.

"You can get dressed," Stephen said finally, discarding his gloves. He faced Theo and Devlin, his expression formal. "Sar's been spotting because of rough intercourse. I'd advise all of you to abstain from that from now on."

"Then why are you looking straight at me?" Devlin said defensively.

"Because it was likely you," Stephen replied. "You don't need me to tell you your own physical realities at your age, Devlin."

Theo's eyes widened like saucers.

"Stop," I said wearily. "I consented."

"Sar, you consent again, and your cervix may give way," Stephen said. "You'll lose the babies if that happens."

Shocked, I turned worried eyes to Devlin.

"I'm telling you I wasn't rough—" Devlin growled at Stephen, his golden eyes angry.

"It doesn't matter if you were or weren't," Stephen said, holding Devlin's gaze. "This is probably what usually happens when you and she have sex. I'm just advising that it can't happen again while she's pregnant, Devlin."

"You're saying I can't be with her until she has the children?" Devlin said, horrified.

"Yes," Stephen said. "You're hitting her cervix, weakening it by repeatedly bruising the muscle."

Theo's eyes almost popped out of his head.

"We'll abstain," I said loudly, flushing dark red.

"Yes, of course," Devlin said softly. "I don't want to risk my child."

Stephen nodded. "Good. As none of you spoke about The Lust, I'm assuming Sar's had no more episodes?"

I kept my mouth shut, unwilling to tell him it was lasting longer this time than it had before.

"That's right," Theo said, taking my hand a squeezing it. "That was rough on her. I'm glad it's over."

"Then you're doing very well," Stephen said, giving me a smile. "Set up an appointment for two weeks." He left.

"Okay," I said, slipping into my jeans.

"I'm sorry," Devlin said, leaning over the table as I put my shoes on. "You never said that I hurt you, Love."

"You didn't," I reassured, giving him a soft look. "I enjoyed what we did. I'm glad we got a chance to do it before we heard we shouldn't."

Theo abruptly leaned in between us, his yellow eyes inches away from Devlin's. "You both fucked her at once last night, didn't you? What kind of sick mind—?"

"It was Sar's fantasy, Theo," Devlin purred, holding Theo's eyes. "Though I admit freely that it was mine and Danial's as well. You should be careful of your words."

Theo turned to me, appalled. "I'll be waiting for you in the truck. Take your time coming out, Sar." He left, shutting the door behind him with a slam.

Devlin was holding me in an instant. "Are you sure I didn't hurt you?" he said hesitantly. "I have had some women tell me—"

I didn't want to hear whatever he was going to say. "This isn't the time for hearing about other women," I said grumpily, putting my finger to his lips.

"Then just tell me last night was as wonderful for you as it was for me," Devlin whispered, nuzzling my neck.

"You felt wonderful to me, both of you." I leaned back into him, the realities of what they had made me feel leaving me tongue-tied. "I….I…"

"What?" Devlin said, looking down at me. "Say it. No one can hear us now except for Lash."

"No one else is like you are," I admitted.

"Are you saying I'm the best?" Devlin said, engrossed.

I just smiled at him teasingly and went to leave. Devlin pushed the door closed and held it shut. I pulled on the handle, then gave him a roll of my eyes. Devlin grabbed me at my waist, sat me back on the table, and then leaned over on me, pinning me with his weight.

"Stop that," I sputtered, trying hard not to laugh. "We've got to get going."

Devlin folded his arms, then, across my upper chest, and rested his chin on them, his molten gold eyes staring into mine. "Not until you answer me. Am I the best?"

I gave him a teasing smile and kept quiet.

He leaned close and whispered. "You don't have to answer with words, Sar." Then he began kissing me hungrily, teasingly, as if his kisses held the answers to all the secrets I'd ever longed to fathom.

How was I going to last six celibate months with him so near? "Stop," I breathed, pushing at him. "Yes, you're the best."

"Why?" He smiled, gesturing with his hands for size as he moved his eyebrows meaningfully.

I shook my head. "No. You'll have to wait another day for that answer."

Devlin reached his hand deftly under my shirt, touching expertly. I closed my eyes, luxuriating in his touch, then stopped him. "Wrong again."

"Ahh," he said knowingly. "My voice."

This was becoming fun. I gave him another smile, and shook my head.

Now Dev was agitated. "Poetry?" he offered hopefully.

"Let me leave," I said gently.

"Tell me," he implored. "I have to know."

"Your words, of course," I said, giving him a smile.

His brow knitted. "You said it wasn't poetry—"

"I like the whole Dev experience," I said, cracking a smile. "But when you tell me how I make you feel, how I feel to you, what you want to do to me as you make love to me. That's what makes you the best."

Devlin grabbed me and kissed me, his hands running up into my hair, his mouth opening on mine. He pressed against me, his hands slipping down to cup my rear. At once, I felt him elongating against my waist. "Stop," I said firmly, pulling away. "Even if we weren't in a doctor's office, we can't do anything for months." I put some distance between us. "I don't want to start what we can't finish."

"They are going to be the longest months of my life," Devlin said throatily. "They are going to feel like centuries. But being with you at the end of the wait will be all the sweeter, Sar." He beckoned to me. "Come. I'll behave."

I followed him out to where Lash waited, reading a magazine. He looked up, nodded to us, then looked down again.

Devlin turned to me. "Don't let Theo make you feel bad for last night," Devlin said. "What we did wasn't wrong and neither was wanting to share that." He smiled pleasantly. "Tell him if he'll remove the stick up his ass, he can join you and I one night playing Danial's role."

I blinked at Devlin, unbelieving. Devlin saw my expression and laughed. "I'll see you this weekend. You don't need to come on Wednesday, as I'll be away."

Would he be, or did he just not want to bother with me now there wasn't going to be sex?

"I'll be late coming back on Friday night. Please be here by eleven, and be waiting for me in bed. I'll be exhausted and looking forward to spending the night in your arms." He took my hand and kissed it. "I'll adhere to Camlyn's orders, I promise."

It would be the first time I had stayed at Hayden that we hadn't had sex. I wasn't sure whether to be relieved that he still wanted me to come or to be dismayed, because I'd still be doing the musical houses all weekend. "I'll come early," I agreed. "I planned to start sewing with Serena, and maybe I can get Lash to show me the outside of Hayden to get some ideas for the gardens."

"Lash will be here at all times, if you should need him." Devlin kissed my cheek gently. "I'm glad you are helping me so much," he murmured. "I love the rooms you painted. I especially like the room of gold and green. If it wasn't so non-secure, I'd make it my bedroom so I could be reminded of you when we're apart."

His words struck me as empty flattery. I managed a smile in return. "I thought you'd like the silver one best."

"I like that one, too," he amended. "I like them all, Sar, because you did them."

I was embarrassed for some reason. Uncomfortable, I looked away. "The filing is taking a while. I'm only about half finished."

"There's no rush," he replied.

"By the way," I said, remembering. "I meant to ask you: I'm finding photos, and other memorabilia, like ticket stubs, play cards, and even love notes—"

Devlin went utterly still, his expression freezing.

"I didn't read them, once I realized what they were," I reassured. "So far I've been putting them in a drawer marked Personal, by year or decade. Is that okay, or do you want me to pick up some boxes like Danial has—?"

"No," he said quickly, embarrassed. "Just do as you are doing. I'll look through them when you're done. Most of them can be burned. The others, I'll put in order or something."

"I could make you a scrapbook," I offered hesitantly, feeling perverse.

"No," he said gently, hugging me. "Some memories are better kept locked away, where they are not easily found by anyone. And some are better just forgotten."

"Okay." *Whatever that was supposed to mean.* "Bye, Lash."

Lash didn't look up from his magazine, or give any sign he'd heard.

Dev let me go. "Go out to Theo, and have a good week," he said. "I love you."

"I love you, too," I said, and then left, walking out into the sunlight.

Theo was waiting for me inside his truck. When he saw me coming, he started the engine. We didn't speak as he drove, even though I could tell he wasn't heading home or to Danial's. Eventually he pulled into a park, and shut off the engine.

"Let's take a walk, okay?" he asked.

"Sure," I said giving him a hesitant smile. "It's a beautiful day."

We walked for a while, hand in hand, not saying anything. The sun was out, and the wind was at our backs, buoying us forward, trying to hurry us a little.. It had to be near sixty-five degrees. The winter birds were out in force: cardinals, chickadees, crows, sparrows of all types clamoring and calling as they swooped. There was even a red-tailed hawk circling far off in the west. I watched it coast for a while, until Theo suddenly spoke.

"Was it your fantasy?" he said.

"Yes," I answered.

"That's all I need to know, then," he said gruffly. "All I want to know, Sar. I just wanted to make sure it was your choice, what happened. I always think Devlin is lying."

"He wasn't," I replied carefully.

"Are you going to abide by Stephen's directive?" Theo said abruptly, looking at me hard.

"Of course!" I said defensively, staring back at him. "I'm not risking my children's lives. How can you ask that?"

"Because I needed to hear you say it," he said, sounding tired. "Sometimes I think you're changing before my eyes, and I need to know that you aren't. I need to know you still love me. Because if there comes a time when you don't, I want to know it before anyone else does."

"You will," I assured him.

Theo looked at me in surprise. It hit me he'd expected to hear me say I would always love him, that there'd never be a time I wouldn't. "You deserved an answer, not a declaration that was a cover instead of an answer," I murmured.

Theo didn't reply. I lapsed into my musing, dismayed that he thought I was changing.

Yesterday morning in Danial's kitchen, I'd sworn my feelings for him were intensifying, that my feelings for Danial and Devlin were lessening. But back at the doctor's, I'd felt like the opposite was true. Now I felt as if that woman teasing Devlin in Exam Room 1 had been someone else. *What was wrong with me?* The only thing I was sure of was that the overwhelming physical and emotional need for Devlin that had been such a big part of our love was lessening. Whether it was the pregnancy or the bond between Theo and I, I wasn't sure. Maybe I just couldn't keep loving someone who was so demanding all the time.

"I looked into going out West," Theo said suddenly, breaking my thought. "I booked seats on a plane for the end of May for you, Elle, and I. We'll be gone a week. Danial has already given me the time off."

I took his hand and squeezed it. "Sounds great."

"I've booked the same house," he said, giving me a hopeful look. "It won't be like before, because we'll have Elle, but—"

"And I'll be huge by then," I said, laughing. "We'll have a great time. My in-laws will like you. I can't wait to show Elle where you were—"

"About that," Theo interrupted. "Can you not tell her about Aspen?"

I nodded. "Theo, you can be the guide. Elle doesn't need to know any more about Aspen than you want her to. I never told her anything."

"Thanks. I don't want her to know."

"Even if she found out, I don't see where it's a problem," I said. "You were under the spell, and even if you hadn't been, we weren't together—"

"Sar, you are thinking of you and me," Theo interrupted. "I thought of the same thing when I came back and saw you with Danial. I should have thought of her instead and let her know I was alive, even if she didn't want to live with me, or ever have anything to do with me." He got to his feet. "We should head back."

"Sure," I said flatly, trying to contain my irritableness. "Let's go."

We made good time back to the truck. But as soon as we got there, Theo stopped a few yards away. He began backing away, pulling his gun, and moving me behind him.

"Get back to the bench."

"What is it?" I said, panicked.

"Men. At least five, maybe more. Armed, I smell gun oil. They are closing in on us."

"Who? Robert—?"

"Drop your gun, Theo, or we'll shoot her!" a voice called.

Closing my eyes, I teleported us to Danial's great room.

"Sar, stay here," Theo said, walking fast to the door. "I'll get Terian and head back—"

"You can't," I called to him. "Terian's out west, looking for his brother's family."

"No, he's not," Theo said, turning to face me. "He came back weeks ago."

"Danial must not have told you," I said with a shrug. "Leri gave him some info and he and Sun left to chase down leads."

"Why would she do that?" Theo said skeptically.

"I asked her to," I said proudly.

"That was good of you," Theo said approvingly. "But we're screwed, Sar. They are going to trash my truck, if they don't just blow it up."

"I can take you back," I offered. "Get some extra clips, and maybe an AK-47 or—"

"It's too dangerous for you," he said, cutting me off.

"Then give me some of the extra body armor," I replied evenly. "I'll only be there for a moment anyway, to drop you off."

Theo looked at me, weighing the options. He stepped closer suddenly, grabbing my hand. "Take us to the were compound."

Seconds later we were in the room I jokingly referred to as the armory. Boxes of ammunition, enough for a war, were stacked on shelves, a rack of assault rifles and miscellaneous handguns covered one wall. The other wall had rows of body armor.

The armor was stacked along the wall, names of the owners above it. Each guard of Danial's had a set, with two sets each for Danial and Theo. "Terian is the only one without armor?"

"He said he didn't need any," Theo muttered. "I'm trying to get him to reconsider. Magical armor isn't 100% reliable." He offered me Janice's vest-

80

like tunic. "Put this on."

We both suited up. The armor was lightweight, made to move in, yet it was hot from all the insulating Kevlar and other round stopping materials. *Good thing it isn't August.*

Theo handed me a gun with explosive bullets. "Strap this on." He grabbed a handful of extra clips then that were pre-loaded, then took my hand. "Go."

We appeared at the clearing's edge, near the truck. There was a man lying underneath with his feet sticking out, hooking something up to the bottom of it. Theo shot him at once, then shoved me behind a pine tree. The man slumped to the ground as bullets fired, spraying everywhere. I crouched behind the spruce, breathing hard, and trying to tell where our attackers were. A few bullets hit near me on either side of the tree, making craters in the earth.

I let out an "Eek!" sound and stayed down. More bullets mowed down small trees, and made huge holes in others, including mine. Finally I began crawling away on my belly, worried that the repeated blasts to the trunk would knock the tree over on me. I made it to another tree just as one of their guys hit the park sign, blowing a ragged hole, the metal curling back with a shriek.

Trying to be brave, I whispered a prayer for good aim and fired, managing to wing one man before he ducked behind a tree. I kept firing with growing embarrassment, missing my target routinely.

Theo, of course, had been practicing right along. He hit everyone he aimed at with deadly accuracy. Within moments, it was over, silence descending as the smoke cleared.

I stayed where I was for another ten minutes, waiting for a signal. "I don't hear anyone else," Theo called finally. "We're clear." He appeared from behind a tree, holstered his gun, and then walked toward his truck, gesturing for me to keep back.

I sat down and waited for him by my tree, resting against it.

"It's a bomb," he called. "I want you to stay back there, while I disarm it."

"I didn't know you could do that," I said admiringly.

"I can build them, too," he replied smoothly. "And set snares, and pick locks—"

"Show me that last one," I asked hopefully "I won't have to worry the next time I'm at Danial's and don't have my keys."

Theo's smiled faded. "I'll teach you." Then he moved back beneath the truck and began working.

I wasn't sure how many minutes it took, but it wasn't long. Theo emerged from under the truck, a bundle in his hands. "All set, Sar."

I came toward him, watching him stow it behind his seat. "Are you saving it for later?"

"Yes," he said, like it was completely normal. "I don't dare leave it here, and it's possible I can reuse some of it."

"You never told me you blew things up," I teased.

"I usually don't," he replied. "But it's good to have the technology, in case you need to."

I nodded. "Can you teach me that, too?"

"Let's work on the locks first," Theo said drolly, gesturing to the side door. "We'll work up to bombs when you've got those mastered. Let's go home."

* * * *

After a shower and some chicken soup, we began playing with the front lock, Theo giving me pointers. Within an hour, he had me working on the lock like a pro.

"It can't always be this easy," I said worriedly. "I always felt so safe locking my door. I never knew it was so easy to bypass."

"Most thieves aren't after old DVDs and firewood," Theo laughed. "We've safe enough, Sar. But always lock the deadbolt. That a thief can't pick, ever."

The phone rang.

Theo's smile faded. "You'd better get that."

It was Danial. "Are you coming into work tomorrow?"

"You know that isn't why you're calling," I replied. "You're calling to make sure I'm okay, because you heard about the scene earlier today from Devlin."

Danial paused, then said. "I heard about it, yes. I had hoped Theo wouldn't find out what we had done."

"Why not?" I said curiously. "You had to know he would."

"I didn't want him to know," Danial reiterated.

"Why?" I said pointedly.

Danial just sighed.

"You're embarrassed?" I asked, slightly shocked. "Why, Danial? Because you enjoyed what you did to me?"

"Devlin told him it was my fantasy as well as yours, he said," Danial said reluctantly. "Did he really say that?"

"Yes."

Danial didn't reply.

"Why did you call, if you aren't going to talk at all," I said, slightly irritated at his sudden guilt.

"Devlin wants me to ask you something, Sarelle."

The use of my full name was never a good sign. "I'm not doing it, whatever he wants," I said firmly. "I need a break, Danial."

"I'm glad," he said, relieved. "I did not want to ask it of you."

I didn't want to know anything more, not after hearing his relief. "Then let's go over the weekend. I'll see you on Saturday. I'll be with Devlin on Friday, all Friday. But I'll come into work Wednesday, to make up for it. Does that work for you?"

"That's fine. I'll be out of town anyway until Friday night. We'll spend Saturday night together. Chuck said he's bringing Poe and Annabelle Lee to my house about seven, so be here by then."

"Sounds good. I'm not going to be able to ride much longer."

"We'll only be walking the horses. If you weren't so experienced, and familiar with your mount, I wouldn't let you ride at all. But I know you enjoy it, and the danger is small."

I did enjoy his gentlemanly protectiveness. "You're sweet, Danial. But I need to go. I'll see you tomorrow."

"Good night, Sar. I love you."

"I love you, too," I said, and hung up.

I went into my bedroom to find Theo reading in bed, nude. He never read much, save gun magazines and that NRA magazine I'd gotten him for Christmas, *America's First Freedom*.

Tonight it was a bullet catalog. "Looking into some new kind of ammo?"

"Just reordering."

"Ready for bed?" I said, letting my gaze linger on him.

"No," he said, putting down the magazine. "I'm worried about you."

"Why?" I said, coming over to sit by him and laying my hand on his arm.

"I'm worried about you staying here with me," Theo said, his blue eyes concerned. "I'm a target, and I don't want to risk you or the children."

"You just told me the locks we have are fine."

"For repelling small time burglars, sure," he replied worriedly. "But Robert could get through them as fast as I did tonight. Much as I don't want you to, maybe you should stay with Devlin—"

"No way," I shouted. "I'm not staying with him!"

Theo turned to me and grabbed my shoulders. "What is it with you?" he said, his eyes hard. "You tell me you love him and you're having his baby. You just had exotic sex with him and his brother at the same time. Yet you don't want to live with him, even if it's just for a little while? You could've been killed today!"

I flushed deep red. "Don't you want me with you?" I asked meekly.

Theo's face softened. "Of course I do. But maybe that isn't the safest place for you—"

"There's danger no matter where I am—"

"Don't argue with me. I'm your husband—"

Suddenly enraged at his presumptuous, patronizing tone, I got up, and left the room.

"Sar!" he called after me.

I didn't answer him. I needed some space from all the men in my life, beginning right now. Grabbing my jacket and my keys, I headed out to the truck.

"Sar!" Theo shouted. "Come back!"

He'd be out here in a few seconds, once he pulled on some clothes. *If I wanted to get away, I had better move fast.* I got in the truck, raised the garage door, and started the engine. Backing out quickly, I drove off, keeping my lights off until I reached the road.

I drove aimlessly for a while, wishing futilely that I had a girlfriend to talk to who would understand. Kat was out: she only had one man to make happy, so she couldn't understand my troubles, plus she'd be appalled. Serena might understand, but she was probably working, as it was night. Suri might have understood, she'd loved two men at once. But she was dead; she had died in my arms last summer.

Screw it, I would go talk to Suri. At least she was sure not to be appalled, dead as she was. I drove to the Chinese restaurant, parked, and then walked to the Eckerd's nearby and bought some flowers. They were green carnations for St. Patrick's Day. Suri would think they were comical, if she was looking down from Heaven. Walking back outside, I strode over behind the dumpster, and teleported to Danial's land. Soon, I was standing beneath the branches of the great oak tree in his cemetery.

I walked to Suri's grave, and sat beside her headstone. "Hi, Suri," I said, laying my hand on her headstone. It was cold beneath my fingers. The wind whispered in the leafless trees, making them sway.

"I'm so afraid. I don't know what to do. Some of my frustration is that there is nothing I can do. I spend most of the time feeling panicked, trapped, and I don't know why. I wanted Devlin. I wanted to be with him. I know I loved him, I felt it! Now that I have him, I feel like I want nothing more than to go back and erase everything he and I shared, and just be with Theo. Then when I'm with Devlin, all I want is him. I feel crazy!"

I blotted my tears with a tissue, hoping I'd hear some ghostly advice, or that an answer would come to me suddenly. But there was nothing, only the wind through the branches of the trees, a gentle sliding and rasping sound that was somehow morose. An owl hooted once, twice, and then fell silent.

With the ghostly advice option gone, the only thing left was introspection. I had come here to find answers. I'd best start looking on my own, or I'd never get anywhere before someone found me. By now Theo had called Danial and maybe Devlin, too. Titus probably had a way to locate me. I'd better make use of my time.

Trying to really meet the needs of three men was too much. There was a one man-one woman statute for a reason, and this was it. It was too hard to see someone once a week and pack enough attention for a whole week into twenty-four hours. Devlin wanted more, of course; hell, he wanted all of my love and attention. Theo was content with what he had, but he wouldn't settle for less, no matter what he said. Danial wasn't as demanding as he had once been, but he, too, wouldn't settle for less. Truthfully, he wanted more from me, if he could have it. There was only so much of me to give. My indiscretions with Lash had made the situation worse in all three relationships.

This had to end. I couldn't take it, not for much longer. So someone had to go, or several someones. *But who? And how?*

For the first time, I sat there and seriously thought about leaving. I could get in my truck, and just disappear. The only thing that stopped me was that I knew that the three of them would combine forces to find me, probably within hours. Devlin would stop at nothing, until he had me back. Lash would be right there, helping him. Then I would be under guard all the time, perhaps even with a collar equipped with a tracking device, so Devlin could be assured I wouldn't escape him again.

That wasn't a real option anyway. I had responsibilities: my pets, my children, not to mention that I was pregnant, oathed and married. I couldn't just leave.

I was strong. I had to find a way to do this until I had the babies, at least. Then…maybe then, if things were still overwhelming, I'd take off. Maybe Theo was right, that Devlin would tire of me. With him out of my life, there would be just Danial and Theo, a much more manageable twosome.

Despair swept me at the thought of losing Devlin, or never having him touch me again. "You are fucking crazy," I said loudly, furious with myself. "You don't want to live with him, but you don't want to lose him. What exactly do you want from Devlin, really?"

I didn't want him to show up, and demand anything of me, but I wanted his protection, and for him not to be with anyone else. *What the hell did I want, for him to love me from afar? To send me flowers as before, and pine for me, and send me poetry, but not be with me?*

My face suffused with shame, bitter tears filling my eyes. That *was* what I wanted of him. I had liked how Devlin had made me feel in the fall, when he had been in Rio, and I just heard from him on the phone, and on e-mail. He'd made me feel wanted, and I'd liked how that felt. I'd liked the illicit romance, the affair we'd had. When we'd moved from storybook romance into a real relationship, something had changed for me in how I felt about him, even though he'd acted the same.

How was that fair to him? It wasn't. Worse, how could I honestly say I loved him if this is how I treated him? I'd liked the bantering, the teasing, the games he and I played. But I hadn't wanted to move beyond the games, and we had, when I'd Oathed to him.

I cried harder, ashamed. I'd known what he was when I'd accepted him, and it was too late to back out now, no matter if my feelings toward him had changed. I had a duty to him to treat him well. He had saved me, and he loved me, no matter what else he was.

Angrily, I wiped my face on my sleeves. Theo was right. I had to stop thinking of what I wanted and do what was best for my unborn children. That meant I had to go to Devlin until Theo handled Robert and whomever had tried to blow us up this afternoon.

Feeling more in control, I got up and teleported back to the Chinese restaurant. I called Danial, and left him a voice mail, telling him that I was on my way to Devlin's. I thought about calling Devlin next, but I didn't want to. *What if he told me not to come?* He had told me not to come this week, but that was to work. But he'd also told me I was always welcome at Hayden…Screw it, fuck it, I didn't care anymore. I was going to Hayden, for better or worse.

* * * *

About eleven, I drove up to Hayden's gates and pushed the button.

"Yes?" said Titus's voice through the speaker.

"Titus, it's me, Sar," I said. "Open the doors, please."

"Okay," he said, surprised.

I drove in the opening doors and used my garage door opener to park my truck in an empty bay. I walked in slowly, wondering what I'd find. What if Devlin was here with someone?

I went into the kitchen, but saw no one. I went to the foot of the stairs and looked up into Lash's reptile eyes. He stood waiting at the top in jeans and a shirt, with no shoes, his hair in all directions.

Had he'd been sleeping, and gotten up for me? "Hi."

"I can't let you in his bedroom," Lash hissed. "Not until Titus clears you."

Titus appeared beside me. "She's fine, Lash." He hugged me. "Not that I'm not happy to see you, but why are you here? Devlin said nothing to me about you coming today—"

"There was an attempt on Theo's life today," I said tiredly.

Titus teleported us to his basement lab, then gestured to a set of huge leather chairs. I sank down into one and he sat down in the other, motioning to me to tell him what had happened. After I recapped the tale, he nodded.

"He's right," Titus said. "No one would try to get you here, it's too fortified. Theo also never comes here, so anyone looking for him wouldn't keep tabs on Hayden." He paused. "Thank you for what you did for Terian. He called today to say he had found his brother's family. Matt's parents and his older brother are long dead, but his sister is still alive. Terian is going to talk to her tomorrow, pretend he is an insurance adjuster and tell her that some money has come to her, finally. That despite whatever reason her brother disappeared all those years ago, he loved her."

I wiped at more tears, but these were of happiness. "God, my face must be a mess."

Titus handed me a black handkerchief from his pocket. It felt very warm, like it had come right out of the dryer. Finding that very comforting, I gave him a smile as I dabbed at my eyes. "Thanks. I'm glad he can finally let it go."

"Let me escort you upstairs," Titus said, getting up. "You must be tired, and also, you need to call Theo to tell him you got here okay."

Oiy. That hadn't been on my list of things to do. But he was right. "Yes."

* * * *

Theo picked up immediately, frantic. "Devlin, have you seen her?"

I felt terrible yet again. "It's me, Theo. I needed to drive for a while and sort some things out. But I'm taking your advice. I'll be spending tonight here—"

"With him," he growled jealously.

I lost it completely. "Make up your fucking mind!" I screamed. "You tell me to come here, that I shouldn't stay with you. Then when I tell you I'm here, you accuse me of what? Abandoning you?"

"Sar, I didn't mean—"

"Yes, you fucking well did, Theo!" I screamed. "What do you want from me? Isn't it enough, I'm having your child? Isn't it enough, that I love you? Isn't it?"

"No, it's fucking well not enough!" Theo roared. "I'm tired of sharing you, tired of you never being home weekends, tired of you fucking that snake—!"

I hung up on him, and went into the bathroom to the Jacuzzi as the phone promptly began ringing again.

There was no way in hell I was answering it. If I'd had somewhere else to go where I'd be safe, I would have gone there. Either Lash and Titus had likely called Dev by now. Once he knew I was here, he'd probably come home tonight, even if he hadn't been planning on it.

I sat in the Jacuzzi and cried until the tears stopped coming. Drained and exhausted, I went to bed, wishing for drugs to ease my frantic thoughts. I lay there for a long time, and finally, I slept.

When I awoke in the morning, I was still alone.

Chapter Seven

I was shocked, but also relieved to be alone. I hadn't woken up alone in a long time. I stretched out my arms, yawning widely. God, I felt relaxed. It was so very nice not to have to get up and do anything, to have to talk to anyone.

Guilt hit me at once over my shirked responsibilities, because someone else was feeding my pets, and seeing to the needs of my children. I rubbed my eyes, then reached for the phone and called Theo.

He picked up on the first ring. "Sar?" he said hesitantly.

"It's me," I said. "I'm sorry about the things I said last night."

"I'm sorry for what I said, too," Theo replied. "I never should have told you to leave. I was just worried—"

"You were right to," I interrupted. "It's safest right now until you deal with Robert."

"I told Danial what happened yesterday. He wants you not to come in this week, to stay there with Devlin."

"I think you should stay with Danial," I proposed. "If Robert's gunning for you, that's the best place to fight him, with an army of guards around you. Send some of Danial's werefox guards to watch our house and pets. Then our house and pets won't be a target."

"I'll find out who was responsible for the attack this week," Theo growled. "I'll see you soon, Sar. I love you."

"And I love you," I said softly.

After hanging up, I looked at the big bed and wondered what to do next. I could work on the filing, sure, but now I had all week for that. I could try Serena; it was after ten, so she should be up. Maybe we could have a long talk, and bake something chocolate. But maybe she was still mourning Vince and didn't want to see me.

Irritated with myself, I picked up the phone to call Devlin. There was no way he knew I was here, or he would have come to me, if only for a few hours, to sleep.

Quickly I put the phone back down. What if he was spending the day in bed somewhere else, with someone else, a someone else he could have some sex with? That was a real possibility. What would I say if a woman answered his cell phone? I'd better have something ready, in case.

I swallowed my pride, rehearsed a quick hello, then called his cell. Dev didn't answer it. I was surprised, then worried. He'd always answered his cell before when I had called.

I'd try Lash. His cell rang for a while, and then an electronic voice came on, saying the caller was unavailable, and to try back later.

Irritated and worried, I got my own cell phone from my purse and hit send on Devlin's cell number. "You damn well better answer."

Devlin answered on the second ring. "Hi, Sar. How are you, Love?'

His voice was slightly out of breath. I'd only seen him get winded doing one thing.

"Yes," I stammered. "I'm good, um…how are you?"

"Fine," Devlin purred.

I tried for a reply that didn't sound accusatory or suspicious. I was still trying when Devlin said curiously, "Why did you call me? Is e-mail down?"

"Perhaps I missed the sound of your voice?" I said curtly, trying to bring myself to ask him if he was with someone else.

"No, something's wrong," he said quickly. "You're calling from your cell, not your home or Danial's. Where are you? Are you okay?"

"I'm at Hayden, in your bed. I waited for you last night, but you never—"

"You have been there all night and didn't call me?" he shouted.

I cringed.

"Stay there!" he yelled angrily. "Don't you dare move! I'm coming to you now." He yelled for Titus and hung up.

If Titus was with him, why hadn't he told him? Shit, he was probably getting threatened with being flayed again for not telling Devlin I was here.

A moment later, Devlin and Titus appeared in the room. Devlin's eyes found mine at once and held. "Leave us."

Titus left, giving me a quick smile. Devlin hastily crossed the room to me, and grabbed me tightly in his arms.

I hugged him hard. "Dev, I…"

"Don't say anything," he said in a commanding tone.

I instantly fell silent. He held me for a few moments more, then let his arms fall and headed into the bathroom. Was he washing off some other woman's perfume? I thought I'd gotten a whiff of something, but wasn't sure.

Telling myself not to think about that, I went back to bed. Sometime later,

Devlin crawled in with me, and laid his head on my chest. Groggily, I put my arms around him, and dropped back to sleep.

I awoke at noon, ravenous, Devlin still on my chest.

I nudged him gently. "Dev."

"What is it?" he said grumpily.

"I need to eat something. Let me up, please."

He looked up at me with his molten gold eyes, then settled back down. "Call Serena and have her bring you up a tray."

Ass. "Dev, I want to go downstairs—"

"Why is that, Sar?" Devlin said nastily. "So you can call Theo out of my hearing?"

"I already called him this morning," I said coldly. "I told him I'd be home Sunday. But maybe I should tell him to come get me now."

Devlin pushed himself up on his arms, looking into my eyes from a few inches. "You're staying all week?" he said in disbelief, his expression hopeful.

"If that's not an imposition." I sighed. "There was another attempt on his life yesterday."

Devlin beamed, overjoyed. He got to his feet and offered me his hand. "Let's get you some breakfast, Love."

* * * *

After a luxurious and very fattening breakfast of pancakes, bacon and sausage, we went back to his bedroom.

"Are you still spotting?" Devlin asked tentatively, turning back the covers. "I feel odd to ask you, but I'm worried after what Camlyn said."

"I'm fine," I replied. "There's been nothing for the last day."

"Will you stay with me here today?" he asked, getting into bed. "I know you probably aren't tired, but I'd enjoy it if you'd stay."

"Sure," I said, relieved. "I felt awkward, just showing up here last night."

"Sar," Devlin chided softly, "I want you here. I always want you here. You're my Oathed One. You have a standing invitation." He beckoned. "Come."

His passion and love was undeniable, yet again I felt oddly uncomfortable. I managed a smile, then got into bed. He put his arms around me and began stroking my hair gently.

"I'll sleep days with you this week and work at night, while you're gone," I said, wanting to hear his response. "Friday I'll try to get the lay of the gardens with Lash, and spend some time with Serena."

Devlin kissed my forehead gently. "Do whatever you want. If you want to go out shopping for more clothes, just ask Lash to take you. You could invite Serena, if you'd like female company."

Shit, he was right. I had no clothes here at Hayden. There was only one pair of jeans and a shirt for emergencies, along with a couple of nightgowns. "That would be nice," I said, then paused, wondering if I should ask him to come. But he couldn't come during the day, as he was sleeping all day and working all night. There was no point in asking. "I do need some clothes for here."

"Go tonight then," Devlin said indulgently. "I'll give Lash some cash to pay for whatever you choose. Buy enough so you feel comfortable here."

I wasn't sure what that meant, but decided a few changes of clothes would be enough. "What colors are your favorite to see me in?"

"Why are you suddenly being so nice to me?" Devlin said, looking at me searchingly.

"Because you deserve it," I replied. "I'm sorry if I made you feel that I didn't appreciate you. I'm having trouble coping with everything. One of the reasons I didn't call you last night was I needed time alone to sort out my feelings." I hugged him tight. "I'm trying hard, Dev, to make all this work. Please understand that I'm trying—"

"Hush," Devlin said, running his hands down my arms. "Don't worry about me. It's enough that you're here with me now, that you're staying with me this week. Now get some sleep."

I snuggled closer, quickly falling asleep in his embrace.

* * * *

The week passed far faster than I thought it would, and I enjoyed myself more than I had thought possible.

Tuesday evening, after Devlin left, Lash took me out shopping, albeit reluctantly.

"I know, I know. Dev asked me to take you," he hissed, making a face. "Just give me directions to this Coldwater Creek."

When we entered the store an hour later, a saleswoman immediately made a beeline for us and then stopped, staring at the scarred bite marks on either side of my neck and the choker above them. Lash noticed and gave her a penetrating look, pushing back the sides of his long wool coat slightly, making the lash of his well-used bullwhip just visible.

She blanched a little, gave him a wide berth, and came to my side. "Anything in particular I could help you find today?" she asked, her eyes on the whip coiled at Lash's belt.

"I need some jeans, and some long sleeved T's," I told her, glad she couldn't see the knife on the other side of his waist. "Nothing embellished and no sequins."

"Colors?" she asked.

"Red, dark pink, white, gray, and green," I said, trying to remember if that was all that Devlin had told me.

"Dark brown, black, and tan," Lash hissed.

The saleswoman looked at him nervously. "Come on back, please."

"You said Dev didn't like those colors," I said quietly, as we followed her to the back of the store.

"*I* like those colors," Lash hissed meaningfully.

I gave him a look. He shot me a grin, then inclined his head, telling me to get to it.

The saleswoman showed me where my requested items were. I began to look through them, Lash hovering over me.

"Don't hover," I said finally.

"What should I do?" he hissed. "There are no men's clothes here, Sar. I feel ill at ease."

I gave him an irritated look, then realized he was serious. "You can sit in that chair there, or you can go and look around. If you see something you think Devlin would like me in, get one for me to try it on. I wear a size medium, or a ten." Lately I was bigger than that, but rationalized Lash wasn't likely to choose the latter option I'd proposed, anyway.

To my surprise, Lash nodded, and walked off, looking around. After looking for gray and black in vain, I quickly grabbed some long-sleeved T's in red, pink, white, green, and then paused, considering dark brown. Rationalizing that it would look good on me, I got one of those, too, grabbed some jeans in my size, and then brought all of them up to the counter. "Please hold these under the name Sar," I said, handing them to the clerk, then went to look around the rest of the store.

Most of the clothes here were too dressy for my normal day-to-day life. Yet I was tempted to buy something special for a surprise. Devlin had seen me in jeans, lingerie, and black-tie eveningwear, but nothing else. By what was in his closet, a few sequins on something velvet would be right up his alley.

After looking at several items, I reluctantly decided not to indulge. Devlin never took me anywhere but Davy's. That was no place for a fancy dress, and getting dressed up to stay home was also not my style. Letting the skirt of the velvet dress go, I turned and began looking for Lash.

He was looking at some of the leather suede jackets. "Try on this," he hissed as I walked up, handing me a long suede duster in a tan color.

It was beautiful. The pieces of soft leather were stitched together in a patchwork pattern; it was elegant and delicate, yet still rugged. Maybe this coat was the answer to my desire for something special for an outfit. I couldn't wear a dress to Davy's, but I could wear this and not feel overdressed. The only problem was that none of the tops I'd chosen would look good with this except the dark brown one.

I went to the counter and asked for the dark brown top, and a pair of the jeans. "I need to try this on as an outfit." The woman nodded, smiling, handed me the clothes, and took me to a dressing room.

I began undressing. As I pulled my sweater over my head, my hand brushed my collar, and it came undone, falling with a clink to the floor.

"Good going, Sar." I'd have to be more careful. If I did that near a sewer grate, I'd be shit out of luck. I picked it up, and refastened it, the links sliding together with a soft clinking sound. Quickly, I slipped on the jeans top and duster.

"Sar?" Lash hissed from the other side of the door. "How does it look?"

I opened the door, and came out. "I think it looks good. What do you think?"

"It does," he hissed appreciatively. "Dev might not have told you he liked the color, but he will like how the clothing fits you."

"You're sure?" I said, going over to look again in the mirror. "I almost never wear brown."

"I'm sure," he hissed, then turned to leave.

"Where are you going?" I called curiously after him.

"Outside," he hissed back without stopping, "before I raise your personal demon here in the store."

Stifling a smile, I went back in the dressing room, then looked at myself again. He was right, they looked great, so great I was tempted to wear them home. Not only did I like how I looked, I liked how the suede coat made me feel. Reluctantly I took them off, telling myself it wasn't nice to tease snakes, even if once in a while they did deserve it.

As I took the clothes off, my choker fell off again. Irritated, I stuck it in my purse, determined to ask Devlin about it that night. I didn't want to lose the damned thing. After putting on my old clothes, I went out to the register where Lash was paying the bill.

As we walked to the Hummer, Lash stopped, staring at me. "Why are you not wearing your choker?" he hissed angrily.

"It fell off twice in there when I was getting the clothes on and off," I said in exasperation. "I was afraid I'd lose it if I put it on again."

"Put it on now, Sar," he hissed. "I'll keep an eye on it. You won't lose it."

Unwilling to argue, I took the choker back out and put it on. I waited a second after, sure it was going to fall off, but nothing happened.

"Do you want to get dinner while we are out?" he said, looking at the dashboard clock. "It's about eight."

"When will Dev be home?" I asked.

"Not until eleven at least," Lash hissed in reply. "He has a lot to do this week. He'd put off some of his meetings because you are staying with him, but there are some he said he just had to attend."

His anger was back, laced with bitterness. It was on the tip of my tongue to ask him what he was annoyed about. But we were getting along well, and I didn't want to ruin it. "Are you hungry?"

"Sar, I only eat raw meat and blood," Lash hissed softly, staring at the dash. "I can eat it warm like when you made me breakfast, but that's all. My hunger is irrelevant."

This had to be one of the side effects of the potion he took as well. "How about raw fish?" I offered.

Lash looked at me strangely. "Raw fish?"

"Sushi," I said, giving him a look. "Can you eat sushi? Rice and meat should be easily digestible."

Lash pondered that for a second. "Maybe," he hissed finally. "I never tried to. Where do they sell it?"

"Take me to the superstore in the plaza down the road," I said firmly. "You can try it. If you like it, there's a restaurant nearby we can go to for dinner."

Lash drove me to the local superstore, then followed me in as I grabbed a hand basket. "They have tuna, crab, salmon, eel, and other things," I said, showing him the display case "What looks good to you?"

Lash crouched down near the display and flicked out his tongue, scenting the air. I grabbed some eel for myself, and some vegetables, too, sticking them in the hand basket.

This was going to be a treat. I hadn't had sushi since I'd first been married years ago. It suddenly struck me as odd that I was sharing this moment with Lash, of all people. But why not? If it made the difference between him being hungry and me having a dinner partner, that was all right. Besides, I'd get some for Theo to try, too. He might like it, though I'd never seen him express much of an interest in fish, other than fried haddock.

I grabbed a small bottle of tamari sauce, then looked down at Lash still crouched down, deliberating. I put my selections in the basket, then hunkered down beside him. "Sooner or later, you are going to have to make a decision," I said with a smile.

"It all smells good," he said finally. "But I may not be able to eat it."

I put my hand on his shoulder. He flinched, looking back at me in surprise.

"Do you want me to just get you some raw fish from the fish display in the back?" I asked gently. "I don't want you to get sick the way Danial does when he has to have wine. You don't have to do this if you don't want to—"

"No," Lash said suddenly. "I want to." He reached out and grabbed about twelve different packages, and dropped them in my basket.

We checked out quickly, Lash again paying. I decided as we walked to the Hummer that if all went well, I'd pay for dinner. I'd brought money of my own in my purse.

"Stick yours in the cooler in back," Lash hissed. "Bring mine up to the front, please."

I put my eel and veggies in the back, as he instructed. There was an empty cooler back there, a giant one. "Is this for emergency rations?" I asked. "Or tailgate parties?"

Lash gave me a smile. "Something like that," he said, opening one of the containers and swallowing a piece.

I watched him try several more pieces, reassuring myself that he should be okay. There was only rice besides the fish, and it should be very digestible. There was seaweed too, but water moccasins were water snakes, weren't they? Water was in the name, so they had to be, right? A little seaweed shouldn't hurt.

He didn't like the eggs, or the tuna much, but he liked the others, especially the salmon and crab. He ate several packages, taking his time. When he had tried the last one, he looked at me, and flicked his tongue at me. "I'm okay," he said. "If I was going to be sick, it would have happened by now."

"Good," I said happily. "But we've got to hurry. Not only am I starving, but if we wait much longer, the restaurant is going to close—"

"Where it is?" Lash said, starting the Hummer.

He followed my directions, driving us there at about seventy miles an hour. Luckily, we saw no police on the way. Lash parked, carefully stashed the last of the containers of uneaten food in the cooler, then grabbed my hand and ran for the front door.

After we were sitting at a table, Lash immediately began to look over the list of alcohol.

"How can you drink if you can't eat?" I asked, regarding him with a humorous smile.

"I don't know," Lash hissed, putting down the list. "But I thank God for it every day."

I cracked up laughing. After a moment, so did he.

When our waiter showed up, I ordered some wine, and he ordered some sake, a Japanese beer. The waiter brought it to us in moments, then asked us if he could take our order.

"Do you want to share a platter, or get your own?" I asked Lash. "I usually get just the eel, but I'll share some with you, if you like."

"Do both," Lash said, his gaze holding mine. "We'll order more, if that isn't enough."

We ordered the sushi for four, the biggest sushi platter they offered, and I got a separate order of eel as well. As the waiter left, Lash abruptly said "Do you and Theo get sushi often?"

Why was he asking me that? "No," I said honestly. "We never have."

Lash regarded me curiously, but said nothing. I was quiet, sipping my wine. Suddenly, I could suddenly think of nothing to talk about. Maybe I should've just gone with him back to Hayden instead of having dinner out.

Why did I feel so ill at ease? This was Lash, and we'd eaten together often, or at least, I'd eaten in front of him. *What was so different now?* That he hated Theo was a given...

Lash spoke again, startling me. "Why do you not like to talk about Theo, if you love him so much?" he hissed. "You always seem uncomfortable when I bring him up."

Was he serious? I couldn't tell, with those flat eyes of his. "Because you dislike each other so much. I hear the hate in your voice when you talk about him."

"Ah," he hissed. "You know why, of course?"

I didn't actually, not on Lash's end anyway. I only knew Theo's reason. "I heard you broke his neck once," I whispered. "That you tried to kill him."

"Yes," Lash hissed. "I broke his neck, but I could have killed him then and I didn't."

"I'm surprised you didn't," I said awkwardly, taking a long swallow of my wine to try to calm myself.

"It wasn't a real fight," Lash said contemptuously. "He didn't challenge me."

I shivered, remembering his ranking in the hierarchy of killers: number one. "What happened?"

"It was at one of Danial's parties, the first one he threw here, when he became Ruler of New York," Lash said, sipping his sake. "Devlin and I came."

"What did you do?" I said, giving him a look that made it obvious I knew he had done something.

"Theo was head over heels for a were named Neoline," Lash hissed, glancing at me. I nodded to tell him I knew who she was, and he continued.

"He was on break from guarding Danial, having something to eat and chatting her up. I thought she was pretty, so I went over to her, and started talking. He didn't like that, and told me to get lost."

I could believe that. "And?"

"I told him to fuck himself, and he went for me with his blade," Lash hissed, giving a shrug. "I told him not to try it, that he was in over his head. He had just started working for Danial a few years earlier, and he was only maybe twenty-two or so. To be fair, he was good with a blade for that age, very good. But I, of course, was much better."

I stared at him, captivated.

Lash sipped his sake, and continued. "He kept lunging for me. I kept sidestepping him, laughing. He lost his temper and attacked me with fists. I grabbed him and broke his neck. Devlin was pleased, but Danial was violently angry. He threw us both out."

I made a face, imagining it. No wonder Theo hated him. Lash had made an ass out of him, not only in front of all the big shots of New York, but also in front of his best friend, and his love interest of the time.

"Danial banned me from any of his later parties," Lash hissed with a smile. "That's why you never saw me until you did."

"I'd wondered about that," I said politely

"The saddest part was that I didn't get the girl, after all that," Lash hissed with a rueful smile. "Neoline oathed to Garrett that same night. I always wondered if it wasn't to stop me pursuing her."

I was betting it was, but didn't say that. "So that's it? You have this animosity over a woman who's dead, who neither one of you really knew anyway to begin with?"

"There were a few other incidents over the years," Lash said vaguely. "Most of them ended the same way, when we actually fought. But that was what started it all. Theo is still angry over it, and probably blames me for her dying how she did." He paused, taking another sip. "Your having been with me only pisses him off more."

There was desire in his tone. I finished my wine in a gulp and then wanted badly to order another. Being pregnant, I couldn't. Why couldn't Lash shut up when I wanted him to? He almost never talked when we were alone. If we were back at Hayden, he wouldn't be talking this much.

"Theo hates Devlin too, maybe more than he hates me, Sar," Lash went on. "He knows that you'll stop being with me soon, but Dev will have you forever—"

"Why exactly is that?" I said, looking Lash in the eyes. "What has Devlin done that Theo hates him like he does? Is it because of Devlin's treatment of

98

Danial? The women he took from Danial over the years?" Lash had to have been around for something like that, being with Devlin for more than a half century.

Lash sipped his sake, and regarded me for a long moment. "The real reason is none of that," he hissed finally. "Theo is jealous. It's hard not to be sometimes, of Dev." Lash eyed me, then looked away, running his hand through his shaggy hair, and settling back in his chair.

"What do you mean?"

"Devlin has an ease with women," Lash replied. "Almost a power. They seem drawn to him like bees to honey. As a man, it's hard not to be jealous a little, even when it's your good friend. I've never had his smoothness, his charm, or his looks, even in my youth. Neither has Theo."

That was sad but true. Devlin's charisma was captivating, at least when he wasn't being annoying, and he was breathtaking to behold.

"There were some women that Danial had, that Devlin seduced," Lash hissed, as an afterthought. "I was only around for the last one, before you. It was about seventy some years ago, or so."

"What happened?" I prodded.

His flat eyes held mine, unblinking. "It's not dinner conversation," he hissed curtly. "And our food's here, so let's eat."

Deciding it wasn't worth it to push, I dug in. My eel was delicious, and Lash seemed to enjoy his platter. As we ate, we stuck to safer topics, like Hayden's gardens. "Can you show me around on Friday morning? The snow's melted some."

"Sure," he hissed. "Just meet me in the kitchen at eight, like usual. Dress in warm clothes."

That reminded me to ask him, "Do you have any mending? Any clothes that need seams fixed, or tears patched?"

Lash choked on his water. He swallowed quickly, then had some more water. "Why? Are you going to mend them?" he hissed finally.

"I'm teaching Serena to sew," I said patiently. "Devlin asked me to teach her. I told her to ask her lovers if they have anything that's ripped or torn, to get some clothes to practice on in real time and—"

"And you're asking yours?" he finished with a grin, his flat eyes meeting mine.

That was it. With a scathing look for him, I got up, walked to the counter, and handed them my credit card. "We're ready to leave, please."

As the hostess handing it back with the bill to sign, Lash sauntered up. I signed it, then handed it to her with a forced smile.

"Ready to go?" he asked.

"Yes," I said stiffly, pushing the door open hard. "Please take me home."

* * * *

We didn't speak the whole trip back, or while carrying in our sushi to Hayden's fridge. But when I went to leave the kitchen, Lash stood in front of me, blocking the exit.

"I'm sorry if I said something I shouldn't," he said quietly. "I'm not always sure how to act around you; where to draw the line between teasing and offending. If I offend you, just say so and I'll apologize."

Why wasn't he being a jerk and telling me the bug up my ass was my problem? "It's okay. Forget it."

"How long will the sushi last?" he asked. "A day?"

"We should eat it by Thursday at the latest. It's not good to let it go too long."

"Will you join me then in eating some tomorrow?" Lash hissed formally. "Around nine, before you start teaching Serena, or filing?"

I froze. There was enough sushi to have for lunch with Theo, and still have enough left over to eat dinner with Lash later on. The problem wasn't that; it was that something else was starting here. I'd heard a different note in Lash's tone just now.

He faced me, waiting silently.

My surety crumbled; we'd always met for lunch the days I was at Hayden. I'd thought nothing of it, so why was dinner such a big deal then? Maybe I was seeing something where there was nothing. "Sure," I said, giving him a smile. "Sounds good."

Lash gave me a nod, then stepped aside. "Goodnight."

I walked past him, grabbed the bag of new clothes, and went upstairs. Clipping off the tags, I put them in the drawer Devlin had cleared out for me and then hung the duster at the edge of his closet, shoving some of his clothes to one side to make it fit.

I was tempted to get dressed in some of the clothes to show Devlin what I'd bought, but nixed the idea. He'd said he would be exhausted when he got home. Instead, I got in the Jacuzzi and relaxed, letting my mind drift.

When I climbed into bed at eleven, Dev was still not home. Phantom, whom I'd not seen all day, jumped up on the bed and joined me, curling up at the bottom. At about midnight, Devlin came in, waking me.

"You and Phantom look so sweet," he murmured. "Let me shower, Love, and I'll come right back," he said warmly.

I said something unintelligible in response, then rolled over and went back to sleep.

When he came into bed, he woke me again. "Lash said you got dinner out," he said softly, stroking my shoulders. "Did you eat enough?"

"Plenty," I whispered sleepily.

"Are you feeling okay?" he said with concern. "Everything is as it should be?"

"I'm fine," I said, yawning loudly. "I'm all good."

"I love you, Sar," he whispered. "I..."

* * * *

I woke up to find Devlin on my chest, dead to the world. A look at the clock confirmed it was late morning. *Sigh.* I'd have to get moving fast if I wanted to meet Theo for lunch.

I looked down at Devlin, then brushed a lock of his hair back from his handsome face. We were curled together so comfortably that lunch and Theo were just going to have to wait. Settling back down, I promptly went back to sleep.

The next thing I knew, Devlin was shaking me. "Sar, wake up," he said loudly.

"I'm awake," I said sleepily.

Devlin let me go. I turned away from him, pulled the covers around me, and closed my eyes again.

Devlin turned me back toward him, then grasped my middle, pulling me up into a sitting position. "Danial hasn't been loving you, has he?" he said softly. "You haven't been with him at all except for last weekend with him and me."

"No," I replied with a yawn, wondering why it mattered. "He and I didn't before, when I was pregnant. He doesn't want to endanger—"

"Kiss me," Devlin said, then brought his lips hard against mine. Hungrily, he opened his mouth, licking me with his tongue.

My brain went from idle to sixty in a split second as my arms went around him, my mouth opening on his, the taste of sweet maple sugar intoxicating.

Something had changed. Dev's blood wasn't just sweet to me; I couldn't get enough of it. I kissed him harder, wanting more. Devlin groaned, then tried to pull away.

"Please, Dev, give me more!" I said hungrily. He groaned for a second time, then kissed me harder, the sweet taste again flooding my tongue.

God, it was so good! It was wonderful, better than sex, better than love, better that anything!

"Stop, Sar. Stop!" Devlin said urgently. He pried me off, pushing me back. As I went limp in his hands, he laid me back on the bed.

I lied there motionless, tired but fulfilled, as if we had just made love for hours and I'd finally gotten release. I stretched out full length, then sighed, letting all my muscles go limp. Devlin sat beside me watching me with affection and smoothing my hair away from my face. Blissful, I dropped back to sleep.

* * * *

I awoke, stretched, then looked over at the clock. *God, why had I slept so long?* It was nearly eight! Pushing back the covers, I got up, grabbing for my clothes. Lash was going to wonder what the hell had happened to me.

"Feeling better?" Devlin queried softly from behind me.

I turned and faced him, the clothes falling from my grasp to the floor as everything clicked into place. "Was I colder?"

"Yes," Devlin said, crossing the room to embrace me. "I thought maybe I was imagining it last night, that you were just tired. But when you wouldn't wake up for me this morning, I knew you needed my blood."

I clung to him like a life raft. "I might not have woken up."

"No, Love, you were not bad off," he soothed gently. "But do tell Danial he must share blood with you when you go to him, that he is to watch you carefully. If you seem sleepy or cooler, he has to give it to you immediately."

"I will." I wasn't likely to forget, with how close to dying I'd come last fall.

"I'll call him tonight, in between meetings, to tell him what happened. He may not know how—"

"He does," I assured. "Don't worry."

"I always worry about you when you're apart from me," Dev said softly, cuddling me against him. "I understand now why Danial always called you every night, and why he calls here if you forget to check in."

"I love you," I said suddenly. "I fell asleep before you finished saying it last night."

"I know," Devlin said, laughing. "I was miffed you missed my heart's outpouring. I'll have to speak it again in the morning." He gave me a kiss, and got up, beginning to dress.

When I got to the kitchen with Devlin in tow, Lash was already there, waiting for me. "Theo called," he said. "I told him you'd call him back when you woke up."

I nodded my thanks as Titus walked into the kitchen. "Ready?" Titus rumbled, his red eyes on Devlin. Devlin gave me a final kiss, and then disappeared with Titus.

"Are you hungry for dinner?" Lash said hesitantly.

102

Hell yes; it was quarter to nine. "Let me call Theo and Danial first," I responded. "Devlin needed to give me blood and I need to remind Danial to do the same on Saturday."

"Take your time," Lash said, nodding. "I'll wait here in the kitchen."

I took that to mean I should use the upstairs phone. Trooping back upstairs, I called Theo. "Have you found out anything?"

"Nothing yet," Theo said angrily. "But it has to be Tasha's father. His name is Karl. I've got the names of the men he hired, but not their base of operations." He paused. "I've got no news on Robert."

"Is everything else okay?"

"The dogs are fine, and Janice and Ivan are enjoying our best wine," Theo said, a smile in his voice. "Other than that, nothing's new."

"Want me to come and meet you for lunch tomorrow?" I asked hesitantly.

"I was hoping you would come to see me today," Theo said softly. "Danial is missing you, too."

"I would have come today," I replied quickly. "But I was getting sick again—"

"What happened?" Theo asked loudly. "Are you okay? What—?"

"I needed more of the virus," I said quickly. "Dev gave me some of his blood."

Theo didn't make a sound.

"I'm okay now. But Danial needs to do the same for me on Saturday night."

"I'll put him on, after we're done. He's hovering right here, anyway."

"I am not hovering," Danial said with irritation. "I heard you say she was sick from the other room, so I came to see what was the matter—"

"Just take the phone," Theo said, laughing. "You're going to hover until you do—"

"Ass," Danial muttered, then took the phone. "Hi, Sar. Are you sure you're fine?"

Faintly, I heard Theo call out, "I love you, Sar."

"Tell him I love him," I said to Danial.

"Aren't you going to tell me you love me, too?" Danial said teasingly.

"Yes, but at the end of the conversation, like usual," I said, half annoyed and half amused.

"Why not now and again later?" Danial teased.

"I love you," I said. "Now tell him."

Danial passed on the message, then said, "I'll give you some when I see you Saturday. Dev called me a few minutes ago to tell me what happened and what to do."

"Good," I said. My stomach growled loudly. "Have a good night, Danial."

"Why are you hurrying off?" Danial asked sharply. "Devlin is gone."

"I'm hungry," I retorted grumpily. "I haven't eaten in twenty four hours. Lash is waiting for me downstairs, maybe eating my sushi right this minute."

"Go rescue your sushi then," Danial said, mollified. "But first tell me you love me again."

"I love you again," I said, then burst out laughing.

"I love you again, too," he said, then hung up chuckling.

Content and satisfied, I put the phone back in its cradle. Things weren't so bad. Maybe I was finally finding a balance in my weird life.

I went downstairs to find Lash right where I'd left him. "Shall we eat here, or in the dining room?" I asked.

"Want to watch a movie with me while we eat?" Lash hissed tentatively, his flat eyes staring intently.

For the second time, I felt a sense of danger, that there was a deeper meaning here that was going to lead to trouble. Again, I brushed it aside, telling myself that this was no big deal. "Sure. But I should check to make sure Serena didn't expect me."

"I'm sleeping days now, since I have to watch you nights," Lash interrupted with a grin. "That means the bears had to guard Dev and you all day en masse, which means Serena is going to be up all night. She's not going to have any time or energy for baking or anything else."

I blinked at him, getting his meaning. "Ah. When will Devlin be home?"

"Not till at least one," Lash said angrily. "Maybe later."

"Why are you so angry?" I said bluntly. "Don't lie and tell me you're not."

"Because he bitches that you aren't here so much most of the time. Now that you are, he's not here taking advantage of it."

"He's working. I don't mind, Lash. He told me he was going to be busy this week—"

Lash looked at me as if he was going to tell me something, then hissed sarcastically, "Then you're a saint."

"Why don't we eat, put in a few hours downstairs, and then watch something?" I offered. "I'm not going to want to work after I get comfortable."

Lash nodded. "Sure."

The sushi was just as good that night as it had been the previous evening. Lash ate twice as much as I did, but that was to be expected. Weres had big appetites, if Theo was typical. After putting our dishes in the dishwasher, we headed downstairs.

* * * *

After a few hours of work, I looked around and congratulated myself. The room was looking much bigger. Half the boxes had been put into the filing cabinets. Devlin's file of personal paperwork was stuffed, so I'd started another under it, but Titus had taken care of the paper trash. Everything was shaping up nicely. It was time for a reward.

"Ready to go up?"

Lash looked up from his usual slouched position in the chair, then closed the Bible he was reading. "Yes, unless you want me to read to you."

"What are you on?"

He shot me a grin. "Song of Solomon."

If he quoted me some of that, he'd raise The Lust for sure. "Movie, please."

He walked upstairs with me. "Do you like art movies?" he asked.

I looked at him curiously. "Like foreign films?"

"Sorry. I meant movies made from graphic novels." He paused, as if ill at ease. "I've always liked Sin City."

I looked at him in shock, and then hugged him. He embraced me, then gently pushed me back. "What was that for?" he hissed.

It was obvious what he was hoping it was for, but I was too thrilled to care. "Because it's one of my favorite movies," I said excitedly, a genuine smile on my face. "Theo likes it now, but he had no idea who Frank Miller was before the movie came out."

Lash was incredulous. "How could he not know Miller in the business we're both in?"

"Forget that," I said eagerly. "Have you read *A Dame to Kill For?*"

"Of course," Lash hissed eagerly. "And *To Hell and Back*, as well as the compilations and the other stories."

Here was a kindred soul, albeit in an odd package. "So have I."

"I have the unedited version on DVD," Lash offered, brandishing it. "Yes or no?"

"Put it on now," I ordered, flopping on the couch.

The next two hours of movie was bliss. But the two hours following were even better. I talked to Lash about how the comics had been brought to life. We compared notes on the parts of the stories that were missing from the film, like Hartigan's talk with Eileen, or Marv's trip home to his mom's house where he gets his gun, Gladys, and then on Miller's other works in the series that hadn't been in the film.

"He did an excellent job though," I said finally with admiration. "You can only include so much of a long book in a movie."

"Not always true. What about *300?*" Lash hissed

105

I nodded. "You're right. They added onto that tale when they made the movie. And yes, I read the comics, when they first came out," I added proudly.

"We can watch that tomorrow, if you want," Lash offered.

"Sure," I said happily. "What are your thoughts on *South Park*?"

"What is *South Park*?" Lash hissed in confusion.

"Stay right there," I instructed, then teleported. The living room at my home was quiet and empty as I walked quickly to my TV. Grabbing the DVD of classic episodes, I teleported back to Lash. "This is *South Park*," I said, handing it to him.

He examined it. "It's a comedy?" he said disdainfully. "I don't like comedies."

"You'll like this one," I assured. "Put it on and see. If you don't like it, I'll pay for another sushi outing."

Lash handed it back to me. "Tomorrow I'll watch some with you, and reserve judgment till then," he said, a faint smile on his lips. "The night's almost over."

He was right. *Where had the time gone?* "Okay," I replied, "Tomorrow."

"Goodnight," Lash said, then walked out.

I went upstairs, and took a quick shower. When Devlin came home, I was waiting for him in bed, asleep.

* * * *

I was emerging from the shower around eleven the next morning when I ran into Devlin. "When will you be back from lunch?" he asked crankily.

Either Theo had called asking where I was, or Lash had listened in last night. "I shouldn't be gone more than an hour, two tops."

"I'll be waiting here for you," he said, yawning. "No rush."

Then why make a big deal when I'd be back? "I'll see you then—"

"Wait," Devlin commanded, his eyes narrowing suddenly. "Why is your choker off?"

"Damn it," I said, going to my side of the bed and rummaging under the sheets. Grasping the cool metal, I held it out to him. "It fell off twice yesterday when we were shopping. I wanted to have you take it to whomever you got it from. Something must be defective."

Devlin took it from me and examined it. "Yes, it must be. I saw you had it on last night. Do you have Danial's on you?"

"No," I said. "It's at his house. I left it there accidentally last week."

"Wear his for today, Sar," Devlin said, laying the choker on the nightstand. "I'll take yours to the jeweler who made it tonight. It's possible with the pregnancy, there is some problem with it staying on."

106

"How can that be? I didn't have a problem with Danial's choker staying on when I was pregnant."

"You weren't so much of a vampire then," Devlin said good-naturedly. "This collar wasn't designed for a vampire to wear. The blood mixture used for humans is different. They may need to rebalance this magically."

"I see," I said, though I had no idea what he was talking about. "Thanks."

"Tell me if his falls off at all when you get home," Devlin said. "I'm curious." He gave me a kiss. "Have a good time with Theo."

* * * *

"This is eel?" Theo said disbelieving, chowing down. "It tastes good, not slimy."

"Then I'll bring you some more next time I go shopping," I said, giving him a kiss. "I've got to see Danial before I go. Have a good day."

Heading upstairs, the bright smile left my face. Theo still hadn't made any new discoveries. While I'd enjoyed the week so far, I didn't know if my exultation would last if a lot of weeks went by. I was already missing my dogs and cats.

Danial looked up as I entered the study. He reached into his drawer, then handed me his choker. "Go ahead. Let's run the experiment."

I clasped it on. "Can you explain what Devlin meant about magical rebalancing?"

Danial nodded in understanding, coming closer. "If you were turning, the choker would need to be altered," he said softly, brushing his lips over my earlobe. "The choker is a magical thing, almost conscious of itself. If a person is turned while wearing it, it will fall off. But don't worry; Dev can have it fixed easily, even have them alter it so you could wear it if you were a vampire. But you may not be able to remove it if he does that, Sar. I know you have gotten used to taking it off when you want to, so I thought you should know."

"Devlin had said Anna was always able to remove hers." But she probably never had, once they were Oathed. *Why would she have, if she only had one vampire lover?*

"Sar, you aren't turning," Danial said soothingly. "But you are changed. That might be enough."

"Devlin wanted to know if yours fell off at all."

Danial smiled in pleasure. "As do I." He ran his hands down my arms, then embraced me. "Shall we test it with some physical activity?"

I cracked up laughing, kissed him eagerly as an answer, then let him lead me downstairs.

Chapter Eight

I woke Devlin when I crawled in beside him. "I'm glad you're back," he said softly. "I missed you."

"I was barely gone," I said lightly, worried he wasn't going to let me go home on Sunday.

"Seemed like days to me," Devlin purred, then pulled me close.

We dozed for another hour or so. About seven, Devlin stretched, looked at the clock, and abruptly swore. "I've got to go," he said, hurriedly pulling on a suit. "I'll be home about one, maybe two. Tomorrow night will be later still."

"No rush," I said, giving him a smile. "I'll be here."

"Good," he said giving me a quick kiss. "Don't work too hard," he called, his footsteps fast on the stairs.

After he left, I lay in bed a while, thinking about how much fun this all was. It was like a mini vacation, even with the filing. Suddenly, going home didn't have the luster it had back this morning.

I sat up, then hurriedly dressed. This had to be the result of the blood Devlin had given me yesterday. I'd better make sure Danial gave me a good bit of his on Saturday. I didn't want to be in thrall to Devlin again.

When I walked downstairs, Lash was on the couch in the living room watching *South Park.* "Hey, you were supposed to wait for me!" I said, cracking a smile.

"You got up for lunch today," he teased. "I thought you might need to sleep in a little. I was just passing the time."

I was getting used to the way he smiled, baring the one fang because of his scar. It no longer unnerved me, or made me flinch. In fact it seemed weird it had ever bothered me.

"I'm well rested," I lied. "Lead me to dinner."

As I ate my soup and Lash his sushi, he suddenly hissed, "Thanks for telling me about this. I never wanted to eat the fish I saw in stores. They were always huge fillets. I liked to catch and eat much smaller fish as a snake. This is more the size I used to catch, though of course the shape and type is not the same."

"Where did you catch them?" I asked curiously.

"When I was little, in the swamps. I was born in the Everglades," Lash said with deep emotion. "I miss it badly sometimes."

I pulled my chair closer to his, studying him. "Do you want me to take you there tonight?"

Lash looked at me in shock. "You have been there? When?"

"Yes," I affirmed. "I went for a field course in college. It was amazing."

"Would you mind, just for a few minutes?" he hissed enthusiastically.

"No," I said, reaching for his hand. "Here—"

"No," he said, withdrawing it quickly. "I need to get my gun and my cell before we go. And you should get some bug spray from the hall closet. Meet me back here in two."

He was right; there would be mosquitoes there. I doused myself in bug spray, then rejoined Lash in the kitchen. "Ready?" I asked.

He took my hand. "Ready."

I teleported us to the southernmost edge of the park. We arrived in front of the hotel near the water. Dusk had just arrived. We immediately got bitten, or at least, I did, but the spray kept most of them off. Lash looked around, then strode off back towards the swamp, me following.

We came to the edge of the saw grass. There was only darkness beyond. Deep, unbroken darkness, and the soft whisper of things moving in that dark as they were hunting and being hunted. I smelled brackish water, green growing things, and the dampness of the ocean farther south. The stars above us were out, the sliver of moon that hung in the sky above us giving little light.

Lash just stood there for some time, his back to me, his form motionless, scenting the air with his tongue, looking into the blackness. I let him have his space, busy covering up all my exposed skin.

After fifteen minutes of this, Lash hissed once in abject longing, and then turned to me. "You should take us back," he hissed softly. "I could stand here all night. This can't be fun for you. You're getting eaten alive."

"I understand the lure of home," I said, oddly emotional. "Take as long as you want."

Lash looked uncertain I meant my words, but he turned back, and scented the air again for another few minutes. When he turned back to me again, he was resolute. "We should go back," he said softly, taking my hand.

When we arrived back, he hugged me gently, then let me go. "Thank you," he whispered. "It was good to smell the mahogany again, and the saw grass."

"Anytime," I replied, giving his hand a squeeze. "But now we've got to get to work."

Lash followed me downstairs where I put in a few more hours filing. This time he didn't read as he always had, but instead looked off into space. He didn't say anything, but I knew he must be thinking of the swamp, and the home he'd known long ago. Was any of his family still alive? He was so old, the answer was probably not. If he had had siblings, their children or grandchildren might be alive, but everyone else had to be dead. Not wanting to hurt him by mentioning it, I stayed silent.

After filing, Lash and I sat down to watch *300*, with me curled up on one end of the couch and him sprawled on the other, not touching. I watched the opening scenes, then put my head down just for a second on my arms, and fell asleep.

I woke up to loud familiar screaming. I'd watched this movie enough times to know the sounds of the final battle. But where was I? I was laying partially on somebody, curled around their lower body. Someone was stroking my hair back from my face gently with callused hands that were rough on my face. There was the scent of leather, autumn leaves, and the faint musky odor of earth.

This was not Theo.

I lifted my head, looked up into Lash's face looking down at me, and froze.

He removed his hand from my face. "You should go up to bed. I didn't want to wake you, but you clearly need sleep. You almost fell off the couch, so I eased you down next to me."

"Sorry," I said, blushing furiously, trying to untangle myself from him. My one arm, woven though the coils of his whip, took me a minute to unwind.

"Don't worry about it," Lash said easily, helping me get to my feet. "I'll see you tomorrow for dinner. We can put the movie on again then, if you want."

We had a standing dinner date now. But Lash was supposed to be guarding me, so it made sense. Also, he'd made no moves on me. He could have tried to raise The Lust when I'd been lying there with him, and he hadn't.

I relaxed. "It's a plan. See you then."

Lash nodded. "You asked me about the clothes yesterday. I left you a pile on Devlin's loveseat. Anything you can't fix you can throw out." He turned and left.

"Thanks," I called awkwardly after him, then headed upstairs.

* * * *

110

The next day was the best one yet.

I had set my watch alarm for eight. When it went off, I got up and threw on some clothes. Devlin grumbled, but when he heard that I was going with Lash to check out the gardens, he gave me a smile, and let me go.

It took a good two hours. Lash showed me all of the gardens, while I scribbled notes furiously. Most of them were raised beds. Not knowing if there were any flowers there beneath last year's weeds, I wrote down a list of possible plants, figuring to wait and see what emerged in the spring.

Lash made no mention of the night before. He was polite, but not overly so. Relieved, and relaxed, I enjoyed the sunshine and his company, deciding finally that I liked him. Maybe he could be a jerk, but he'd been decent with me when it counted. That was what mattered.

Afterwards, I went back to bed, and spent the rest of the day sleeping with Devlin. When I awoke with Dev at dusk, I was rested. He dressed, kissed me once warmly and then went off to work with Titus. I got dressed, then called Theo at Danial's house for an update.

"He isn't here, he's working," Danial said crankily, when he answered. "And I hope you'll be back to work next week, too, Sar."

"What's the matter?" I asked, surprised.

"I finally put up the Solutions Inc. website," Danial answered grumpily.

"That's great!" I said excitedly. "You've wanted to do that for ages." I'd looked at so many designs with him over the years, I'd suspected this day might never come. Danial was always the perfectionist; it had to be perfect, or he wasn't happy. But whatever he did do usually got great results. "So what's wrong?"

"Sar, we had a hundred emails our first day!" Danial said loudly. "I deleted the junk, but there are over thirty people to call. That's just from today." He paused. "I need you next week."

Sigh. "I'll be there Monday at eight. Tell Theo I called."

Hanging up, I put the looming work to come out of my mind and went looking for Serena.

We spent an hour sewing. Using Lash's clothing, I showed her the basic stitches, and how best to repair clothing needing mending. There were a lot of Lash's clothes in the pile, more than I had expected. The heavy cotton, denim, and wool were all in black, which made my work easy; I didn't have to change my thread color once.

Serena got the hang of it quickly. Nosy about the men who'd given her clothes to mend, I snuck glances at the fabric, but the dark navy blue shirts, single red shirt, white socks, and brown jeans didn't give me any clues as to whom their owners might be. Asking flat out seemed in bad taste. But I made a mental note to pay attention to who wore blue shirts here.

Some of what we worked on was normal wear and tear: socks needing darning, pockets that had ripped out, frayed cuffs, and unraveled seams. But several others were from fighting, though I didn't see any bloodstains on the ripped and sliced cloth.

Lash came in as we were finishing. "You fixed them all?" he hissed, surprised.

Serena grabbed her clothes and edged fast towards the door. "Thanks, Sar. See you later." She darted out.

"Bye, Serena," I said brightly, handing the clothes to Lash as if her behavior was perfectly normal. "It's not hard to do mending. It's just tedious sometimes. Yours was easy." I gave him a knowing look. "Maybe you should be more careful when you fight."

Lash gave me an odd look in return. "Dinner?" he hissed.

"Sure," I said, making a face. "but we're out of sushi. Do you want—"

"I got some more for us today, while you and Dev were sleeping," Lash said, going to the fridge and handing me several packages of eel, and one of vegetables.

"You didn't have to," I said awkwardly. I got a plate, and filled it with sushi, wondering again if there was more to this sudden thoughtfulness, and if that more was a bad thing.

Lash followed suit. "You need it." He paused. "It's probably the closest thing to raw meat that you can tolerate eating. Wereanimal children need a lot of protein. My mother always made sure we ate a lot of meat and fish. It is good for your werechild to eat this. You should try to eat it at least a few times a week, to give the baby what it needs to grow."

Suddenly, I wasn't just awkward, I was an emotional mess, too. "Thank you," I managed.

"I told this to Devlin, but he is vampire and doesn't understand," Lash hissed furiously. "But most vampires don't understand weres, or want to, other than to tell us what needs doing."

What was his issue with Dev? I'd absorbed from my time with Danial and Dev, not to mention the other Rulers, that most vampires looked down on weres, and that most, if not all, weres knew this and expected it, though they didn't like it. Danial had always treated Theo pretty much as an equal, but he hadn't thought of the foxes that way until I had called him on it. Even then, it was adopting Elle as his daughter that had finally made him realize that his employees had their own needs, personalities, and desires. It was clear from Dev's comment when I had insisted on telling Serena about Vince, not to mention his treatment of Elle, that he thought of weres and even Titus as just creatures who were there to work for him, or make his life easier. But Lash I'd thought an exception, especially with Lash's bedroom right next door to Devlin's.

"Did you two fight?" I asked finally, worried.

"No, but we're going to soon," Lash said bitterly, then lapsed into a brooding silence.

"Then let's leave the work for tonight," I said, taking my plate into the TV room. "Put on *South Park*, please."

Lash liked it at once, though he was shocked at the language. "These are children?" he said, flicking his tongue at me. "Children talk like this now?"

"Third graders, no less," I said, laughing.

"I feel old," he said ruefully.

We were watching the episode about the Starbucks coffee house, when Dev called.

"Sar's fine, Dev," Lash hissed angrily, after he answered it. "We are watching TV."

There was silence. Lash didn't speak, but whatever Devlin was saying was pissing him off, as he began flicking his tongue rapidly, like a rattling angry tail.

I had to shut this down. "Tell him you know what happened to his underwear," I said quietly.

Lash looked at me, and his mouth dropped open. I laughed, then gestured to the screen where the underpants gnomes were singing songs and stealing underwear. Lash began roaring, laughing so hard he was choking. That set me off, tears streaming out of my eyes as I howled.

"What is so funny?" Dev's voice screamed out of the receiver.

"We're sorry the gnomes got your underwear," Lash hissed contritely, giving me a wicked grin. "We managed to fend them off ourselves. We feel sorry for you."

I wiped at my eyes, the tears flowing like water as I gasped for breath. "Stop!" I yelled. "I can't breathe!"

Devlin sputtered on the other end of the phone. "I don't wear underwear by choice! No one stole it! It was not worn in my time, you idiots! What the hell are you talking about? What's going on there?"

"You'd know if you were here," Lash hissed, venom flowing in every word. "But you're not, so you won't." He hung up the phone.

"I solved one old mystery at least," I said, grabbing for a tissue. "But he'll be pissed you hung up on him."

"He'll get over it," Lash hissed, smirking. "That was great, Sar. He was so pissed, because he thought we were having fun here without him."

"Well, we are," I said, snickering. "Hit play."

We watched a few more episodes. Soon it was after midnight. "I'm going to bed," I said finally. "I don't want to fall off the couch like last night."

To my surprise, Lash didn't take the opening to banter. "Okay. Do you mind if I keep the DVD for a while?" he said formally. "I'd like to watch the rest."

"Go ahead," I said, oddly awkward again. "I'll be coming back sometime soon." I walked off waiting for Lash to call goodnight after me, but he didn't.

* * * *

It was close to two in the morning when I awoke. Devlin was not back yet. Guilty over the prank I'd instigated, I lay there sleepless thinking about it, wondering if he was delaying returning on purpose as a sort of punishment. Telling myself that was stupid, I decided to go get a drink of water. Irritated I'd forgotten to bring up a glass from upstairs, I put on my robe and headed for the kitchen. I was just starting down the stairs when a hissing voice cut the silence.

"Where are you going?"

I turned. Lash closed his bedroom door behind him, and came towards me in the semi-darkness, framed in the weak outside lights shining through the downstairs windows. He was wearing a black motorcycle jacket and his jeans, his face in deep shadow.

"You shouldn't wander downstairs alone," Lash continued, coming closer. "What do you need?"

*Did he sleep in those jeans? No, most likely he slept naked as he had at Danial's. Probably he had nothing on underneath them...*The Lust came roaring back like a tidal pool, drowning me in seconds.

He's probably warm like he'd been that night I'd fallen asleep with him. I want that warmth, to curl around him, and smell his scent, to roll myself in it until I'm covered with it. I want to surround him with my body, to cover him with my scent, until everything meshes into one!

I went up the stairs in a lunge, my robe dropping to the floor. I reached out for him, but he evaded me like before, sidestepping quickly, his hands grasping my arms. He pressed my back to the wall, turning me to face him. I reached up with my hands, and brought his lips down on mine, opening my mouth eagerly. Lash responded immediately, sliding his forked tongue to mine fervently, tasting me as he pressed his body to mine, his erection forming quickly at my hip. I reached down and caressed him. He let out a soft groan, breaking the kiss.

"Is this for me?" I said seductively, stroking him.

Lash pressed himself against me hard, rubbing and thrusting. "All for you, if you want it," he hissed. Then he kissed me, the unyielding press of his fangs

114

quickly lost to the soft kisses on my cheeks, then my neck as he reached his arms up under my nightgown to slide his callused fingertips up my naked back.

The feel of his rough hands on my smooth skin inflamed me. I reached down and grabbed his ass, pulling him hard against me and squeezing. "I want it! I want you," I moaned insistently, overcome by the pleasurable sensations of his lips and tongue caressing my skin.

"What do you want?" he hissed softly in my ear. "The same as before?"

"Yes," I said, reaching for the front of his jeans. "Now."

"Come with me," he said, trying to lead me to his bedroom. "We can't do it here, or Serena and Nick may see us. They are in her room—"

"No, not there—"

"Where?" Lash said hungrily, kissing me lightly again on my neck.

I grabbed him by his hair, and jerked his head back from me. "Davy's," I said roughly, kissing down his neck. "I want you to take me as you used to take Cin."

"Take us there and I will," he answered, raw lust uncoiling in each word.

I closed my eyes, teleporting us. But instead of ending up inside, we ended up before the closed doors of Davy's, in the parking lot. The harsh light of a streetlight shone down on us. The cool night air was cool on my skin, raising goosebumps down my arms.

Lash shrugged off his leather jacket, then draped it over me. "My bad," he hissed. "Davy's is shielded when it's not open, so no one can teleport in and have a private party." He grinned. "Demons have a taste for booze."

"I want in," I said harshly, then let my tone shift to sultry. "Don't you?"

"Yes," Lash hissed, baring his snake fangs. "And I get what I want, Sar. Come here."

I pushed into his arms, my arms going around his neck. Lash grabbed my wrists, then held me to the brick wall, kissing me as he rubbed his groin on mine. My breaths came raggedly, my consuming desire for him building uncontrollably. I raised one knee, bending my leg to pull him closer, the sudden added stimulation of his erection making me moan with longing. *Yes, he could take me right here, against the wall. I wanted his fangs in me, along with his cock...*

Lash shuddered, then pushed back from me. He went to the doors and with a well-aimed kick, sent them crashing open. Returning for me, he led me into the main room at Davy's. In the blackness of the early dawn hours, nothing was visible, not even Lash beside me. I stood still and let my eyes adjust, afraid if I moved I was going to stumble over something. Lash gave my hand a squeeze, then began walking towards the yawning deeper blackness of the back room. I followed him slowly, suddenly angry that my night vision that had once been so enhanced had not returned with the recent influx of Devlin's blood. But the fire in my veins turned to desire as I was led though the dark by Lash, the knowledge of where he was leading me, and what he would do to me when we got there intensifying my arousal with every cautious step.

Lash paused in the back doorway as if getting his bearings. A dim emergency light above the bar revealed two pool tables and a couple tables with a few chairs around them. Everything else was in deep shadow.

I was frantic by now with need, tremors wracking my body. "Please," I whispered, running my hands up, then down his arms. "Please, Lash. I need you—"

He made no answer, only grabbed my hand again and started walking. When we reached the furthest table, he lifted me in his arms, setting me on the edge. With a swipe of his arm, he sent the pool cues and the balls behind me clattering to the floor. The noise of their rolling disappeared as Lash kissed me insistently, his long tongue twining with mine as he parted my legs and pulled my hips hard against his straining jeans, letting out an eager hiss. I clung to him, my mouth devouring his, even as I reached down and unzipped his pants.

Lash hissed, then grabbed my arms, stopping me, and pushed me backwards down on the table. I watched his shadowy form as warm hands pushed my nightgown up, then parted my legs all the way open. Those hands ran down my belly and over my hips, then stroked my thighs softly.

I moved involuntarily under his hands, trembling hard. "Please!"

I tried hard to hold still in sweet anticipation, waiting for a hard thrust. Instead came the sensation of his tongue licking at my vagina, then his fangs brushing my skin. Even in my lust, I felt a sudden shiver of fear. Involuntarily, my legs tried to close. His hands clamped down around my thighs tightly, holding me still. I went to stop Lash, drawing breath to cry out. Instead a sigh escaped my lips as his warm tongue curled up within me, and began stroking gently.

A few seconds later, I was jerking for him, moaning as he stroked me over and over. My hands went into his hair, kneading and grasping. Lash knew what he was doing. I had never felt anything like this, not with anyone else, ever. With his long forked tongue, he could do movements that couldn't normally be done, creating unbelievable stimulation when he'd kissed my mouth. What he was doing to me now made those kisses seem like nothing.

Waves of utter pleasure hit me. I jerked beneath him, crying out over and over with every touch. Lash kept stroking me, kissing me, the pressure building until I felt I was going to die if it went on much longer. Then I erupted, screaming in climax as I arched up off the table into him. He held me fast with his hands, still moving relentlessly, wresting every last tremor of my orgasm from me.

Panting, I relaxed back onto the table. There was the whisper of falling cloth, then the light abrasion of skin on skin as Lash leaned onto me, almost undulating, kissing my skin as he worked his way upwards. Taking my nightgown in his hands, he ripped it down the front, then pushed it to either side. With a wooden creak, he easily boosted himself onto the table, laying between my legs. As the pool table groaned again under our combined weight, I went rigid, worried it was going to collapse beneath us.

"Shh," Lash hissed. "It will hold us."

Holding himself up on his elbows, he kissed me again, harder this time, sliding his erection back and forth over my thatch. As I tasted myself in his kiss, I groaned, feeling the sudden slipperiness as my body told him I was ready. Preparing to guide him in, I eagerly put my hands on his chest and felt warm scales beneath my fingers.

Lash went motionless.

This was what he had been afraid of me feeling that last time we had been together. But my breaths were fast from excitement, not fear. I liked the feel of him under my hands; I wasn't afraid he was different. I slid my hands over his chest, caressing his scales a few times, then reached my hand down, pushing his erection into position to enter.

With a grunt, Lash drove himself in, bringing a cry from me. He lowered himself onto me, kissed my throat, and then there was a prick as his fangs slid in. I convulsed at the sensation, and Lash made a muffled groan as I tightened up, squeezing him. At once he began moving in and out of me in rhythm, his mouth fastened on my neck, sucking gently.

I clasped him to me, barely registering the slight pain. All I could hear was his heart beating fast, much faster than mine, and my own gasps. I ran my hands over his back, his ass, loving the feel of his muscles contracting under my hands, loving how he was driving so deep with each thrust.

Suddenly, I was there. As I took a breath to scream, he covered my mouth with his hand tightly. I shook hard in the throes of my orgasm, screaming into his hand, my muffled cries quiet in the stillness. Lash's body stiffened as he drove himself into me deeply with a soft hiss.

His body gave a few spasms on mine, then relaxed. Giving me a chaste kiss, he pulled out quickly and eased down on his back by my side. We lay there for a while, not speaking, as our breathing calmed. Lash made no sounds, except soft hisses of pleasure, as I slowly came back to myself.

As I did, I began to shiver. It wasn't fear of him, but fear of myself: I'd rarely felt so sated in my life, even after hours of lovemaking. What he had done to me that first time, it had been like no oral sex I'd ever experienced. It had been a goddamn epiphany…

A wave of guilt hit, telling me I was wrong to have enjoyed his touch so much. Anxiety followed; Lash had said he didn't like being with women who weren't weresnake, as he was. But Devlin hadn't given him a choice, he'd just told Lash what needed to be done and expected him to just do it. Given another option, Lash wouldn't have touched me in a million years. It was a safe bet he hadn't had an epiphany, only a pleasant day at the office.

I knew what it was, not to have a choice. I let out a deep breath. "I'm sorry—"

"Don't apologize after," Lash hissed sharply. "Don't make more of this than it is."

Tears flooded my eyes. That he was right didn't matter. I'd used him to slake my lust, just like the slut Elle had accused me of being. Worse, he wasn't mellow or sated like me; he was angry and unfulfilled. I turned my back to him, trying not to make any noise.

With a hiss that sounded like a sigh, Lash put his arms around me, and pulled me close to him. "Shh," he said softly. "Don't cry."

"I'm sorry I made you—"

"You didn't make me do anything but come," Lash hissed in my ear. "Don't be sad about that or regretful. That's all I meant."

I turned to face him, then touched him gently on his chest, again stroking his warm scales. They were leathery and smooth to the touch, the ridges where one overlapped another just noticeable under my hands. "Is there a pattern on them?"

"Of course," Lash said mockingly. "I'm not an albino cottonmouth. I thought you were a big animal lover."

Not sure how to answer, I put my hand over his heart. The beats were still coming fast, though his breathing had quieted. Lash's chest was hard beneath my fingers, his wiry arm muscles like steel bands around me as I stroked his scales.

"It's the potion I take," Lash hissed after a moment. "I can't come all the way back to human form anymore. But it's better than dying."

He was embarrassed his body wasn't fully human for some reason. Was he worried I'd recoil?

"I don't mind," I whispered. "I've always had a fondness for snakes." I kissed him gently on his chest, putting my lips to his scales.

Lash let out a sharp hiss and pushed me back gently from him. "Unless you want to go again, stop that."

I hugged him, and didn't reply, taking comfort from his nearness.

Lash shifted slightly. "We should get back to Hayden. Dev will be back soon."

As he moved, he brushed my hip gently, his erection thick and solid. The Lust came roaring back, possessing me completely. I reached down and took hold of him with one hand, sliding it down over his shaft, squeezing gently.

"Not so fast, Lover."

Lash whipped his head around, then relaxed back on the table, pulling me astride him. I worked his penis in my hand rapidly, as he groaned and contracted his hips. Lowering myself into position above him, I teased him, rubbing my body on his. Lash reached up and grabbed my hips, bringing them down quickly to receive him, his hiss of pleasure loud in the silence. His mouth devoured mine, his hands gripping me hard as he began to thrust.

The Lust ruled me, my lips whispering to him to kiss me, to take me, to fuck me. But despite my impatient demands, Lash took his time, his hands caressing my breasts, curling his long tongue around my nipples as he suckled them, his gentle bites not breaking my skin. I rode him relentlessly, my body sweaty and starving for climax.

"Deeper," I hissed at him angrily. "Do it!"

"I'm in you to my balls," Lash hissed back, then groaned, moving my hips on his faster.

My muscles tightened as the first tickles of orgasm hit me. "Come," I commanded harshly. "I want you to—"

"You come," Lash commanded, then rolled over onto me, his organ driving into me furiously. I came at once, my scream muffled as he quickly covered my mouth with his hand, his movements jagged as he orgasmed.

Lash lifted his upper body on his forearms, his eyes glimmers in the heavy gloom. "Are you done?" he hissed softly. "Do you need it again?"

He was saying he was only done if I wanted it to be done. I reached up and caressed his scales, then rested my hand on his chest, The Lust slowly abating as the minutes passed.

Lash shifted, his still-hard penis withdrawing slightly. I breathed in abruptly, blinking rapidly to clear my head of The Lust's influence. "I'm okay, I think."

Lash quickly pulled out, then rolled onto his back beside me. I lay there, trying to think of what to say as the silence stretched. I wanted to tell him how good he'd been, but I couldn't seem to get the words out. Not only was I embarrassed, I was wondering why the hell I'd come without him biting me.

"You're heart is racing," Lash hissed softly, his tone teasing. "Lover."

My pulse shot up. I looked over at his form with just my eyes, watching as his hand slowly reached over and caressed my pubic hair. I shifted uneasily the moment he touched me, then began to writhe, The Lust engulfing me again as his skilled fingers worked their way deeper, his mouth closing on my breast.

I grasped his head, pressing him to my chest. "Slide in," I whispered seductively, spreading my legs, my hips pushing upwards. "I want you to—"

"No." Lash pressed me flat to the table with one hand, the other rubbing my clit. "I want to see you come."

"You bastard," I snarled, reaching for his throat. "Take me or I'll kill you."

"Don't threaten me," Lash hissed, grabbing my wrists as he maneuvered on top of me. "Don't ever threaten me—"

I wriggled under his body, moving from side to side. "Get off me!"

Lash shifted his hips back and forth, then suddenly bore down hard, penetrating me. I gave a jerk, then began moving frantically, trying to dislodge him. He trapped me under him, his hands on my wrists, his hips moving fast on mine. I fought him, pushing at him with my hands, kicking and cursing until the moment he bit down into me. At once compliant, I relaxed back to the table, moaning and sighing.

Lash drank and made love to me as I luxuriated beneath him. Then he stiffened, thrusting deeply, his hiss of pleasure bringing a gasp of sudden ecstasy as I clasped his ass, kneading as the familiar surge of pleasure washed though me. Sated, I finally went limp, my chest heaving.

Lash pushed up from me, then waited there above me, watching.

I shuddered under him, coming back to myself, ashamed of how I'd acted.

Lash waited in silence, unmoving, tense as a coiled spring.

"I'm sorry," I whispered, wiping at my eyes. "It's...it's like that sometimes."

Lash rolled onto his back again with a sigh beside me and didn't answer.

I stayed quiet, too, my mind working furiously. Lash's refusal had brought out the worst of The Lust. But why was it raising repeatedly over and over after being sated? Maybe it had needed him to drink some blood like he just had? More important, how were we going to get home if it rose every time he touched me?

"I should've just done what you asked," Lash hissed, letting out a breath.

"It's not important," I answered absently.

"You didn't scream."

I looked over at him, wondering what he was talking about.

"If you'd have screamed for me to stop, I would have," Lash added. "I thought what I was doing was okay." He touched his fingertips to my arm just perceptibly. "I didn't meant to scare you."

"You didn't," I assured him, then paused, the sudden urge to tell him how much I'd enjoyed the first two times undeniable. I wrestled with my conscience a few seconds, then decided screw it, he'd been fucking amazing, and after making me feel like that he deserved to know it. "What you did to me…it…it was wonderful. It was amazing."

"Good," Lash said, moving closer. He put his arms around me, then squeezed gently.

The Lust ebbed, then disappeared completely. As it did regret filled me; not at the sex itself, but for how it had complicated our relationship. I'd wanted to get along with him. I thought maybe we were becoming friends. Now this had to happen.

"I'll miss this," Lash whispered in my ear, "when you're back to normal."

Guilt and regret washed over me, because I couldn't reply the same. "I thought you didn't like to be with any women who weren't weresnake," I said hesitantly.

Lash grunted. "Non-were women want nothing to do with me, now that I can't hide my snake nature," he said a little too casually. "Any female were that isn't snake is the same. Serena said up front when Devlin asked her to come and see to everyone's needs here that she wasn't going to let me touch her. If he hadn't agreed to that, she wouldn't have come to Hayden, no matter what he paid her."

I knew he didn't want my pity, so I didn't reply. But it was evident now why Serena feared him and why Devlin had gone to lengths to match Lash up with another lover after Cin left. "She doesn't know what she's passing on, barring you from her bed."

"Most women don't like snakes," Lash said bitterly. "They don't want a man who's part snake next to their naked skin, much less inside them."

There was no answer that wouldn't hurt. "That's probably true—"

"You are the first non-were I've been with like this in decades, Sar," Lash hissed, running his hand from between my breasts up to clasp my neck, and then my face. "Even then, they didn't want me like you do in the throes of your lust. Hell, no one has ever made me feel as wanted as you have, the times we have been together. If Dev didn't love you, if you weren't pregnant with his child, I would change you, here and now. It would feel so good, to coil together with you in snake form, to feel your scales sliding under mine—"

I didn't want to be werecougar; I sure as shit didn't want to be weresnake. I recoiled, moving towards the table edge.

Lash grabbed hold of me, bringing me back into his arms. "Sorry, I shouldn't have said that. I'm no good at this after-part. I'll stop talking."

I reached up, and ran my hand over his scar on his cheek. Lash froze.

"How did this happen to you? I thought you were born a were. Were you turned when you were very young—?"

Lash took my hand, and gently removed it from his face. "I was born were.

This happened in Rio, months ago." He paused, as if gathering himself. "The scar's healing, but very slowly. The wound was deep. My regenerative powers have ebbed almost to that of a human. It's the potion I take that regenerates me, Sar. My body can't do it anymore. And the potion is taking longer to work these days."

"Does Devlin know?" I asked.

"No. I told him the blade was laced with poison; that is why it's taking so long to heal. He wouldn't let me risk myself if he thought I couldn't regenerate. I have to be extra careful not to get injured when I fight now. But I'm not going to spend the rest of my life sitting on the sidelines, thinking about the good old days." There was determination in his tone, and more than a trace of sorrow.

"Can't Titus heal you? Or give you something else to try?"

"He's done all he can," Lash said quietly. "I'm grateful that he has helped me to live this long."

Something in his tone told me that this was deeper than just a wound that was taking a long time to heal. As I turned toward him I understood all at once that he was telling me that he was going to die soon. I didn't love him, but I liked him and didn't want him to die. He was my lover, even if I hadn't wanted him to be. Besides, Dev would be devastated.

I hugged him tightly. "I'm sorry."

"It won't be for a while yet," Lash hissed uncomfortably. "Titus has told me the time is coming; that he can't hold it off any longer. Another ten years or so, at most."

That seemed so short. No wonder Lash had been so angry I was going to live forever and not age. "Can't we ask someone else to give a second opinion?"

"Don't you dare say anything to Dev," Lash hissed hotly. "I don't want him to know. I don't want anyone to know. I—"

"I won't say anything, not to anyone," I assured him. "I give you my word. It's not anyone's business but yours." I reached down and squeezed his hand in mine.

After a moment, he squeezed back. "I give you mine, too," Lash hissed. "I won't tell anyone this happened tonight unless you want me to, though I'd like very much to brag about bedding you again."

"Thank you," I whispered. "No, don't tell anyone."

Lash turned me toward him, then kissed me softly, moving his hips against me lightly, his rigid throbbing length pressing insistently against my side. "Once more for the road?" he offered, sliding his hand down to caress my hip.

My Lust roared back. I brought his lips down on mine as my answer.

* * * *

We finally got back to Hayden about six a.m. Once more had turned into twice, then thrice, The Lust rising every time I touched him to teleport us home. At first, Lash had enjoyed being in demand, but the later it got, the more we both worried someone was going to come in and find us. Finally, after a quick brainstorm session, Lash rolled off the side of the table, slipped on his jeans, and walked into the darkness. He was back shortly with a greasy apron that he'd draped over him, hiding his head, chest and arms from my sight.

"It's worked so far," I said, pulling the remains of my nightgown around me. "Don't say anything." I walked closer, then grabbed his hand, teleporting us to Hayden.

We arrived in Devlin's bedroom. Devlin was sitting on the bed, fully dressed, reading a file which he immediately closed. "You know better than to leave Hayden with her without telling me, Lash." He paused, taking in the state of our undress. "Again?"

Lash tore the apron off his head and threw it aside. "You know about The Lust and you know we didn't have much of a choice, so stop bitching."

Devlin looked over at me. "Go ahead and use the shower, Sar."

I cast a quick glance at Lash, then went into the bathroom. When I emerged later, Lash was gone and Devlin was in bed sleeping. As I got into bed beside him, he opened his eyes, then turned toward me.

"I burned your torn nightgown," Dev whispered. "Lash told me you wished that no one know." He paused. "Even me."

"I thought I was done with this and I'm not," I replied irritably. "I don't know why it's lasting so long this time."

"It'll pass," Devlin consoled, resting his hand on my belly. "And it's worth it, Sar."

Because it's not happening to you. "So you're okay with what happened?"

Devlin nodded. "Of course. Lash told me what happened, how you brought him to Davy's and had your pool table adventure." He chuckled. "He said he was surprised you got so violent so quickly." He shook his head. "He should have expected that, refusing you like he did."

Lash had left out a hell of a lot when he'd related the night's events. He'd kept his promise; as much as he could, anyway.

"I think he wanted you to chase him around again," Devlin purred. "Tell me, is there any damage to the bar I have to pay for, other than a new apron and locks for the front door?"

I shook my head. "He contained it."

"You sound almost fond of him," Devlin purred, a new dangerous note suddenly apparent.

"I'm grateful to him," I corrected. "Please, let's get some sleep. We're both tired."

I expected a barb from Devlin about Lash tiring me, but oddly enough he just hugged me and said nothing.

Chapter Nine

Things went wrong from the first on Saturday morning.

Someone pounded on the door, waking me with a start. Devlin also woke, his bad mood from last night still evident. "What the hell is it?" he yelled.

"Phone call from Danial," one of the bears growled back. "He demands to talk to her."

"Figures," Devlin said bitterly. "It's always something."

I stretched, feeling the soreness of my body, scenes from last night coming back to me. God, Lash had been amazing…

"—or someone," Dev finished, giving me a look that said he knew what I'd been thinking of . "Pick it up, Sar."

I grabbed the phone. "I'm here," I said quickly. "What is it?"

"Be here by noon if you can," Danial said with a sigh. "We have another seventy emails, Sar. At least half look legitimate—"

I flopped down on my back in bed, dismayed at the thought of the hours in front of the computer that amount of emails would translate into. "Danial, what are we going to do?" I said stridently. "You can't take all these cases. You're only one man, and Terian is still gone—"

"He'll be home by Wednesday. Besides, Theo is going to step up. I'm going to start sending him on some cases with Terian without me. He can work days, and I can't."

I was shocked. Danial had never mentioned this to me before, nor had Theo. "But he can't do the programming you can. He's not computer savvy to the extent you are. Neither is Terian—"

"No, but they can do the other cases, especially the ones that only entail watching, or catching someone in the act, or figuring out what happened to some missing files—"

That was certainly true, but it didn't answer the big question. "Danial, you've always been ambitious about your business. But you've never wanted to expand it like this. You don't need the money, so why are you doing this?"

"I want Theoron to join me as my partner when he's an adult," Danial answered with pride. "I have hopes that he'll want to run the business with me, Theo and Terian. There needs to be enough work to keep us all occupied. At the rate he's learning and growing—"

This was crazy. "Danial, he's a child. He may not want to do what you do—"

"Sar, he has to make a living," Danial said defensively. "Something may happen to me one day; I'm not invulnerable! I want him to have respect, and enough power to not be interfered with, as I do. He can make good money doing this, far more than he could make as a simple bodyguard."

I closed my eyes, and counted to ten.

"I didn't mean it how it sounded," Danial added quickly.

Yes, you did. "I'll see you this afternoon," I said and hung up on him.

Devlin took the phone from me. "I knew this would happen," he said, setting it back in its cradle. "Danial wanted his mortal son to follow in his footsteps also. Nothing has changed."

"I guess I always knew Danial was hoping to have a father and son business," I said, rubbing at my eyes. "It's just way too much, too soon."

"Sar, Theoron has eternity," Devlin said soothingly. "He can get degrees, be whatever he wants. There is time for him to decide, and for him to be what Danial wants him to be, at least for a little while, before he decides how he wants to live his life. He can change his mind and be something else when he tires of whatever he has chosen."

"Can he?" I said brokenly. "I think Danial has his future mapped out for him."

"That's a father's way," Devlin said, touching my belly possessively. "I'm looking forward to showing my son many things, Sar. He can do what he wants for a living, but he's going to learn to sing and get an education, particularly in history and art. Perhaps piano as well, or some other instrument, if he shows promise in one—"

"It may be a girl," I said, relaxing. "But she can do that, too."

"I want a son, Sar," Devlin said, taking my hand. "I want you to try with me to have one, if our first child is a girl."

I blinked, then turned my head very slowly to face him. Devlin looked at me calmly, regarding me with his golden eyes.

"Our...first child?" I said finally.

"If it's a boy, we can just have the one," Devlin said, kissing my neck. "But I want a boy, Sar. Sooner or later, if we try long enough, we'll get a boy. Even if it takes years, and we fill Hayden with girl children—"

I pushed him away with a sob, and bolted out of bed. "You said one was enough!" I screamed, tears running freely from my eyes. "You said you'd help me get fixed!"

Devlin didn't look ashamed, or drop his eyes. "That was before. Harriet is pregnant again. Samuel is the father. He's keeping her in bed, carefully protecting her. She's either going to deliver the child, or die this time."

"What does that have to do with anything?"

"He's already suspicious!" Devlin shouted. "If she dies, he'll figure out what I did. If Camlyn gives you the operation, he'll find that out, too!"

"Stephen would never betray me."

"Perseus, Zane, and Samuel will question him thoroughly, regardless of what happens with Harriet, when they learn about your inability to have any more children!" Devlin yelled, eyes flashing. "They'll torture him to make sure he's telling the truth, because they want so badly for it to be a lie. Camlyn will cave under the pain. Your deception—our deception—will be exposed."

"You never planned to help me," I whispered, closing my eyes tight. "It was all just bullshit."

Devlin embraced me. "Sterilizing you won't keep you out of their clutches. Having other children together will. Samuel will understand my desire for a son. Or even for a daughter, if a son is born to us first. They would not attempt to take you from me if you're pregnant and Oathed, Sar. So that is how you must be until we can find another solution—"

I felt sick, lightheaded, as if I was going to faint. *This couldn't be happening.*

"Part of me wants a girl as well, one that looks just like you, Sar," Dev murmured in my ear. "With my fair coloring we have a good chance of that, though she may get my eyes instead of yours."

His eager words unhinged me, and I broke away from him in horror at his betrayal. "No!" I screamed. "I agreed to try once! I'm not only risking my life, Dev, but I'm losing my mind! One will have to be enough for you! I'm not going through this again, not ever, not for anything!"

"I'm telling you now that it's not enough!" Devlin hissed coldly, his eyes red. "And you will try with me, as many times as I ask you to. You are mine, Sar. You promised yourself to me."

I ran for the door. Devlin grabbed me, then brought me back to the bed, holding me down as I struggled and screamed.

"Hold still!"

"Let me go! Let me go!"

Dev swore angrily, then climbed atop me, holding me down with his weight as he tried to grab something beside the bed. "Hold still! You're mine,

Sar!"

My mind raced frantically. Dev couldn't be with me the normal way, but he could do something else to me, something I didn't want him to do. He was reaching for lubricant.

I shrieked in terror. "Don't do it! Stop! Stop it!"

With a loud crash, Lash kicked the door in. He looked down at us from the doorway, irritated. "I heard screaming," he hissed. "But you're not in danger, I see. Keep it down. I'm trying to sleep."

"Go back to bed," Devlin snarled, turning from him. "We're fine."

"Let me go!" I screamed. "Get off me, Dev! I won't do it, not ever!"

"What is the matter with her?" Lash hissed, coming closer.

"Just hold her," Devlin said, furious. He let me go and kneeled beside the bed, rummaging under it. "I need to put her collar back on."

I ran for the door. Lash grabbed hold of me and I began screaming again, yanking at his hands.

Lash shook me hard. "Stop it," he hissed. "No one is going to hurt you."

I yanked again weakly, then collapsed to the floor, crying hard. Devlin knelt beside me, fastening his choker above Danial's with a soft clinking sound.

"Get hold of yourself," he said sternly. "You're acting like a child. Get up and get dressed."

Lash turned to Devlin, his flat eyes cold and hard. "What did you do, worse than you have already?" he hissed, folding his arms across his chest. "Sar was not like this all week; she was happy. She's terrified of you now."

Devlin ignored him. "Sar, get dressed. Lash will take you to Danial. But you will understand something right now." He helped me stand. "You will be coming back to me on Monday. Bring your pets if you like, and anything you want from your house. You can help Danial with his business from here, I'll have something set up. You can see Danial on Saturdays and Theo on Sundays—"

"No," I gasped out. "I won't do it—"

"You will, and you'll do it gladly!" Devlin snarled. "Or I'll rescind my order to Samuel, and tell him it's okay if he kills Theo. He still wants to kill Theo, Sar. Badly. All I need to do is let him know I don't care if he does it, and it's done."

"No, I don't want to—"

"I don't care if you want to be with me!" Devlin yelled. "I want to be with you, and I'm not going to wait anymore for you to come around. The games are over, Sar. You are coming here to live where I know you're safe. We will be happy together. You'll adjust in time."

This was a nightmare. It had to be a nightmare. Everything had been going so well.

"And Sar," Devlin continued in an icy tone, "If you enlist Theo to try a daring rescue, Lash will kill him. And if he doesn't, I will."

Warm hands grasped my arms, then propelled me forward. Lash opened the bathroom door, then shoved me in. "Stay here. I'll bring you some clothes." He closed the door behind him as I huddled there on the bathroom floor, trying not to cry.

"Stop coddling her, Lash," Devlin spat. "She's a big girl—"

"Stop being stupid," Lash hissed. There was the sound of clothing rustling. "All you are going to do is make her hate you more than she does already."

"She loves me," Devlin said angrily.

"Does she?" Lash hissed sarcastically. "She loves Theo and Danial. But does she really love you, Dev?"

"She doesn't love you," Devlin replied cruelly.

Lash laughed back at him. "I never asked her to," he said easily. "I'm not the one desperate for her love, Friend." There were more sounds of clothes rustling, hangers being removed, and drawers opening and closing.

"Then why do you still smell of her, Friend?" Devlin purred. "You wear her scent like a badge of merit—"

Lash let out a sharp angry hiss, yet his next words were casual and calm. "I want to relish her scent on me, so I can always remember how good she felt under me, how she cried out so softly—"

"Get out!" Devlin shouted furiously. "Shut up and get out!"

Lash didn't reply, his footsteps coming towards me. As he opened the bathroom door, my clothes in one hand, Devlin tried to come in past him. Lash gave him a sudden shove backward, knocking him sprawling.

"Sar," Lash hissed sharply. "Shower fast and put these on. Open the door when you're ready; I'll be right outside." He shut the door hard.

Devlin said something in a low voice. Lash angrily hissed something back to him, but it was either in another language or so soft I couldn't make it out.

It didn't matter anyway. I had bigger problems to handle, like how to ensure once I left Hayden that I never had to come back.

* * * *

"You look nice," Lash hissed softly, startling me.

We were in his truck heading to Danial's, him driving and me running scenarios through my mind, none of them good enough to warrant a plan of action.

I nodded, unwilling to confront him about the clothes he'd picked out for me; the tan duster, black jeans, and dark brown top. At least the underwear had been white cotton.

"We don't have to go to Danial's immediately," Lash continued. "If you want a while to get yourself together, that is."

I glanced in the side mirror. My face was blotchy, my eyes bright green, evidence of a good cry not quite done. "No, it's okay."

Lash suddenly pulled in to a bank's empty parking lot, and shut off the truck. He turned to me. "No, it's not," he hissed softly. "But there's nothing I can say that'll make you feel better."

"No," I said brokenly, starting to cry again. "There is nothing you can say."

"Then take us back to the Everglades," Lash hissed quickly. "It will be warm there. We can sit awhile in the sun."

I blinked at him in disbelief. "What?"

"You need to get lost for a while," he replied, cracking a smile. "And I would love some sun. Danny can wait a few more hours for you to answer his email." He held out his hand. "C'mon. The weather down there has got to be paradise next to this late winter shit."

I used one hand to wipe my eyes, and grasped his warm hand in the other. Instantly we were there, the sun's heat and light engulfing us immediately.

Lash led me past the park office to an empty spot of grass. Taking off his long black coat, he spread it on the ground, then plopped down on it. I took off my duster, already sweating, and sat down beside him.

The sun's warmth felt wonderful. I closed my eyes and basked in it, not talking. Lash shrugged out of his overshirt, made a pillow out of it, and stretched out on his back with a groan. I waited a few moments, then did the same, quickly flipping over on my stomach to hide my eyes from the bright light.

"If I notice you burning, I'll tell you," Lash hissed. "You'll be more sensitive to light. Your lasting youth comes with a price."

I didn't answer, looking off to the shoreline. The slight waves relaxed me. It was a beautiful day, not a cloud in the sky. There was a gentle breeze off the ocean. Some tourists were walking on the paths, taking pictures of the pelicans and a group of four anhingas, a type of water bird that was basking in the sun as they dried their feathers.

I thought for a long time about what to do and came up with nothing that made any sense that I also could live with. In my desperation, I looked over at Lash and suddenly was tempted to ask him to bite me.

There was only one way to run away and stay free; enlist him to help me. He'd wanted to make me snake last night. The only problem was his two reasons he'd spoken for not doing it were still in force. He'd refuse if I asked him. I'd have to startle him somehow and get him to inject poison so he'd be forced to turn me or let me die...

Letting out a huge sigh, I sat up and told myself to stop the crazy daydreams. There was no running away with Lash. I had to face this and find a solution.

Lash stirred. "Ready to go?" he asked, not opening his eyes.

"Not remotely."

"Then lie down and rest," he hissed. "You were up most of the night. Think of nothing but your body being relaxed. Let the sun warm you. You'll feel better."

I stretched out on the warm grass, and closed my eyes. For a short while my mind raced. Before long I fell asleep, lulled by the warmness of the day and the heat of the sun.

When I awoke, the shadows had lengthened, and there was a chill in the air. Lash and I were wrapped around each other, lying half on his coat, half on the grass mixed with dew. I burrowed closer to him, trying to get warmer, then dragged my duster over my shoulders.

"I'd like to stay, too," Lash hissed in my ear. "But we have to leave. Danial expected you hours ago.."

I blinked my eyes, then groggily got to my feet. "Why didn't he find us?"

"We were lucky," Lash hissed, yawning. "There are tracking devices in our cell phones. Devlin likely doesn't know we didn't arrive. But he will soon, if we don't get back and Danial calls him. I don't need the bullshit I'd hear about that and neither do you."

Tracking my cell had been how Devlin found me the night I'd been taken. "Why on your phone? I understand mine, but—"

"It's a standard feature," Lash hissed, slipping into his shirt and coat. "I removed mine right after I was given the phone, though keep that to yourself. I just thought I should remind you that if you run from Devlin, Sar, you can always be found."

"And it will be you that comes for me, won't it?" I accused.

"Probably," Lash hissed, offering his hand.

I shot him a glare, then teleported without taking it. Lash grabbed my hand before I could vanish, appearing beside me in Danial's great room. Danial was there, pacing the floor, talking into the phone angrily.

"You can calm down," I said loudly, my voice reverberating. "I'm here."

Ghost and Darkness came barreling into the room and jumped on me immediately, almost knocking me down.

"Down!" I said firmly. They obeyed grudgingly, whining, their tails wagging. "Someone has been letting you get away with bad behavior," I teased, crouching down and hugging them, running my hands in their thick fur.

Danial hung up and strode over to me, annoyance radiating off him like heat. "Where have you been?" he said stridently.

"With—" I looked around for Lash, but he was gone.

"You left Hayden back around noon. It is now past five," Danial said. "I repeat; where have you been?"

I ignored him and went into the kitchen. After skipping breakfast and lunch, I'd be damned if I started working without eating first.

"I asked you a question," Danial said quietly, his fury obvious.

"With Lash," I answered, opening the fridge. "I needed time to think things over. I have to make some choices."

Danial waited a moment, then cautiously replied, "What things?"

"Devlin blew up and demanded I live with him," I said wearily. "He said I could see you and Theo on the weekends—"

"Over my dead body!" Theo said hatefully from the doorway. "You are not living with him, Sar! You are—"

"Shut the hell up!" I screamed, making both Theo and Danial jump. "I need solutions, not blustering orders." I turned to Danial. "That's your business, isn't it; finding solutions? Either help me find a way out of this or get the hell away from me!"

Theo and Danial left at once, the scrape of chairs in the dining room telling me they hadn't gone far. When I'd made my lunch, I brought it in to join them.

"—I was afraid he would do this eventually," Danial finished. "He—"

"Sar doesn't want to live with him and I don't want her there," Theo interjected. "But I'm worried to have her home with me. I still haven't tracked down Robert. Karl's men have also kept their heads down—"

"She can stay here with me for now," Danial said decisively. "Samuel will not act against a fellow Ruler, not with us being Oathed." He looked over at me, then back at Theo. "Both of you go home and pack anything important. I'll have the foxes watch your house for you."

Theo shrugged. "Maybe that would work, but where would we sleep? We could sleep in the basement, but you'd need to feed some evenings. I suppose we could sleep at the were compound—"

"Sar will stay with me in my bedroom, as she always has," Danial said, his eyes on Theo. "You are welcome to stay there as well."

Theo's eyes got huge. "What are you saying?"

"Theo, close your mouth. We are not going to be having sex," Danial said patiently. "I don't wear pajamas," Theo said, blushing hotly.

I bit my lip, trying not to laugh.

"I have some you can borrow for tonight," Danial offered. "We only need bottoms anyway."

Theo blushed harder, and looked at the floor.

Danial rolled his eyes. "Theo, for all the times I saw you coming in at four in the morning after you had changed form in my forest, you think I don't know what you look like naked? You've seen me naked, too, on occasion. Just because we're in bed doesn't mean something is going to happen—"

But Danial wanted something to happen with the three of us; it was obvious. Not that the thought wasn't interesting. Now that Devlin had made us realize the possibilities, we'd both found that we enjoyed experimentation. But that possibility wasn't something Theo needed to face right now. We had more important things to think about besides fantasies.

"We should all be clothed," I interjected, coloring. "I don't need to have any temptation, Danial. If we all have some clothes on, it will be that much easier for everyone."

"You should leave as soon as possible," Danial urged. "We can discuss night clothes later."

"Is Terian back?" I asked, carrying my dishes to the kitchen. "We need his help—"

"He is, but he's no match for Titus," Theo replied. "Just like I'm no match for that snake."

It was on my lips to tell them that Lash was dying, that Theo might be able to beat him now in a fight. But I said nothing, remembering how he'd broken Vince's neck and bit Kev. Lash might be failing, but he was still deadly enough to kill Theo.

"Go," Danial commanded. "I'll contact Terian. Speed is of the essence."

* * * *

Four hours later, Theo and I were on the road back to Danial's in separate cars, having left Ivan and Janice in charge of our home. I was lost in thought, replaying the scene at our house when we'd arrived.

Theo had been teasing Ivan for Janice's nickname for him, Van. Janice had countered with a dig at Theo's full name, Theopolis, leading Theo to reveal that his mom had been reading a religious book about Ireland, researching his family roots when she was pregnant. That had led to a brief foray into babies names and how activities during pregnancy influenced them. Suddenly the conversation had ceased, Janice and Ivan no longer meeting my eyes. I didn't know if it was because one of my babies was Devlin's or because of Lash. I'd blurted some thanks for them watching our house, and then they'd left to get lunch in town.

What had bothered me most was that the packing hadn't made me emotional at all. I'd been gone so much these past few months that no place was home anymore. But my pets would be there; all three cats were in stacked cages beside me on the seat meowing loudly. Theo, Danial, and my children were there. That was my family. That was all that really mattered.

Chapter Ten

The minutes dragged by as I followed Theo in the truck to Danial's. Desperate to assuage my depression and the loud cat pleas for release, I flipped on the radio.

...your love is like a shadow on me all of the time....

Bonnie Tyler's *Total Eclipse of the Heart*. I'd loved this in high school. I turned it up.

Once upon a time, I was falling in love, now I'm only falling apart.

There's nothing I can do, a total eclipse of the heart.

Once upon a time there was light in my life, now there's only love in the dark...

I flipped it off, irritated. "I don't remember those lyrics. Some love song." I rode the remainder of the trip in silence punctuated by loud meowing.

As we pulled into Danial's long driveway, it began to snow. Winter was reminding us that it was still in control. There would be a few hard months before we found ourselves in the warmth of spring.

How had so much gone so wrong? I'd thought having Theo, Danial, and Devlin would be paradise, had even wished for it last fall and winter. I'd wanted Devlin to really want me, for Theo to leave Tasha and come back to me, for Danial to drop Monica, and love only me. I'd gotten my wishes, all of them, and the reality was nothing like I'd thought it would be.

I pushed my thoughts aside, angry with myself. It was past time to stop griping, and start taking control of my life back. I'd share it with whomever of the guys was willing to accept my terms. I knew I could count on Danial, if not Theo and Devlin. He and I could handle this, so long as we stood together.

* * * *

Hours later, I put the last shirt away and sighed with relief. Danial's dressers were bulging with the clothes Theo and I had brought, but everything had fit. Theo's hand-carved chairs were now in the great room, giving it a rustic touch. My cats Jesse, Cavity, and Ash weren't fighting with Briar, though Briar had seemed leery of Ghost and Darkness. The Cougar and the Woman were safe in the corner cabinet with Theo's other carvings.

"Do you feel like a late dinner?" Theo asked from the doorway.

"Yes," I answered. "Can you make some sandwiches? I'll be right out."

Halfway through my sandwich, my mind began to wander off Theo's chitchat. All I could think about suddenly was that I'd rather be eating my sushi back at Hayden.

"—I'll be gone tomorrow," Theo continued. "If you want, I could pick up some new DVD's or books for you."

Maybe I should call Dev. He'd been so angry and jealous over Lash. He'd just reacted like he had because of that.

"I know you have a lot of email work, but I'll try to schedule my meetings so we—"

Dev would be so happy if I called him. I could imagine his rich voice laughing, and teasing. He loved me. *Maybe it wouldn't be so bad, if I lived with him...*

"Danial!" I shouted, making Theo jump. "Come here quick!"

There was several thumps on the stairs, then Danial appeared. "What is it, Love?" he asked, coming to me. "Do you have contractions?"

"I need your blood!" I said frantically. "Quick!"

"Why?" Theo said, leaping to his feet. "What's happening?"

"Devlin's blood is working on me, calling me back to him," I said, my eyes wide in fear. "I need Danial's blood to keep me rational—"

"Won't his work the same way in you?" Theo said quickly.

Danial leaned down and kissed me deeply, opening his mouth on mine. I kissed him back desperately, not caring that Theo was watching. A sweet coppery taste flooded my mouth laced with an undercurrent of spice, that same hint of nutmeg I often smelled on Danial's skin.

In a few seconds the taste vanished, and Danial broke the kiss. "Do you still want to go to him?" he asked.

I closed my eyes, examined my feelings, and then opened my eyes with a snap. "Yes. And I know why. He's been careful to give me his blood as often as possible and as much as possible since Christmas. It was his intention all along to keep me in thrall to him with his blood!"

"Then how'd you break his thrall now?" Theo began suspiciously.

Danial's eyes tinged red, and he kissed me again, harder, his tongue delving deep into my mouth, the spice no longer a trickle, but a torrent. I swallowed over and over blissfully. Danial suddenly went to his knees, pulling me down to the floor with him as my chair fell over with a crash.

"Stop," Theo growled. "You've given her enough!"

The thought raced across my pleasure-laden brain that he was right. Danial should be stopping me. But I didn't want him to. *Not ever...*

The torrent slowed abruptly. I burrowed into Danial's lips with mine, trying to get more.

Danial broke away, pushing me back from him. "Stop, Sar! Stop!"

Groggily, I got to my hands and knees, then started towards Danial. Theo grabbed hold of me.

"Let—ahh!" I snarled, falling back to land on my ass.

"No," Danial whispered fearfully.

"Danial, what have you done?" Theo said in a strangled voice, staring at me.

"Sarelle, go look in the mirror," Danial ordered. "Now."

At least he didn't sound afraid anymore. I got up and went into the bathroom, the bright light making me wince. My reflection wasn't a surprise to me: luminous skin, bright green eyes, and dark pink lips with blood on them. But when I went to wipe the blood away, I cut my lip.

I opened my mouth hesitantly, bracing myself for fangs. But my teeth appeared normal. A casual light touch that sliced open my finger reveled they weren't. My teeth were as sharp as Danial's now.

Rationalizing that this was the price for being lucid, I grabbed a pen and paper from Danial's night stand and went back out to Theo and Danial.

"I'm fine," I wrote. "This is how I looked at first when Devlin saved me. My teeth are sharper, though."

"I felt them," Danial said with a faint smile. "You bit me, trying to get more of my blood."

"Sorry," I wrote, then squeezed his hand.

"Do you feel him calling to you now?" Theo asked.

I shook my head, then wrote, "Ask just yes or no questions, please."

"Tell me if that changes," Danial said. Giving me a light kiss on the cheek, he went back upstairs.

I thought about whether I should write a note that told him I'd help him tomorrow, then let out an irritated sigh.

Theo came over to me and took my hand in his. "Are you sure you are okay?"

I nodded, then pointed back at our uneaten food. Theo nodded, and we went back and resumed eating.

That didn't last long. I bit myself a few times on the tongue on my first few tries. Irritable, I'd given up and fed the sandwich to Ghost and Darkness, who had gobbled it down greedily, wondering how much harder eating would be if I'd grown a true set of vampire fangs. The cuts had healed almost immediately, but they'd hurt a lot.

Motioning I was going to bed, I left Theo with his third sandwich and went into Danial's bedroom. Lying down on his bed, I let myself drift into sleep.

Sometime later, Theo woke me when he entered. "I hope you feel better," he said, coming to sit beside me. "You had a rough night."

I made a face carefully and nodded.

"I talked to Elle; told her we'd be staying here for a while. I told her it was because of Robert, but I think she knows I left something out."

Someone, you meant. I nodded again, then patted his hand.

Danial came into the bedroom and shut the door. "Any change?"

Theo shook his head.

Danial walked to the dresser, opened a drawer, and then tossed a pair of pants to Theo, taking out one for himself. He began to undress.

Theo dropped my hand, got up, and went into the bathroom.

Danial put on the bottoms, and then got into bed. "Come to bed when you're ready, Love."

I took off my clothes, got into a long flannel nightgown that covered everything, and then went into the bathroom to brush my teeth. Theo was sitting on the toilet, looking like he was sixteen and about to take his first driver's test. The silk pants were in his hands.

"Why'd he give me red?" he whispered. "I hate red."

I wanted to laugh, but didn't. I made motions with my hands that indicated there was nothing to be done about the situation, and went about my business.

"What if I touch him in the night?" Theo whispered.

I gave him a look that said there were many more important things to be worrying about.

"I don't want him to touch me!" Theo said, making a face.

I snorted with laughter, then sighed and took out my pen and paper. "Look, it is obvious neither of you are gay!" I wrote, "What are you afraid of? Danial is not going to seduce you. You know him, you've been friends for years."

Theo took the pen and paper. "But I can see this turns him on," Theo wrote back. "He likes the idea of us together in bed."

He was writing his response because he hadn't wanted Danial to overhear his words. "So what if he does?" I wrote. "You're an adult who can make choices."

Theo looked at me in shock. "Do you like the idea?" he wrote, adding three question marks.

I wanted to tell him that Devlin had, but decided that would be cruel.

"Theo, until the children are born, nothing is going to happen," I wrote. "We can discuss this in the morning, when I'll hopefully be normal again."

Theo gave me an uneasy look and sat down on the edge of the bathtub, pants still in hand. He made no move to get undressed.

I was too tired for this. Giving him a kiss on the cheek, I patted his arm with my hand and left.

Danial was waiting beneath the covers. I slipped in beside him, and he turned and embraced me, snuggling close. "I heard you talking," he said softly. "This was why I didn't want him to know, Sar. I worried he would be uncomfortable around me if he knew."

I was not getting the paper and pen again. "You showed him pics of you and Dev with women years ago," I managed, talking very, very slowly.

"Seeing pictures is one thing. Actually being in bed together with a woman is another."

I nodded, then closed my eyes to tell him I was done talking for the night.

For once, Danial didn't take the hint. "I must tell you something," he whispered.

My eyes snapped open. Whatever this was, it was serious. I turned to face him, expectant.

"I wasn't here for Christmas," Danial said. "I expected with your curious nature that you would ask me about it, especially after all your questions on our trip to Letchworth. I feel awkward bringing this up, after so much time has passed. But I wanted to tell you I was sorry that I had missed Christmas with you, that I hadn't been there myself to give you the earrings and the poem."

Reluctantly, I reached for the pen and paper. Danial handed them to me.

"Well?" I wrote, then crossed it out, flushing at my bluntness. "You were on a job," I wrote. "I assumed it was dangerous, too dangerous to come home?"

Danial nodded. "A demon was being set by a corporate climber to knock out competition. I was hired only to discover who. But when I knew the real cause, I couldn't turn the information over to the client, who had no idea how to handle a demon."

I waited, expectant.

"Terian tracked down the demon, and helped find it's human master. Then I called in a professional to handle things."

Did I want to know anymore? And why was Danial telling me all this now? "Is the demon alive?"

Danial shook his head. "The professional was as good as his references made him out to be. I tell you this now because I'm not sure that demon won't show up again someday. While almost all demons stay far away from those who they knew when they were last out of Hell, a few sometimes come looking for revenge. Terian received word today that this demon has been summoned out of hell. I wanted to warn you, just in case. If you feel blackness, don't assume it's Terian."

"Titus said the same thing," I wrote. "I'll be on my toes."

"Good," Danial said, taking the paper and pen from me. "Terian has wards in place, so no full demon except his father can teleport here. But it pays to have everyone aware. You were my last to be warned." He paused. "I would not have let anything keep me from Christmas with you if I could help it, Sar. I needed you to know that."

I squeezed his hand, then kissed his cheek, telling him I knew that.

Theo was in the bathroom for so long, I fell asleep waiting. Danial nudged me gently when he finally appeared an hour later.

Theo looked to die for. The red pants had been made to be loose-fitting on Danial, who was much less bulky. In short, they clung to my husband in all the right places, the outline of the little they hid visible by the bathroom light. Theo's chest was bare, the deep V of his chest hair shining in the light. His muscles rippled as he leaned in and turned off the bathroom light, cloaking him in darkness, then he padded towards us barefoot.

"I feel your heart racing, Sar," Danial said seductively, excitement in his words.

Theo stopped still.

"Get in here, Theo," I said, praying that The Lust didn't take this moment to show itself.

Theo took a deep breath, let it out slowly, and then got into bed. But he stayed over near the edge, and didn't come near us.

"Theo, I'm not going to bite," Danial said, mirth in his words. "You can come closer to Sar, if you want."

"I'm fine where I am," Theo squeaked.

"Suit yourself." Danial pulled me a little closer to him, and then relaxed.

I touched Theo on his shoulder with my fingertips, making him jump. When he saw it was me, he turned over on his side facing me, and put his hand in mine.

* * * *

When I awoke, the dynamic had changed. I was now in Theo's arms, clasped tight against his chest. We were in the middle of the bed, where we usually slept when we were in our own bed. But we weren't alone. Danial was behind me, his body pressed to my back, his arms also around me underneath Theo's.

Danial felt me wake, and woke up. He kissed my cheek. "Any change?"

I carefully probed my teeth with my tongue. "Back to normal," I said, relieved.

"Then wake him up," Danial said wickedly. "I'm dying to see his face."

I leaned up a little and kissed Theo. "Theo," I said softly.

He didn't stir.

I kissed him again. "Theo, there's bacon."

Theo shifted, but didn't open his eyes. Then he said sleepily "I don't smell any, Sar."

"I'll make you some, if you let me up," I said, trying hard not to burst out laughing.

"No," he said, squeezing me and Danial. "I want you to stay here with me. I missed you. I want you. I know we can't do the normal way, but we could—"

"Theo," I said stridently. "We are not alone."

Theo's eyes flew open, registering he was holding both Danial and I. He pushed back hard with his arms, trying to get away.

Danial moved fast, his hands clamping on Theo's arms to hold him where he was. "Careful," Danial said sharply, holding him still. "You may hurt Sar in your fear of me."

Theo was breathing hard now, clearly afraid. "Let me go."

"No," Danial said patiently. "We need to get past this." He paused. "I'm not going to touch you as I touch Sar. When I and Devlin were together with her, we touched her together, not each other. There is nothing for you to be afraid of. I have never wanted a male lover. I'm not about to change after four hundred and twenty some years."

"Then why does the idea of you and I sharing Sar together excite you so much?" Theo replied. "I can smell that it does."

"I liked what Devlin and I did together with her," Danial replied. "I liked it very much, much more than I expected to. I have shared women with Devlin before, but never one that either of us loved. It was just sex, and it wasn't that good, not for me, anyway. But being with he and Sar was different." He paused. "What we did that night, I...I'd never done it before. I hadn't known how good it could be, watching another man make love to her, and helping him love her. I saw what it did for Sar, how much she loved what we did to her." Danial paused again. "At my age, there is very little that is new, especially in love or sex. That this was so good and I'd never known of it...well, I'm looking forward to next time." He glanced over at me. "If Sar in interested, that is."

"I can tell she is," Theo growled, either from jealously or from my not being on his side. "But why me and not your brother?"

"You are like a brother to me. I think it would be as good with you as it was with Devlin. Maybe better even, because I know how much you love her."

My love for Theo aside, I didn't agree. Devlin had been the ringmaster of our threesome, maneuvering us all masterfully. The reason it had been so good was that he had been the one in control. But I didn't say any of that.

"Why do you really object?" Danial continued. "Your views on sex have never been Biblical."

"I just...I just never considered it," Theo whispered. "It seems immoral to me. It seems wrong somehow."

"If it's something we all want, I don't see how it's wrong. We both love her, and she loves us. Who are we hurting by doing this with each other?"

"No one," Theo whispered reluctantly.

"Then please consider it," Danial said, letting Theo go and gently moving me aside so he could get up. "Not until after the babies are born, and Sar's well enough for it. But perhaps then, if you are interested, we might try it."

Theo moved to the far side of the bed and didn't answer.

Danial put on his bathrobe, and turned to us, fastening the tie. "You said you wanted her, Theo. I'm going to use Elle's shower. She and Theoron are at their lessons by now. No one will hear you, including me." Danial got some clothes out for himself, gave me a passionate kiss, and then left, closing the door gently behind him. Once his footsteps receded, all was quiet.

Theo's expression was petrified. I reached out and grabbed his hand. "Relax. There's no pressure. You don't have to do anything you don't want to, and I mean here with me now, too."

Theo turned and kissed me gently. "You can talk. Your teeth aren't sharp anymore," he said, very relieved.

"Good thing, too," I said with a smile. "I'd make a bad vampire. I'm very bad at being careful." My smile became suggestive. "And you'd be out of luck."

"Say it for me," Theo said lustily, pulling me close.

"As many times as you want me, Theo. As many times as you want me."

* * * *

Feeling sated and stuffed with bad breakfast food, I made my way up the stairs to Danial's study. Terian and Danial were both hard at work at their computers.

"What first?" I asked. "How many emails are we up to?"

"I've done the more pressing ones," Terian answered. He gestured to some piles on a small desk. "We set that up for you to use."

Making a fake cheery face back at him, I got to work. "How was your trip out west?"

"Good," Terian answered, flashing me a smile.

He looked better than good, he looked more relaxed than I'd ever seen him, as if a weight had been lifted from his shoulders.

An hour later, Terian shut off his computer and got up.

"Quitting early?" I teased.

"I've been working since eight a.m.," he replied, smirking. "Despite all the disturbances."

He had heard Theo and I. "I hope we kept you entertained," I said drolly.

He laughed, nodded, then left.

Danial also got up from his computer, grabbing a few papers from beside his desk.

"You leaving, too?" I asked

"My donor is downstairs waiting," Danial answered. "I've left the internet window open, so when you're done filing, you can begin answering emails. You already know what to do; the only new thing is that we have a new signature for you that includes the web address. I've logged you on, so that will be automatic."

"I'm almost ready to switch to that," I said. "I'll see you later tonight."

Danial gave me another kiss on the cheek, and then left.

A few minutes later, I began to go through the emails for Solutions, Inc. There were a bunch of good leads. I printed off at least thirty emails, and then gave them case numbers. There were more than a few that were junk, so I deleted them. As usual, there were also a few that had to be sent to Devlin.

As I attached them all to one email to him, I wondered what Dev did exactly with everything I sent him from Solutions, Inc. He'd had all these meetings this week, but who was he meeting? Devlin had credited his vast wealth to his investments. He'd initially been given this branch of the business by Danial in an attempt to get back some of the respect and fear power he'd lost when Danial had disposed him as Ruler, not for the money it would bring in. Now as the new Ruler of Canada, Devlin no longer needed additional respect. Devlin also never had indicated he was working these cases at all, so who was? Lash?

I reclined back in the chair, puzzling over this mystery. Danial had said once that Devlin was handling the work we sent his way very well, without a lot of bloodshed. I'd just accepted that vague answer at the time, because back then I'd been happy not to know. But things were different now.

What was going on? Had Dev been killing people those nights he had left me to go out? If he had, were they justice kills, righting wrongs? I remembered Devlin's answer to Danial at stake point years ago, telling him that he'd take care of Danial's hits for the Italians, so Danial wouldn't have to do them anymore. Had Dev paid off the mob or had he been killing people for them? If he had, what had happened to that arrangement when he'd left for Rio, then reappeared here months later?

Where did Lash fit into all of this? He had to be involved somehow; likely he did some of the contract killing. But why do them for Devlin, not for himself? Did Devlin approve them for him? Did they split the money? That seemed unfair to Lash, if he did all the work. That bitter comment about being told what to do all the time had been important and meaningful. So had the ease with which Lash had disposed of Kev and Vince, two trained and powerful men much younger and in peak shape.

Where did Titus fit here? He seemed too nice for contract killing. Yet if he ate people, that was way too generous an assumption, even if he was a relatively good demon.

The nights Dev had gone out, he'd worn suits half the time and jeans the rest. Had he been doing jobs on the casual nights, and meeting clients on the dressy ones? Or had he been collecting payment in jeans and killing more upscale people in a suit? Or was this all just a bullshit smokescreen and he'd been meeting a woman—or women—to satisfy himself? I knew Dev's appetites; he'd been far too relaxed all week to not have had any sex.

Angry at myself for my sudden surge of jealousy, I focused again on the business end. Devlin had given me the filing to do. He'd said they were all of his records. So where were the business records: the cases, the expense reports, all of the details? I'd only found various employees' wage listings, old receipts for household expenditures, some handwritten investment records, and a whole lot of love notes.

I was having his child. If that child was in danger because of what Dev was doing, I needed to know. Now.

I picked up the phone and called his cell. The phone rang twice before he answered.

"Hi, Love," Devlin purred. "I've been missing you."

I didn't reply, debating what to ask first and how best to ask it.

"What have you been doing all day?"

"Cut the shit, Dev," I said calmly. "We parted on bad terms. Don't act nice to me now, just because you probably got laid a few minutes ago."

"I was not with anyone today, Sar," Devlin said gently. "I'm just happy to talk to you."

"So talk."

"I want to say I am sorry for how I said what I said—" Devlin began vaguely.

"So you aren't sorry for saying it," I stated.

"I want more than one child with you, if we have a girl first," Devlin said bluntly. "Things were going so well, I thought that you might like the idea. I know you haven't got to working on the nursery yet, though I liked the colors and suggestions you have been showing me—"

"Things were going well," I said coldly. "The word is 'were', Dev."

"I should have just told you the choker was fixed. I shouldn't have forced you to put it on. I am sorry I scared you."

"No, you aren't!" I said bluntly. "You have said that many times, and it's simply not true, Dev! You like my fear. And I don't like to be afraid of the people I love."

"Then you still do love me." Devlin's tone was relieved.

"Not enough to live with you," I said bluntly. "I'm staying here with Danial and Theo."

"Lash will be sad to hear that," Devlin teased. "He missed eating dinner with you last night."

I felt a pang then, because I did miss Lash. But not enough to come back to Dev. "He'll understand," I said firmly. "He saw how upset I was yesterday morning."

"I want you to come on Monday morning, and stay until Thursday afternoon. Danial talked to me last night about this. I am amenable to the idea, especially as you are safe at his house, and I won't worry about you so much when you are not here—"

This was probably the best deal I was going to get, but I wasn't agreeing just yet.

"—I'll send Lash to get you," Devlin continued. "Say about ten, or maybe a little later?"

"I'll agree to that for next week, on one condition," I said finally. "You and I need to talk, Dev."

"About what?" he said curiously. "I've always encouraged you to ask me anything."

"I need to understand your business better. What do you do with these cases I send you, for starters?"

"You should know that well," Devlin said, bemused. "You've sorted through a ton of my files."

"And found only employee records, tax stuff, lots of documents, and love notes enough to drown in—"

"There were not that many, Sar," Devlin said, laughing. "I went through them today. That file is cleared out for you now. I kept only a few important mementos. The rest I had Titus incinerate."

Not good enough. "Dev, you are talking around my question."

"Sarelle, haven't you gone through any of the white boxes? I was sure you had."

"What are you talking about—?"

"The white boxes are cases and other business records," Devlin said patiently. "The other boxes had everything else."

I hadn't known what the different colors meant. "I started doing the brown ones, because I thought they were all from the same period of time," I said. "I'll go through a white one next time I come."

"Monday. You can do it Monday. And if you have any questions, just ask me."

"Okay."

"Do you forgive me?" Devlin asked, very serious. "I didn't mean what I said, about Theo."

I took a deep breath. "Yes, you did. You'll threaten me again with it, probably."

"No," Devlin said tiredly. "I will not. There is no point. You know I won't do it. I'm too afraid of you hating me."

"You're right, I would."

"For all I wanted to be under your skin, it is you who have gotten under mine," Devlin whispered longingly. "I desire you more than anything. I lose my temper far too easily with you."

"No shit!" I said flatly. "It's not any fun to be on the receiving end of your anger, Dev, no matter that you don't actually hit me."

"I know," Devlin said reluctantly. "I have asked Titus to look into making something for me that would make me more…mellow, I guess is the word. At least for the time you and I spend together."

"Vampire Valium?" I asked, disbelieving.

"Something like that," Devlin said with a chuckle. "I keep apologizing, but even I can see that I'm not controlling my jealousy and possessiveness enough. I need to do something before I drive you away from me."

Had Lash been talking to him about this when I had been in the bathroom showering yesterday? Or had Titus or Danial said something to him? "That's a good step."

"I need to go," Devlin said suddenly. "But I'll call you later."

"When?" I said, looking at the clock. "It's six now. We'll be going to bed about eleven or so, probably."

"I heard you three were sleeping together," Dev said longingly. "I wish I could join you one night. Ask Danial, when you have a chance."

Was he kidding? "I'll ask him," I replied, knowing I would not.

"Good-bye for now, Sar. I'll call about ten-thirty. I love you."

Well, he was trying. "I love you, too," I said softly, then hung up the phone and got back to work.

I said to hell with work at eight. There was more to do, but I was exhausted. Besides, I wanted to see the kids before everyone went to bed. It was time for a little normalcy.

I walked downstairs. Theo was in the kitchen, making dinner. He looked very tired as he stirred the vat of Campbell's tomato soup, and flipped some grilled cheese sandwiches. Elle was talking to him, Danial and Theoron absent.

As I came into the kitchen, and took over from a relieved Theo, it occurred to me suddenly that this was how Theo had wanted our life to be; the three of us together, preparing a meal as a family. Then Elle asked me a question and the moment passed.

Danial and Theoron came in a few moments later, as I was serving dinner. After gulping her dinner, Elle asked, "Does anyone want to go for a walk?"

Theo promptly downed the rest of his. "Sure."

It had been a while since he had changed form. I declined, both to avoid the cold and give him the time to bond with Elle. Danial did also, saying he had to put Theoron to bed. Theoron protested, so Danial picked him up and carried him off, loudly protesting.

As I cleared the plates and loaded the dishwasher, Elle changed in her room. Theo let her outside in her lion form, then a moment later he was pawing at the door, looking at me expectantly. I let him outside, with a quick stroke of my hand over his fur. He gave me a throaty purr, and then bounded away. There was a roar, followed by an answering one in the darkness. I smiled and shut the door, locking it.

I went into tuck Theoron in and found Danial beginning a game of Peanut Butter and Jelly, Theoron's favorite, which my son quickly persuaded me to join. Theoron won over Danial, but only because Danial lost a turn on an unlucky role of the dice. I was way behind, Lion having eaten all my bread several times.

As Danial and I tucked Theoron in, I again had the odd thought that this was what Danial had probably imagined long ago for us: being with our son, spending time playing together, putting him to bed, and kissing him goodnight. Because this is what families did when they loved each other. This is what parents did, when they loved each other and their children.

Moved suddenly, I decided it was best to stay here until I gave birth, at least. I hadn't planted a garden yet back at my house. I would plant one, but it would be here at Danial's home. At the end of the summer, maybe Theo and I would stay here with Danial. We were safe here. Theoron and Elle were growing fast; I was missing their childhood, being anywhere else but here. I would never get this night back. If not for Robert, I'd have been home with

Theo. Neither of us would be with our children here, only with each other. I had to take this opportunity and so did he, before it was gone.

After we said goodnight, I walked with Danial out to the great room. "Would you like me to read to you?" he asked. "We haven't done that in a long time."

I made a face, then went down into the basement. "If you want to follow me as I do laundry." I walked to the machine, then began loading clothes. "How's Mary?"

"She's very sad," Danial said solemnly. "She's been taking her daughter to chemotherapy all week. There isn't much hope now."

Mary had been gone a lot in the last few months, as doctors tried many last-ditch efforts to save her daughter. Danial's house showed it. Though Cia was managing to keep the were compound clean somehow. I knew Janice was helping her when she could, but she was busy herself with the plans for her mating ceremony that was later in the summer.

"So you're going to turn her daughter?" I asked. "I know Mary talked to you about retiring before all this happened."

Danial nodded. "I've delayed hiring another housekeeper, being worried about security with Robert and Karl's threats. But if things go where they seemed to be heading, we'll have a new vampire housekeeper soon enough."

I nodded. Until this played out, I could certainly pitch in a little to help. It would probably be only a month or two, horrible and cold as that sounded.

As Danial helped me fold the dry clothes, I suddenly felt a kick. "One of the babies kicked," I said excitedly. "Danial, feel me."

Danial put down the shirt and came over to me, putting his hand on my abdomen. We waited a few minutes expectantly and nothing happened. The longer we waited, the surer I became that it had been a fluke. The baby was not supposed to be kicking this early.

Out of the blue I felt it again, a tiny flutter within me. Danial felt it, too, his face breaking into a wide smile. "I feel him, Sar," he said excitedly. "It's always so amazing, to feel that little kick."

As much as I was grumpy about it, there was one other who needed to share this news. Devlin wouldn't want to miss this. "Danial, do you mind if I teleport quick to Devlin's house to see if he's home yet?"

Danial looked at me carefully. "So long as you aren't going to be angry at what you might encounter there."

"Dev said that he was going out tonight," I said, very careful with my words. "He was probably seeing someone, I know. But he said he'd call me at ten-thirty. It's almost that now."

Danial nodded. "He's likely home then. Go ahead, Sar. Just call me if he's not there, and you are going to wait more than a few minutes."

"I'll be right back," I said, giving him a wide smile. "I'm too tired for a long talk, or anything else."

I teleported and ended up in the hallway before Devlin's bedroom. As I raised my hand to knock, Devlin cried out in pleasure from within.

"I know how much you like that, Dev," a woman said sexily.

Devlin spoke harshly, lust heavy in each word. "Get over here."

There was the sound of bodies moving, sliding across fabric. Then Devlin began to cry out repeatedly, in rhythm, a woman's voice joining him.

I knew what he was doing in there with her. But I had to see it for myself, to see with my own eyes how he'd lied to me, because even now I wanted to believe there was a reason. There had to be something more important than he'd just wanted sex, and didn't care about what he'd promised me so ardently.

I took hold of the knob, and twisted it slowly, opening the door inches at a time.

The room was dark, but the glow from the fire illuminated their bodies on his bed. Devlin was on top of the woman, her back to him, her long blond hair that was so like mine spread across the pillows. She was bracing herself on the bed, the whole thing rocking slightly with Devlin's vigorous movements.

He was thrusting hard into her, crying out with each thrust, holding her hips to his. Just like he had held mine, many times before.

I moved into the room slowly, shutting the door behind me. Leaning heavily against the wall, I watched them copulate, wanting to remember this, to hold onto my anger through the image, and never forget it. I wished then for a poisoned dagger to stab him in the back with, like he'd been stabbed so many years before. That woman had just been doing it for money. I had a better reason: he'd broken my heart.

Devlin thrust faster into her, and then came with a loud cry, jerking on top of her. She came, too, screaming his name in her passion.

"Dev! Oh Dev!"

Obviously, she knew him well. Or perhaps he asked all his lovers to call him that, so he could remember who he had fucked, and who was still on the "to do" list.

There was the sound of links sliding, and my choker with the bear emblem fell off my neck to land on my crossed arms. I looked at it in shock, and then back up at them, my fury building.

This was why it had fallen off. The excuse he had given me to explain it was bullshit.

"Was it good for you?" the woman said huskily.

He laughed low, and kissed her. "It's always good for me with you," he said, each words heavy with satisfaction. "Though I wish you would relent, and let us meet elsewhere."

"I want you here in the bed you turned me in, all those centuries ago," she whispered. "I want to pretend it's that night all over again. I loved you then, and I still love you, D—"

"Ah, Catherine, you're such a sentimental soul," Dev said with sarcasm. He chuckled, then made to move off her.

"I'm not done yet, lover," Catherine said, turning beneath him to face him. She saw me watching, but her eyes flicked over me without pause, giving Devlin no warning.

Her face had a resemblance to mine, though she was more buxom. She was also a vampire. That together bothered me. Had he been attracted to me because of her and their past?

Catherine reached down and squeezed his penis.

Devlin groaned. "Again, so soon?" he said, immediately aroused. "We have all night—"

"Do we? Doesn't your Oathed One expect you soon?" Catherine countered teasingly. "I wouldn't want her to be denied her fair share."

The bitch was playing some game, but for whose benefit?

"Not tonight," Dev said softly, then sighed. "I'll need to leave to call her in a few minutes. She's with Racklan."

"No, she's not," Catherine said with a grin. "She's over there, watching us." She cut her eyes to me, grinned, and then went down on Devlin.

Devlin froze, then looked over and saw me. His mouth fell open.

"There is nothing to say, so don't!" I yelled furiously, opening his bedroom door. "You won't be seeing me again, Devlin. Get your cock sucked as much as you want!"

"Sar, wait—"

I went to slam the door in his face, but he moved too fast, wedging his foot in the crack. I let the door go to teleport home and he grabbed my arm.

I couldn't teleport with him hanging onto me, unless I wanted to take him with me. That was the last thing I wanted. "Get your hand off me!" I hissed. "I can see how much sleeping beside me means to you. We've slept together all week, and you've only been content because you've been fucking someone else—!"

"You let *her* sleep with you?" Catherine said, shocked and hurt. "You've never let—!"

"I couldn't understand why it kept falling off!" I screamed, tears running down my face. "This is why! You broke your promise to me!"

"Sar, you weren't supposed to find out—"

150

"I found out, Devlin. We're done. Goodbye—"

"We will never be done!" he shouted harshly. "I love you. You're having my child—!"

"What are you talking about, girl?" Catherine said, coming towards us. "Dev took no oath of fidelity to you—!"

She was wearing my robe! Bitch! "Yes, he did!" I screamed, pulling the shreds of my pride together. "He promised to be with only me here. No other lover was supposed to share his bed here, you cunt!"

"Dev, is this true?" Catherine said coolly. "No wonder you came to me at my hotel all this week and wanted to take me to a hotel tonight instead of here—"

I headed for the stairs. "I don't need to be here for this!"

Devlin tightened his grip on my arm. "You are going nowhere!" he hissed. Then he turned to Catherine. "But you are. Get your clothes on and leave. Don't ever come back, Catherine. I never want to see you again."

"Bastard!" Catherine hissed, baring her delicate fangs.

Devlin tried to pull me back inside his bedroom. "Sar, come back inside, please—"

I held onto the doorframe with all my strength. "No. I don't want to see you ever again—"

"You never have to, girl," Catherine said with a smirk.

Chapter Eleven

Catherine's eyes flashed. "Dev promised to only be with you, to not have other women here in his bed. Is this true?"

"Yes," I grunted, still gripping the doorframe hard. "Yes."

"Shut your mouth, Catherine," Devlin growled, his eyes red tinged. He let go of me and started towards her. "I'll warn you just once."

"He broke his Oath to you, child," Catherine said gleefully as she backed away, her eyes glaring furiously at Devlin. "You're free of him. If the choker fell off, it recognized what he had done, that the Oath was irreparably broken—"

"Get her out of here, Lash!" Devlin yelled.

Catherine was yanked backward, snarling and struggling. Lash grabbed her hands, knotted them together in one of his, and began dragging her down the stairs. She was swearing at Devlin, and fighting, but Lash was stronger than she was.

I turned back to Devlin. "Let me go!" I demanded.

"No," he said, drawing me into his arms. "I love you, Sar. I just needed—"

"You don't love me, and you never did," I said slowly, deeply hurt. "I was a fool to think you could, that I meant anything to you."

"Don't say that," Devlin said raggedly, tears welling in his eyes. "You mean everything to me."

"Stop lying!" I screamed, and threw his choker at him. He caught it in his hand, snatching it out of the air.

"I want you to know something," I said hatefully. "You won't ever see this child, not ever. It's clear you aren't fit to be a father. Danial can help me raise him—"

"You can't keep me from my child!" Devlin roared, his eyes glowing red. "You have no right, Sar! How dare you even speak those words!"

"I have every right!" I screamed back at him. "You lie about everything,

Dev. All you know is seduction and sadism, and how to manipulate people! Nothing and nobody truly means anything to you, except maybe Lash."

Devlin glared at me, his face contorted and terrible in his anger. For a split second, I thought he might strike me. Instead he took his hand off my arm.

The second I was free, I teleported back to Danial. He was on the couch waiting. As soon as he saw my face, he hugged me. "Did you find him with someone?" he asked.

"Catherine," I said emptily. "He called her Catherine."

"She was the first woman he turned," Danial said. "I'm not surprised he was with her, though I am surprised he would choose to do that particular act with a vampire—"

"He was having regular sex with her, not oral sex. He broke his Oath to me."

Danial held me tighter.

"I confronted them, Danial. Catherine said I was free of my Oath, that it was broken."

Danial pulled back from me, his brow knit in confusion. "That's not true, Sar. Only Devlin can dissolve the Oath. And he would never—"

"She said that was why the choker fell off, Danial," I said accusingly. "That is why it's been falling off all week. That crap about rebalancing was just an excuse to cover up that he's been sleeping with her."

Danial abruptly sat me on the couch and headed to his study. "Stay here, please. I need to check something."

"What?"

"I need to know if she was telling the truth."

Was he going for his copy of the vampire law book? Must be, odd as it sounded.

I made myself some hot chocolate. The warm liquid soothed me, even as I berated myself for being a fool. At least Theo hadn't been here to see it. Once he knew, it was going to be one big "I told you so." And the worst of it was he was completely right: I'd been an idiot. I'd known exactly what Dev was, and I'd loved him anyway. I'd thought he'd change for me, that I'd be the one to tame him, when I was old enough to know better.

After finishing my cocoa, I went into Danial's bedroom, slipped into pajamas, and went to bed. Today had been bad. I wasn't giving it the opportunity to get any worse.

* * * *

Danial was shaking me. "Wake up, Love, please."

I blinked, then yawned. "What is it?"

"Sar, it's true," Danial said emptily. "You are free of him. The Oath is broken."

Relief crashed down on me. I sank back down on the bed and relaxed utterly. I didn't have to have any more children. I didn't have to go to Hayden tomorrow. I'd miss Lash and Serena, but not enough to go back there. Maybe Serena could visit me here. As for my friendship with Lash...I'd think about Lash another day. What mattered was I no longer had to do what Dev told me, or worry he wasn't happy. I wasn't bound to him anymore. I'd been so tense for so long. Now suddenly, my chief source of tension was gone.

Danial still was looking at me miserably in silence.

"I'm not free of you," I said, opening my arms to him. "And I wouldn't want to be."

"He accepted for me. There is a gray area, Sar, as he is the one you actually Oathed to."

"My choker with your symbol is still in place."

"I can see that, Love. But it doesn't mean the Oath we share isn't broken."

"I acknowledge your rights to me, Danial Racklan," I said softly, as formally as I could. "I Sarelle O'Connor, swear to you that I will take no other vampire lover, save you—"

"Save I and my brother," Danial said quietly.

I gave him a furious look, and stopped talking.

"Sar, he did it for me," Danial said apologetically. "I couldn't do less for him."

"Then you will have to stay in your gray area," I said flatly. "I'm not opening that door, Danial, now that I've finally been able to shut it. I'm not letting him back in my life."

"Sar, you love him," Danial said cajolingly. "He's the father of your child. There is no shutting that door, not now." He touched my shoulder, then slid his hand to my hip. "You have his mark beneath your very skin."

I turned away from him, and didn't answer. A few moments later, I felt him lowering himself carefully next to me in bed, so he could spoon me. "I'm sorry," he said softly, hugging me. "I'm just worried about losing you."

"You aren't going to lose me," I replied. "I'm going to need your help, Danial. When the dhamphir is born, I'll have to leave him with you until they are old enough for me to handle safely."

"What?" Danial said, shocked. "Dev can't have agreed, Sar. He's wanted a child of his own for so long—"

Who cared if he agreed? I sure as hell didn't. "Danial, we can't just let him take the baby, when he's so irresponsible. What if he decides he needs to have sex and leaves the baby alone?"

"He won't do that," Danial said patiently. "But in any case, I will not help you keep Dev's child from him. That is as blunt as I can say it. "

"You don't have to keep him away," I said stridently. "Just don't let him just take the child to Hayden. I'll never see it—"

"You will have to go there and visit your child," Danial said firmly. "And you will have to face Devlin. You are having a baby with him, and you are an adult, Sar. The baby will need him; need his guidance as its father. You don't need me to fight your battles for you, at least, not this kind of battle."

I didn't answer, fuming. As angry as Danial's refusal made me, without his help I'd have to let Devlin take the baby, and visit it at Hayden. The only possibility was that if Dear Dev screwed up enough, maybe Danial would come to his senses.

The phone rang. Danial picked up the phone. "Stay silent," he instructed me, then he pushed the speakerphone button and said, "Hello, Dev."

"I don't understand how this happened, Danial," Dev replied, his slightly distorted voice irritated. "I've never heard of a collar falling off before, not when it was the vampire who'd—"

"Dev, you broke your word," Danial said edgily. "Sar is within her rights not to see you for a while, if not to dissolve the Oath entirely."

"The actual Oath had nothing about other lovers for me in it," Devlin said quickly. "The Oath still stands. There must be some problem with the collar. I'll take it back to the jeweler—"

"Be as that may, it doesn't really matter," Danial retorted. "I've checked the laws. According to the choker, you broke your Oath. It couldn't bind Sar once you did. Every time you broke your word to her, it released her by falling off. She kept refastening it. By doing so, she was telling it that she accepted what you were doing. But now she has refused to refasten it. She gave it back to you, so she's not bound to you anymore, though the Oath to me still binds her."

"It does not," Devlin said dangerously. "Don't quote me law as if you know it all, you who have Oathed, what, three women in your four hundred plus years of life? I took her Oath. You were not even there to consummate it! I acted in your stead. You would never have dared to—"

"The same jeweler made the choker with my emblem, Dev," Danial said angrily. "Mine has never fallen off by itself. Never. At the least, Sar is marked as my lover. As such, it's within my rights to protect her, to make her happy. As she doesn't want to see you, I forbid you from coming here until she instructs me otherwise!"

"You could ask that she see me," Devlin said hesitantly. "By law, she has to, if you ask."

"I won't ask her to," Danial said coldly. "Sar will see you when she's ready to.”

“Danial, please—”

“Dev, you should have either never promised to be faithful to her, or you should've kept your word. I have no pity for you, not after how you acted. I'm sure you are very sorry now. You always are, *after* you've been thoughtless! But you never learn—”

“Danial, please tell me you won't keep me from my child,” Devlin said, panicked.

“You know I won't,” Danial said gently. “And I'll keep you abreast of any doctor appointments or developments. But Sar is not going to come to you, or stay with you at Hayden. Not this week. Maybe not ever again.”

Devlin didn't reply.

“And don't issue threats about telling Samuel,” Danial said flatly. “You would never want it known Sar was not Oathed to you anymore. We will not say anything, and I know neither will you. You love her too much to risk her falling into their hands.”

“I do love her, Danial,” Devlin said brokenly. He began crying. “So much it tears me apart.”

“I know you do,” Danial said gently. “But you got yourself into this. You will have to deal with the consequences of your actions.”

“Keep her safe,” Devlin said reluctantly. “And make sure you give her enough blood to keep her well. If she is not seeing me, she'll need you more than she has before.”

“I gave her blood last night,” Danial said easily. “She was radiant after, almost glowing. And her teeth got sharp, like mine. Would you believe, she actually bit me—”

Devlin made a strangled sound.

“What?’ said Danial.

“Don't give her that much again,” Dev finally got out. “You'll turn her, Danial.”

I almost let out a scream, but clapped my hand over my mouth.

“You said she could not *be* turned!” Danial shouted at the top of his lungs.

“I never said that!” Devlin yelled back at him. “I said she was not turning back in the fall. She wasn't turning when I saved her. No amount of sex can do it, it's true. But our old blood is potent, Danial. Sar is very resistant to the virus. Did you hear what I said? Resistant, not invulnerable. A massive amount could turn her. If her teeth got sharp, she was close—”

I gritted my teeth. *Why was it always Devlin who had to have the answers I needed?* Danial was just as old. What the fuck had he been doing all those years, that he hadn't learned any of this? Damn it!

I made myself breathe deeply. Not knowing wasn't Danial's fault; he'd only had the power to turn humans for a few years now. And he had never had a woman like Annabelle for a companion. Devlin knew most of what he knew regarding me because of her, and the decade or so they had spent oathed to each other.

Thinking that, I wondered what Anna had looked like. Devlin had said she didn't look like me, but it seemed important to know somehow. She had died hundreds of years before I was born, but she was responsible in a way for saving my life.

"I didn't know," Danial whispered, breaking into my thoughts. "I won't do it again."

"Are her teeth normal again?" Devlin said forcefully.

"Yes," Danial said.

"Watch her skin, as you give her the blood next time," Devlin commanded. "When it begins to get luminous, stop giving it to her immediately. You are much stronger than she is. Pry her off you, do whatever you have to, but don't give her that much again!"

"I won't," Danial said in a small voice.

"Now put her on," Devlin said commandingly. "I should warn her about this, too."

"Forget it!" Danial said loftily, his tone changing immediately. "I am not going to, not tonight. Sar's tired, and it's been a long day, besides her having to see you screwing around with your old flame." He paused. "I need to be going to bed, Dev," Danial continued slyly. "Sar is waiting for me. I can't wait to touch her soft, warm skin."

"You don't have to rub it in," Devlin said crabbily. "Call me tomorrow, and let me know how she is." He paused. "Call me every day, and let me know how she is."

"I will," Danial said gently. "Goodnight."

He hung up, then said, "Sar, I'm sorry. I didn't know about the blood."

"I didn't either. But we do now, and we'll be careful. Go to sleep."

Ten minutes later, both of us were still wide awake. "You sure couldn't wait to rub it in, that you were with me," I said teasingly, to break the oppressive silence.

"I couldn't help it," he replied, stroking my arm. "Dev always rubbed in when he was with you, and what he was going to do to—"

I reached down on impulse, and caressed him gently.

Danial let out a sigh. "Stop, Love," he said reluctantly, removing my hand from his swelling organ. "I meant what I told you. I don't want to endanger the babies. It isn't worth it, much as I'd like to."

"Danial," I said seductively. "There are other things we can do, besides that."

Danial looked at me in surprise. "We never did that, when you were pregnant before," he said, his voice already husky.

"Do I take that to mean you don't want to try doing it now?" I asked teasingly.

"Sar, we have done that as foreplay. We have never taken it all the way."

"Would you like to?" I began blatantly.

Danial was already out of bed, locking the door. He darted back to me, taking me in his arms. "Sar, you know I can't do the same for you because of my fangs. I might cut you. I'm sorry, but it's going to be pretty one-sided. Are you sure you want to continue, knowing that?"

I thought about telling him that I knew someone with fangs he could take lessons from, but decided it was better to hold my tongue. "I'm sure. Lay back for me."

"No," he said lovingly. "I want to kiss you for a while first, Love." He paused, giving me a meaningful look. "For what has the night to do with sleep?"

His intended purpose had been teasing seduction, yet I felt oddly that there was some other meaning as well. But the thought left my mind the moment his lips touched mine. Soon Danial was kissing me ardently, and I was burning up inside from the fire kindled from each feather light touch.

* * * *

In spite of Theo beginning the night positioned at the edge of the bed, the three of us woke up again the next morning holding each other. But Theo took it more in stride this time, though he remained uncomfortable. It helped that he was hurrying to make an appointment, and that Terian was already outside, waiting for him.

"Our first solo case meetings are in an hour and a half," Theo said as he put on his shoes. "I'll be back sometime this afternoon. Wish us luck."

I gave him an encouraging smile, hiding my worry inside. Theo was rash sometimes, and he didn't know how to finesse people. Terian had experience from running his online order business years ago, sure, but he hadn't dealt with many people face to face. There was a big difference between talking on the phone and meeting in person. But I didn't say any of that, not wanting to imply I didn't have utter confidence in them. They were both nervous enough.

I gave Theo a kiss. "Good luck."

I watched them drive off through the morning sunlight, feeling cheered by the good weather. It was supposed to be a nice day, sunny and clear. Hopefully spring was coming early this year. I'd had more than enough of winter.

I closed the front door and went into the kitchen. Elle and Theoron were there getting breakfast, Elle helping her brother. From the easy way she did it, I assumed that she did it most mornings. I was hesitant to help her, and instead just watched from the sidelines, eating my cereal and giving her points for how well she got him to keep moving without yelling.

Danial came in briefly and then headed up to his office, after giving us all a hug and a kiss. Afterward, I teleported Elle and Theoron to the were compound for their lessons. Their tutor had already arrived and was waiting. With a forced smile for me, he quickly hurried off with them.

His name was Bill Winger. Though he was very intelligent with a very impressive list of titles and degrees, he and I had never really hit it off. He tended to stare at my bite marks a little too much. I'd also seen revulsion on his face, though I wasn't sure if that was for the marks or because he knew what the choker meant and abhorred the custom. Danial had never seen the revulsion, or he would have fired him immediately. Yet I'd never brought it up to him, as Elle and Theoron both liked him immensely. Bill did his job well, with how much he had managed to teach them in the short years he'd been their tutor. For that I was willing to overlook the fact he was a jerk.

The morning flew by as Danial and I checked email and contacted clients. At noon, he took my mouse from my hand. "Why don't you take the afternoon off, and rest?" Danial said, giving me his now customary cheek kiss. "I have conference calls for the rest of the afternoon anyway."

This was a welcome surprise. "Are you sure?"

"Of course," he said, gently giving me a push towards the door. "Have some lunch, and take a walk. It's supposed to be a beautiful day, with highs in the high sixties. Elle and Theoron are taking a trip to the Alan's Creek Nature Preserve this afternoon with Bill, Brian and Demi. They won't be back for a while. Take a nap, if you want."

"You won't make me work harder tomorrow?" I teased.

Danial shook his head. "You're going to have to start taking it easier in the next few months anyway. Just tell me if you leave the grounds."

"Agreed," I said, flashing him a smile.

I went downstairs, thinking happy thoughts about sending one of the foxes for takeout. I checked the refrigerator, but nothing looked appealing. Takeout it was.

As I began dialing my phone, there was an odd noise out front. *Was someone yelling outside?*

I opened the door and looked out. Lash was there waiting, leaning against his truck, staring at me. Per usual, he was dressed all in black, his whip and knife on his belt. He didn't speak.

Despite my breaking up with Dev, and everything else that had happened, I was glad to see him. He'd been decent to me and I thought of him as a friend now. The intimacy we'd shared gave me a little pause, sure, but he'd always been decent about that, too. "Hi," I said in a friendly tone. "Why are you here?"

"I came to see if you wanted to go to lunch," Lash hissed.

I looked at him oddly. "You came all this way for that?"

"No," Lash hissed, opening his truck door. "I came also to give you your leftover sushi, before it spoiled, and to return your DVD." He handed both to me, the former in a small Styrofoam cooler. "I liked it so much I bought my own copy."

I took them from him. "Gnomes can be addictive," I said, smirking.

Lash smiled, baring one fang. "Yes, they can," he hissed.

"What did you have in mind?" I said awkwardly, remembering his special diet restrictions. "There isn't a sushi place near here."

"There is one now. It's near the movie theater now outside Alan's Creek," Lash hissed. "Tell Danny we'll be gone a few hours."

He hadn't just shown up, hoping that I wouldn't already have a lunch date. "You know Theo isn't here," I said slowly.

He nodded. "Yes, I know."

Was Brian still reporting to Devlin, or was it someone else here? Probably Brian. He was deathly afraid of Lash. If Lash had asked him a question, any question, Brian would have told him whatever Lash had asked him.

"First, assure me you are not here to try to kidnap me and take me to Dev," I said flatly.

Lash narrowed his eyes and said nothing.

"Tell me. Say it, and I'll believe you, Lash. But I need to hear you say it."

"Only lunch," Lash hissed. "Then maybe a short walk, if you are up to it."

"Then I'll be right back," I answered, turning and going back inside.

After stowing the sushi in the fridge, and marking it with my name so Theo wouldn't eat it all, I left the DVD on an end table and headed upstairs to Danial.

He was sure to throw a fit, and I was tempted to not tell him, to just come back in a couple hours with no one the wiser. But if something happened because of it, I'd kick myself later. Also, I wanted to meet Lash again for lunch in the future. Danial might not find out once, but he would if it happened twice. It was better to be up front and get it over with

Danial concluded the conference call as I entered. He hung up, and looked over at me, surprised. "Did you already have lunch?"

"Lash is here. I would like to go out with him to lunch."

Danial's eyes went red immediately, glowering. "If you are asking permission, the answer is no. He'll take you to Devlin—"

"I'm not asking permission," I retorted. "I'm telling you because I don't want you to worry, or think I'm somewhere I'm not. But I want to go and I'm going."

Danial gaped at me. "You *want* to spend time with him?" he said slowly. "Why? You can't enjoy his company."

"I surely do," I replied saucily. "He likes the same things I like—"

"No, Sar; take one of the foxes with you instead."

Time for the prepared speech. "Danial, if The Lust rises, I'd rather not do a complete stranger, or one of your employees. Now just tell me to have a good time and get back to your work."

Danial's eyes went red again, but he didn't speak.

"This is no big deal," I said more contritely. "I'll leave my phone on. We won't be gone long. A couple hours at most."

"If Theo was here, he would not let you go—"

"I know," I interrupted. "Just tell me it's okay already."

Danial looked at me out of the corner of his eye, raising an eyebrow. "Is there more to this, Sar?"

I flushed. "For all the bad things I've heard from you and Theo, Lash has never treated me as anything but his best friend's girl," I said hotly. "He could have easily made moves on me dozens of times, or tried to bring The Lust. He's never once tried to take advantage—"

"Go ahead then!" Danial said, throwing up his hands. "You will anyway."

"Thank you," I said curtly, and went downstairs. Danial didn't follow me.

It had taken so long with Danial I thought Lash might have left. But he was waiting, leaning against the truck. "Ready?" he hissed.

I nodded.

"Get in then," he said, opening his door.

* * * *

Lash was silent until we'd reached the restaurant and been seated. Even then, all he asked was what I wanted when the waiter came, his eyes fixated on the sake list. The place wasn't too crowded, being a Monday, but there were enough people there eating to encourage me that the restaurant might make it.

Lash said nothing for many minutes, his eyes never leaving me. That behavior wasn't outside the norm for him, though, so I just relaxed and enjoyed being out with someone who wasn't pressing me for anything, not even conversation. Most of the people I spent time with weren't quiet. Even Danial, the quietest of them all, was always on the phone, giving orders, or coordinating something. It was nice to share silence and not try to please anyone but myself.

When our food came, I noticed he'd gotten a few pieces of eel. "You branching out?" I asked.

"You liked it so much I wanted to try it," Lash said, making a face. "But no, I don't really care for it." He motioned to his plate. "Help yourself."

I wasn't turning down extra eel. "Thanks." I moved his pieces to my plate. "But why did you really come here?" I asked, giving him a smile with serious Don't-Bullshit-Me eyes.

"You know why," Lash hissed, eating a piece of salmon. "Devlin wants you to come back to him. I'm his best friend. It's my duty as such to come to you, and ask you to take him back."

I'd suspected this, but didn't want to believe it. "You want me to forget what he did?" I said, disbelieving "You've got to be kidding."

"I am," Lash said drolly, and then he laughed, baring his fangs.

I gave him a look to let him know he was being strange and to knock it off.

Lash leaned over the table. "Take your time letting him back in, Sar," he hissed. "You need to show him he can't treat you badly, and get away with it. That's understandable. I'm not saying what he did was okay. It wasn't. And you shouldn't forgive him quickly. He needs to earn your forgiveness."

I was feeling odder by the minute. "When you were angry…was it because you knew what he was doing?"

"I checked her for weapons before she went inside. I knew what she was there for," Lash hissed angrily. "It wasn't right—"

"Why do you care how he treats me?" I said, my eyes narrowing. "You didn't seem to care about how he treated Catherine. What's it to you?"

Lash gave me a long look. I held his gaze as long as I could, then looked down.

"Because you are having his child," he said finally. "You are risking your life, Sar, to do this for him. Dev made you promises. Promises should be kept, or never spoken at all."

"That's pretty profound of you—" I began sarcastically.

"But he does love you, Sar," Lash continued, talking over me. "Don't use this as an excuse to shut him out of your life forever. Give him another chance to make things right between you when you're ready. That's all I'm asking."

"I can't do that," I replied. "I had enough trouble trusting him the first time around. I don't think I can ever trust him enough to be in a relationship with him again. All I can think of is he and Catherine in bed together."

"You know he doesn't love her," Lash hissed insistently. "He never let her sleep beside him. I have never seen him let anyone sleep with him, save you.

162

Not even in the same room. Not in all the years I've known him."

Well, at least that part had been true. "So what? That doesn't give me a lot of comfort."

Lash regarded me silently for a moment, and then ate more of his sushi. I finished mine, and sat back, wondering if I should leave.

"Are you still hungry?" he hissed suddenly. "Do you want some of mine?"

He did have some avocado he wasn't going to eat. "If you don't mind."

"Please," he said. "Let me know if you want more."

I was tempted briefly to say I always wanted more, but decided that was way too inappropriate even for me. We weren't that close, even if my imagined retort had been pretty funny. "Thanks."

Together, we finished up the last of his platter. When the bill came, Lash took it.

"I am paying half," I insisted stubbornly.

He ignored me, giving the waiter a solid black credit card. "You are not paying," Lash hissed with authority. "I asked you and I am the man."

I rolled my eyes. *Another male chauvinist.* "Thanks for lunch then."

"Do you want to go for a walk?" Lash hissed. "It's a beautiful day. We have another hour until Danny sends out the trackers."

I couldn't help cracking a smile. "Sure, that's—"

Suddenly, it registered I'd heard my name in the hum of the people around us. I looked up with horror and saw Theo and Terian following a waiter to the table next to ours. They were smiling; their meetings must have gone well. I had a split second to think regretfully that this was going to ruin their day.

"Tears, you are going to love this stuff. Sar got me to try it, and it's wonderful—"

"Raw fish?" Terian said with disdain. "Can't we go and get Chinese food instead?"

"C'mon," Theo encouraged, laughing. "Where's your sense of—"

Everything happened at once.

Theo's blue eyes found Lash and me and held fast, the blue lightening and shifting to yellow. He went for his gun, but Terian grabbed hold of his arm. Theo shook him off with a growl, and kept coming. Lash was already on his feet, his whip unclipped, the thick coil in his hand. His other hand held his knife.

"Get away from her—"

"Stop it!" I said shrilly, causing the nearby patrons to dash for cover, screaming.

"Theo, not in the restaurant!" Terian shouted.

Lash alone said nothing, just waited for Theo with eager menace.

163

I had to stop this. Lash would hurt him, if not kill him. I reached over quickly, my hand closing on Lash's arm, and teleported us both outside near his truck.

"We're going to have to wait for another day to walk," I said anxiously. "Go, before he gets out here."

"I am not afraid of that cat, Sar," Lash hissed angrily. He uncoiled his whip and faced the restaurant entrance, his knife still in his hand. "Just stay out of the way."

"You are not hurting him!" I yelled angrily. "No one needs to fight."

Theo burst through the door and headed toward us. "Yes, we do," he said furiously, his words difficult to understand because his fangs had grown. He brandished a long survival knife. "Get away from her, you scarred son of a bitch!"

Lash got in front of me and braced himself. "Do you need another lesson on which of us is better with a blade?" he hissed. "I've given you quite a few over the years. But I think you need reminding."

Terian came up beside Theo, his eyes red, blackness boiling out of him. "Stop this!"

I got between Lash and them. "Yes, stop. Lash is leaving," I said, glaring at Theo. "We just had lunch."

"Why?" Theo growled. "You missing something you're not getting?"

Terian clapped his hand over Theo's mouth, flushing faintly.

I gave Theo a look of death, then turned back to Lash, resisting the urge to tell him to leave with me. "Please go."

Lash looked at me, and then back at Theo, obviously dying to wipe the parking lot with him. Instead he resheathed his knife, coiled up his whip, and clipped it back on his belt. "Be seeing you," he hissed politely, then his eyes came back to me.

Theo started for Lash again, and Terian grabbed hold of him.

Lash gave me a twisted smile, then got in his truck, opening the window. "Bye, Sar."

"Thank you for lunch," I said politely, resting my hand on his open window. "And for bringing me my stuff. Be safe going back."

"Thank you for coming to lunch with me," Lash said politely, his flat eyes holding mine.

Then he put his hand on mine, caressing gently, his tone shifting to insinuating. "I was glad you came."

My shock hit me like a slab of ice in July: Lash was trying to raise The Lust.

Theo let out a crystal-shattering roar. "Get your fucking hand off—!"

I took my eyes off Lash for a moment, turning to Theo. Lash used the opportunity to cup my head with his hand and yank me forward, his lips banging into mine. My lips parted in a gasp and he used that, too, his tongue sliding in to lick me playfully, a soft hiss of pleasure escaping.

For a moment, I lost myself in the kiss, remembering how good he'd been. Then reality crashed down and I pushed back from him. "What are you doing—?"

Lash pulled back in surprise, blinking.

Terian yanked me away, pulling me off my feet and out of the way as Theo's fist came right past my head to smash into Lash's face, knocking him back into the truck.

"Don't ever fucking touch her again!" Theo screamed, leaning in the truck window. He grabbed at Lash with clawed hands, trying to drag him out of the truck to beat the shit out of him.

There was a harsh click. Theo went still, then slowly leaned back out of the window, Lash's gun against his temple.

"You shoot him, Lash, and you're dead!" Terian growled, a ball of blue fire appearing in his hand. "I'll cinder you."

Lash's expression was livid as he wiped at the blood running down his face with his sleeve. "You fucking cat. You had to come in right then. You couldn't have waited another few minutes, picked a different fucking restaurant?"

Theo growled at him softly. When Lash didn't shoot, he growled louder.

Lash licked his welling blood off his cut lip. "I always let you live and what's it gotten me? Why don't you challenge me for real, Theo, so I can just kill you? Let's end this bullshit once and for all."

He was going to kill Theo. "Lash, please don't."

His eyes cut to me, looking at him in revulsion, and he eased the hammer up, then took the gun off Theo's forehead.

"As if she would let you have her again!" Theo shouted. "But you're just like your master. You don't care if she wants you, you know she doesn't! You would never have gotten near her otherwise, and you know it! You were going to try to force her today after lunch, when you were alone with her, weren't you? I think you planned the first time it happened, just to fuck with me! Hell you probably put those bears up to grabbing her, for the same reason—"

That wasn't true, none of it. I'd been the one who'd gone after Lash. He'd done everything he could to avoid my advances. He'd never have forced me, never. But instead of standing up for him, I looked at the ground, ashamed.

Lash's eyes slid off Theo to me, then back to Theo. "Don't disrespect her, Cat."

"Stay away from her," Theo finished. "You come to Danial's again, and I'll kill you."

"And I'll help him," Terian added. "Get out of here, Lash. Now."

Lash's eyes came back to me. "I'll let Dev know that The Lust is done with," Lash hissed, "Good-bye, Sar." He started his truck, put his gun down, and drove off in a squeal of tires.

Theo swore again, still furious. "Son of a bitch!"

Was he angry for the kiss, or because Lash had gotten the drop on him yet again? I was disgusted, either way. "I'll be at the house."

Terian grabbed my arm before I could teleport. "Are you okay?"

"I'm fine!" I shouted. "Why wouldn't I be?"

"What the hell were you doing here with him?" Theo yelled back.

"Having lunch," I said sheepishly. "Talking."

"Talking about what?"

"He and I've had lunch together for weeks now, whenever I went to Hayden. I like to talk to him."

"What could you possibly have to talk about?" Terian said, abhorred. "You have nothing in common besides Devlin."

How would you know, Tears? "Movies. Books. Music," I said, counting them off on my fingers. "The gardens at Hayden. Some of the bigger nursery items that I'd still needed to buy—"

"Fine," Theo said gruffly. "What about the kiss?"

"He never did that before," I said angrily. "I can't believe he—"

"Let's get out of here," Terian urged quietly. "We've got an audience."

There were a few spectators looking at us now from behind the restaurant windows, their faces pressed to the glass. Well, more than a few.

"Someone's called the cops by now."

"Relax, Tears," Theo said gruffly. "Danial's got it covered. The PD gets paid to look the other way, so long as no locals get hurt. You should know that, especially after the attacks last year."

"He never mentioned it to me—" I started.

"Someone always reports the automatic weapon fire," Theo said, rolling his eyes. "It's less trouble this way, with the police staying out of it." He made a face. "It's either that or move again."

Had Danial left Colorado and relocated here because of trouble with police? It sounded that way. Paying for ignorance made sense, both in practicality and for why we weren't in cuffs right now. The sheriff's office was five buildings down from the parking lot, yet no police had arrived.

"C'mon, Sar," Theo said, grabbing my hand. "Let's go home. I'm not hungry anymore for sushi."

I yanked my hand free. "Then I'll see you back there." He reached for me again, but I evaded him, teleporting to Danial's.

* * * *

Hours later, Theo came into the kitchen as I was finishing up the rest of my sushi.

"I'm sorry if I scared you," he said. "I saw him with you and freaked."

I didn't answer.

"I told Danial that The Lust was gone," Theo went on. "He—"

"Where are the kids?" I asked pointedly.

"In Elle's room, watching a movie."

I'd made Elle and Theoron dinner earlier when I got home. They'd known something was wrong when I didn't eat with them. They'd eaten quickly and excused themselves. I'd been so relieved to have a moment to think by myself I hadn't checked on them since pouring myself a small glass of wine. "Good."

Theo looked at me uneasily. "Lash brought you that?"

I didn't answer. I'd had some time to think, not that it had taken a lot of thought to understand Lash's motives. He'd tried to raise The Lust because having Theo watch me throw myself all over Lash would've cut Theo deeper than any blade. As much as I was relieved that The Lust was finished, I felt terrible that Lash had used me that way. *You're a fine one to talk about disrespecting me, Lash.*

"Do you...um, did you want him to—?" Theo said finally, his words like shattering glass.

"Theo, shut up," I snapped. "I don't want to talk about it."

"We're going to talk about it," Theo retorted. "I need to know right now. He's my enemy!"

"I'm pissed at both of you," I said. "You're both jerks; him for trying to start something he had no business starting, and you, for doing the same."

"Then why are you eating food he brought you?"

"He said were children need a lot of protein, ass," I snapped. "It wasn't about him, or me—"

"Bullshit."

"Your baby, Theo. Not Devlin's baby, not for any kicks, just because he was concerned about me."

"I don't believe that," Theo spat. "He hates me. Why would he care about my child?"

Lash had cared about me, until his hatred got the better of him. "I'm not sure," I said honestly. "But I'm eating this anyway, because it tastes good."

"Fine; eat it. But I don't want you seeing him again. Not for lunch, dinner, or anything else."

"Don't worry," I said heavily. "I won't be going to Hayden anytime soon. He won't be coming here. So that's that."

* * * *

That night, I lay awake a long time, alone in bed. Theo was putting in some late practice with the werefoxes, and Danial was above me in the study, on a conference call. I was glad of that. I wanted some time alone, to think about my next steps.

I'd trusted Lash, and he'd betrayed that trust. Sure, the wound wasn't as deep as the one Devlin had given me, but it still hurt to think I'd extended my hand in friendship, and he'd taken advantage. Maybe Theo and Danial were right about him. In any case, I shouldn't have to spend any time with him again, so that would make it easier.

Devlin would not be so easily handled. Danial was obviously not only hoping for a reconciliation between his brother and I, he was avidly working for that in all he did. Some of that was likely to cement his own rights to me, but more of it was he wanted Devlin to be happy. I smiled, thinking with just a trace of bitterness that I'd wanted to rectify their brotherly rift, and accomplished it too well.

The question wasn't could I forgive Devlin, because I certainly loved him enough to forgive him. It was why should I forgive him, when being separate would likely be better for us both? He could have what he needed, and I...I could, too. I'd wanted him to love me from afar and pine for me, hadn't I? This was me getting my wish again. I just wasn't enjoying it, because all I still visualized when I thought of him was he and Catherine together. It would take me a long time to get over that hurt. Right then, I wasn't sure I ever would.

He didn't love her. He loved you, Sar. Only you. He said so.

I believed that. I did. But Danial hadn't loved Angelica, either, and it had still hurt to think about the night I'd come to see him and she had answered the door in my robe, smirking. Just thinking about it upset me again, no matter that she had been dead for years now, and Danial only wanted me. I'd never thought of myself as a jealous person before meeting Danial and Devlin. Maybe I'd just needed the right stimulus to bring it out in myself. Or maybe all the vampire blood I'd had in the last few years was giving me some of the bad qualities of the donating vampires.

You were jealous of Theo and Tawny, too. And don't forget the two bitches, Tasha and Aspen.

All right...maybe my possessiveness and jealousy had nothing to do with vampires, only with my own feelings...

No maybe about it. And it's past time you pulled yourself together and stopped feeling sorry for yourself. It's your life, Sar. Only you can fix it.

That was true. Maybe my circumstances were bizarre, but I had got myself into this situation. I would find a way to make it work. Danial might have his own agenda with Dev, but he wouldn't do anything that would compromise my safety. He had always been my shoulder to lean on, a support I had been and remained grateful for. With him helping, I could not only safely deliver my twins, but also find a way to care for them both.

Theo was clearly not happy about our current situation, but he had been unhappy about how things were since we had returned from out west. That still made me feel guilty, but I shoved that guilt down, and told myself for the first time that it wasn't my problem, it was his. He knew how things were. If he didn't like it, he could leave.

Could he really, though? You bound him Sar, helped strengthen the bond you had so now it's unbreakable.

Did Theo stay out of love for me, as he said, or because he couldn't break the power of our thrice shared magical dream? I sighed, knowing that unanswered question was where my guilt really stemmed from. Only time would tell, as neither Titus nor Terian seemed to know for certain.

Feeling guilty over what was already done wouldn't help anyone. Making some goals and a plan to get there would.

I went over some ideas, then sketched a quick mental plan.

I would do everything possible to make sure the next few months were as stress free as possible. Until I delivered, my twins had to be my priority, just as Theoron had been my first concern when I was pregnant this time last year. The Lust was done, so the worst third of the battle was already over. If the cooling or heating problem presented itself again in the months to come, I had Terian to help me, and easy access to ice. Camlyn would be there for other questions, this time with data on my first pregnancy. We were no longer operating blind; this time he had tested my blood from the first. Not only was I going to be much safer this time around, but with everything documented, Titus might have enough info to really make another woman—maybe even Harriet—like me. The idea of the other Vampire Rulers leaving me alone instantly buoyed my hopes, flooding me with relief.

I would be courteous to Devlin, but avoid him as much as possible. Danial would not let him come here without my permission. That would take care of seeing Lash, too. If I kept my distance from Devlin, Theo was bound to relax. That would not only give Danial and I some peace, but also allow him to focus more on the death threats against he and Danial, not to mention his pending challenge with Robert.

The only sad aspect to my plan was my friendship with Serena, which had begun well and was now effectively cut off. Maybe I could arrange for her to visit me here? At the least, I could find a way to send her a letter. I would work on that tomorrow.

I snuggled into the pillows, relieved. Though my plan only got me to the birth of the twins, it was still a good start. I would take the next few months to figure out what came after that. Whatever path I chose, I promised myself I was going to do what was right for me.

Danial came in, shutting the door. "You're not asleep."

"Getting there," I said, then yawned.

He took off his clothes, slipped on some bottoms, then crawled into bed beside me, hugging me. "Your mood seems better. I'm glad to see you so relaxed."

I hesitated, then told him all of what I had been pondering.

Danial listened, then nodded. "Having a plan always comforts me. If you doubted I'd help you, let me assure you that I'm here for you, whatever you need."

"I know that," I said, hugging him happily. 'I know that, Danial."

Chapter Twelve

March became April, as winter faded into Spring. The hardest part of those weeks was seeing Devlin, and Lash, who was always with him.

The first few times Dev came to the doctor appointments, I refused to look at him. He didn't speak to me directly, nor did Lash, but I heard the questions he asked as he played the part of the concerned parent, asking how the babies were developing. Eventually, as time went on, I was able to look at him, though every time I did, I remembered him and Catherine. The sadness in his eyes didn't change anything between us.

Dev had sent me fire and ice roses with a card the day after Lash and Theo had locked horns. I had kept the flowers, and burned the card, unopened. I would have thrown the roses out too, but they were living things that had been cut just so that they could bloom for someone before they died. It seemed wrong to me not to give them a chance to live as long as they could. And I admitted reluctantly that I loved their heavenly smell. Danial watched me burn the card, though we didn't talk about it. A week and a half from then, when the roses began to die, another dozen arrived. Again, they were fire and ice, but there was no card on them this time, or any that arrived after them at regular intervals.

I didn't talk to Devlin at all; not at the doctor's appointments and not on the phone, though Danial talked to him every day, telling him about the baby's kicking, or how I was feeling. Devlin also didn't come to the house, though Danial begged me weekly to relent. But I'd had enough of Dev, and Lash too, and refused to see either of them.

Theo and I were getting along well now. It was a huge relief to have him around most of the time. He and Terian routinely went out together on jobs now, sometimes by machine, and sometimes via teleportation, but they were never gone for more than overnight. Together, they cleared out a lot of the simpler cases, leaving Danial to deal with the more complex ones. With my help on the clerical duties, the Solutions, Inc. team kept pace with the steep increase in workload. Danial had never advertised for his business before, relying on his reputation to bring cases to him. The new website and portal continued to surpass even his expectations for new clients.

The extra money was nice, too. Danial shared the wealth. Everyone got a hefty raise, including me. I happily socked most of my paycheck away, though I made Danial take some of it for household bills, now that Theo and I were living with him. He resisted at first, but then accepted. Theo also gave a good bit of his pay to Janice and Ivan for watching our house, by way of taking over their salaries from Danial. Weekends, I took the dogs back to spend some time at our house, sometimes with Elle, Theoron, and Theo. I missed my land, missed being there in the spring, missed the garden I wasn't planting. But I also felt like that farmstead wasn't where my home was now, leading me to take Theo aside on one of the trips.

"Theo, I know Danial is getting used to us being there with him," I began, trying to think about how to word my proposal.

Theo gave a me a look. "I'm sure he is. So?"

"Do you think it's safer to stay with him, after our baby is born?"

Theo looked at me in surprise. "Sar, are you saying that you think we should live with Danial, stay with him? Sell your house?"

"I'm asking what you think," I said, putting my hand on his arm. "I can't give an opinion, Danial is the only one giving me blood now. Some of his desires have become mine. I miss my home, but I'm content at Danial's, living there with him, and you. And I know I probably wouldn't be, if I was getting blood from Devlin as well. So I need you to tell me what you think, because I want our baby to be safe, and you to be happy, and you aren't in thrall to anyone."

Theo hugged me tight to him. "I want to live here with you, and our baby, but not until its safe. Robert hasn't tried again, but he's biding his time, Sar. So is Tasha's father, Karl."

"So we shouldn't make any decision now, is what you're saying?"

"Maybe in the fall," Theo said finally. "Terian is helping me go over leads regarding both of them in our spare time, though we haven't turned up anything yet. We will, Sar, but we need more time."

* * * *

By May first, I was huge. Stephen informed me during my weekly checkups that the babies were growing faster than normal. Theo was afraid, remembering what had happened to Tawny, but Stephen reassured us that he was planning on doing a C-section, so there was no reason to worry.

On the second of May, we had a huge birthday party for Theo at the were compound. Everyone had a great time. Theo had said no presents, but everyone had gotten him something, like boxes of bullets, or an extra pair of jeans. I had given him a heavy terrycloth bathrobe of his own to wear, as he'd reluctantly been wearing an extra of Danial's that was satin. Theo was more of a cotton kind of guy. Danial had also gifted Theo with nightclothes: a few pairs of loose-fitting silk pajama bottoms. While Theo, Danial and I were pretty much used to sleeping in the same bed after a month, both gifts were sure to ease Theo's persistent homophobia.

Watching my husband, and how much he was enjoying this, I wondered if Theo had ever a party before. I didn't ask, because it didn't matter. Theo was going to get a party every year from now on, complete with a three layer red velvet cake big enough to feed a crowd, like I'd baked him this year.

And he wasn't the only one. Danial also was getting a party every year from now on. From his own words, his birthday had never been celebrated, not even back when he was mortal. So a week later, on Theoron's birthday, I made sure to make Danial his own small cake.

Danial's real birthday was sometime in September, but he'd asked that his son's birthday be the day of celebration. "I was reborn the day you had Theoron," Danial had said softly to me one night. "Let that serve as my birthday, Sar."

That party came together perfectly. Theoron had run amok, tearing through his presents in a flurry of paper, the blunt horns Terian had grown for him sticking out of his forehead, and the devil's tail sprouting from his lower back lashing in excitement. I'd given Terian raised eyebrows over making my son a devil, but Terian had just shrugged, and said that that was what Theoron had asked him for. When it came to Theoron, Terian was as bad as Danial was at spoiling him. But my mother and stepfather were just as bad.

Titus had teleported them to the party. My mom had been very uncomfortable with his blackness, downing an entire glass of wine at her arrival. It hadn't helped when he'd asked her—if she didn't mind too much—to put her cross under her shirt. My mom had complied, then she'd gone for another glass. Seeing his effect on them, Titus had given me a quick hug, and then teleported back to Hayden. Once my parents got over the shock of their delivery method, they had a great time, loading Theoron with fishing gear, and L.L. Bean clothes. "He's our only grandchild, so far," my mom said meaningfully. "Of course we're going to spoil him."

My mother was dropping hints in her usual blunt way, but she had no idea her wish for a brood had already come true. I still hadn't told her that I was having twins, or that one was Devlin's. I knew there was a better than even chance that the baby would get Devlin's eyes. They had only to see the eyes, and they'd make the connection in a minute. *I had to tell them, but how?*

Compounding my stress was that Devlin had been invited to Danial's party. He brought Lash, of course, and the two of them spent the beginning of the evening talking with my parents. I'd noticed it, then dismissed my worry, rationalizing it was normal for my parents to talk to the only other people here they knew. What I failed to notice was that my stepfather had brought a tasting pack with him: a group of small bottles of at least seven different scotches. My stepfather's pride in his extensive collection proved to be my undoing.

The first hint was Lash sidling up to me. "Sorry. I let it slip one of the twin's is Dev's."

I glared bloody murder at him. "You asshole."

"Sar, they wouldda had to know eventually—"

"Sar," my mother called stridently. "Come over here a minute."

She knew, and if I didn't get over there, she would be dragging me over there by my ears in front of everyone. She'd had a fair bit of wine, too, meaning her normal verbal boundaries, already low, had probably shrunk to nothing.

I headed over, smiling fakely. Theo came over quickly to meet me in front of my parents, sliding his hand into mine, while managing an almost inaudible growl at Lash.

My mother got to her feet, and launched in without preamble. "Is it true, Daughter dear?" she said with a bared-teeth smile and hot eyes. "You are having twins with more than one father?"

I opened my mouth to speak, but Theo was faster. "Yes, ma'am. It's true."

"How could you do this?" my mom yelled furiously.

The room went silent, all eyes on us.

We had to get her out of here before she said any more. We needed Titus. I glanced around desperately for help, meeting Terian's eyes. He nodded, then disappeared.

"How could you let her do this?" my mom yelled at Theo.

I squeezed his hand, to tell him not to say anything.

Titus appeared behind my parents, grabbed one in each burly arm. "Hayden," he rumbled, and then they were gone.

I grabbed Theo, Terian grabbed Devlin, and we teleported to Hayden, arriving in the kitchen. Luckily, no one was there. Devlin nodded, then gestured to Titus and Terian. They went into the basement, leaving the five of us in the kitchen.

"Where the hell are we?" my stepfather asked.

"My estate," Devlin replied, grabbing a bottle of wine from the counter. "Its name is Hayden."

"Its name?" my mother asked, casting him an odd look.

"I own two thousand acres, give or take a few hundred," Devlin said casually. "When I came here, there was only land. But by the time the house was built, I thought it should have a name."

My mom, of course, was not impressed. "Why is Sar having your baby? She is Theo's wife. You are Danial's brother. Is there something I'm not seeing?"

"Have a glass of wine," Devlin said, handing her one. Then he handed one to each of us.

I swallowed half right off. "This is good," I said, savoring the taste.

Devlin froze, then looked over at me hopefully. I looked away, damning myself for breaking the wall of silence between us.

"It's a Shiraz called Groom," Dev answered. "It's my favorite."

"I'll ask one more time, Mr. Dalcon!" my mother said at top volume. "Why is my daughter having your child?"

"The simplest answer is because I told her that I wanted her to," Devlin said, locking eyes with my mother, then my stepfather. "Your daughter is the only woman known who can have a vampire's child, ma'am. That makes life dangerous for Sar—"

"What danger is she in?" my stepfather asked, an edge to his words. "And from whom?"

"Surely you don't think my brother and I are the only vampires in the world?" Devlin said casually, making it clear of the conclusion that was supposed to follow his words.

"Others want her," my mother breathed. "They know about Theoron."

"Yes," Devlin said. "Danial isn't powerful enough to protect your daughter from others of our kind. He doesn't have the experience, or the ruthlessness. I do." Devlin had been charming up until now. But he uttered those three sentences with enough cruelty and malice in his voice to melt steel. Both of my parents recoiled from him. My mother gave him a look that said she believed it.

"What he said is true," Theo added roughly. "He saved Sar's life at least three times now, risking his own in the process. Your daughter wouldn't be standing here with you today, if not for him."

My mother came and hugged me. A moment later, my stepfather did the same. But when they separated from me, my mother was all business again.

"So you made her have the baby with you in exchange for protecting her?" my mother accused.

Here was the big question I'd been dreading. *How would Devlin answer it? Would he tell the truth? And if so, which version?*

Devlin took the last swallow of wine, and rolled the empty glass in his hand, looking at it as if it held the answers to my mother's questions. "I gave her a choice," he said softly. "I told her I loved her. I told her I would protect her. And I asked her in return to let my brother and myself into her life again. To try to have a child with me. She agreed."

"What kind of a choice was that?" my mother said shrilly. "She either gave you what you wanted, or you let her get used, passed around! This is the reason we saw her that night with Danial—!"

"Stop it, Tina," Theo growled.

Everyone turned to look at him.

"With all due respect, Tina, you are not dealing with the world you know," Theo continued carefully. "It was Sar's choice, and she made it. And if I had been her, been in her shoes, with all that was going on at the time…" He trailed off, looking at me with sadness.

He meant his leaving me, my dying, the Gathering, all of it, in those last weeks of the old year.

"I would have made the same decision," Theo finished. "There wasn't another one to make. Not if she wanted to stay my wife, or ever see you or her children again."

Devlin said nothing, his golden eyes fixed on my parents.

"Please take us home," my mother said, anger and a little weariness creeping into her tone. "I think we've had enough of the world Sar's chosen to live in, at least for tonight."

"No," Devlin said cruelly. "I want you to see my house, now that you are here. Sar's done a lot of painting here, put in a lot of work. I want you to see the nursery, before you go."

"If it's all the same, we'd really rather not—" my stepfather said politely.

"It is not!" Devlin snarled, baring his fangs, and throwing his empty glass hard against the far wall to shatter in a spray of glass.

Theo grabbed me tight. My stepfather grabbed my mother.

"You made a scene at my brother's first birthday party in over four hundred years," Devlin growled, his eyes glowing red. "He saw it. My nephew and niece saw it. Anyone that means anything to him saw it."

My mother let out an "Eek!"

"Everyone knows that Sar and I are Oathed, and about the baby, so there is no lasting damage," Devlin went on, the red in his eyes diminishing. "But you didn't know that. You thought before you spoke, Tina. And I want you to think next time very carefully before you say anything within my hearing."

My mother was hugging my stepfather, the latter glaring at Dev like a cornered badger looks at a grizzly bear.

I had to do something before this escalated. I let go of Theo's hand, and

176

went to my parents. "Come, please," I invited, touching both of them on their shoulders. "I would like you to see Hayden before you go. It is beautiful, and you might not get to visit often, because it's dangerous."

"Dangerous how?" my stepfather asked flintily. "Theo said you're protected."

"Devlin and Danial are big shots in the vampire world," I said carefully. "They have a lot of enemies. That's why I never met you at either of their homes, or invited you there on holidays. No one wants any of their enemies finding out about you, or using you to get to them. We have enough problems with that happening to me."

My parents looked nervous, but at least they weren't as scared.

I steeled myself, then went to Devlin, and took his hand, hearing his intake of breath when I touched him. "Lead on," I instructed.

Devlin beamed at me, then put my arm in his. For the next half hour, he led us around Hayden. We didn't go into the bears' quarters or the basement, but he showed them the completely restored ballroom, which was breathtaking, a grand piano now shining with luster on the stage beneath the double staircase. I debated asking him to play for us, knowing music would help to relax us all but decided against it, not knowing if Dev would agree.

Dev also showed us the rooms I had painted and the nursery. While they were still not furnished, the nursery was complete and perfect, from the pastel walls to the many stuffed toys and books all the way down to the little acorn wind chimes above the crib.

"Do you like it?" Devlin asked, very hesitantly putting his arms around me. "I went with Pooh, as we don't know if it's a boy or a girl."

"I like it very much," I responded, flashing him a quick smile.

Devlin gave me a gentle kiss on the cheek. I shifted, uncomfortable, then tried to relax.

"You said Sar is Oathed to you," my mom said boldly. "What does that mean? She's Theo's wife."

Devlin looked at her, his arms tightening possessively around me. "It means that your daughter promised my brother and I that we would be the only vampires she would ever be with as lovers," he said frankly. "Your daughter is part vampire now, from having Danial's son. She needs—"

"Sar needs them," Theo said, cutting Devlin off. "Sar needs their blood regularly to stay alive. And by giving them this promise, all other vampires have to leave her alone. That keeps her safe. That's why she wears that gold necklace. That's what it means."

My mother looked at me, grief in her eyes. Behind that was anger that all this had happened to me, that someone was responsible for allowing it to happen. She blamed Danial for dragging me into his world and changing me, for wanting the baby, for having a monster of a brother like Devlin. "May we go home now?"

"As you wish." Devlin led us back downstairs. "Titus will take you."

Titus emerged from the basement with Terian. "You told them everything?"

"Not everything," I said softly. Taking my mother's hand in mine. I teleported us to her house.

"You can do what they do?" my mother said, horrified.

"I'm part demon, too," I answered. "I got some blood on me years ago, Mom. It was an accident." I gave her a winning smile. "But I'm still me."

"You aren't," my mother said with disgust. "The daughter I raised would never have fallen in with a man like that Devlin. Bad enough to even know someone like that, Sar, but you're having his baby—"

"You have no idea what I have been through," I interrupted angrily. "Don't blame Danial for this, not for any of it. He has been the only one who stood by me since I met him, Mom. The only one."

"He hit you," my mother spat. "Or did you forget?"

"I deserved it, for what I did," I retorted.

She blanched. "If you can say something that stupid, then I know you've changed—"

"Shut your mouth!" I yelled.

My mother stared at me, mouth open.

"I love Danial. I forgave him a long time ago for what he did. You are the only one who remembers it, who won't let it die. How long are you going to make him pay for a mistake he made years ago?"

My mother began to reply, but I talked over her. "Theo tried his best, Mom, but he couldn't protect me. Danial couldn't either. Devlin did, but he had to go through a lot of pain and hassle to do it. He had to send men to their deaths."

"You're describing a war," my mother said harshly.

"It was going to be a war," I said, letting all of my memories flood my words with emotions. "Devlin made a preemptive strike. He stopped it before it started. But the danger isn't gone. All Devlin has to say is that I'm no longer Oathed to him and you would never see me again, because some other vampire would lay claim to me, one who didn't care I had a husband, or children—"

"Stop," my mom said, crying.

"No, Dev was right!" I yelled. "You can't just speak or act rashly, Mom. You have to be careful in what you say and do. Everything has repercussions." I took a deep breath and let it out. "It took me a while to learn that. I found it a harsh lesson. I'd rather you didn't have to learn it the way I did. So I think you should take some time and think about how involved you want to be in my new life. Because this is my life now. I can't go back to the way I was. But you don't have to join me."

"Please, Sarelle," my mom begged. "Please don't shut us out of your life, or your babies' lives."

"I won't," I relented, hugging her. "I'll call you tomorrow. I've got to get back to Danial's party. And I love you as much as ever, Mom. Don't think I don't, because we fought."

As my mom went to reply, she looked over my shoulder and suddenly stopped.

I turned to look. Devlin stood there, along with Titus and my stepfather.

My stepfather went to my mother. "Come inside, dear." They both went inside the house leaning on each other.

Devlin and Titus came over to me. As soon as Devlin got near enough, he grabbed my hand, then linked to Titus. The driveway disappeared, replaced by Danial's great room. Titus nodded to me, then disappeared again.

"We checked on the party," Devlin said. "Theo's there. Theoron's still running around in his horns and tail, and Danial's chasing him. Everyone's having a good time."

"Good," I said, relieved.

Devlin brought me closer. "You handled yourself well, Love."

As much as I longed to lose myself in his arms, to kiss his inviting lips, I pushed back against him. "That's close enough."

"Promise me you'll stay and talk, and I'll let go," Devlin replied. "You can understand I'm afraid you'll bolt."

"I'm not going to run," I said, sitting down heavily. "I don't feel like rejoining the party. I'd just be a downer, in the mood I'm in."

Devlin clasped my hand in his loosely. "I think you did and said what needed to be done and said," he said evenly.

"I didn't want them to know all that. I didn't want them to have to deal with the darker side of things."

"Like me, you mean?" Devlin said, annoyed. "Like our deal?"

"No," I said. "I didn't want my mother to worry about me. I didn't want her to know I could teleport, that I was part demon. She goes to church regularly. Even though she's not a zealot, she can't help but be influenced now by what I told her. She's going to look at me differently."

"But you are different than you were," Devlin interjected. "You're also right in that there is no undoing it. You would have had to tell her, sooner or later."

His words reminded me of Lash's, the jerk who'd started this whole mess. "And where's your henchman? I hope you didn't leave him at the party to add to this mess."

Devlin squeezed my hand, then let it go. "Do you want me to punish Lash for telling them?"

"No. Just tell him not to talk to my parents again. The last thing I need is for them to find out about him, me, and The Lust."

"I'll take care of it," he said, then inclined his head slightly. "Do you want me to leave, or stay?"

I looked back at him, wanting him desperately to stay, to make love with me, to sing to me, to love me. I took a long shaking breath. "Please go."

"Will you allow me to come and see you?" Devlin, taking my hand again. "I've missed you, Sar." He stroked my wrist, then my arm. "I lie awake at night wishing you were with me."

Go now, or you'll give in to him. I got up abruptly. "I'm sure by this time you've found someone to ease your loneliness," I said spitefully, then strode into Danial's room.

I waited there, not sure if I wanted Devlin to come after me, or not. When a knock sounded some time later, I hesitantly called out, "Come in."

It was Danial, not Devlin. "Dev told me what happened. Tina is never going to let me forget what I did," Danial said miserably. "As if I could anyway."

"She'll forgive you, Danial. Just give her time." I gave him a bright smile. "How was the party?"

"Much enjoyed," Danial said, flashing a smile. "But we were talking of your mother. Why do you forgive so easily, and she doesn't?"

"Because I've done a lot I needed forgiveness for. I've been lucky, in that most of the people I wronged forgave me. I try not to withhold forgiveness, if someone is really contrite."

Danial looked at me pointedly.

"Sometimes there is just too much to forgive," I said softly, then went into the bathroom to shower.

"Never can true reconcilement grow where wounds of deadly hate have pierced so deep," Danial intoned softly. "I hope in time you'll reconsider, Sar."

I didn't answer him, biting my lip.

* * * *

By June first, Stephen announced my babies would most likely be born in mid-August.

"But that is over a month early, right?" Theo said worriedly.

"The dhamphir would have matured a little early in any case," Stephen said patiently. "But the werecougar is developing much faster than it should, Theo. As this also happened previously with your daughter, it's likely due to something with your physiology."

"Is the were going to endanger my child?" Devlin asked.

Stephen didn't immediately reply.

"Answer me, Camlyn," Devlin said roughly. "Now."

"Probably not," Stephen said finally. "It's the dhamphir who is a danger to the werecougar."

"What?" I asked, confused. "Why?"

"The babies are close together, Sar. Every day, as the were child gets bigger, it presses more and more against the dhamphir, whose fangs are already forming. Sooner or later, the dhamphir is going to realize that it has a source of nourishment right next to it—"

I let out a scream, remembering Perseus's idle comment. "No!"

"What can we do?" Devlin said. "Will giving her blood help? If the dhamphir is getting enough blood, it should negate the desire to feed, like it does in a vampire."

"I'm going to prescribe some capsules of blood," Stephen said, nodding. "It's our best chance, I think. Sar, I want you to take them every day. It might mean the difference whether both babies survive."

"I'll take them," I promised, squeezing Theo's hand in a death grip.

"Is everyone ready?" Steven said brightly, smearing goo on my abdomen.

I nodded. Today we'd find out if the twins would be boys or girls.

Stephen began the ultrasound. "There they are."

The blobs were bigger, but I still didn't really see anything that resembled a baby.

"Devlin, Theo, we can tell now which child is which. Theo's is in cougar form, see the tail there?"

I looked and saw nothing resembling a child, or a tail, or anything else recognizable. "Sure."

"That one's a boy, according to the blood—"

Theo squeezed my hand hard.

"The other there is Devlin's," Stephen finished, pointing.

"And mine?" Devlin asked hopefully. "Is it a boy?"

"Devlin, your child will be a girl," Stephen said, beaming.

I couldn't look at Devlin. He had to be disappointed, especially as Theo was getting a boy, and Danial had had a boy. But I was thrilled to be having a girl, my heart light and happy.

Devlin tentatively touched my hand, then clasped it. I gently squeezed his hand. He squeezed back gently once, then let me go.

* * * *

In the last week of May, as we'd planned, Theo, Elle, and I took a plane, and went to Wyoming. We stayed in the house that Theo had lived in.

There were a few awkward moments. The first was when Theo and I picked up the keys from the landlord, and he warned us to tell him if we saw any prowlers. "Some jackasses broke in one night, and tore the place up," he said grumpily. "They ripped both phones out of the wall and broke them, and cut the cords. It looked like someone had tried to tie someone to the bed."

I pretended to be appalled and looked away, trying to keep the heat in my face from rising.

"That's bizarre. Sure, we'll be careful," Theo said neutrally, then shot me a disbelieving look. Later he told me that he thought the man was making up that story, but that he couldn't figure out why anyone would. I agreed, shrugging my shoulders.

On our last night in town, we went out to dinner, and had the second awkward moment. We were perusing our menus when a voice said, "Theo?"

I knew that voice. I looked up to see Aspen standing there. Worse, she wasn't alone. She was holding a little girl that looked about three or so. A beautiful girl with brown hair and blue eyes.

All the blood drained out of my face, and Theo's.

Elle looked at her with interest. "You must be Aspen?" Theo shot her an unhappy look, then gave me an accusing one that said I'd told. I shrugged and made a face in response that said I hadn't.

"Yes, I'm Aspen. This is my daughter, Heather. You must be Elle."

"I'm her husband, John," a gruff man said, appearing from behind her and extending his hand to Theo.

I breathed a huge sigh of relief, as did Theo. "Good to meet you, John," Theo said, shaking his hand. "This is my wife, Sar, and our daughter, Elle."

"You smell a little odd. Are you cougar too?" Elle asked John.

He gave her a smile, and nodded. "Aspen changed me," he whispered, giving his wife a look of love. "It was love at first sight. She felt the same, but she was worried I wouldn't love her because of what she was. I let her change me that night. We married the next week."

I thought my marriage had been fast, or my Oathing to Danial. I guess I just needed a comparison point like this one to feel better. "That's very romantic."

"We live in Colorado," Aspen said, giving Theo a smile. "We came up here to get away for a while."

"Same here," I said, smiling as good-naturedly as I could under the circumstances. "We were seeing relatives, too. This is our last night."

"Give her to me," John said, holding out his arms for Heather. "I'll go get us a table. You need to sit down too, honey."

Aspen looked at him adoringly. "I'm only a week late. It could be nothing."

"I hope it's something," John said meaningfully, then looked at us. "It was good to meet you."

I watched him move off, wondering if he always was so forthcoming to strangers. Maybe it was just because he knew about Theo being an ex-boyfriend.

I noticed Aspen had stayed, and was looking at Theo. "Theo, why don't you go outside for a minute? Elle and I will wait here."

Theo nodded to me and then headed outside, Aspen following. Elle let out a growl, watching them leave.

"Knock it off," I said, handing her some money. "Go play the crane machine for a while."

"She tried to break you and Theo up. I don't like her."

"Terian told you about her, didn't he?"

She nodded.

I was going to have to have a talk with Tears when I got back. "Elle, Theo has things he needs to say to Aspen, things that he didn't say to her back when he left. It's okay if he says them to her now."

Elle didn't reply, she just took the money and headed to the machine to play.

When Theo and Aspen returned a half-hour later, it was obvious they had both been crying. But there was also an air about them both that something had built for a long time had finally been resolved, bringing not only relief, but also a sense of peace.

The rest of the meal passed in a rush as we hurried to make our flight. When we were driving to the airport, I noticed Elle didn't have her toy. "Where's your lion?"

"I gave it to Heather," Elle answered, "She was making it roar. Didn't you see?"

"I did," Theo said, choked up. "That was a very kind thing you did, Elle."

I didn't say anything, just squeezed his hand in mine.

* * * *

As we were flying home, I reflected on the trip, and how well it had gone. My in-laws had been supportive and loving, the white water rafting on the

Colorado River had been exhilarating, and we'd resolved the whole Aspen issue, too. There was only one thing bugging me: piano lessons.

My in-laws had a piano. My mother-in-law had helped Elle learn a few keys during our visit, then encouraged me to send her for lessons. The trouble was the piano wasn't one of Tutor Bill's skills, and letting another human in on Danial's home's coordinates wasn't an option. And I knew already who Danial would push for the moment Elle asked him for lessons: Devlin.

* * * *

"You know what I'm going to ask," Danial began hesitantly.

"I do," I answered, closing the bathroom mirror. "If you want him to give her lessons, it's okay with me."

"Are you sure?" Danial asked. "That means him coming here, as I don't want Elle at Hayden."

That had something to do with Lash, though what the real reason was for Danial's hatred of him, I wasn't sure. "I'm sure. Dev will be a good teacher. He was when he taught me to sing."

"All right," Danial affirmed. "I'll ask him tonight."

Even with his neutral tone, I could tell Danial was very pleased, that he thought this was my first step toward a reconciliation with Devlin. I didn't have the heart to tell him there wasn't going to be one, no matter how much he wanted it.

It had become apparent in the months I hadn't been with Devlin that my feelings for him had faded. I'd always desire him for his gorgeous body, and his beautiful eyes, and the tender way he could be when he wanted to. But I was much happier with him not in my life. I didn't miss his volatile personality. I was also worried that as soon as I popped out his girl, Devlin would start pushing for another child. He hadn't given up on his desires. He was just biding his time.

Chapter Thirteen

In the second week of June, Serena finally came to visit me via Titus.

The first thing I did was show her the garden that was just beginning to sprout. "Just because I'm not at Hayden doesn't mean that I can't teach you gardening," I said with a smile. "We can talk as we dig weeds."

"We have three new guards, all single males. I'm busy," she joked. "That's all my news."

I chuckled. "That's—"

"Why don't you condemn me like everyone else?" Serena asked me suddenly.

How had we gotten so deep so fast? Probably because she'd had no one to talk to. "It's not my business what you choose to do with your life," I said with a shrug.

"But how can you be so permissive—?"

"Do you like having sex with the men you're with?" I said bluntly.

She looked unsure.

I held her gaze. "It's an easy yes or no answer."

"Yes," she said finally. "I always liked sex. My partners are considerate and the sex is safe. And the pay is a hell of a lot more than I could make being a short order cook, not to mention the protection working for Devlin offers me."

"Then you enjoy your work, you make good money, and you get paid to do something you love," I summed up. "I'd say that was better than most people's careers."

"You are the oddest woman I think I've ever met," Serena said, tilting her head. "And I've met some odd ones."

"I get that a lot," I said, grinning. "I'm not sure why."

"There's also a new maid," Serena said. "She's a werewolf."

That was a little much for me, a real werewolf. Strange that the idea was so peculiar to me, when I was surrounded by all kinds of other real life nonhumans. "How is she?"

"Robin's nice," she said. "She does a good job cleaning and keeps to herself. We've been spending time, as the bears don't really like her—"

Wait, a werewolf named Robin?

"—she's living in the basement, she said she prefers it, it's more like a den to her."

Well, whatever made her feel at home. I hoped she wasn't spending time in the dungeon. "That's good, then."

"Sar, are you ever coming back to stay?" Serena said. "I miss you."

"I don't know," I answered. "Most likely not anytime soon."

Serena looked at me sadly, then turned the conversation back to gardening.

* * * *

Over the next few weeks, I put in long hours with Danial's business. It kept my mind off Dev. My attraction to him had seemed so easy to forget with his absence, but it had returned in full force now that he was here most days giving Elle lessons.

She had rebelled at first, refusing him as a teacher. But when Danial had threatened that it was either Devlin or no lessons at all, Elle had relented. A small upright piano had arrived the next day. Danial had had it placed just outside his bedroom. He'd done that deliberately; I heard the music from start to finish, no matter which room of the house I was in.

Danial's scheme worked. It was hard for me to know Devlin was there, so close to me, and not go see him. Devlin had skill with the piano; it sang for him, the music both breathtaking, and heartbreaking. But despite his attempts to lure me, I resisted. Each time I thought of going down to him, I made myself remember him and Catherine together. And I never went down to him.

Lash stayed away, too. When Serena mentioned on one of her visits that he was helping clear the gardens of weeds, I gave my folder of garden ideas to her, asking her to give to Lash for me. I'd proposed roses of fire and ice, as well as regular red and white, plus red and white tulips, white flocks, red bee balm, white violets, and black pansies for the empty spaces between; someone might as well use my ideas. Serena didn't want to bring them to him on my behalf at first, but she finally agreed.

Janice and Cia had been running around like crazy for the whole month of May, trying to get the former's mating ceremony and reception planned out. I helped as much as I was able, like putting the ribbons and dates on the fox-shaped cookie cutter wedding favors. It was fun, and got me some samples of wedding cake as a bonus.

My weight was up, but I still took walks in the forest, while the treadmill gathered dust. Now that the ice and snow had melted, there was no way I was staying inside. Experiencing the sheer exhilaration of spring becoming summer was not an opportunity to be missed.

Danial continued to ride, but now it was Elle who joined him, with Theoron sometimes riding in front of her. Danial had wanted them both to be good in the saddle, and Elle took to it like she was born to it. The greater problem had been getting the horses to accept her werecougar scent. But with time and a lot of gentle persuasion, Poe and Annabelle Lee did. It was a pleasure, to sit on the wraparound porch on a Saturday evening, and watch them cavort in the front yard.

I also sat down Theo early one night when Danial was away, and asked him what he thought about names. "Did you have your heart set on anything? Theo Jr.?"

"I don't know," he replied. "I talked to Danial, and proposed naming the baby after him. But he said he would rather we didn't. You know how he feels about his past."

I nodded. "Any second choices?"

"Why don't you pick the name?" Theo replied. "You haven't been the one to make a lot of the decisions regarding your pregnancy. You should at least get to choose the name."

"I will then," I agreed happily. "Let me do some searches online and get back to you."

* * * *

On the sixth of June, Nineva showed up for his visit. Theo, Elle, and I went to meet him at the airport.

I almost didn't recognize him getting off the plane. When I had seen him last years ago, he'd just been through horrible grueling torture. Now he was beaming with health, his dark skin shining, his long hair in dreadlocks to his shoulders. Elle raced into his arms as soon as she saw him.

"Look how big you are!" he exclaimed, his brown eyes shining with emotion.

Theo came over, and offered his hand. Nineva just hugged him. Theo hugged him back, both of them a little teary, remembering the circumstances of the last time they had seen each other.

"I'm glad you got out," Theo managed finally.

"If it hadn't been for you, I wouldn't have," Nineva replied. He turned to me. "Sarelle." He hugged me very gently, careful of my huge belly. "You look wonderful." He turned back to Theo. "I see you've been busy," Nineva said with a laugh.

Theo and Elle spent most of the two weeks running around Danial's forest with Nineva. He was completely recovered from his ordeal, nothing like the pale shadow he had been when I had seen him years ago. His lion form was magnificent: all golden fur, wild mane, and tufted tail, with the loudest roar I'd ever heard.

With Nineva staying with us for his visit, it quickly became apparent to him that Danial, Theo and I were sharing the same bed.

"I told him, Sar, when he asked me," Theo said one night. "All of it. And he said if you ever needed to hide, to get away, he would do his best to keep you safe. No matter who it was you were hiding from."

I was touched, especially knowing how much Nineva hated violence. "That's sweet of him. But it wouldn't work. He doesn't know what the other Rulers are like, or what Lash and Dev are capable of—"

"And Titus," Theo added, glowering. "Don't forget that monster."

"What do you have against him?" I said, putting my hands on my hips. "He saved you from that love spell. He saved you from poisoning—"

"He also eats people, Sar," Theo said coldly. "He ate Neoline, probably drank her blood first, just like a damned vampire."

"How can you say this?" I said, aghast. "A vampire is your best friend!"

"Danial tries never to kill," Theo replied abruptly. "I know he has, but he tries not to. But Titus has to. And if a being is so evil that it has to kill to live, maybe it's better for the world if that being wasn't in it—"

"So you hold against Titus that he was born a demon," I said angrily. "You're blaming him for something that he didn't have any choice in?"

Theo looked at me, his expression conveying that he had never thought of it that way before. I nodded once, then walked away, leaving him to think of the similarity between Titus and himself.

* * * *

When it came time for Nineva to leave, none of us wanted him to. Danial even offered him a job, which Nineva declined. "I like the quiet life," he said, giving Danial a smile. "I'll help you if you ask, if you need me sometime, of course. I owe you a great debt, for what you did for me. But I don't like violence, or killing."

I was glad then Terian wasn't around to hear that. Nineva sounded like Terian once had, before his human nature had been influenced by his demon side. Saying good-bye to Keriam and putting his past to rest had helped Terian heal old wounds. But there was something darker about him these days. I wanted to think it was Sundown, that being with her had changed him. He swore a lot more frequently and easily, and he could be both cruel and sarcastic now, where he had not been before. Most of the fault lay with Solutions, Inc., or so I concluded. Theo and Terian didn't kill people for profit as Lash did, but they had killed in self-defense several times in only a few months. And Terian made no pretenses about enjoying it now.

Titus seemed to give no sign of awareness of the change in Terian, though I talked to him about my concerns.

"Terian hasn't changed," he replied. "He's steadfast in his morality, Sar. I do wish he would let his mother back into his life, though."

I cringed. Terian still refused to talk to Leri, or see her, though Titus was back with her now. "Devlin said you were thinking of building a small house for her and you on the outskirts of Hayden."

"Dev won't let her live in the main house," Titus replied. "Dev's balking at my proposal, too, but I've sweetened the deal with something he won't refuse."

"What?" I said, my tone saying that it had better not have anything to do with me.

Titus smiled. "I offered to work the next year for him free of charge."

That was bullshit, but I didn't call him on it. I had no proof. Besides, even if whatever he had offered Devlin did have something to do with me, I had nothing real to threaten him with anyway.

* * * *

Life remained relatively peaceful until the afternoon before the end of June, the day before Janice's ceremony to Ivan.

I was harvesting the garden with Serena's help. Not much was ready yet, except a few little carrots, and radishes. This was more for me, because I shared a lot with her that I no longer could share with my one-time best human friend, Kat.

I'd avoided Kat all spring because of The Lust. But sometimes even if you avoided people, they found you. We'd run into one another, one night when Danial, Theo, I and the kids were all out together getting ice cream with my parents. She had seen me and come over to say hello. The moment Theoron had looked at her, she had known he was my son. Hearing him call me "Mom" a minute later had cinched it. She had also seen I was pregnant.

She and Brett had been polite, then excused themselves. After that, she'd stopped taking my calls, though I tried her every day for the next three weeks. While I kicked myself for not trusting her, for not telling her, I rationalized this was for the best. She didn't need me in her life, and the danger I would bring her and her family. We'd more than grown apart in the years since I'd met Danial; we were in totally separate worlds now. And like I'd told my mom,

189

there was no going back.

Theo hadn't understood what her loss meant to me. He'd only had Danial for most of his adult life. He'd told me that I had a lot of friends, and not to let it get me down. But Serena had understood.

"She was the last part of your old life," she had said softly.

I'd nodded, feeling the tears come. "Yes," I said, brushing them away. "I've lost touch with most of my neighbors, and the people I used to work with. An elderly woman I was close to died, and her son, who I was also close to, has gotten married, and moved away. I never had a lot of friends. The only people I'm still close to that I even knew back before I met Danial are my parents." I took a breath. "My life has changed so much, from knowing Danial. I'm happy, but I also feel like I've lost a lot of friends. I'm not who I was, and that bothers me."

Serena hugged me. "It was the same for me, when I came here. My mother died when I was young. It was a problem with having me, because of the two types of were. My father loved her very much. After she died, he crawled inside a bottle, and stayed there until I was ten."

I hugged her back hard, imagining what her childhood must have been like.

"We moved to Rio," she continued. "He tried to get clean. He stopped drinking, and got a job in the engine room of a cruise ship, and he was gone most of the time. He met a nice woman, a human. She took good care of me."

I could tell by her tone this wasn't the end of the tale. It was too happy a conclusion for a voice that empty. "What happened?"

"He fell off the wagon. She was lonely because he was gone so much, and began to suspect he was seeing other women. She was right. I smelled them on him sometimes when he came home. Sometimes we both could smell the alcohol on him." She paused. "When I was sixteen, she packed her bags and left. He got drunk on the ship that night and fell over the side. No one saw him, or missed him. It wasn't until they found his body washed up on the beach."

I hugged her. "You don't have to tell me the rest if you—"

"No, I want to." She paused, then began again. "I got a job at the diner. I was a decent cook, from fending for myself when I was little. And Rosa had shown me some recipes when she took care of me. It wasn't great, but it was a job."

I waited, hoping her story got better because I was thoroughly depressed now.

"Years passed that way. Then one night, back in the late fall, Jazz came in, with Vince and Nick," Serena said quietly. "They knew at once I was were. Before they left, Vince asked if I'd consider being with him and Nick for a price. I was flattered. Vince was good looking, to me anyway, and you've seen Nick."

Yes indeed, I'd seen Nick when I'd visited Hayden. And if I were single, I would have liked to have seen a lot more of him. "Yes."

"The money they offered was more than I made in a month," Serena continued. "I hadn't been with anyone before, not ever. But I was desperate for rent money, so I took their offer."

I hadn't expected to hear this. "You were a virgin?"

Serena saw my expression before I could cover it up. "I know," she said. "They were shocked, too. But they were also pleased because I was a clean slate. I was young and naïve." She made a face. "I didn't know back then there were some things most women usually balked at doing."

Let her not tell me what they did with her, God. "So then Dev offered you a job?"

Serena nodded. "Devlin came to see me and proposed this job. I accepted." She shrugged. "And here I am."

Serena had gone from tons of detail to almost none in her last sentences. That meant one thing. "He was with you, wasn't he? Dev?"

Serena gave me an uneasy look. "Are you mad?" she asked. "I didn't want you to know about that. It was only that one night, late last fall."

Why was I mad, or even surprised? "I'm not mad. It's just that Devlin lied about being with you. He said he never was."

"It wasn't for love or even for lust, Sar," she said with a sigh. "It was instruction. He simply asked me to demonstrate to him what I knew. He had been told I wasn't experienced, that I was a virgin. He gave me pointers to make sure I was able to perform my new job."

I closed my eyes, feeling suddenly inadequate. None of the men I'd been with had ever complained about my knowledge, or lack thereof. But I didn't know much more than what I'd learned from books and my own limited experience. That wasn't a hell of a lot, really. It wasn't surprising Dev had turned to Catherine, a woman with hundreds of years of experience, to satisfy him. *How could I have competed with that, ever?*

"Sar, I'm sorry," Serena said emotionally. "I can smell how hurt you are."

"You didn't do it," I replied, hugging her. "I'm not angry, Serena. I'm glad you're here, that you're my friend. It's just that I feel sometimes like I'm in so far over my head. "

Cia and Janice came around the corner. "Sar, who are you with?" They began walking fast towards us.

"Should I go?" Serena said quickly, looking as if she wanted to run.

"No," I assured. "They're nice."

Cia came to an abrupt stop five feet from Serena and me, her expression darkening as she rapidly sniffed the air. "I smell coyote," Cia growled. Janice hissed, baring her fangs at Serena.

A werecoyote bounty hunter had killed Cia's family years ago, leaving Cia as the only survivor. But I had never expected her to hate all werecoyotes because of that. "Stop it, Cia," I said firmly. "Serena is part fox—"

"I smell a bloody coyote!" Cia growled loudly, infuriated. "This what you learned at Hayden, to keep company with murderers and whores? What a surprise, Sar."

If I didn't love Cia so much, I might have decked her. Instead I gave her a solid shove, knocking her into Janice. "You don't talk to her that way!" I said furiously. "Don't say another word!"

"You keep company with trash like this and we aren't friends, anymore, Sarelle," Cia said coldly. "Don't come and bake with me anymore. If you need help with that demon inside you, call some other fox to mind your brat—"

Enraged, I started for her. Serena grabbed my arm. "No don't, Sar—"

Janice grabbed hold of Cia. "Come on." They left, both of them glaring at me.

"I'm so sorry," Serena said, tears sliding down her face.

I hugged her. "Don't be. It's not your fault. And it's not mine that I am who I am, either."

The scene with Cia having glaciated our fun afternoon, Serena and I picked up our tools, and she called Hayden for demon transport. After Titus teleported Serena home, I went inside to shower. After I got the water running, I turned on the radio. Meatloaf's "Anything for Love" had just began.

When I got out of the shower a few minutes later, the song was almost at the end. Happy that the retro channel I'd been listening to was playing the real version, not the abbreviated one, I began belting out the female's few lines, proud of my voice. It wasn't Sarah Brighton's, but it was decent.

Suddenly, I heard, "I can do that. Yeah, I can do that," in a rich rolling voice outside the door.

That had to be Devlin. I sung the next few lines, and again came the assent.

"Will you cater to every fantasy I've got?" I sang. "Will you hose me down with holy water, if I get too hot? Will you take me places I've never known?"

"I can do that now, Love, if you let me in," Devlin sang, his voice reaching in through the door to wash over me. "I will take you places you've never dreamed."

I opened my mouth to tell him to go to hell. But instead, I smiled, cruelly.

The next lines were good enough. "After a while you'll forget everything. It was a brief interlude, and a midsummer night's fling. And you'll see that it's time to move on—"

"I won't do that!" he protested in song. "No, I won't do that—"

"I know the territory, I've been around. It will all turn to dust, and we'll all fall down. Sooner or later, you'll be screwing around." I sang it with emotion, putting all my hurt into each note.

"I won't do that!" Devlin sang, a mix of anger and hurt. "No, I won't do that."

"You already did," I said loudly.

Only silence answered me. When I finished dressing, I opened the door, but there was no sign of him.

Later, I asked Danial if Devlin had been here today.

He just looked at me. "Elle didn't have a lesson today."

I folded my arms over my chest. "That's not an answer."

He gazed at me in silence a moment, then said, "Abashed the devil stood and pined his loss."

My guess was the line came from one of the books he and Devlin had been reading that morning in bed after our threesome. Unlike Dev, Danial never mentioned where he was getting these quotes he kept peppering our conversations with. I was sure he left the mystery because he wanted me to ask him, just as I was sure that the conversation would then turn to Devlin, and Danial pushing in his gentle way for a reunion. So in spite of my curiosity, I resisted temptation. "Neither is that, Danial."

"It's the only one you're getting," he replied. "Go to sleep, Sar."

I turned away from him, irked but resolute. I was not letting Devlin back in, period.

* * * *

The day of the ceremony dawned clear and sunny. For once, everything went off without a hitch.

Cia was still not speaking to me, but that didn't make Janice and Ivan's ceremony any less beautiful. It was held out on Danial's front lawn, under a tent. The ritual was very like a wedding, with the usual promises spoken, though there was a bit about "not letting others into their den," which I thought interesting.

At dusk, the reception began. Danial, Elle, and I sat together, as Theo was on duty that night with Terian. Still, I got in a few slow dances. Terian also found a few moments to dance with Sundown. His style was similar to Theo's, and I concluded, watching him move, that Theo had been the one to teach him.

Like all magical things, the reception came to an end at midnight. After saying goodnight to everyone that was still speaking to me, I walked inside with Danial.

"So Janice and Ivan are leaving tonight for Acapulco?" I asked as I took off my earrings.

"Yes," Danial answered. "They'll be gone for a week or so. Warren is staying at your old house." He paused. "He asked if you wanted him to start laying in wood for winter. I said I'd ask you your plans and get back to him."

What he was really asking was if Theo and I were going to stay with him after the babies were born. I brushed my teeth, not daring to answer. In my heart, I didn't want to leave. But I knew those feelings weren't solely my emotions anymore, they were his, too.

Theo came in a few moments later, and began pulling off his clothes. "We need to talk," he said. "Elle's sleepover is coming up."

I'd forgotten all about that. "The first week in July, right?"

Theo nodded. "She's adamant."

"We did promise her," Danial said with a sigh from the doorway. "Why don't you see if you can borrow some of Devlin's bears to guard you? You can do it at Sar's old house again."

Theo nodded. "I'll ask him when he comes next week to give Elle her lesson." He slipped on his bottoms. "How's the financial end of things?"

"Better than good," Danial said proudly. "We are clearing almost 200K a month, after expenses. Gross is more like 500K a month."

"I'm asking because I want you to know that when the babies are born, Sar and I won't be able to work as hard as we've been working," Theo said firmly. "I missed Elle's cubhood. I can't miss my son's, too."

Danial nodded. "I know that, which is why I hoped you both might consider staying here, while the baby is young." He looked over at me. "Devlin will take his child to Hayden to raise. Sar will need to resume her visits to him to see the child. It's going to be hard enough for Sar to go between two places. Three will be that much more difficult."

"She can teleport," Theo said. "Travel time that way is nothing—"

"Sar may lose the ability temporarily, if not permanently," Danial interrupted. "You can't rely—"

I let out a gasp. "How do you know this?" Theo demanded.

"Terian," Danial answered. "Titus showed him some old scroll about dhamphirs, and it fits with what Stephen told me happened before. After Sar has the child, the virus in her body is going to spike, even with no help from me. Until her blood returns to what is normal for her, she won't be able to teleport. If the virus spikes high enough, she'll lose the ability permanently, unless she gets more demon blood. Dosing her again would be tricky; when she was exposed before, it was accidental. I doubt she remembers how much got on her hands the first time."

"Why didn't Terian tell me about this?" I demanded. "Why is he always telling you instead of me?"

"Shit!" Theo swore. "It makes things a lot easier, her being able to teleport."

"If you stay here, things will be easier," Danial soothed. "You would both have to bring the baby here every day anyway."

"I thought Sar could stay at home—" Theo began.

"Unguarded?" Danial said, incredulous. "Alone with just your cub?"

"Damn it!" Theo said loudly. "This is that bastard's fault! If only it wasn't taking so long to find Robert. I don't know why the fuck he just doesn't challenge me right off."

"Yes, you do," Danial retorted. "He knows Karl is after you, too. He is hoping to catch you weak, after you've sustained an injury."

"Danial, we can stay here, but you need to accept that we aren't going to live with you permanently," Theo said hesitantly. "We have a home—"

"Is it really because you have a house, or is it because you are both in my bed?" Danial said cuttingly. "That you are afraid of something happening between the three of us?"

"Danial, Sar is my wife. I want to sleep with her, live with her. Just her and me and our child. I love you, but—"

"But you don't want to share her with me," Danial stipulated.

"No, I don't," Theo answered. "I never wanted to, not from the beginning. I'm grateful to you, for all you've done for me, for her, and for our children. But I want time with her alone. I know she has to come to you, Danial. I know Dev will probably demand his rights, too."

"Sar will have to resume her visits," Danial agreed. "Devlin is not going to wait forever, Theo. It doesn't matter to him that the Oath was broken." Danial glanced at me, then back to Theo. "He'll just get another one from her."

"I'm not immortal," Theo whispered.

I took a swift intake of breath, my eyes wide. "What are you saying?" I asked shrilly.

"There is going to be a day, probably a few decades from now when I'll go out on a job, and not come back," Theo stated. "You can't retire in my line of work, Danial. Not once you're ranked."

"I know," Danial assented neutrally. "I've always known."

"You'll have Sar all to yourself then," Theo stated bitterly. "She'll probably still look the same. I've seen your pictures of Annabelle and Dev. She didn't age at all in that decade she was with him." Theo sighed. "You'll look the same, too, and so will Dev. But I won't, no matter how much I work out."

Danial was silent.

"I didn't understand how Sar felt, years ago. I told her she should just love you, spend time with you while she was young, that it wouldn't matter when she was older. That you loved her enough not to turn from her, as she aged. But I understand completely now."

Danial reached out and put his arms around Theo. "I'd change that if I could. All I can say is that how I feel will not change, no matter how you age."

How would it feel to see Theo founder? To take care of him while I remained young and he slipped away from me by inches? "There must be something we can do."

"I don't want you to see me crippled," Theo whispered. "I'll stay as long as I can, until my body begins to fail. And then I'll go out, and when I draw down on a mark, I'll do it slow enough to take care of things—"

"You will not!" Danial said sharply. "There are potions that can be taken."

"I'm not ending up like that fucking snake," Theo growled. "Half man, half monster. You know what he eats, Danial. You know it's not just Titus that takes care of Dev's human liabilities."

"Hush, Theo," Danial said abruptly. "Sar doesn't need to hear this."

"I think I do," I answered slowly, sickened. "Are you saying Lash eats people? I know he drinks blood, but—"

"Yes," Theo said quietly. "Titus said something in front of me once, years ago. I'm not going to repeat it to you, but the inference was made."

When Lash had said he could eat only flesh and blood, I'd concluded he meant animal flesh and blood only. He hadn't. Likely the blood in his flask hadn't been from an animal, or a donor, either. It also explained why he'd asked Devlin for some of my blood the night he'd met me, and why he'd been so eager to drink my blood during our liasons, with barely any encouragement from me. Revolted, I didn't reply.

"We should all get to bed," Danial said. "Next week is going to be busy."

The three of us got into bed, both of them hugging me. But none of us slept for a long, long time.

Chapter Fourteen

As the sleepover I'd been dreading approached, I made trips back to my house to mow the lawn, and weed a little bit. While I could have asked Warren to do it, I still thought of this as my home. It mattered to me that the guests coming find it presentable, if not enviable. Theo did his part out in the woods, using my tractor and wood-splitter to begin laying in a wood supply for us. As it was, by the time I would be able to help him we'd likely end up cutting the last of it ankle deep in the first snow.

Theo was still adamant about moving back in here in the fall. Danial hadn't said another word about it, but he held me tightly now when we slept. There had been more than one afternoon that he had joined me in my now daily nap. I clung to him, too, no more anxious than he to part ways after so many months of being together.

I was also concerned about Elle. Sometime in the last few months, she had matured from looking about nine to thirteen. She had gotten taller and leaner, and there was a sway in her walk that hadn't been there before. Her clothes she picked out and favored were all tight, and when we went shopping, guys as old as eighteen noticed her. When I glowered at them, they stayed away, but I knew they wouldn't for long. Her body was developing slowly, most of it lean muscle, but the curves were emerging. Soon, sleepovers were not going to be enough; it would be dates and boys.

When I brought up my concerns to Theo, he brushed me off, saying that she was too young, and that there were no young men at Danial's home, so there was no reason to worry. That only made me worry more, because there were single male werefoxes there. Even if they were a decade older, they were still male. And no matter what anyone said, they were not getting taken care of by anyone like Serena. So a few days later, I mentioned something to Danial.

Unlike Theo, he took me seriously. "I'll talk to all of the single males," he said, his eyes glinting red. "I doubt anything would happen, Sar. Elle is still too young to be thinking about that."

I gave him raised eyebrows. "We don't know how old she is, really. And this has more to do with hormones anyway."

"I understand that. You're right, the time is going to come soon when she needs to begin to look for a mate." Danial sighed. "She faces the same problem that Theo faced years ago. There are no werecougars in the Northeast. She'll have to go west."

"She could change someone," I said, sitting down across from him, suddenly tired. "It worked for Aspen."

"John was an unusual man," Danial said, running his fingers through his shoulder length hair. He had stopped cutting it short for me months ago, when I'd told him I'd liked him just as he was, and it shone from his earlier feeding in the light from his desk lamp. "It's hard to find a human who is accepting like you. It's easier for weres to find one who already is one of their kind for a companion. And turning can fail, if it's not done right."

"Mom!" Elle yelled, snapping me back into the present. "Susan's here!"

It was the day of the sleepover. Susan had arrived, and Violet was right behind her, both of their parents following.

The moment I met Susan, my worry for Elle increased. She wasn't the plain, reserved girl Violet was; Susan was a knockout like Elle was becoming, with teenage arrogance in her dark blue eyes. Her mom was of the same type, a bleached blond with too much makeup, her overly dressy clothes expensive and tasteful.

"Violet, Susan, you can go right in to Elle's room. Hi," I said brightly. "I'm Sar."

"Hi, I'm Diane, Susan's mother," she said coolly. "I've got to be going, I'm afraid."

I politely exchanged pleasantries, thinking to myself that we weren't the same kind of woman. Diane didn't spend her days getting her hands dirty, and had probably never wanted to. But that was fine; likely I'd never have to see her again.

Cathy, Violet's mother, was just as nice as I remembered. After chatting with her a few minutes, I saw her out, and then went to check on the girls.

The rest of the night went well, in spite of my worries. Elle and her friends spent most of it in her room giggling. But as Susan felt no desire to wear Elle's choker, and Violet had tried it on already, that problem didn't repeat itself.

In the morning, it was Violet who woke first. When she wandered out into the kitchen, I offered her breakfast, which she readily agreed to. With a smile, I lifted out a newly done pancake, and then began putting fresh pancake batter into the pan.

"Where are the dogs?" Violet asked shyly. "Something didn't happen to them, did it?"

Startled, I replied, "No, um, they're at Elle's other father's house. I wasn't sure whether Susan liked big dogs." I dished some butter onto the pancakes, the handed her the plate. "They'll be here if you visit again. Syrup is there on the table."

"I don't know if Elle will invite me again," Violet said softly, taking the plate. "They were talking by themselves a lot of last night."

At their age it was so easy to feel excluded, and to hurt others with a careless word or gesture. "Elle likes you, Violet," I said, putting my hand on her shoulder. "Of course, she'll invite you again."

"We don't see each other very much anymore," Violet said sadly. "She's in another dance class now. Whenever I invite her anywhere, she says she can't go. We mostly just talk on the phone now."

This was the first I'd heard of Elle being invited anywhere by Violet. Even with Danial's protectiveness of Elle, we had to start letting her spread her wings. She was rapidly becoming a woman. "Violet, you go ahead and keep asking Elle," I said, giving her a smile. "Her other dad almost never lets her out of his sight. But I think that if you want to meet her at the mall, or at the movies, she can probably go, at least once in a while. I'll talk to him, okay?"

"Okay," Violet said, giving me a tentative smile.

After the girls went home, Elle went back to her bedroom, and began packing her stuff up. I went after her with a purpose, Theo following me, his expression a little mystified over my intense expression.

"Elle, I need to talk to you," I said, sitting down on her bed. Theo came in behind me, and leaned against the doorframe. "Violet's worried you no longer like her," I said gently. "Is it true?"

Elle gave me a guilty look. "She seems so young, Mom. Susan knows so much more."

"What does she know?" Theo said, giving her narrowed eyes that said he could guess the answer.

"She knows about boys!" Elle said excitedly. "She said she's kissed this one she knows, who's sixteen—"

Theo's eyes had gone yellow. Mine would have, too, if I were werecougar. "Elle," I said firmly. "You are too young yet for boys."

"Damn straight," Theo growled. "You are maybe eleven, Elle. You aren't dating until you are sixteen. And even then, I'm not letting you go out with anyone that I haven't met and approved first."

Elle got up off the bed and faced us. "I'm old enough," she said suggestively, her eyes rebellious. In her tone was her mother Tawny's boldness, as clear as a bell.

Stay calm, Sar. Breathe. You knew this was coming. "Enough," I said calmly. "I think you are old enough to be given some more freedoms—"

Theo looked at me like I'd lost my mind.

"—but I want you to remember something. Danial has many enemies, as does Theo. There is never going to be a shortage of people who might like to kidnap you—"

"Yeah, I know, and torture me!" she said, rolling her eyes. "I've heard it all a million times—"

I grabbed hold of her roughly, and shook her. "You are a young woman, Elle," I said sharply, my eyes flashing. "There are other things that can happen to you now that you aren't a child anymore. As you just said, you *are* old enough."

Elle's face went white, and tears formed in her eyes.

"Sarelle," Theo said, aghast at my implication. "You shouldn't say that to her."

"Don't cry!" I said sternly to Elle, ignoring Theo. "Just remember what I said, and be careful. Don't trust boys that aren't your own age, Elle. Or any men besides Brian, Aran, Ivan, Terian, Theo, Danial, Devlin, or Lash."

Theo growled when I included Lash, but I didn't take it back. Lash might be an ass, but he was not going to hurt a child. At least, not Danial's adopted daughter.

Elle nodded. "Okay."

I hugged her tightly. "Don't be afraid of men. I know that might seem at odds with what I just said. I just want you to understand that some men are not going to want what is best for you. I want you to find one who does, who respects you and treats you well. And I want you always to be conscious that just because you think someone isn't going to hurt you, it can still happen."

Theo put his hand on my shoulder, and squeezed a little. "Your mom is right." He went to Elle and hugged her. "I wish she wasn't, but the world is sometimes a hard place, Elle. We love you, and we want you to be safe."

She was quiet for a moment. "Can I go to the mall next weekend?" she said finally. "Violet asked me, before she left. Dad always says no. Maybe Theo could chaperone—"

"Yes," I said, glancing at Theo. "Terian will tail you, Elle. You won't know he's there, but he'll watch you. But if he does come up to you and tell you it's time to go, you have to agree to go with him without a fuss. Understood?"

"Sure!" Elle said happily hugging me.

What I didn't add was that I would be giving a description of Violet to

Terian, because if Elle was planning on meeting Susan instead, Elle wouldn't be making any more trips to the mall without me as a chaperone.

* * * *

Danial hit the roof, of course. "What were you thinking, Sar?" he yelled. "She's not going alone, even with a tail."

"Elle is getting older, and in another few years, it's going to be time for college, Danial," I said firmly. "You need to loosen the apron strings."

"Elle is not tied to me," Danial glowered. "I just want her to be safe."

"Terian will watch her," Theo soothed. "Sar's right, we have to let her get her feet wet. She can't live here with you for the rest of her life, no matter how much you want her to."

Danial grumbled, but after talking about it at length, he agreed that it was a good decision. While I was relieved that the sleepover had gone so well, and he'd come into agreement with us over Elle, I was nervous about what was still to come. Elle wasn't the only child who was changing fast.

During July, Theoron had aged another five years. He outgrew his clothes almost overnight. Now he was as tall as Elle, also made of lean muscle, and the spitting image of Danial, save for my green eyes. He was going to break some hearts with his stunning good looks and the inherited charm that was just beginning to make itself felt in the way he asked for things with easy smiles. He wouldn't be running around with horns and a tail ever again.

While I found it sad my little boy was growing up so fast, I was also relieved. He would have the strength of his father, and my ability to walk in the daylight. And I had enough to worry about as the day of the birth of my twins approached.

* * * *

I knew something was wrong the morning of August second, when I was making tomato soup for Theo. He'd asked me to, as his mother had made it for him when he was little. I'd agreed before he casually mentioned he didn't have the recipe. After trying recipes all that week, I finally came up with one that was right, or at least was close enough, according to Theo. As I was stirring the paste into the broth, I began to get warm, then hot.

Theo came over to me, worried. "What's wrong, Sar? You're sweating like you're in the sun."

"I'm too hot," I replied. "Probably from being in the kitchen."

"Go lay down," Theo said, taking my spoon. "I'll check on you in an hour or so."

I went to our bedroom to lay down, thinking he was overreacting. When I woke up, I was slick with sweat, and too weak to move. "Theo!" I said as loudly as I could.

Theo didn't hear me in the kitchen, but Danial did, working in the study above. He came down the stairs quickly and into the bedroom. One look at me had him yelling for Theo.

"You're burning up," Danial said, laying his hand against my brow. "When did this start?"

I tried to get closer to him. His skin was cool, wonderfully cool against mine.

Theo burst in. "What's wrong?" Then he saw me. "Danial, what's wrong with her?" Theo shouted. "She's got a fever.

"This happened before to her," Danial said. "But never this late in the pregnancy. Call Devlin right now."

Theo hesitated. "Maybe we should call Camlyn."

"Call Devlin now," Danial roared at him. "Get him here now!"

Theo left. A few minutes later, Devlin came in the bedroom, embracing me immediately. His body was also cool, marvelously cool like ice water on a one hundred degree day.

"What happening, Danial?" Devlin asked, worried. "She's far too warm."

"You said he'd know," Theo said as he came in, irritated.

"Have Titus teleport Stephen here," Danial said to Devlin. "If you don't know, we need him to tell us what's happening."

Titus was dispatched to Stephen. A few minutes later, Stephen showed up, looking disgruntled. He checked me over thoroughly. "She's too hot," Stephen said.

"That's genius," Theo growled. "What's causing it?"

"That doesn't matter," Stephen replied. "We've got to get her temperature down, or she'll not only lose the children, she'll lose her life. She's a hundred and three degrees, and her temperature is rising." He turned to Devlin. "Get ice and run cold water in the bathtub—"

"Why is this happening?" Theo shouted, his eyes yellow.

Devlin dashed for the bathroom. Water began running.

"Last time, the dhamphir had trouble controlling its temperature as it developed," Stephen said. "It was too hot first, and then too cold. This time, I'm guessing the werecougar fetus has been keeping the dhamphir's temperature steady. But the werecougar is too big now. It's making the dhamphir overload on heat. Sar's body is overheating because of—"

The water abruptly stopped. "You know what we need to do, Danial," Devlin said quickly. "Come with me. Titus, take us to the guard barracks here."

I passed out then and don't remember much of what happened next. I

202

heard later that Theo put me in a bathtub full of cold water, and packed ice around me with Cia and Terian's help. Though that stopped my temperature from rising, it didn't make it go back down. Within a half hour, the ice had melted from my body heat and I was delirious.

When I came to, I was in fresh clothes in Danial's bed lying next to a body as cold as a block of ice. I was cool though, wonderfully cool. It flowed into me, easing away the heat, letting me fall back into a deep sleep.

Sometime later, I woke back up, feeling much more like myself. Danial was beside me, awake and freezing cold to the touch. When he reached for me, it took him a long time to move his arm. I eased my body closer to him, then hugged him. "Thank you."

Danial hugged me back. An hour later, he'd unthawed to the point he could talk and move normally. "Are you feeling better?" he asked slowly, his voice raspy. "Are you still hot?"

"Yes. But I'm not anywhere as bad as I was. I felt like I was cooking."

"You were," he said, afraid. "Devlin and I froze ourselves. Our bodies don't absorb heat easily, and we lose it rapidly. He thought this would work, and it did. He is there now, doing it again for you. Titus should be bringing him back within moments."

Just as Danial finished, Titus appeared with Devlin in his arms, and quickly laid him down next to me on the other side. Then he disappeared, before the heat from his demon body undid what we were trying to do.

I eased myself closer to Devlin. His eyes were shut. There was ice in his golden hair, and on his eyelashes. His skin was covered in a layer of frost, his arms folded over his chest, with more heavy frost coating his clothes.

"He can't move," Danial said softly. "He won't be able to talk to you, Sar, not for an hour at least. But he can hear everything we say." He got out of bed. "I'll go tell Theo that you're okay. Stay here with him, and call out if you start to get cold. Stephen is outside, waiting to make sure you are fine before he leaves. He said once you got cool that you should be fine, but I'm not taking any chances."

I clasped his hand, then kissed it. "I'll be okay now, I think. I'll call out, if I'm not."

Danial kissed me softly once on the cheek, then left. I moved back close to Devlin, letting his coldness soothe me.

"Can you hear me Dev?" I said softly. "I hope you can."

Devlin didn't move.

"Serena told me that you had been with her. But I understand why you said you hadn't been. To you, what you did was necessary, to make sure she would do what you hired her to do. It wasn't sex for pleasure. I'm telling you this because I want you to know I know, and I understand it. But you still should have told me you had been with her before. I would have understood, if you had told me why it had happened."

Devlin didn't move, or give any sign that he had heard.

"I'm sorry that you aren't getting the boy you wanted. But I'm glad to be having a girl. I'm not going to have any more children, Dev. No matter what you say. Not after this, all of the last months, everything with Lash, and The Lust. It's been too much. But I thank you for having this child with me. I wanted a girl very much. She'll be beautiful for certain, with your genes. And I hope she has your eyes, Dev. They are so much more beautiful than mine."

Again, Dev gave no sign he had heard.

"It's funny," I said, snuggling close to him. "I feel more loving toward you like this than when you are awake. I know like this, you aren't going to be angry with me, or say something cutting when I don't do as you say."

I felt bad immediately, hearing my words aloud, even if they were true. I reached up and touched his face gently. Even like this, covered with frost and motionless, he was utterly beautiful.

"I'm sorry, if I ever made you feel like I didn't care about you. I do care, very much." I paused. "I do love you, and I never stopped. But it's better if we aren't together, because when we are, we hurt each other. I have missed you, these months we have been apart. I appreciated the flowers you sent me, and the lessons you have been giving Elle. I used to listen to you playing and think about—"

I stopped abruptly. Here I was getting charmed just thinking about him. He hadn't changed. In an hour, he was going to be his same old demanding self. "Thank you for doing this, for being here for me when I needed you," I said softly. "It means a lot to me." I laid my head on his shoulder, and slept.

When I awoke hours later, I was alone, and Devlin was gone.

* * * *

I didn't talk to Danial in the days that followed about what had happened. I could see he was waiting for me to ask about Dev, but I didn't, knowing Danial would press me to let him visit. The heat didn't return, for which I was grateful.

In those last days of my pregnancy in the dog days of August, I was absolutely miserable. I felt swollen, too uncomfortable to move. Adding to that were Theo and Danial, who were afraid to leave me alone anymore. They took turns lying in bed or watching TV with me. Danial read to me as well, mostly poetry from his older books, the ones I'd put by his bedside years ago when I'd first moved in. Most of them were the older poets, like Byron, Frost, and Tennyson. And the inevitable happened.

Danial and I were lying in bed one morning, him reading to me from a collection of poems, when I heard the following familiar lines:

"We have lived and loved together, through many changing years.

We have shared each other's gladness, and wept each other's tears,

I have never known a sorrow that was long unsoothed by thee,

For thy smiles can make a summer where darkness else would be—"

"Jefferies, right?" I interrupted, glancing at him.

Danial stopped and looked over at me. "You know this?" he said innocently.

It was a plot; a brotherly plot, no less. "Danial, if you want him here, say so."

"Only if you want him here, Sar," Danial said neutrally. "I told you I would not make you see him unless you wanted to." He looked at me out of the corner of his eye.

"Tell him he can come if he wants to," I said, letting out a sigh. "He has a right to be here. Any day now, it's going to happen. He should be here when it does."

Danial beamed, then got up immediately and left. I turned onto my side, away from the door, groaning as I shifted my weight.

Minutes later, the door opened. I breathed in Devlin's scent, that scent that was better than all other scents almost, the scent of myrtlewood trees. He lay down next to me, behind me, but didn't speak. While I was debating how to open a conversation with him, I drifted back to sleep.

I awoke with a gasp, feeling sharp pains across my stomach. This was it. "Dev!" I gasped, another contraction hitting me. "Dev, wake up!"

Devlin woke up immediately, his sleepy expression changing to excitement and panic. "Is it time?"

Another contraction hit me, making me groan. *Why were they so close together already?* "Yes! Get me to the doctor."

Devlin picked me up carefully. "Your water has broken. Lie still." He got me to the door, shouting, "Danial! Theo! It's time! Get down here!"

Suddenly, everyone was there. Terian and Titus got Devlin and I to Dr. Camlyn's office in record time. As they carried me inside, I saw Lash was there, too, talking to Devlin. He was dressed in black armor. As I was carried into the delivery room, my last view was of Lash shutting the doors behind us, a wicked looking automatic rifle with a scope in his arms as strode away.

"Get me some drugs," I hissed.

"Stephen's coming," Devlin assured me. "Lash and Titus are outside on guard. Just relax."

"I'll relax when I get some drugs," I replied grumpily.

By the time Stephen arrived a half hour later, I was screaming, crying, and swearing, the sweat pouring off me. Then Stephen administered the anesthesia, coupled with a magical sleeping spell, and I dropped right into a blissful sleep.

* * * *

When I woke up, it was over.

Theo was holding a tiny cougar cub in his arms, feeding him from a bottle. The cub was squeaking a little, and lashing his tail, his eyes closed. Theo looked every inch the proud father.

Devlin was also cooing over his child, Danial right next to him. I wanted to ask if the baby girl had his eyes or mine, but then I remembered it was probably too soon to tell.

Stephen came over. "How do you feel?"

"Tired but good," I said, managing a smile. "Did it all go okay?"

"Yes," Stephen whispered, nodding. "Everything went fine. And I tied your tubes, also. You won't get pregnant again."

I breathed a sigh of relief, then fell back asleep.

* * * *

When I awoke again, I was back at Danial's house, lying in his bedroom. Theo was beside me, our child sleeping in his arms.

"What do you want to call him, Sar?" Theo said softly. "Your time for picking a name is up."

"Devon," I said hesitantly. "Would you mind if we called him Devon?"

Theo looked at me, curiously.

"It was my father's middle name," I said with emotion. "He didn't like his first name, so he went by his middle name."

"Of course," Theo said, relaxing. "Devon is a great name. We'll call him Dev, for short."

"No," I said firmly. "We'll call him Devon."

* * * *

In a few days, when I felt well enough, Terian took me to Hayden. "Titus said he would bring you back," Terian said with a smile. "I've got to go and meet Theo."

I nodded, though inside I was grumpy. I needed people to transport me now. As predicted, I had lost the power to teleport when the vampire virus within me had spiked. Worse, the virus would increase, according to Stephen, so my power wasn't going to return anytime soon. It sucked, big time. I'd almost forgotten how to drive, and now it took hours to get anywhere. But I held onto the hope that soon I'd have it back when the virus eventually declined.

Serena was there to meet me. "She's beautiful, Sar," she said, hugging me. "She looks like you."

Hesitantly, I walked upstairs to the nursery, but found it empty. So I went to Dev's room next.

He'd put the baby's crib in his bedroom. I thought about remarking something about that cramping his style, but thought it too rude, even for me. Especially as he was there feeding her, looking as enthralled and loving as I'd ever seen him.

"What are we going to call her?" I said finally.

"Come in, please, Love," he said softly. "Come see our child."

I went over hesitantly, and looked down at the little girl with her wisps of light golden hair. Her eyes were closed. "She's lovely, Dev."

"I'm…um, we're going to call her Venus," Devlin said happily. "If that's okay with you."

He had to be kidding, right? "You are not naming our child after a Bananarama song," I said, putting my hands on my hips. "Pick something else."

Devlin rolled his eyes. "I would call her Aphrodite," he said, "But everyone uses nicknames around here. I don't want her going by Fro, or Aphro."

I chuckled. "Yeah, that would be bad."

Devlin gave me a tentative smile. "It's after the Greek Goddess of Love, not the song. Though I imagine she'll like the song, when she hears it."

"Why not Athena, then?" I asked. "She's bound to be feisty—"

"Because I've had enough of war," he said, his molten gold eyes staring meaningfully into mine.

I held his eyes for a second, and then looked back down at our baby. "We'll call her Venus, then. She's certainly beautiful enough."

"She is," Devlin whispered, stroking Venus's tiny face. "She is going to look like you, Sar. She has your hair." He put her down on her back in the crib.

"It's not my hair," I said, trying to smile. "It's yours, Dev. Mine is highlighted to be this color. Yours is naturally lighter."

"Sar, I've seen pictures of you when you were little," Devlin said happily. "Your hair was this light then. It got darker as you aged—"

"Who showed you pictures of me when I was little?" I said in alarm. "When?"

"That night I stayed to watch you for Theo, more than a year ago now. When you went to bed, I was bored, so I looked through your bookshelves. Although one shelf was interesting—"

I blushed, knowing what shelf he meant. *My softcore romantic porn shelf.*

"—I didn't see anything worth reading. But your photo albums were there, and your baby book. I looked through them, to find out more about you."

I was horribly embarrassed. He'd seen my most embarrassing photo, that picture where I'd put my pants on my head when I was six and was pretending I had long hair. I'd been raised like a boy in my youth, and my hair had always been cut in a pageboy style. So I'd used pants. I flushed deep red and redder, thinking of the many embarrassing pictures he had to have seen. I'd thought no one would find them there on the bottom shelf. Worse, Devlin seemed to remember every single one.

"You were so cute, Sar. Dressing up your tricycle with jewelry, and your girl dolls with their horses, swords, and shields, and the strange costumes you dressed up in."

I got more even red, if that was possible.

"I think you were trying to be a belly dancer, maybe?"

"I was trying to be an Amazon. And you were not supposed to ever find out about that," I said, biting my lip. "No one was supposed to see those pictures, ever."

"You are embarrassed?" he said curiously. "Why?"

Duh. "I'd had pants on my head. It's kind of self-explanatory."

"You should not be embarrassed," he said lovingly, coming closer. "I loved seeing the woman you are taking shape in the little girl you once were—"

He was making his move. "I'm going to head out," I said, backing toward the door. "But thank you for letting me visit with her—"

"Sar, wait, I—"

Go now. "Have a good day, Dev," I said quickly. "Please take care of her. I'll be back in a few days." I got out and shut the door quickly, then hurried downstairs.

To my relief, Devlin didn't follow. But Serena wasn't there and neither was Titus. Deciding the safest place to wait was down in Titus's lab, I went to the basement and got into one of the big leather chairs, pulling a heavy blanket over me.

It was quiet down there. For a while I thought about Devlin, and then about Danial. Just as I was dozing off, I felt a hand on my arm.

"Sar?"

I opened my eyes. Lash was beside my chair, his hand on my arm.

"It's good to see you," he hissed.

It was hard for me to meet his eyes. Seeing him brought back all the embarrassing things that he and I had gone through during The Lust, plus the bad experiences with Dev's men. I wanted to forget who I'd been with him, like

I had when I had fallen out of love with my first boyfriend in high school. Months after we'd broken up, I'd seen him one day in the hallway and I'd wondered what the hell I'd been thinking. That I'd been the one to pursue him so desperately just made it worse. I felt the same way now about Lash; uncomfortable and ill at ease.

"Venus is beautiful," Lash hissed gently. If his voice could have affection in it, it had it now. "She looks like both you and Dev. She has his eyes."

While I thought she looked more like me, I was happy to hear that Venus had gotten her father's golden eyes. "I hoped she'd get his eyes," I said, trying to smile.

Lash squeezed my arm a little. "Would you be interested in some sushi?"

I shifted in my seat. "Um...no, not just—"

"Sorry," Lash hissed immediately, withdrawing his hand. "I won't touch you again."

Guilt flooded me. Lash hadn't been in the grip of anything; his desire for me had been powerful and real. It hadn't ebbed, as mine had. "I'm sorry, Lash," I said, biting my lip. "I used you—"

"Stop," Lash hissed sternly, some of his old nastiness back in his tone. "We both got what we wanted out of the time we spent together. It's over now, and that's that." He stood up abruptly, and turned to go.

"Lash," I said hesitantly. "Do you want me to talk to Titus, see if he can't take my blood—"

"No," Lash hissed in a low, low voice that somehow was worse than if he had shouted the word. "Keep your blood. I shouldn't have taken what I did from you."

"I don't want you to be in pain—"

Lash turned in a split second, and leaned over me menacingly, his hands on the arms of the chair, his face inches from mine. I shrank back into the seat. "Shut your mouth, Sar," he hissed in that same scary low voice, his words venomous. "You don't talk about that, not to anyone, remember?"

"I remember," I squeaked.

"Good," he hissed. Then he turned and left, without a backward look.

I sat there for a moment, trembling, and then Titus came in. "Everything okay?" he rumbled in his bass voice.

Everything was not okay. But there was no way to fix it. It was just as well Dev and I were done; now that he had what he wanted from me, he would forget me. There was no going back for a do-over to make Lash into a different man than he was, someone I could have called friend. There was only going forward, away from Hayden and the paradise I'd hoped to find here. I'd make a new life with Danial and Theo. With time, remembering the dreams I'd had would sting less. That would have to be enough of a plan. The rest I'd figure out on the way.

"I just had a bad dream," I whispered. "But it's over now. Take me home, please."

About the Author

Tara Fox Hall's writing credits include nonfiction, horror, suspense, action-adventure, erotica, and contemporary and historical paranormal romance. She is the author of the paranormal action-adventure *Lash* series and the vampire romantic suspense *Promise Me* series. Tara divides her free time unequally between writing novels and short stories, chainsawing firewood, caring for stray animals, sewing cat and dog beds for donation to animal shelters, and target practice.

Other works by the author with Melange Books, LLC

Return To Me
Surrender to Me
The Origin of Fear in Spellbound 2011 Anthology
Night Music in Midnight Thirsts II Anthology
Partners in Midnight Thirsts II Anthology
Kink in Wicked Christmas Wishes Anthology
The Oath in Wicked Christmas Wishes Anthology
Bedtime Shadows Anthology
Make Me Behave Anthology
Latham's Landing, An Anthology

The Promise Me Series
Promise Me, Book 1
Broken Promise, Book 2
Taken in the Night, Book 3
Taken for his Own, Book 4
Promise Me Anthology, Book 4.5
Immortal Confessions, Book 5
Her Secret, Book 6
Point of No Return, Book 7
Lost Paradise, Book 8 of the Promise Me Series

Coming Soon

Dark Solace, Book 9 of the Promise Me Series